SLAB CITY BLUES

SLAB CITY BLUES
THE COLLECTED STORIES

ALL FIVE STORIES IN ONE VOLUME

NEW YORK TIMES **BESTSELLING AUTHOR**
ANTHONY RYAN

TABLE OF CONTENTS

SLAB CITY BLUES

I WAS IN the forest with Consuela when Father Bob patched the call through. We were having The Discussion and she was at the "just throw the switch you selfish sonuvabitch!" stage.

"Inspector McLeod?" Father Bob, terrific timing. He's a great guy. I'd die for him.

"Yes Father?"

Consuela crossed her arms impatiently. "Alex."

"Superintendent Mordecai for you."

"Alex!"

"Patch her through."

Consuela turned away and stomped off through the undergrowth, losing herself in the trees.

"Alex?" Sherry Mordecai, nervous, guilty. She hated calling me here.

"Sherry. What's kicking?"

"Got a flatline for you. Yang Thirteen, Quad Delta."

Yang Thirteen - Spliceville. "What species?"

"Human."

"Unusual."

"Very. Get here." Sound-off click leaving staring after my wife, my hawk-faced Spanish wife who hated me for making her live in paradise.

"Jack me out please, Father."

*

Father Bob pulled the leads from my temples and I straightened up with backache adding to post-immersion nausea and the added disorientation of the old face/new face swap-over. When I jacked in for the first time the war was six months over and I'd actually forgotten I had a new face. I'd left the old one behind when a spent-uranium tipped shell tore through our shuttle during the Langley Raid dust-off. Several centuries of surgery later and a stranger stared back at me from the mirror with a French woman's idea of what Englishmen are supposed to look like. If they'd known I was the son of a Russian mother and Scottish father I'm sure I'd have come out as a cross between Rudolph Nureyev and Sean Connery. My new face was beautiful, no lines or scars. I hated it. Apparently, so did Consuela.

"Who the hell are you?" she said that first time. I jacked out and Father Bob left the room so I could cry in peace. Next time I brought a disk with an old 2D so he could render a convincing mask.

Consuela lay on the next couch and the sight of her still chilled me - implanted leads, waxy skin, a lump of machinery grafted onto her chest, making her breath, making the blood pump through her veins, making her live. But it couldn't heal her, couldn't bring her back to me.

The private immersion suite of Yang Twelve's Neo-Catholic Chapel was supposedly reserved for visiting Cardinals who wanted to commune with the Saviour Himself in moments of spiritual crisis. When Father Bob arrived he reported the neural enhancers defective, knowing no repair crew would venture into this neighbourhood, and converted it into much needed office space. When he heard Medicalis ("Because We Care") were going to cancel Consuela's insurance, he called and offered free, indefinite usage. Did I tell you he was a great guy?

"She asked again, Father," I told him.

He didn't look up, busy thumbing through Revelations for a spark to inspire the morning sermon. "Yes, Inspector. But did you hear her?"

"You think I should do it."

"I think it's between the two of you."

"Sometimes I think she hates me."

"She loves you, you silly fuck." He picked up my gun from the desk with a thumb and forefinger, holding it out at arm's length. "Go to work."

*

Blood seeped out from under the edges of the sheet covering the body. Some days are worse than others on the Slab. I had a feeling today would be a gem.

Fabio Ricci grimaced as he lifted the sheet to cast his pathologist's eye over the corpse. "Sheesh! Someone really wanted to see this Jed's backbone."

The morning rain was washing the blood away. Slab rain, streaming in ugly miniature waterfalls from the girders and ceilings. I suppose they didn't care about the condensation factor when they designed this place, given that the current population exceeds the original estimate by six hundred percent. All the thousands of unfortunates crammed in here, sweating, breathing, fighting, screwing. Steam rises and having risen must fall. Slab rain falls hard, pooling to reflect dim streetlights like a thousand unpolished mirrors. I hate the rain.

"Dead," said Sherry Mordecai.

"Flatlined," I agreed.

"Chilled," Ricci, not wanting to be left out. He lowered the sheet. Sherry and I exchanged expectant glances.

"Nasty," she said.

I shrugged. "Nasty but quick. Couldn't've taken more than a couple of seconds. Doesn't fit any known MO either. Slashers like to take their time and keep it private. And they usually slice off a chunk or two as a souvenir. Unusual weapon too, look more like claw marks."

Sherry turned to Ricci. "ID?"

He was already running the scans through his smart. "No match. Either he's got no priors or he's had some expensive remodelling work. Might get a hit when I scan his neural cortex. The one thing you can't change."

I crouched down and lifted the sheet. Oriental male, late twenties. I checked the arms and what was left of the chest. "He's a Shuriken, Black Lotus."

"You're kidding." Sherry bent down to take a look. I pointed out the two dragon tattoos on the inside of each forearm, one black one white. With a bit of imagination the design on what was left of his chest became a lotus. He'd served a hard apprenticeship - over twenty kills to get his dragons and a high profile hit for the lotus.

"Hey." Ricci held something up for inspection, a thimble sized plastic vial with a needle protruding from one end. "Had this under a false skin patch on his sole." He handed it to Sherry.

"Ampoule," she said. "Bliss maybe."

"Nah." I took it from her, turning it over, no markings. "Shuriken like to stay pure, use that zen mind-control crap to shut out the pain if they get hit. Could be poison but that's not their style." I handed it to Ricci. "Let me know when you get a make on the contents."

This was the first murder of the day. The daily average for the 28th Precinct was six. One hundred and eighty a month, two thousand one hundred and ninety a year. Ninety five percent are cleared up in the first five hours. The last five percent are my job. I suppose it's flattering.

I scanned the crowd. We were in the market district. A satyr in a raincoat haggled with the dire wolf who ran the fruit stall. An orang-utan with a reverse baseball cap made bets on the Tyger Joe vs Ortega the Puma title fight, speaking into a smart whilst peeling a banana with his feet. A pack of wolf cubs roller-bladed past in a high-speed babble of Slab-slang and juvenile howls. Spliceville. At least it's never boring.

I wandered over to a jewellery stall where a young vampire couple sold under-priced platinum trinkets.

"How's business, Jed?" I asked the guy vampire.

"It's Antonius." Pale and sullen. He didn't look at me. No-one liked being seen talking to the Demons.

"What about you, Jedette?" I asked the girl.

"Calpurnia."

Latin names. A high-status vampire thing. These were two genuine lace wearing, turn to cigarette ash if you expose them to ultraviolet, blood drinkers. Oh the wonders of science.

"See him?" I jerked my head at the Black Lotus under the sheet. ""How long's he been there?"

"Couldn't tell you," Antonius said.

"He here when you set up this morning?"

"Didn't notice."

"Say Jed, where'd you get the metal for these things?" I fingered a dolphin shaped brooch hanging from the stall. Consuela had always preferred platinum to gold. Our wedding rings were platinum.

"We buy it wholesale," Calpurnia said. "Jed from the lower Yin resyk bins comes round with a sackful every few weeks."

"That's good. Nice and legal. Not like if you bought it from those kids who crawl around the hull scraping precious metals from the cables."

"No. We don't do that."

"It's easy enough to check. My fat Italian friend over there, he's a genius with this stuff. It's all in the purity levels apparently. The recycled stuff is like, total crap."

"He was here when we set up," Antonius said.

"When was that?"

"Eight or eight thirty."

"That's three hours ago. Didn't you feel even a small urge to call us?"

"Switch on, Demon man. Flatlines are a banquet round here. We call it in we'll be lying next to him two seconds later."

"You two didn't take the opportunity to have a little snack did you?"

They bared their fangs in a unison smile. "Dead meat's no good to us."

"So I heard. How much for this?" I held up the dolphin brooch.

Calpurnia sighed. "It's on the house."

I took out some European green and handed over a couple of hundred. "Buy yourselves some o-neg on me."

"Anything?" Sherry asked as I wandered back. Spliceville heating systems never work properly and the chill made her scars angry red stripes across the paleness of her face. I never asked why she hadn't had them fixed.

"Been here three hours at least," I told her. "The local Jeds picked him clean so forget about finding any of those little knives they carry."

Ricci had bought a taco from a nearby stall and spat corn and pepper as he spoke. "No defensive wounds on the arms. This was over before it began. Must be someone special whoever it was, taking down a Black Lotus like that. Could make a killing this side of the Axis, literally."

"Veteran?" I wondered.

Sherry dug her hands into her raincoat. She didn't like to talk about the war. "Could be. Certainly narrow the list of suspects if it is. Not so many of us left."

"I'll speak to Colonel Riviere, do the tour of the Vic affiliates, see if anyone's heard about a big contract on offer recently."

She nodded. "Let me know what you get. Ricci, we're done here. Get this thing shifted."

I took the Pipe to the Axis. Some overweight Australian tourists, still jaded by the obligatory Yang-side sleaze tour, started fumbling for assorted souvenirs as the gravity lightened up. A Blissful sleeping it off on the floor floated up to the ceiling and banged his head on the fluorescents. He didn't wake up.

A Yin-side girl watched the sports on a portable hol. The Multimedia Entertainment Corporation had announced the postponement of Tyger Joe's latest fight. The smiling MEC PR lady explained how the big guy had sustained an unfortunate injury during training but they expected he'd be back on his feet soon and anyone with tickets for the fight would receive a full refund. Somehow, I doubted the orang with the baseball cap would get his stake money back. Ortega the Puma was explaining how Joe was a gringo faggot running scared from a real fighter when the Yin-side girl noticed I was watching, got scared and moved seats. I have that effect on people, pretty face or not.

As the Pipe crosses into Axis territory it passes the sky-view window on the roof of Yang One and there's a ten second panoramic glimpse of the Slab's interior. Imagine Hawksmoor had designed a shopping mall and got MC Escher to touch up the sketches and you'll have an idea of what it looks like. In orbit it's almost majestic. A tall, spinning, gothic rectangle above the blue green jewel of mother Earth. Once it had the inglorious title of Orbiting Housing Enterprises Luxury Apartment Complex No. 5. After the war it became Lorenzo City in honour of our glorious leader, the second city of the Confederation of Autonomous Orbital States. Now, everyone called it the Slab. A hard, cold prison for the poor where rats grow big and sweat falls in rain. Hard to believe we fought a war for places like this. Harder still that my wife died for it.

*

I got off at Axis Central, propelling down the tube and flashing my badge at the border checkpoint. They let me in without the mandatory customs search and I floated through into the Axis.

Inside it's beautiful, a vast cavern of spherical hab-pods tethered together with miles of cable and crawlway. Micro-grav hydroponics give rise to spider-web extrusions of cherry blossom and maple lit by countless floating glow orbs. The antithesis of the hard-edged simplicity of most Slab architecture, even the higher Yin levels couldn't hold a candle to it.

I drifted for a while, enjoying the view. No rain here. The Axis Provincial Council had set aside sufficient funds for moisture extraction gear. I started to move, old trooper's hands reaching instinctively for the ladders, propelling myself towards the VA pod.

I drew a few glances from some of the Axis folk, even a couple of salutes. Here I wasn't a Demon or some Yang-sider you didn't sit next to on the Pipe. Here I was a Vet, a Langley Vet at that. Here I was a hero.

Most Axis folk are amputees or paraplegics from the war who got tired of waiting for the COAS Feds to cough for decent prosthetics or nerve reconstruction and decided to annex the Axis. They'd stormed the place, throwing out the leisure loving Yin-siders who gathered there for micro-grav sports, and declared themselves an autonomous province. The City Council, peeved at the loss of prime real estate, ordered the Lorenzo City Police to clear the area at once. Two months later, when the mayor (a rich but stupid Chechen who got flatlined last year when his bribe-fees became excessive) asked Police Chief Arnaud why the squatters were still in residence he received a "Nah, fuck that," by way of reply. No-one had mentioned it since.

Colonel Riviere is a living, breathing monument to the nature of war. His arms are two Daewoo Mark II prostheses, his vision a Nikon sonic-sight implant, no good in a vacuum but you can't have everything, and his legs end below the knee where Medicalis ("We give you peace of mind") decided they'd squeezed enough publicity out of war heroes and moved on to orphans with a conveniently short prognosis.

"Whoever it is," he said, "they're not here and I don't know where they are." He lit a cigarette, which is a disgusting habit at the best of times and truly appalling in micro-grav. I'm sure he only does it to annoy me. We'd never got on. He thought Consuela was too good for me (hey, he was right). I suppose it was understandable. She was his daughter after all.

"Consuela sends her love," I said.

He didn't say anything. If he had said anything it would have been "My daughter is dead", but the last time he said that I broke one of his arms. It was a heat of the moment thing and I'd forgotten it wasn't real. The pain receptors worked OK though.

"Black Lotus got chilled in Spliceville this morning," I continued. "Killer displayed signs of pronounced combat expertise. Thought you could give us some pointers."

He shrugged. "Fewer Shurikens taking up good air the better."

I held out my smart. The moment stretched. He sighed smoke and took it, called up Ricci's shots of the body.

"No other wounds?"

"No."

"Make on the weapon?"

"Not yet."

He grunted and handed it back. "Saw something similar during the war, but only once. It was in the early days, we had this Splice in our cell. This was when we were trying to target the Downside security chiefs. The Splice, he could rip them apart with his hands... well, claws. Handy because we didn't have enough weapons to go around. Looked like this Black Lotus of yours when he was done. Not as neat, but similar."

"What happened to him?"

"Got scragged in the first UNOIF counter-offensive. Saw it happen. Pity, I liked him."

"What was he?" The smoke made me cough. "What species?"

My father-in-law smiled as I choked. "El tigrĕ."

*

I did the stool-pigeon tour around midday. Two hours of cajolery, bribery and intimidation later and I wasn't any nearer to whoever killed the Black Lotus. No-one knew anything, or if they did they weren't willing to sell, which is so unlikely as to be impossible.

I was on my way to the office when Madam Choi called me.

"I have trouble Inspector."

"Sorry to hear it."

"Can you come?"

Madam Choi ran a joint on Yang Ten, one of the more Oriental levels. She saved my life during the war and never tired of calling in the favour.

"You know I'm always there for you, Matsuke." I sounded off before she could say anything else. Her real name was Matsuke Hiroka but, the denizens of Nippon being about as popular as small pox on the Slab, she had changed it to Choi Soo Ying. Madam Choi was the living definition of pragmatism.

*

It was called The Heavenly Garden, at least that's what the cheap hol above the door said, but everyone called it Madam Choi's. The name was kind of misleading anyway because it had no garden and no sentient being could call it heavenly.

Near the door two elderly Chinese were shouting at each other over a Mah Jong board. A Blissful was negotiating desperately with a pusher at a corner table and Marco, the elderly lobotomy case who did the shit work, was mopping blood from the floor. Madam Choi was waiting behind the bar with a double Glenlivet. She kept it just for me.

"Thanks." I drank it down and slammed the glass on the bar. "So?"

Madam Choi wrapped her talons around the bottle and poured me another. "It is a delicate matter, Inspector. A matter requiring tact."

"So why call me?"

She smiled her Dragon Lady smile. I suppose she was beautiful, pale skin, long silken hair, lips red like cherries, all that good stuff. Personally, I'd always found her about as attractive as a scorpion.

"You are my friend," she said.

I picked up the whisky. "I'm listening."

"There was an incident last night. A regrettable incident."

"You mean this?" I gestured at Marco ineffectually pushing his mop around the bloody floor.

"Oh no. That was something else. This concerns one of my rats."

"One of your fighting rats?"

"Indeed. You understand the confidence I have in you that I feel I can share such information."

"The honour of your confidence is overwhelming."

Despite the obvious attractions of Madam Choi's establishment her real profits came from gambling. Dice, roulette, Mah Jong, cards and above all rat fights. Strictly illegal due to the obvious (and disturbing) intelligence displayed by Slab rats, being more physically and mentally developed than their Earthly cousins. They're about the size of a family dog with problem solving abilities on a par with dolphins. So it seems a little inhumane to force them to fight to the death in a backroom arena. No-one knows what the rats think about it. For all we know, with their enhanced IQ, they might see it as an intellectual challenge.

"Someone doping the competitors again?" I asked.

She shook her head. "Someone has stolen my champion."

"The Emperor?"

"Exactly."

The Emperor was a legend in rat fighting circles. Big as a pit-bull, fox cunning and cobra fast. Victor of a thousand fights, eventually the odds on him had dropped to nothing so Madam Choi was forced to give him early retirement.

"Thought he was out to stud."

"He was. However, recently a consortium approached me with a highly profitable offer. They had a rat truly worthy to contest with the Emperor. It was a great opportunity. We held the bout in the old ore processing works on Yang Three where the gravity is lighter. It makes for a more interesting contest. Select patrons only, drinks, Bliss and Blues on the house and ring-side betting at even money. It would have been a profitable night if that Splice had not turned up."

"Splice?"

"Big species. Predator. Bear maybe."

"You couldn't tell?"

"He was wearing a cowl, as they often do when they venture away from Spliceville. He came out of nowhere just as things were reaching a climax. Poor old Emperor was out of condition, he put up a valiant fight, but his end was surely coming. Then the Splice jumped into the ring, pulled the competitor off and picked up the Emperor. I expected him to be torn to shreds but a strange thing happened, the Emperor just curled up in his arms, like a child."

"I take it you didn't just let him walk out."

"Indeed not. My associates tried to stop him but he was very quick and skilful. He scarred several of them quite badly, but he seemed careful not to kill anyone."

"Scarred? So he had claws?"

"Oh yes. Also, his fur, it was red."

"When was this?"

"Two nights ago. If the Emperor can be returned to me I would be very grateful. There is a substantial finder's fee."

I ignored that. She knew she couldn't buy me and must've been desperate to try it. "I'll see what I can do. But in exchange I want some information."

"Of course. You wish to know about the Black Lotus who was killed on Yang Thirteen."

"Word gets around."

"I know little except that he was hired from Downside. A very big contract. He was a Dai Wei of the Red Sun Circle, a Vietnamese affiliate."

"You think the Vics have some stake in this?"

"They have a stake in most things."

"Yeah, I've noticed."

*

I went to see Consuela after leaving Madam Choi's. The beach this time. The settings were her choice and the immersion software had a pretty big library. Somehow though, we always seemed to end up in the forest or on the beach. She sat watching the evening tide roll in while the sun dipped into the horizon. She had probably been watching the sunset all day.

"How was father?" she asked as I sank onto the sand next to her.

"Been speaking to Freak again?"

"He likes to have someone to confide in?"

"It."

"What?"

"You said he. Freak doesn't have a gender."

"I suppose that depends on your point of view."

"Your father is well. He sends his love."

"No he doesn't. He thinks I'm dead. And he's right."

"Con, please…"

"It's OK, I'm tired of the argument. You never listen. And why should you? I'm just a ghost after all."

"You're not a ghost, you're my wife. If you can just hang on.

A few more years. They're coming up with new treatments all the time…"

"When, Alex? A year? Ten? Twenty? A couple of centuries maybe? And will you still be waiting for me? This place, these dreams I live in…" She scooped up a handful of sand, opening her fingers to let the grains drift away in the wind. "Perfect, no glitches, no clues, nothing to tell me it's not real. But I feel it, I know it in my soul. This isn't paradise, this isn't heaven. This is a prison where you keep the ghost of your dead wife. And the worst thing is I'm not haunting you, you're haunting me."

My smart started bleating. I shut it off and threw it into the sea.

"You better answer that," she said. "Someone still breathing might need your help."

*

It was Sherry. "Alex, we've got trouble. Two suits from CAOS Federal Security just left my office with everything we've got on the Black Lotus. They also purged the mainframe of all pertinent data and we've got a signed order from Chief Arnaud to desist from further investigation."

"And those are your instructions to me?"

"Why else would I be calling?"

"Very well. I hereby acknowledge your instructions to desist from investigation into the Black Lotus case."

I signed off, hit the encryption icon on the touch screen and tuned to the private channel where she was waiting. "What can you tell me?"

"Not much. The ampoule we got off the body, Ricci says it's not poison, quite the opposite."

"An antidote?"

"Cardeferon, they use it to treat heart defects."

"Did the Shuriken have heart trouble?"

"Ricci says no. Look this is bad news, Alex. This whole thing. If you want to drop it..."

I sounded off and called Colonel Riviere. "I want to see Freak."

*

Freak is the mother of all enigmas, the daddy of all Splices and most humane individual alive. I could've spoken to Freak over the smart but s/he prefers the personal touch.

Freak lives in a big pod at the centre of the Axis, myriad tentacles jacked in to every system on the Slab, reading every smart transmission, financial transaction and data entry. Omnipotence personified, Freak is a cyber-god. Colonel Riviere never told me where he found Freak. There are rumours about a raid on an orbiting Russian research lab but no-one knows for sure. Where ever s/he came from Freak was our salvation. Once he managed to establish communication with his discovery Riviere persuaded it to tap into the UN Orbital Intervention Force mainframe and download the security overrides that made the Langley raid possible.

Two hundred of us fanatical freedom fighters dropped on CIA HQ, fought our way into the communications centre, downloaded every byte they had and shot it to Freak in a concentrated data-squirt. Freak had it all decrypted and distributed within five seconds of transmission: troop dispositions, battle plans for the next twelve months, even the keys to every code they used. A month later the UNOIF was on its knees and our glorious leader was sitting at a conference table with the Secretary General discussing terms for the formal recognition of CAOS. The rest is a history lesson. As for the brave two hundred, me and Consuela were two of the six who made it out.

If you want to know what Freak looks like I can't tell you for sure, s/he's so enmeshed in the machinery now it's difficult not to think of a giant squid in collision with a computer factory.

"Alex," Freak's soft, androgynous tones echoing from the multiple speakers as I floated in. "Nice to see you. I visited with Consuela earlier."

"So I gather."

"Ah, our intimacy angers you. You are envious that she finds companionship with a monster…"

"Freak."

"…when she constantly rages at you for keeping her alive. But she is so lonely—"

"Freak! This is official business. I need your help."

Something stirred wetly in the wall of flesh and circuitry, folds parted to reveal an eye the size of a basketball, iris contracting as it found the focus. "How handsome you are. I'm surprised Consuela prefers you ugly."

"Ugly is who I am."

Freak is fickle. God-hood will do that to you, I guess. Omnipotence makes everything clear, every action and reaction. Positive acts have negative consequences and vice versa. So Freak will help or s/he won't, and an explanation is never forthcoming either way.

The eye closed. "What can I do for you?"

"Is Tyger Joe on the Slab?"

"Yes. He arrived four days ago on a freighter from the Texan Republic and has been hiding out in Spliceville."

"So he killed the Black Lotus?"

"Yes."

"And stole Madam Choi's rat?"

"Yes."

"Why?"

"He killed the Black Lotus because he had been hired to keep him alive. I have no idea why he stole the rat."

"The Black Lotus was hired to keep him alive?"

"Yes. The ampoule Dr Ricci recovered contains a drug used to control heart defects. Tyger Joe's heart was surgically weakened when he signed his contract with MEC. He must receive regular doses of cardeferon or he will succumb to myocardial infarction. MEC sees this as an incentive to loyalty. I assume the Black Lotus tried to inject Joe with the drug and died in the attempt. This would indicate an eagerness on MEC's part to retrieve their champion. He's worth over six billion in Universal Accreditation after all."

"How close are they?"

"They lost him at Madam Choi's rat contest."

"How long before his heart gives out?"

"Assuming he doesn't have a cardeferon supply of his own, about fourteen hours."

"What's he doing here, Freak? Seems a long way to come just to steal a rat and have a heart attack."

"The Slab is currently home to ex-Doctor Mariel Janus, one time Nobel laureate who pioneered accelerated de-Splicing techniques before losing her licence after several patients died during treatment. As you know, de-Splicing is a lengthy and expensive process, taking several months. Dr Janus's technique enables a subject to become fully human in a matter of hours. I have information that she is continuing to perform the procedure, quite illegally of course, and at an inflated price."

"MEC know about her?"

"Oh yes. Of the forty MEC operatives on the Slab, twelve are engaged in surveillance of you. The remainder are attempting to locate Dr Janus. I estimate they will find her within eleven hours."

"I don't get it. Joe's the best, that Puma guy won't even scratch him. They treat him like a god. Why throw it all away?"

Something shifted in the wall of flesh, some small spasm of discomfort. "Do you remember the time before the war, Alex? Do you remember what it was to be a slave?"

Memories clouding - pain and fear and hate. I shook them away. "Yeah, I remember."

"I too was once a slave, as Tyger Joe is a slave. What do all slaves dream of?"

I pulled my gun from its holster, a standard issue Sig 4mm, checked the magazine and made sure I had my spares. "Twelve, huh?"

"Yes. Comms indicate they're getting desperate and will use extreme measures. MEC has already offered me a large sum to provide information. Naturally I refused."

"Well they don't know you like we do. I'll need you to jack into the security net and do the tactical. Like Langley, remember?"

"Of course."

"So where do I find this Dr Janus?"

*

Quad Gamma of Yang Fifteen is mostly deserted in the early evening when the devout neo-Catholic locals troop off to mass leaving a perfect shoot-out set.

"Ready?" Freak via the smart's earpiece.

I reached into my jacket, gripped the Sig. "Yup."

"Targets one, two and three directly behind you. One: red shirt. Two: blue raincoat. Three: suit and tie. Be advised: Jeds in the area."

"Got it."

I stopped abruptly and turned. They were good, barely a flicker. Red Shirt just kept walking. Blue Raincoat and Suit veered off to the right. They'd walk on by and let their colleagues take over the tail.

There was a time when policemen had to give a warning before they shot someone, which is a pretty good idea when you think about it, ethically speaking.

I put the Sig's laser-dot over Red Shirt's throat and pulled the trigger. A pre-programmed ten shot burst of 4mm caseless is usually pretty messy and Red Shirt was no exception. His head stayed on though, which is unusual.

The few Jeds on the street vanished like ghosts. No screams or panic. Fucking Demons, shooting people again...

I caught Blue Raincoat with the second burst and swept Suit into a shop window with the third.

Freak in my ear: "Four at three o'clock. Reading weapons: H&K Mark Six tazers. They want you alive, Alex."

I took cover behind a newsstand, firing as they rounded the corner. I could tell they were professionals by the way they didn't bother to pull their wounded into cover.

"Three more on the rear flank."

Pivot and fire, Sig's inhibited recoil feeling like a dentist's drill, making them dance and spin and fall, provoking a fierce blaze of war nostalgia.

"On the grocery roof, six o'clock."

Drop, tazer dart shatters on the pavement, pivot and fire, sniper spinning on the roof. Magazine fires empty and ejects. Slam in a new one. Scan for targets. Bodies, some wounded moaning, dropped weapons, and blood of course. Hey, even a sad sack like me is good at something.

"Freak?"

"That's it."

"You said twelve. I count eleven."

"There's nothing on the scope. You better get moving."

I ran to the Pipe and took the Grey line for the Extremity.

*

I checked my watch: 2030. Joe had about ten more hours before his heart went bust.

"Alex, I'm reading an encrypted transmission from the Extremity to MEC Orbiting HQ on St Rowan. Running decryption now... It's tough stuff, very expensive work."

"Let me guess. She's selling him out."

"Decryption complete. I'll patch you in."

A click then a woman's voice, educated Downside vowels grating on my underclass ear: "-uarantee my reinstatement with the UN Medical Ethics Committee?"

Male voice, not so educated: "Our Chairman plays golf with the Secretary General, Doctor. He's a very compassionate individual, and a Christian. He knows the value of forgiveness."

"Well, what I have is also very valuable."

"You have my personal assurance. And if you check your Zurich account you'll find a substantial gesture of good faith."

A pause as Janus checked her smart. "I see." Her voice was actually quivering. "I am now transmitting the whereabouts of the item."

"Get me there, Freak," I said.

"Clear the carriage."

I looked around. Four Jeds, a couple of them too Blissed to care either way, but Freak has this morality problem. I waited until we pulled into Yang Twenty then showed them the Sig. Had to slap the Blissfuls around a little before they followed the others onto the platform.

"OK."

"Hold tight."

A lurch as Freak diverted the carriage from the main line to one of the rapid access tunnels. The Pipe main lines run around and through the Slab in gravity-change friendly spirals but the techs need to move around the system quickly hence the vertical tunnels intersecting the network. First time I used one I found out the true meaning of free-fall. I gripped the nearest hand-hold with both fists and braced myself against the wall, mentally saying goodbye to my lunch.

"You're not going to scream again, are you?"

"Let's go!"

The floor tilted, my guts tried to wrap themselves round my spine and I screamed. I couldn't help it.

*

The Yin Extremity is a symphony of architectural elegance and a wonder of engineering where dolphins play in shimmering pools and young lovers stroll the tiered forests hand in hand beneath a square mile of pre-tensile glass revealing an endless canvas of stars.

The Yang Extremity is equally spectacular but it's also a garbage dump. There are mountains of the stuff, all the stinking, unrecyclable crap we're not allowed to flush into space any more. A few years ago several tons of junk collected into a ball and failed to burn up on entry, leaving a pretty big crater in Toronto.

Unsurprisingly, the Extremity is one of the places Demons generally avoid which makes it an attractive locale for Slab fugitives. They're grouped together in three unhappy, constantly feuding shanty towns called Faith, Hope and Charity. Whoever said criminals have no gift for irony? If you thought Yang-side was bad you should take a walk down here, just don't expect it to be a long one.

Freak guided me from the Pipe exit, through the foothills, stumbling over non-biodegradable shit and keeping a wary eye out for an opportunist with a crossbow. Janus's place was an aluminium hab-pod surrounded by razor wire, floodlights and automated mini-guns. "How the hell do I get in there?"

"I've already cut the power. Left the lights on to keep the locals away."

There were a few corpses in advanced stages of decomposition littering the no-man's land between the hills and the pod, testament to the fact that Extremists took a long time to learn some obvious lessons.

The outer gate was on an electronic seal and swung open at the first touch. "How many inside?"

"Just Joe and the Doctor. She's jacked him into an immersion couch, we've been having an interesting conversation."

"Glad you've made a new friend." I kicked the door in. Janus, tall and Downside elegant in an obligatory white coat, was speaking into her smart. Joe, four hundred pounds of fur and muscle, lay on a couch with a king size drip in his arm and immersion leads on his temples.

"Hello, Doc" I said. "You're under arrest for conducting an unlicensed medical procedure. Hope there's enough in your Zurich account for a good lawy–"

This was when MEC Security Operative Number 12 shot me in the back with a tazer. I never heard a thing. Very slick.

Tazer shock feels a bit like being hit by a jackhammer travelling at a hundred miles an hour. It also makes you piss yourself and gibber around on the floor, all very embarrassing for tough guy detectives.

I was still in paralysis when I resurfaced. Janus was predictably dead with a hole in her forehead and Number 12 was staring down at me. He had those perfect teeth no-one is born with and a leathery face that didn't match the dentistry.

"How you feeling, Inspector?"

"Schlumph," I replied.

"Never mind. Won't last much longer." He wandered over to Joe, still sedated into oblivion on the couch. "Will you look at the size of this guy? Don't appreciate it when you see him on the hol. But up close like this he's really incredible. Had six hundred riding on him for the Ortega fight…"

He droned on as I swivelled my eyes about desperately. The Sig was on the floor a few miles away. Something was scratching nearby, something out of view because I couldn't turn my head.

"… that mega-mutant of yours has shut down the pipe so my colleagues are having to climb down here. It'll take a few hours so I thought I'd pass the time with you."

"Thnshks."

"You're welcome. You know, that job you did on my team was remarkable. 'Course, none of them had our experience."

My eyes flicked up at him.

"Yeah, I'm a Vet too. On the other side of course. Still, all over now eh? No hard feelings."

He was wearing a stealth suit of non-reflective, insulating fabric. That's why Freak missed him. All he had to do was stay in the shadows while I scragged his friends then follow me to the Pipe. Latched onto the carriage somehow when Freak put it in free fall. Real hard-core space commando shit. He must have killed dozens of us in the war.

The scratching got louder. I had regained enough mobility to crane my neck a fraction of an inch. There was a large white box under the operating table about three feet away. The scratching stopped, started, stopped again. I heard something sniff the air.

"...after the war I had some trouble reintegrating into society. Not that there is much of what you'd call a society anymore. You should see it down there, Jesus..."

There was a catch on the front of the box and I was starting to lose the numbness in my arms. But Number 12 was certain to kill me the nano-second I moved.

"...I mean the poverty, you wouldn't believe it. There I was, a three times decorated war hero for Christ's sake, and what do they offer me? Refuse disposal specialist. I guess that's when my anger management issues first manifested themselves..."

"Alex?"

I'd forgotten about Freak. "Yspls?" I kept it to a whisper. Number 12 probably thought I was throwing up.

"I can see the box on the room scanner. If I give you a diversion can you move far enough?"

"Uh."

"OK. Just a sec."

The box was starting to shake as what was inside got angry.

"…one day this MEC suit turned up at the psych ward with a contrac-"

Joe moved, not much, just a spasm as Freak ran a pulse charge through the immersion leads, but it was enough to get Number 12's undivided attention. "What the fuck!"

I lurched across the floor, trailing saliva and piss, scrabbling at the box, finding the catch more through luck than judgement. Number 12 was already putting the laser dot on my forehead when a streak of black erupted from the box and latched onto his face.

The Emperor was trained to put on a show so it took longer than it should and Number 12 made some disgusting noises before it was over. The Emperor sat on the body, licking blood from his snout and regarding me with the cold, baleful stare singular to rats. I knew he was smart enough to tell friend from foe but he was such a vicious little bastard he might kill me just for the hell of it. After a few seconds he turned away, hopped up onto Joe's massive chest, curled up and went to sleep.

"I estimate you will regain full mobility within two hours. That provides us with an adequate window to move Joe and destroy this place before the arrival of MEC Security. I can provide transport but we're lacking a destination. Colonel Riviere has refused asylum for Joe in the Axis…"

"Ishokay."

"Pardon?"

"Isst's OK. Uh've got shumwer fer im."

*

"I don't really know why I did it," Joe was saying. "I saw the little guy was about to get torn to pieces and I just couldn't leave him there." He paused to look around. "Nice place."

"The Black Forest," I said. "As it was in the thirteenth century. There's a wide selection in the library if you want a change. Just ask Freak."

"Thanks, Inspector. How long will it take?"

Shorn of his fur and muscle it was surprising how ordinary Joe was. Big and tough, certainly. But nothing special. I mean that in a nice way.

"About seven months. Standard de-Splicing period. You'll be pleased to know you died in a shuttle crash last night. Along with most of your management team."

"These things happen."

I smiled. "Gotta go, Joe. I'll come and visit soon."

"I'd like that. And hey, remember what we talked about, you know, about Sniffy."

"I can't believe you called him Sniffy."

"He likes it."

I shook my head. "Jack me out please, Father."

*

I was standing over Joe's body. The machine grafted onto his chest was already starting the programmed alterations: blood change, DNA realignment, everything he needed to make him human again. In the meantime he could stay here with Father Bob.

I pulled the leads from my temples and turned to Consuela's couch, laid my hand on her face, traced her profile.

"Would you like me to leave?" Father Bob asked.

"No." I bent down and kissed her forehead. "The blue switch, right?"

He nodded.

I looked down at her hawk face for the last time. I had always liked to think she looked as if she was sleeping but I knew now she just looked like a dead woman plugged into a third-rate life-support system. She was right. I had made her a prisoner, a slave. And what do all slaves dream of?

"'Bye, Con." I hit the switch and she sighed, face going slack, head lolling to one side. She sounded relieved.

*

I carried the box to the air ducts on Yang Twenty-Four. They lead directly to the mid-outer hull, Rat Country. I undid the catch and stood well back as he ambled out, stopped at the lip of the duct to sniff the rush of air, ears pricking up at the scent of so many brothers and sisters. He glanced back with that same glittering, baleful stare, then was gone.

I dug my hands into my pockets, feeling something cold and sharp, realising I'd forgotten to give Consuela the dolphin brooch. It was raining as I walked away. I hate the rain.

END

A SONG FOR MADAME CHOI

DOC OWUGA CAST a dubious eye over the old 2D I'd given him then took a long look at my face, propped none too comfortably on a chin support in front of his dermal scanner. "You sure?" he asked.

"Sure I'm sure, Doc," I said brightly. "Surer than sure."

Doc Owuga rechecked his screens, he hid it well but I noticed his hands were trembling a bit as he punched the keyboard. We'd done some business back in the war and I guessed I'd left a lasting impression.

"This," he waved at the screens where the face that I wore revolved in all its flawless glory. "This is art. This…" he glanced at the 2D, "…is -"

"It's me, Doc," I told him. "You remember me right?"

Doc Owuga sighed and sank into a swivel chair that was two parts duct tape to one part faux leather. "Sure, you're a tough guy Demon who killed a shit-load of people during our glorious revolution and a shit-load more since."

"And you sold the Resistance anti-biotics at a three hundred percent mark-up, when you weren't trafficking organs to both sides of course."

"There was an amnesty…"

"Not from me." I undid the velcro strap from my forehead

and freed myself from the scanner. "I can pay. You want the work or not?"

Doc Owuga had been through eight faces in the time I'd known him, each more youthfully handsome than the last. But whilst the faces grew younger the rest of him didn't, he was pot-bellied with liver spotted hands and an old man's stoop. The face he wore now, darkly handsome and reminiscent of some old action-movie star I dimly recalled from late-night free-flix reruns, looked like a particularly bad joke.

"Hear they're doing accelerated, full-body remodelling on the Downside," I pushed. "Asking price is twenty thousand in folding green if you know where to go, and I'm sure you do."

He arched an eyebrow and I got a part fix on the face. Roves was it? Reeves maybe? "Where's a Demon get twenty thou in green?" he asked.

"Fuck d'you care?"

"Why not go to a Yin-Side clinic? Nice and clean and legal."

"There are… ethical issues, apparently. Cosmetic surgeons have a legal code of practice. Who knew?"

He glanced back at his screens, sighed and stood up, moving to the coat rack to toss me my jacket. "Half now, got expenses."

I nodded, peeling bills onto his desk.

"Mind if I ask why?" he said as I went to the door. "What you're wearing would cost a lot, and you got it for free."

Consuela's eyes, that first time, taking me in, scars and all, liking what she saw… "It's not my face," I said, yanking the door open. "See you in a week."

*

I bought noodles from a vendor near the Yang Four Pipe entrance, sat on a bench and watched the crowd as I slurped. Yang Four used to be mostly normo but there were a lot more Splices these days, hence Doc Owuga's new surgery. Youthful vamps and cats eyed each other warily from street corners and overpasses, horned and scaly hellspawn muscled past waif like elf maidens, all genres represented in the genetic soup.

My smart buzzed as I wiped away soy with a napkin. ID withheld. That's never good.

"Yeah?"

"Alex." Flat even tones, cultured Yin-Side vowels. Voices from the past, I hate them.

"Mr Mac. How's the criminal overlord business?"

"Fair to middling. We need to meet."

"No we don't. I'll kill you on sight, you know that."

"Not today. Got an opportunity for you to play the hero, be the knight errant, save the day, et cetera. There's even a damsel in distress."

I tossed my empty noodle carton into a nearby hopper. "There's always a damsel in distress around you, y'fucking psychopath."

A pause, maybe I'd hurt his feelings, as if such a thing were possible. "It's a child."

I stared at the crowd, noticing how even the pseudo-demons avoided my gaze. Mr Mac and I had been playing this game for five years and there were rules. Mr Mac was always a stickler for rules, number one being you don't lie to me. He would conceal, omit, prolong or carefully phrase. But he wouldn't lie.

"Where?" I said.

*

The last time I'd seen Mr Mac he was repelling from a second storey window, nimbly hopping between lines of SWAT team tracer. I was out-ranged with the Sig but fired off a whole clip anyway. He'd waved as he touched down, no irony or affectation, just the friendly greeting of an old friend. I was sprinting towards him, slamming in a fresh clip, when the building he'd just exited blew up, taking most of the SWAT team with it. The blast earned me some new scars, oddly none to the face, and a week in hospital. It's fair to say the experience hadn't made me like him any better.

Mr Mac's new abode rested in a corner of Yang Thirty-Three, one of the commercial levels clustered around the main freighter docks. Warehouses and bland two-tier office blocks, anonymous and thinly populated, just the way he liked it.

I circled the place twice before approaching the entrance. It was a mid-size warehouse with flickering holos proclaiming itself the home of Fairweather Import Export: Customs Clearance Specialists. I counted ten unremarkable grey-green boxes on the roof, positioned at the corners and mid-way along the edges. Auto-guns, I decided, noting the inter-locking fields of fire. Each box contained a 7.62mm minigun and sufficient ammo to turn any assault into a Somme rerun. Every passer-by would be scanned and relayed to Mr Mac's smart who could and would deal out instant death with a thumb-flick if your appearance aroused even the slightest suspicion. For someone in his position, paranoia was an essential survival trait.

The doors slid open as I approached. In the lobby Nina Laredo waited with two blocky security types, obvious weapon bulges creasing their suits.

"Nina," I said. "Not dead yet?"

"Inspector." She inclined her head, perfect Latin features impassive. Unlike me Nina's beauty was all natural, though like me, entirely skin deep. Six years at Mr Mac's side, uncountable kills to her name and she never picked up a single scar, nor apparently, anything resembling a human emotion. The Department's criminal psychologists had her pegged as either a sociopath or an ultra-rationalist personality. I preferred my own diagnosis of Grade A Evil Bitch.

"Your weapons, please," said Nina, holding out a hand, short nails, impeccably manicured, no rings. Nina had no need of ornamentation.

"Fuck you," I replied amiably.

"You know he won't harm you. It's for his protection."

The knowledge that she was right and I was entirely safe here did nothing to improve my mood. I unholstered the Sig and handed it over, followed by the tazer in my inside pocket and the knife strapped to my forearm.

"I better not find a tracer on these later," I warned her, knowing it was a redundant threat. Mr Mac had no need of tracers.

"This way please."

Mr Mac's office was a picture of Victorian elegance, as much as an ignorant Jed like me understands Victorian elegance. Antique real oak-wood desk, leather bound books on the shelves, horse bronzes and automata, actual oil paintings on the walls. If knowing he would have to move everything as soon as I left perturbed him at all, he didn't show it, coming from behind the desk to offer his hand, smiling warmly. "Alex!"

I ignored the hand, gesturing at the office. "Where'd you get all this shit?"

"Downside auctions mostly. Passion of mine for a while now."

I made a mental note to profile a customs search on future antiques imports and sank into the chair opposite his desk. "So? This child."

Mr Mac smiled tightly, resting against the desk, arms folded, dressed in sweater and slacks. He's a tall man, Mr Mac, every inch the blond, good-looking Yin-Sider. At his age he should have been running Daddy's procurement division, making partner or approaching the climax of a sporting career before commencing a run for political office. Instead, here he was, quite simply the most feared organised criminal on the Slab, which potentially made him the scariest gangster in the populated solar system. He came over the Axis during the war, running medicine through the blockade, then joining up with our Active Service Unit. For three years we blew stuff up and killed people together. Even back then I could tell he was really enjoying himself. He disappeared shortly before the Langley Raid, we all assumed he'd been pinched by Federal Security. A year or so later, not long after I joined the Department, rumours started circulating about a Yin-Sider gang boss with a ruthless attitude to conflict resolution.

"I heard about Consuela," he said. "I'm very sorry."

"Yeah, mention her again and I'll beat you to death with one of your bronzes." It had always irked me greatly that Consuela had liked him so much. "Tell me about the kid."

He took a smart from his pocket, thumbed up a holo and tossed it to me. The holo showed a pretty little girl, seven or eight years old, Eurasian features.

"Name?" I asked.

"Don't have one."

"Nature of distress?"

"She arrived twelve hours ago, economy-class ferry from the Jakarta Hub. Accompanied by a twenty-something male of European appearance. They walk through Customs and security without a blip and promptly disappear. Two hours later the accompanying male is found dead in a dock-level warehouse along with two others, both armed. No sign of the girl."

"Manner of execution?"

"Neat made to look messy if I'm any judge. You can double check with Doctor Ricci."

The little girl's image revolved in my palm, it was a still shot but the sadness evident in her face was unnerving. Kidnap or not her expression told me she needed protection. I wondered briefly if she was an avatar, imaginary bait on Mr Mac's hook, but then he didn't lie. Not to me.

"What's she to you?" I enquired.

"A child in need of rescue."

"From what?"

"Nothing good, Alex." He'd moved into dissembling mode. No lies, but no more truth either.

"If I find her, there's no way I'd ever hand her over to you."

"If you don't find her, I strongly believe she'll be dead very soon."

I switched off the holo and pocketed the smart. No need of tracers.

"I need more to go on than this," I told him.

"Come on, Alex." He laughed and shook his head. "No you don't. You never do."

I levered myself out of the chair and went to the door. "Have fun moving your stuff. And tell Nina, if I see her within a mile of this, I'll put her out the nearest airlock."

*

"See it?" Ricci pointed a gloved finger at a patch of slightly discoloured skin.

I shrugged. "Not really."

"Needle mark. Easy to miss, if you're not me." He eased the corpse over onto its back. European appearance, mid-twenties, extensive blunt-force trauma and penetrative injuries to the face and torso.

"Bruises don't look post-mortem," Sherry Mordecai observed. She wasn't looking at the body. She was glaring at me over the autopsy table and she wasn't happy.

"Syteline on the needle," Ricci told her. "Paralysing agent. Somebody froze our boy up before doing all this."

"Easy to come by?" I asked.

"Syteline? Shit no. Fast acting synthetic weaponised compound. Strictly controlled and very expensive. Haven't seen it since the war. Federal Black Ops types liked to use it when they disappeared someone."

"ID?" Sherry asked.

"No documents found. No make on any database. His prints

are grafts though so I guess he's been a bad boy somewhere along the line. DNA sequencing indicates a high probability he originates from the Mediterranean basin." Ricci paused, he always tries for dramatic effect when he can. "Specifically southern Sicily. Can anyone else smell spaghetti and meatballs?"

"They don't come here," I said. "There's a treaty."

"With Mr Mac?" Sherry asked.

"Yeah," I grated, more forcefully than I intended. "With Mr Mac."

Sherry bit down her anger and turned to Ricci. "What about the other two?"

"Same thing. Syteline needle to the neck, extensive injuries to the upper body. I'm guessing a low velocity dart gun."

Three precisely placed shots in barely two seconds to put them all down so quickly. Using a weaponised compound favoured by Federal Black Ops no less. This wasn't shaping up well.

"Did manage to ID them, though," Ricci went on, calling up files on his wall screen. "No-one you've ever heard of. Fairly long entries on CrimInt, violent assaults and robberies in their youth, numerous criminal associations and a few drug busts as they grew into fully fledged gang-members. Affiliated with one of the more high-end Yang Ten crews. CrimInt says they tend to sub-contract a lot, security and courier services."

"Take a team to the crime scene," Sherry told him. "Full work-up. See if anything got missed. Alex, let's talk."

*

The Bosnian café near the morgue sold cevapi - chopped up sausage meat in pitta bread with a yoghurt dressing. Sherry loved the stuff but I always found it a little bland. We sat next to the window, the blue holo-sign outside making her scars stand out, red and angry. There were four of them, traced across her face like badly drawn tiger stripes, the legacy of some wartime escapade she never talked about. She'd been a marine, an archaic term adopted by the poor bastards who put on armoured pressure suits and tried to fight their way into Fed ships and defence stations. Their casualty rate had been predictably appalling and the few survivors tended not to bother with reunions.

"You got a take on this?" Sherry asked around a mouthful of sausage and pitta.

"Hand-over gone wrong and Mr Mac's got the contract to clean up the mess." It's what he does, Mr Mac. He deals no drugs, doesn't steal, doesn't smuggle. All societies require rules and the enforcement of rules, criminal society being no exception. That's the service he provides and anyone who does business on the Slab is required to put him on retainer. It's not just a protection racket, it's a genuine insurance policy, for times like this.

"Hand-over?" Sherry said. "The girl you mean?"

"What else?"

"Child prostitution? Organ trafficking?"

I shook my head. "Plenty of home grown fodder for that. This is something new."

She washed down a mouthful with a gulp of Dragon Fire, the only beverage produced on the Slab that could rightfully lay claim to the title of beer. "We're handing this off to the SOCU."

Specialist Organised Crime Unit. A parade of time-servers with an average case turnaround of three years if you were lucky. I took out Mr Mac's smart and called up the little girl's image, placing it on the table between us, her sad face revolving in slow accusation. Sherry gave it the briefest of glances.

"I don't like you dealing with that evil piece of shit," she said. "I especially don't like you meeting him face to face with no back-up."

"He'd never kill me, you know that."

She snorted. "Code of honour bullshit."

"No, I saved his life a few times true enough, but it's more than that. He genuinely believes we're friends. Probably thinks my repeated attempts to take him down are just a bad patch we're working through."

Sherry took another pull of Dragon Fire and wiped her mouth with a napkin. "There's something else, had a call from Professional Standards."

I straightened up a little. My welcoming attitude to life-threatening experiences gives me a generalised immunity to most fears, but to any Slab City Demon the words Professional Standards always provoke a certain unease.

"If it's about Nielson, he was dead when I got there..."

"Not that. You made a large cash withdrawal from your personal account two days ago. You know they profile stuff like that."

Doc Owuga's twenty grand. Should've taken it out in smaller batches.

"There's an innocent explanation, I'm sure," Sherry pressed.

"My face," I said.

"Ah." She sat back, beer bottle clasped in both hands, eyes appraising. She'd never seen the old me, our working relationship was entirely post-war and if perfect male beauty ever stirred her womanly loins she'd been expert in not showing it. "You'd have to go Downside for that." No judgement, no surprise. I remembered she knew what it was like to carry a disfigurement.

"Yeah," I evaded, knowing my consult with Doc Owuga wouldn't go down well and she was sufficiently pissed at me already. I gestured at the holo. "So?"

She gave the girl another brief glance. "I'll give you a day. Then we're handing it off. Need anything?"

"Yeah, I need to borrow Joe."

*

I found Joe cleaning up after the regular bi-monthly riot on Yang Eighteen. At first glance he seemed like an unusually large Demon in riot gear, dragging narc-gassed suspects to the holding pens with barely any sign of exertion, but look closer and the splice heritage was obvious. The cut-price desplicer I'd hooked him up to had given out after only three months, taking the fur and claws but leaving him with patches of discoloured skin on his face and most of his body, plus an enlarged musculature and prominent canines. I'd offered to send him to the African Fed to complete the treatment but he refused, said I'd done enough already. With his impeccably forged new identity, plus a personal recommendation from me, it had been easy to find him a place on the riot squad. Six months in he was already a Section Leader.

"Inspector!" he greeted me as I picked my way through the inert bodies littering the main concourse.

"Joe." I waved a hand at the carnage. "What was it this time? Politics or religion?"

"Worse, economics." Joe heaved the two unconscious rioters over the temporary shock fence and onto the growing pile of compadres beyond. "The Level Council raised the housing maintenance rate by half a percent. Doesn't take much to kick things off round here."

"How about a little holiday? Got a case and I need some back-up. Chief Inspector Mordecai cleared it with Commander Kurtz."

Joe smiled, showing a wall of brilliant white enamel and for a moment it was like he'd stepped out of one of his ads from the old days, when he was a champion and the whole world knew his name. "You know you don't have to ask."

"It's only polite. Get changed, civilian gear, and put this on." I tossed him a Sig newly drawn from the armoury.

Joe regarded the Sig with a mixture of distaste and contempt. "Don't go much for guns."

"Regulations, Constable. See you at the Pipe in ten minutes."

*

We started in the most obvious places. Contrary to popular fiction, police work is largely a matter of pursuing the obvious. The Slab was home to a few specialised human-trafficking gangs, some with a sideline in supplying children. It's a ruthless and grimly efficient aspect of organised criminality and none too easy for someone like me to trawl for intel on a missing girl. Luckily, I had a few well-placed informants who prized continued good health and liberty above prudent silence. A few hours intimidating our way through the grubbier corners of the lower Yangs and it was clear that whoever had the girl wasn't interested in channelling her to a niche market brothel or porn studio.

I took a call from Ricci having just finished turning up squat on Yang Ten. I'd hoped to extract some intel from the compadres of the two gang-members for hire who'd died alongside Mr Spaghetti and Meatballs. Sadly their gang-mates had disappeared themselves as soon as the news broke, leaving only blank faced hangers on and relieved shop owners who didn't have to cough up protection money any more.

"Just finished the work-up on the crime scene," Ricci said. "It's pretty clean but I did find an interesting trace sample." My smart showed some kind of molecular diagram, donut shapes swirling about each other in a lazy dance.

"Been a while since chemistry class, Ricci," I said. "Looks like blood."

"It is, but with a difference. Look." Ricci zoomed in on a red blood cell revealing small, yellowish protrusions on the surface.

"What is that?" I asked. "Some kind of blood disease?"

"Nah, it's diacorteline, in inert form so it won't show up on a blood test. Only picked it up cos I ran a visual scan. It's present in every cell in the sample."

"Diacorteline?" Joe asked.

"Blues to you and me," I said.

Bliss and Blues are the principal drugs of choice on the Slab. Bliss will send you to heaven on a wave of ecstasy. Blues puts you on a slow burn of pain free oblivion. The thinking junkie's drug.

"Is it extractable?" I asked Ricci.

"Sure. Run it through a standard blood cleanser and add acetic acid. Voila, usable, saleable Blues."

I sounded off. A Blues and blood compound. Something new alright. There was someone who knew the Blues trafficking world a lot better than I did but I owed her enough favours already.

"Shit," I sighed, making for the Pipe.

"Where to?" Joe enquired.

"Joe, my friend, prepare yourself for a trip to the Heavenly Garden."

*

The place was early-afternoon empty save for a few endurance athlete drunks. Marco was keeping bar with heavy-browed concentration.

"Inspector," he said in his too precise and overly loud voice. There was a multiple scraping of chairs as the remaining patrons decided to take their custom elsewhere.

"Where is she?" I enquired as Marco poured the Glenlivet, two glasses.

"Upstairs." He stoppered the bottle and stepped back, brow creasing further as he considered his options. "I'll tell her you're here." With that he stomped off towards the stairs.

I took a sip of scotch and gestured for Joe to follow suit. "It's the only free drink you'll get working with me."

Joe seemed distracted, head angled, eyes closed. "Prefer Bourbon. You hear that?"

"What?" I couldn't hear anything but empty bar and muffled street noise.

"Someone's singing." A faint smile played on his lips. "Beautiful."

A door opened upstairs and there was a brief snatch of vocal melody, pure and resonant. Joe was right, it was beautiful. The rumble of Marco's voice cut through the song shortly followed by Choi's answering bark. She sounded pissed. A brief pause then the heavy plod of Marco descending the stairs. "Be right down," he reported before taking his usual place by the door.

"Bourbon," I informed Joe, "is a bastardisation of my heritage."

"Scotch is the Devil's privy water. My grandma always said so. She should know, drank herself to death on Kentucky Red before she hit fifty."

Choi appeared after a few minutes, all dragon lady elegance as usual. "Inspector," she gave a short bow.

"Choi, this is Joe. A colleague."

"Yes." Choi's smile was flinty. "He stole my rat." Despliced or not, she never forgot a face.

"Liberated you mean," Joe rumbled.

"Play nice kids," I cautioned. "We're all friends here."

Choi inclined her head, moving behind the bar and pouring me another measure of scotch.

"You auditioning?" I asked.

Her porcelain smooth brow creased a little. "Your pardon?"

"The singing. Joe was quite taken with it."

"Ah." She blinked. "Merely an old recording. I like to listen to music when organising my accounts."

"Right." I paused a little before reaching for the recharged glass. All the years I'd been coming here, there had been no music. No piped in crap-pop, no jukebox, no performers. Just the soft aria of alcoholic despair punctuated with the occasional drum roll of violence.

"How may I serve, Inspector?" Choi enquired in her perfectly faked Mandarin-tinged tones.

"Anything new in the Blues world? Big splashes and ripples. You know the kind of thing."

"As far as I can tell the balance is in order. Gangs trade, co-operate, kill each other and profit accordingly. No one group ascends above the others for long. No leader endures beyond a few months. The balance is in order."

"Nothing recent? Rumours of a big buy maybe? Something new coming up the well?"

"There is talk of a substantial purchase tonight. I was approached with a view to contributing a portion of the purchase price. I declined as my current stocks are sufficient."

Joe shifted a little, uncomfortable with her frankness. The other informants we'd visited today had all displayed the requisite amount of reluctance or obfuscation. But Choi wasn't really an informant, she was a career criminal who spoke to me without fear of arrest because I owed her a favour and we were useful to each other.

"Where?" I asked.

She reached for a notepad and scribbled down the details. Choi had a healthy aversion to electronic media. "Security will be tight," she cautioned, handing over the note. "The groups involved are very professional."

"Then they'll see the value in coming quietly." I threw back the rest of the scotch. "What d'you call that song anyway? The old recording?"

"Redemption Song," Joe said. "Bob Marley. Favourite of my grandma's."

"Kentucky Red grandma?"

"Nah. Grandma Deane, my dad's mom. Used to be a musician. Never seen so many tattoos on an old lady."

I pushed back from the bar. "Ersatz daylight's burning and desperadoes await justice. Later Matsuke."

She barely flinched when I used her real name. Normally

I could see her biting down the anger. "A true friend is always welcome, Inspector," she said with a smile.

I was out on the street before it hit me. Her smile actually had some warmth in it.

*

The buy was set for 7 pm at an abandoned manufacturing plant on Yang Thirty, a mostly derelict level sparsely occupied by vagrants and rats. Prime drug deal territory. Sherry was able to scramble a SWAT team at short notice and we set up on the level ceiling, micro-cling gloves and knee-pads sticking us to the crete, kitted out in thermal-masking stealth suits and night vision gear. All very ninja. Sherry had opted to assume the role of Team Leader. I wondered if she was missing her marine days or keen to keep tabs on me.

"Got ten suspects on the plot," Sergeant Manahi reported over the scrambled net. "All armed. Eight on perimeter security, two inside."

Buyers or sellers? I wondered surveying the grey-green silhouettes below. They were all disappointingly adult-sized, no little girls, huddled and awaiting rescue.

"Movement," one of the SWATs reported. "Five more approaching from Quad Delta." A pause. "No children in sight."

"Could still be in there," I said. "Concealed maybe."

"Hold until they get inside," Sherry ordered. "We don't bother waiting for the hand-over on this one. Remember, tazers only, exercise extreme caution. Possible infant in danger."

I hung from the ceiling in a lateral pose, repelling cables hooked up and ready to go, watching the newcomers approach the block, a brief exchange with the guard on the door then two went inside, the three others lingering on the street, good spacing, loose formation, eyes constantly scanning. Choi was right; professionals.

"OK," Sherry said. "As per the briefing I'm primary infiltrator. Sergeant Manahi is secondary. Alex, Joe, clean and sweep for the girl. Let's go."

I punched the button on my chest and went into rapid descent. The height of every Slab level is a standard two hundred metres. Experience has taught SWAT over the years that to have a reasonable chance of taking down a group of armed suspects you had to cover the distance in under three seconds. In practice this means a dizzying 110kph fall to the floor followed by a jarring, just soft enough not to dislocate your lumbar vertebrae, deceleration.

I juddered to a halt five feet above a perimeter guard with an Ingram 5mm under his jacket. He was just starting to glance up when the tazer dart smacked into his cheekbone. I hit the quick release and landed astride his twitching body, looking round to see Joe choking another guard unconscious, meaty arms wrapped tight around his neck and mouth until he spasmed and went limp. Joe dropped the guard, caught my reproving eye and gave a silent shrug. Don't go much for guns.

We sprinted for the main entrance amidst the multiple phut phut of the SWAT team's tazers as they took down the remaining guards. Inside it was already over, two unconscious forms on the floor and another two disarmed and cuffed, wincing from Sherry's none too gentle interrogation.

"Where is she?" she demanded, holding up the holo of the little girl and handing out painful cuffs when she didn't get an answer.

Joe and I swept the building finding only dust, some industrial plant that wasn't even good for scrap and the stale smell of disuse. Back on the ground floor a SWAT was running a scanner over a caseful of vials whilst his team-mate checked a holdall full of green.

"Half a mil," she said and whistled. "Clean too. Numbers all coming up as legitimately sourced."

"This is good stuff, Inspector," the SWAT with the scanner

said. "Eighty percent purity. Your intel was a little off though." He held up one of the vials containing an opaque, greenish liquid. "This is Bliss, not Blues."

I went to the prisoners, chose the tallest and dragged him to his feet, drew the Sig and jammed it in his mouth, held up Mr Mac's smart with my other hand, close to his eyes, wide and terror filled.

"My name is Inspector Alex McLeod," I said. "Heard of me?"

Faint twitch of the mouth around my gun, eyes widening a little more, a nod. "Good, then you'll know it's very important you give me a truthful response." I held the smart even closer. "Have you ever seen this girl?"

Instant head shake, eyes imploring in a sweat slick face. No sign of a lie and I knew how to spot a lie from a man with a gun in his mouth.

"Shit!"

I removed the Sig, wiped spit away on his jacket and moved to the door beckoning Joe to follow. "Fire me if you have a problem," I said to Sherry's glare of disapproval.

*

"She lied! She fucking lied!" I fumed on the Pipe, prowling the aisle, fists clenched. The carriage was empty apart from Joe, our fellow passengers wisely having decided to vacate a few stops back. "How many hours have we wasted on this crap?"

"Dunno," Joe said. "Four maybe."

"It's a rhetorical question." I slumped into the seat opposite. "She's never lied before. Not to me."

"She was kinda right, just got the wrong commodity…"

"You don't get it, she doesn't get things wrong. She deliberately wasted our time."

"She did seem kinda pissed. Taking a little revenge maybe? For her rat I mean."

I thought it over. Choi certainly had a vindictive streak, there had been enough bodies on the ground over the years to attest to that. But not to me, we had too much history of shared dependency, however much we both resented it.

"Y'know, Inspector..." Joe began.

"Alex, I keep telling you."

"Yeah. You look like a man in need of a drink."

*

Joe's apartment was on the fourth floor of a mid-price block on Yang Twelve. Mid-price in this neighbourhood meaning the elevator worked one day in five and the Super kept the stairways clear of Blissfuls and Blues Heads. The apartment itself, kept so neat and well-ordered I wondered if there wasn't some military experience in Joe's back catalogue, boasted an en suite bathroom, fold-out bed and kitchenette slash living room. Plus a very large rat sitting on the couch.

"You remember Sniffy," Joe said, closing the door.

"Yeah." I found myself edging closer to the wall as Sniffy licked his snout and favoured me with his signature baleful stare. "Kinda thought he was enjoying life in the outer shell."

"Guess he didn't take to it." Joe hung up his coat and moved to open a cupboard over the sink. "Been around people too long. He turned up a couple of weeks ago. Must've tracked my scent through the ventilation ducts."

"Uh huh," I said, calculating the chances of getting to my gun if Sniffy decided he didn't like visitors. I'd seen him move with a purpose before and didn't think much of my odds.

"Here we are." Joe extracted a bottle and two shot glasses from the cupboard and went to the couch. "Off you!" he told Sniffy. "Bed time."

Sniffy gave me a final stare then hopped off the couch and into a blanket-lined box under the window.

"Kentucky Red," Joe said, pouring a measure. The bottle

was square shaped with a picture of a running horse on the label. "Twelve years old. Got a contact at the docks puts a bottle aside for me. All legal of course, excise paid at import."

"I'm sure." I sat on the couch, unhooking the uncomfortable weight of the Sig and dumping it on the coffee table.

"Cheers." Joe handed me a glass.

"Slange."

Kentucky Red had a complex texture and a pleasing burn on the tongue leaving a rich wood-smoky aftertaste. "Pisswater," I told Joe.

He grinned. "Thought you'd like it."

I relaxed into the couch, thinking about lost little girls, pretend Dragon ladies and the enticing prospect of reacquiring my old face.

"How long since you slept?" Joe enquired.

"A day or so. I'm fine." In fact I wasn't sure when I'd last slept. My apartment had gradually morphed into a junk-food carton filled mess that felt more like a prison cell with every increasingly infrequent visit. There was no mystery as to why of course, since Consuela died I'd seen little point in domestic trivia. For that matter, I'd seen little point in much of anything. I worked, I hunted through this orbiting slum for murderers, rapists and sundry human drek, but I was going through the motions. It was only when I took a look in the mirror and finally decided I'd had enough of seeing a stranger there that I started to feel like maybe I had a life to live after all. Then Mr Mac called.

"What is it with you and Choi, anyway?" Joe asked, pouring more bourbon. "Didn't used to bump uglies did you?"

I barked a laugh. "Shit no!"

"OK. Just thought I sensed a little tension is all."

"Mutual dislike, my friend. What's between us is that she saved my life. I like to pay my debts. Plus she and the missus were compadres during the war." I paused, in truth Choi and

Consuela hadn't really been that close, more politely professional than anything else. They co-ran the Yang-Side intelligence cell, Con was analysis whilst Choi ran the informants and took care of any security leaks with typical efficiency. She'd detected a last minute compromise as I'd led my cell against a Fed-Sec safe house where some of our people were supposedly being tortured. It was a trap, forty Fed-Sec Commandos lying in wait on the surrounding rooftops. Choi had killed her way through the outer perimeter and wide-cast a warning over the open net. The resultant shit-storm was pretty ugly but most of us made it out. Like I said, I like to pay my debts.

The sound of Joe's humming broke my reverie. Redemption Song. Bob Marley. Since when did she like music? And she barely flinched when I used her real name.

Probably the one thing that makes me good at the whole Demon biz is the innate inability to let things go. Consuela used to say it was like a form of autism. Consuela used to say…

I put down my shot-glass and picked up the Sig. "You got any sober-up?"

"Sure, the drawer next to the sink."

I got up and retrieved the pills, dry-swallowed two and tossed him the pack. "Back on the clock, Joe. Take yourself off to Madame Choi's. Exterior obs. Comings and goings. Try to be unobtrusive."

"Erm, OK. Where you gonna be?"

"Need to consult with my priest."

*

Sober-up does what it says on the pack but it also brings on an instantaneous hangover leaving the user bleary-eyed and grimacing from a pounding headache.

"You look like shit," Father Bob commented as I wandered into the chapel. He was placing hymn sheets on the pews for the late night mass. "Been drinking?"

"Only during working hours." I hesitated. We hadn't spoken much since Consuela died. "How's things?"

"Need new plumbing if you'd care to contribute to the collection box."

"Sure." I pushed some green through the slot. "Would've been round sooner…"

"Save it, Alex. You don't believe so why would you come back? It's OK, got my hands full with the sins of the faithful."

"There's a little girl, kidnap case…"

"Whatever you need."

"I need access to the copy. I assume you made one."

Father Bob gave me a sidelong glance, kept placing hymn sheets. "What makes you think that?"

"The soul resides in memory, memory resides in the soul. Preservation of human memory is therefore the holiest of acts." A quotation. Cardinal Eduardo Mendez, ex-communicant, apostate and founder of the Neo-Catholic Church.

"Didn't know you read scripture."

"Consuela did. She was the believer after all."

Father Bob sighed and put down his hymn sheets. "Come on, it's in the office."

*

"It won't be the same," he warned, spooling up the immersion couch. "It's just a construct, an interface for accessing memories, don't expect too much."

I nodded, swallowed, realised my hands were shaking.

"Do you really need to do this?" Father Bob asked.

I closed my eyes, exhaled slowly, refilled my lungs. Four repeats. An old pre-combat routine. "Let's get on with it."

*

I'd opted for the docks as a setting, the viewing platform overlooking the ore freighter bays. It was where I'd first seen her. She hadn't seen me that first time. I'd been hiding in the air ducts, on the run and waiting for an opportunity to stowaway on her father's tug. They ran it together, family operation, had since she was little. But she longed for the freighters, long hauling out to the Belt and back, and would come here to watch them berth or launch. She was watching now, older than the first time, the age she'd been when she died.

I tried to speak and faltered, coughed, forced the words out. "Hello, Con."

She turned, there was a brief moment of blankness then a bright welcoming smile. "Alex." A pause. "You haven't been to see me in nine months and eight days."

I nearly jacked out then and there. Father Bob was right, it wasn't her. Perfect face, perfect voice, but all wrong. Just not her.

"I'm sorry," I stammered. "I'm here now, and I need your help."

Blankness again as the construct programme processed my response. "Of course I'll help."

"Choi," I said. "I need to know about Choi."

"Choi, Soo Ying. Real name Matsuke Hiroka. We served together during the war."

"What do you know about her life before the Slab?"

"Veteran of the Sino-Nippon War. No surviving family members. Served in Japanese Air Force Intelligence then covert ops. She was an entertainer before the war, part of the Tokyo Teen Pop revival, a singer, gave it up when she got married and had a daughter."

A daughter? All this time I had no idea. I'd always assumed Choi spent her entire life either killing people or dealing drugs. "What happened to her family?"

"Killed in the initial Sino assault wave." The construct's face became sombre. "That's very sad."

Looking at this perfect but grotesque facsimile of my wife I couldn't help but conclude Cardinal Mendez had got it wrong. There is no soul in memory, no ghost in the machine.

"Thank you." I couldn't bring myself to say her name. She wasn't there to hear it. "Jack me out please, Father."

*

I was hurrying back to the Pipe when Sherry called. She was using our private channel which didn't bode well. "Problems, Alex. Tech just found a mobile bug latched on to the Department's main comms data feed. Looks like it's been lying dormant for months. Must've cut its way in when they did the last systems upgrade. Very high spec, bespoke engineering."

Mr Mac, he always hired the best. "How much did it get?"

"At least seven hours' worth of comms data, all squirted out in a data-burst less than twenty minutes ago."

Seven hours ago, when I met the sonofabitch. Wind me up and let me go then track my progress a few hours later. Like I said, Mr Mac had no need of tracers.

I check-listed every call I'd made in the previous seven hours. Luckily I hadn't mentioned Choi at any point but I had called Sherry to arrange the SWAT team just after leaving her place. He knew of our association, he knew she dealt Blues and he knew the intel she gave me was a blind. If he hadn't put it together by now he soon would.

"You need to get as many Demons as you can to Madame Choi's place," I told Sherry, now sprinting for the Pipe. "Give them Nina Laredo's ID specs. Advise to shoot on sight."

"Won't be easy. The bug uploaded a virus to the Departmental data core the instant the tech's found it, a really nasty one. Yang-Side police comms are seriously screwed for at least another hour."

"Do what you can." I sounded off, ran onto the axis-bound platform and scraped through the carriage doors a fraction before they closed.

I forced myself to take a seat, checked the Sig then exhaled slowly, refilled my lungs. Four repeats. Pre-combat routine.

*

Joe had secluded himself behind an over-flowing dumpster in the alley opposite the Heavenly Garden, crouched in the shadows, hooded against the sweat-rain, large hands resting on his knees. I wondered if he had any idea how threatening he looked.

"Anything?" I asked.

He rose, shaking his head, rain drops flying from the hood. "Nothing in or out since I got here. Place is closed up. Lights on upstairs though."

I glanced up at the slitted yellow rectangle over the door, knowing whatever awaited me there wasn't likely to be pretty.

"We're going to have company," I told Joe. "Plenty of it and not friendly. No back-up for at least a half hour. You don't have to stay."

Joe's only reaction was a slightly raised eyebrow, but he was the kind of guy who could say a lot with an eyebrow.

"Sorry," I said, drawing the Sig. "Stay close."

The door was locked so I got Joe to bust it open, went in gun raised, blinking in the gloom, finding Marco unmoving on the floor. I went to him, fingered his neck for a pulse. Slow, regular. The sweat dewed pallor of his skin told the tale. Drugged. Syte-line maybe? He wouldn't leave so she put him out.

"Find a closet for him," I told Joe. "Then watch the door. I'll be upstairs."

I lingered at the foot of the stairs, peering up at the half-rectangle of light showing she'd left the door to her office open. Why didn't you run, Choi? I sighed and started climbing.

I gave the door a gentle push, kept the Sig held low. Choi was kneeling before a large sheet of rice paper, dressed in an all-white kimono, guiding the hand of a little girl as she painted Japanese symbols with a bamboo brush.

"This means tree," she told the girl who smiled a little. "You try."

The girl took a firm hold of the brush and tried to copy the symbol, a frown of deep concentration on her small face.

"Very good," Choi complimented her. "Don't you think so, Inspector?" She looked up at me, face absent of any fear or concern. There was also no sign of a weapon within reach. Just a Satsuma-ware tea set with a half-empty bowl.

"Yes," I said, putting the Sig away, coming in, forcing a grin at the girl. "You're very clever."

She gave a shy smile and burrowed into Choi's side, snuggling close.

"Choi," I said, keeping my voice as light as possible. "We don't have much time…"

"Will you sit Inspector?" Choi gestured at the couch opposite. "I'm afraid I have no more tea to offer."

It was clear she had no intention of going anywhere so I went to the couch and sat down. "What's her name?" I asked.

Choi smoothed the little girl's hair back from her forehead. "I doubt she has one. I've been calling her Satomi. She seems to like it."

I didn't need to ask to know Satomi had been her daughter's name. "Let me see if I've read this right. You got wind of a major Blues exchange but didn't know what the package was. You surveilled the hand-over to see if it was worth stealing. Mr Spaghetti and Meatballs turns up with Satomi here. You kill him and the security, hack up the bodies and take her back here to play house."

Choi just smiled and tweaked Satomi's nose, drawing a strange rasping giggle. "She can't laugh," she explained. "Or talk. They made her without vocal chords. The courier had a data stick with all the details. They took a little girl and made her into a narcotics production facility."

I remembered Ricci's call. "Her blood."

"Yes. Her endocrine system has been altered to synthesise Blues. The perfect courier. She's worth billions. And she will never grow old, they took her ageing genes. But she will die, eventually. Blues is a carcinogen, even now she shows early signs of non-Hodgkins lymphoma. She has perhaps another two years."

"That why you didn't run?"

Choi looked at me squarely and I noted a faint sheen of sweat on her forehead. "Where would I run to? I knew who they would send after us." Her voice was a little strained and her hands trembled as they cradled the girl, who now seemed to be sliding into sleep. My eyes flicked to the half-empty tea bowl.

"Choi…"

"My name is Matsuke Hiroka," she said. "I know we have not exactly been friends Inspector, but I am glad you are here to witness my final act. I have lived a life of deceit, crime and violence. And now I have a chance to give it meaning." She held Satomi closer. "If they take her they might save her. Save her for the life they made her for."

An urgent whisper from Joe hissed in my ear. "Movement outside. Counting four so far."

"I can get you out of here," I told Choi. "Get treatment for her…"

"There is no treatment." Her eyelids were drooping but she forced them open, fixing me with an imploring glare. "Consuela worried for you during the war, did you know that? Not for your life but for your soul. The many lives you took, your fierceness. She worried that with the war over there would be no place for you, no path to redemption. But here you are, no less fierce but a force for good. You have your redemption, Alex. Let me have mine."

Joe again, "Getting pretty busy down here, Inspector."

Choi closed her eyes and began to sing, soft, melodious, that old Bob Marley tune again. Satomi shifted a little in her arms, rested her head against Choi's breast, her lips moved as she tried to sing along.

"I'll be right down," I told Joe.

*

Nina Laredo was waiting outside, alone in the middle of the street. The nightly sweat-rain was starting to ease off and the holo-lights reflected off the slick paving like scattered jewels. There were a few hirelings lurking in the corners and no doubt a few more I couldn't see.

"Wait for the signal," I instructed Joe. "Then lay down fire on the right flank. Concentrate on the rooftops."

"What's the signal?"

"It'll be hard to miss." I went outside.

"Inspector," Nina greeted me with the usual professional courtesy, keeping her H&K flechette carbine pointed at the ground. "I am instructed to permit you to vacate the vicinity peaceful-"

I quick-drew the Sig and shot her in the stomach. After that things are pretty hazy.

*

The Heavenly Garden Shoot Out (or Massacre depending on who's telling the story) has since become something of a Yang-Side legend, a story to scare infant crims at bedtime. All about how the big bad Demon gut-shot the most feared hired gun on the Slab, took a flechette burst in the face as she went down but that only seemed to piss him off. There are lurid and improbable tales of extraordinary marksmanship as he went on to pick off the snipers on the rooftops with single shots to the head then engage the survivors in hand-to-hand combat. The ending varies a little but most agree he had to be prevented from further abusing the corpse of Nina Laredo by a large fellow Demon who knocked him unconscious.

Whether or not any of this is true I can't tell you. I honestly don't remember anything after I shot Nina.

*

I woke up in the hospital finding Sherry Mordecai gazing down with an expression I'd never seen on her face before. Pity.

"Don't do that," I croaked, feeling like my oesophagus had been replaced with sand-paper. I blearily fumbled for the water jug next to the bed. Sherry gently pushed my hands away and poured a small amount into a cup, holding it to my lips.

"Thanks," I said, slumping back into the mattress. I met her gaze. "Choi?"

She shook her head. "And the girl. Ricci says sodium thiopental, fast acting and mostly painless."

"Joe?"

"He's fine. Feeling guilty. Thinks he may have hit you too hard. I told him where you're concerned there's no such thing as too hard."

She took something from her pocket and placed it on the bedside table. Mr Mac's smart. "He's been calling. Thought I'd leave it up to you."

She went to the door then hesitated. "Oh, it seems Choi made a will. She's left you the Heavenly Garden, and everything else. It's a shit-load of money and I'm not sure how much of it Professional Standards will let you keep, but for the moment, you're a rich man. Congratulations." With that, she left.

I stared at the Smart for a long time before picking it up and thumbing to the missed calls. He picked up immediately.

"Alex, are you OK?" Genuine concern. No anger or frustration.

"I killed Nina," I said. "Blew her guts out."

"I know. Nina had a professional awareness of the risks inherent in her occupation. I'll miss the contribution she made to my business. But employees are replaceable, friends are not."

"Try and get this, you fucking nutcase, I am not your friend!"

"Of course you are, Alex. As I am your friend. Why else would I give you the opportunity to resolve this?"

A cold realisation gripped my chest. "You knew, you already knew Choi had taken her."

"No, I suspected it and you confirmed it. Being aware of your connection I thought it only fair to at least give you a chance of saving her. Pity how it turned out. I always liked Choi..."

A chance of saving her. "Her name was Matsuke Hiroka and she didn't need saving," I said. "She'd saved herself. Don't call me again. If I see you I am going to kill you." I switched off the smart and tossed it into the water jug.

I suddenly became aware that there was an adhesive bandage on the right side of my face, a big one. The cause of Sherry's pity? I struggled out of bed and wobble walked to the mirror over the sink. A handsome man I barely knew stared back from the mirror. He'd clearly been through some bad times, tired red-tinged eyes set in a pale unshaven mask that was, nevertheless, still unfeasibly attractive.

I reached up and began to unpeel the bandage. Flechette wounds have a signature all their own, the way they score the flesh leaving straight line scars that might have been left by a scalpel. Nina's final shot had carved deep channels in the skin from my jawline to the top of my ear which had been partly sheared away. The medics would have treated the scars with re-growth enzymes but the damage was too severe for a full repair. Without surgery or a complete facial reconstruction I'd be wearing this disfigurement for the rest of my life.

"Now," the handsome man grinned in the mirror, "that's more like it."

END

A HYMN TO GODS LONG DEAD

CHAPTER 1

THE VAMPIRE CAME to the bar just after the Yang Seven lights dimmed to a deeper blue to signify the onset of evening. She was tall with the standard night black hair and alabaster skin, but her clothes were unusual; no lace or leather, just practical grey-green combats, a loosely fitting unbranded t-shirt and a stay-clean jacket of pale blue. No tats either, another surprise, as was her smile. It had none of the cunning or predatory calculation they spent hours perfecting in the mirror - and yes, they do show up in mirrors, gene-splicing has its limits. There was an openness to it, extended canines notwithstanding.

She took a seat at the bar, the tone of her greeting as bright as her smile. "Hi!"

I said, "I don't stock plasma or blood subs."

There was the smallest twitch in her smile. "Water's fine."

"Sparkling or still?"

"Whatever's cheapest."

I met her gaze as I poured the water, not liking what I saw: recognition. *Please, not another killer-Demon groupie.*

I noted a mark on the porcelain of her wrist. A faded pattern too heavily lasered to make out, but the size and location said a lot. Family sigil tattoo on the wrist - second generation vampire thing. *She's probably older than I am.*

She sipped her water, eyes twinkling a little. She was happy to see me.

"I don't do autographs," I said. "I'm not available for freelance employment and I'm on sabbatical from the Lorenzo City Police Department."

She put down her water glass. "I know. I'm sorry to come here, but there wasn't anyone else…"

The jukebox roared to life, Long Tall Sally raising the heads of the few sober patrons. The regulars barely noticed. It was a genuine Wurlitzer, payment for an old debt, and tended to exercise a certain autonomy over when it chose to entertain my customers. One of my first management decisions when taking over the Heavenly Garden was to reverse the former owner's strict no music policy. Something I was beginning to regret.

"That's very loud," the vampire said, wincing a little.

I went over and kicked the Wurlitzer to silence, picking up Blue Nancy's empty glass for an unasked for refill on the way back. "Lord'll reward ye iffin I don't, Inspector."

I held the glass to the Kentucky Red optic, it had become my best seller since Joe procured me a pallet-full from his friend at the docks.

"As I said…" the Vampire began.

"As *I* said, I'm on sabbatical." I handed Blue Nancy her drink as she shambled to the bar. "It's a polite way of saying they fired me but haven't filed the paperwork." I ran a cloth over where Nancy had spilt just a little before returning to her usual place by the long out-of-order pinball machine.

"I run a bar," I told the vampire. "Demon days are over Cornelia or Althea or whatever your fucked in the head parents called you. Whatever it is, I can't help you."

The smile hadn't gone completely, but she wasn't showing her teeth anymore. "Thomas DeMarco," she said. "Ten months ago. You were the lead investigator."

DeMarco. I didn't need to dig through too many memories, it had been a bad one... and unsolved.

"You a relative?" I asked, thinking it unlikely.

"No, just... an interested party." She reached into her jacket, coming out with a cheap smart and placing it on the bar. I noticed her nails weren't overly long, no black enamel varnish either. "All I ask is that you look at this." She eased herself off the bar stool. "Contact details included if you want to talk some more."

She gave me a final look, oddly warm in its appraisal given what a prick I was being, tapped her unvarnished nails on the bar and left.

The Wurlitzer blazed into life again as I contemplated the smart. "Fucking hell!" I realised I was reaching for the Sig in my belt with every intention of blowing the glass-chrome monster to pieces. Except the Sig wasn't there, Sherry Mordecai had taken it after handing over my notice of suspension. I contented myself with wrenching the Wurlitzer's power lead from the wall then picked up the smart with every intention of tossing it in the garbage.

"Kindly girl," Blue Nancy was saying, mostly to herself, gazing at the door. "Kindly girl calls to the warrior, smile like summer, his heart like flint."

"I told you before, Nance," I said, without any real conviction. "Any more haiku and you're barred."

My thumb pressed the smart's command menu, calling up the contacts file: Dr Janet Vaughan, PhD, Emeritus Professor of Classical Studies, Lorenzo City University (Yang Faculty).

"Janet?" I said. "What kind of vamp is called Janet?"

*

I pushed out the regulars a few minutes before closing time, told Marco to go home, he could clean up in the morning. I went upstairs in company with a bottle of Red and the vamp's smart, checked my own for messages - one from Joe, three from Sherry - and settled onto the futon making the thousandth firm resolution to buy a couch tomorrow.

Dr Janet's files were neatly arranged in a web-matrix familiar to anyone who'd ever seen a crimint report; lines interlinking subject nodes with time stamps. Thomas DeMarco was highlighted in red. I opened the file finding a brief bio and a crime report of sorts, all open source stuff missing the more lurid details, but I had a vivid memory of those already.

Thomas DeMarco, aged sixty-two, father of three daughters, self-styled King of Curry as owner and CEO of the Pipin' Hot lamb curry franchise, third largest home delivery and restaurant chain this side of the Axis. A rich fellow by Yang-side standards, when he went missing it was naturally assumed he'd been kidnapped for ransom, a tradition of the small but vibrant Mexican criminal sub-culture in our fair city. Except no ransom demand was forthcoming. Six days and no calls, no notes, no body parts in the post. Which is not to say Mr DeMarco's case was a dismemberment free zone. A worker in one of his slaughterhouses on Yang Thirty found an unlogged barrel of rendered animal fat in a quiet corner of the yard, inside was Thomas DeMarco, all six pieces of him, bobbing in the grease like an underdone stew.

The family was rich and demanded the best from Chief Arnaud. He gave them me and Sherry, and we found nothing. Granted I'll confess my mental state was nothing to boast about at the time, Consuela's death was only three months gone and my apartment was beginning to resemble the cage of a gorilla with a serious fast-food problem. But I would like it on the record that I did my detectively best for poor dis-constituted Mr DeMarco.

He'd last been seen paying a visit to a handsome young man in a nicer corner of Yang Thirty-Two. DeMarco had an active sex life and, not one to discriminate, maintained an expensive stable of young men and women scattered throughout the Yang levels. Mrs DeMarco was clearly an understanding wife, evidenced by the fact that many of these specialist employees were invited to the funeral and eager to help with enquiries. The young man who had last enjoyed DeMarco's company was a square-jawed youth of muscular proportions whose evident grief didn't prevent him slipping me his smart ID when Sherry's back was turned. DeMarco's visit had been routine, if apparently vigorous, the King of Curry spent a lot on rejuve treatments, and he left in company with two bodyguards at nearly midnight. The bodyguards were both ex-military, highly experienced and working under strict Duress Protocol. They boarded an empty Pipe carriage for the journey home. Ten minutes or so later the lights went out along with the security cams, and the carriage came to a sudden and jarring halt, throwing both guards off their feet. Sixty seconds later the lights came on and they were looking at the space where DeMarco had been. Both claimed to have neither heard, smelt or felt anything, a testimony which stood up to some hard grilling and a court-ordered dose of sodium pentathol.

We ran intensive forensic scans over the Pipe carriage and found nothing. Same for the remains and the barrel they came in. Ricci's autopsy found no trace of sedative or poison, though he advised that death had been caused by the first dismemberment, inflicted with a standard-grade automated power saw of the type used in the production line at the very slaughterhouse where the remains had been discovered. Tests of the plant confirmed it. DeMarco had been put through his own mincer.

DeMarco, like most Yang-side businessmen, had his fair share of enemies, largely among his competitors who couldn't disguise their delight at his demise. But none of them had the stones, or the contacts, to arrange a hit of such precision and brutality. All alibis checked out and whilst we found plenty of financial irregularities, enough in fact to land a few in the Slab

City slammer, there were no mysterious payments to numbered Latvian accounts or unexplained withdrawals of folding green in mixed denominations.

Sherry and I worked it for a month, coming up empty on every lead and getting only blank stares or desperate lies from informants. Eventually, word came down from the Chief to hand it over to Major Cases, where we knew it would languish in the desk of some time-server for a few years before being quietly filed away.

I remembered I hadn't liked handing it off. Something was very wrong about the whole thing, beyond the obvious gruesome torture and murder stuff, of course. It didn't fit any template, too anonymous and savage for a professional job, too clean and efficient for a psycho / sociopath. It rankled but we were getting slammed with a series of gang killings on Yang Forty so I filed it under 'to be continued if I ever get the time', knowing I never would.

I skimmed through Dr Janet's amateur crime report, noting the phrase 'three daughters' had been highlighted. Did she have something on the daughters? We'd checked them out, all in their twenties, two were law-graduates with top level positions in the family business, ironically in charge of the slaughterhouse division. The third daughter was living comfortably on a trust fund on the other side of the Axis. They were all convincingly traumatised with equally convincing alibis.

I checked out the other two subject nodes, picking the one with the oldest date stamp - September 28, 2240. The files consisted of another crime report and a 2D of a grinning young man, holding an antique looking guitar in one hand with his arm draped over a smiling girl. The background indicated some Downside desert-ville. The crime report told me his name was Dwayne Francis Rickard, musician (this was highlighted), age nineteen, denizen of Ribera, New Mexico Territory. From the press reports it seems Dwayne had been suffering from severe depression following the death by Bliss overdose of his girlfriend, presumably the girl in the 2D ('girlfriend' highlighted). When he went missing the local sheriff immediately suspected suicide, a reasonable theory he was forced to discount when Dwayne's head washed up on the banks of the Pecos river ('river' again highlighted). His mutilated and headless body was found in a drainage ditch ten miles upstream.

I wondered if this might be another unsolved case but noticed a file marked 'convictions'. The local sheriff, an efficient fellow, ran down three suspects in as many days, all young, female and well known Blissfuls. They claimed to know nothing of Dwayne's demise but the forensic evidence was overwhelming, DNA found in their hair, under their fingernails, in their mouths, between their teeth. It seems poor old Dwayne had got the worst of the deadlier of the species. The girls had been convicted and executed within the month - New Mexico Territory was renowned for swift and merciless justice, none of that leaving them to stew on death-row for ten years stuff anymore.

I re-read the report for any connection to DeMarco but could see nothing beyond the dismemberment of both victims. One was a disorganised murder by brain-addled junkies, the other an expert abduction and motiveless act of savagery.

The third and final node held the least information and was also the most recent. Ygor Karnikhov, aged forty-two, Slab resident and employee of Exocore Mining. Found dead two days ago in the central asteroid processing plant on Yang One. The details, cribbed from a police announcement, were sketchy. Homicide was confirmed and the phrase "brutal and senseless killing" used along with "no suspects currently in custody." The only highlight on this node was a snippet from Karnikhov's bio: "keen volunteer for various charities", and an image file. It was a poor quality 2D, probably taken on the move and well short of crime scene quality, but the contents were clear enough if you looked closely: a man chained by his arms and legs to what appeared to be a wall of rock, slumped and lifeless, with a large incision in his side and a chunk of his guts hanging out.

I looked at it for a long time, feeling a faint murmur of the same sensation of wrongness that had plagued me during the DeMarco investigation. *This doesn't fit.*

My own smart was buzzing, dragging my attention away from the blurred image of Ygor Karnikhov's corpse. The caller ID was blank and the message read: "You need to talk to the vampire." I thumbed the reply icon but received an instant "ID non-existent" bleep, which was as good as a signature; no-one else could wipe a call so quickly.

"Freak," I murmured to my empty apartment above my empty bar. "What are you about now?"

CHAPTER 2

THE NEXT MORNING I locked up, put a 'closed - get drunk somewhere else' sign on the door and caught the Pipe. The contact file gave an address on Yang Eighteen. Not a salubrious neighbourhood, but far from the worst. I called Sherry on the way.

"Finally," she said. "Three days I've been leaving messages."

"Been busy. Drunks don't serve themselves, y'know."

A brief silence and I knew she was stopping herself say, *You should know.* Instead she said, "So can you make it?"

"Make what?"

"Please tell me you did actually listen to my messages."

"Erm…"

"Christ!" A part muffled sigh of exasperation. "My place, tonight, eight pm. Bring a bottle." *Should be easy for you,* she didn't say.

"What's the occasion?"

"It's my birthday, you prick."

"Can you remember my birthday?" I asked, getting pissed. "Can't really recall any card or gift-giving rituals being part of our almost entirely professional relationship, boss."

"Well now it is. Besides, I want you to meet Sam."

Sam was her new squeeze. Truth be told, as far as I knew, Sam was her only squeeze. Sherry didn't talk about her pre-

Demon days and in the time I'd known her she'd always been way too much of a workaholic to accommodate a relationship. Recent months had seen something of a change in her, not a softening exactly, more a loss of the tense defensiveness I liked so much. It left me a little resentful of the as yet unseen Sam and not inclined towards an evening of enforced socialising. But I needed a favour and was already in a weak negotiating position.

"I'll be there," I said. "Listen, what do you know about the Karnikhov case?"

"I've got Red Wing on it. Pretty nasty, leads are thin on the ground." A pause. "Why the interest, Alex? You got something?"

I pulled the vampire's smart from my pocket and called up the blurred shot of the crime scene. *Wrong. Doesn't fit.* "Maybe. Probably nothing."

"I'm listening."

"I want to work it a little first. Since it's probably nothing."

"You are aware you have no legal standing just now, right?"

"Fully aware, thank you." My tone was harder than I intended and she lapsed back into silence for a moment.

"Well don't kill anybody. My place at eight. Bring wine." *Not that bourbon you're so fond of,* she didn't say. The line went dead.

"Can't kill anybody," I muttered. "You took my gun."

*

The vampire's hab was the upper half of a prefab block otherwise occupied by an oriental spice shop. Approaching the place I took in the hard to miss sight of a large multi-tattooed youth - bare brawny arms, black wife-beater, shaven head - standing stock still on the walkway outside. It was the stillness that caught my attention, the rigid, sweaty tremble of his stance was out of place, as was the large dark stain on his combats and the puddle lapping at his boots.

"Public urination's a crime, Jed," I advised, ambling up.

I didn't have an ID to show him but with his type I didn't need one.

"Nnnn..!" said Shave-head, not meeting my gaze, jaw tensing a little, drool staining his lips.

I frowned, this wasn't going how it should. Whatever he was on it was something new. I moved closer, shouting into his ear: "Go away, fuckhead!"

"He's not allowed." It was an elderly Asian lady, clutching a broom in the shop doorway, eyes cautious. She didn't need to see an ID either.

"By who?" I asked.

She flicked her gaze at the upper storey window then went back inside. I gave Shave-head a final curious glance then followed her, fishing the cheap smart from my pocket. "I'm looking for…"

"I know. She's expecting you. Take the stairs at the back." The old woman put her broom aside and moved behind the counter. The shop had a rich aroma of mingled spices, not unpleasant but surely a shock to anyone with gene-enhanced olfactory senses.

"How long's she been here?" I asked.

"Two months, give or take."

"Good tenant?"

Her gaze became suspicious, defensive. "She's a good person. Doesn't deserve any trouble from you."

I could tell she knew who I was. The Heavenly Garden Shoot Out (or massacre, depending on who you ask) ensured an unwelcome celebrity these days. "Nice to know."

I moved to the back of the shop, finding the stairs. She opened the door before I could knock, same bright, open smile as before. "You came! I hoped you would." She stood aside. "Come in, come in."

Her furnishings were elegant if sparse, a few objets d'art, mostly Asian ceramics, some tasteful twentieth century prints.

No 2Ds or holo-stills, of her or anyone else. And books, a whole wall of books. Clearly Dr Janet was something of a traditionalist.

"Get you anything?" she asked, closing the door. "Coffee, tea..."

"Who killed Thomas DeMarco?" I said.

She paused then laughed a little. "Straight to it. I should've expected that." She went to her couch, low set and fake but still expensive leather, perching on the arm, long legs crossed. "I don't know who killed him but I think I might know why."

"And the Downside musician kid?"

"Him too."

"And Karnikhov?"

"Yep."

I went to the window, looking down on Shave-head. "There's a man outside standing in his own piss, too scared to move. Know anything about that too?"

She shrugged, a little sheepish. "He was upsetting Mrs Yeung. Demanding money with menaces I believe it's called."

"What did you do to him?"

"I told him to stand there. Some people still have a superstitious view of my kind. Flash them some fang and they'll convince themselves you've put a hoodoo on them."

I met her gaze, seeing only a small flicker of worry in her too perfect face. "When I leave, tell him he can go. Tell him I said not to come back here. That should be enough."

She pursed her lips and nodded. "Don't you want to hear my theory?"

"If you have information about the Karnikhov case you should take it to Chief Inspector Mordecai, LCPD Homicide Bureau."

"I've been messaging for days. When I finally got through to the case officer, Redwin or something, he told me not to waste his time and hung up."

"We get a lot of wierdo calls, cranks, fake psychics, wannabe amateur sleuths and the like. All convinced they've got the vital insight that'll break the big case. What makes you any different?"

She laughed again. "I don't know. Maybe nothing. You can be the judge when you've heard what I've got to say." She rose and went to an old writing bureau positioned so it faced her wall of books, lifting a live-text sheet from the desk and holding it out to me. "It's all here, if you want to read it."

"Tell me instead."

She tilted her head a little. It was the first predatory mannerism she'd exhibited, focused, feline and more attractive than I wanted it to be. "Easier to tell if I'm crazy or lying if you hear me say it, right?"

"That's right."

"Fair enough." She sat in the swivel chair in front of the desk, putting aside the live-text. "What do you know about the Greek legend of Medea, Inspector?"

"I'm not an Inspector these days. And my formal education was a little limited."

"Medea was a sorceress and Priestess of Hecate, daughter of King Aeetes, ruler of Colchis and keeper of the Golden Fleece. When Jason arrived with his Argonauts to claim the fleece she fell in love with him, helping to steal it and fleeing with him on the Argo. They sailed back to Iolcus in triumph, for Jason had been promised the kingship of the land if he managed the impossible feat of stealing the fleece. But when they arrived jealous King Pelias refused to give up the throne. Medea, beautiful and wise but also cunning and ruthless, promised Pelias the secret of eternal youth. Killing and butchering an elderly goat she placed the pieces in a cauldron from which a young, healthy goat sprang a moment later. Pelias' daughters, seeing this and keen to honour their father, fell upon him with knives, cutting him to pieces and throwing them into the cauldron, expecting a new youthful king to emerge. But, of course, they had been tricked, and Pelias was truly dead."

She had the voice of a natural story-teller, strong and compelling. I supposed it went with her profession.

"What happened to Medea?" I asked. "Did they kill her?"

"No. Some legends say she and Jason ruled Iolcus together, but Euripides has her murdering their children a few years later when he dumps her for a younger woman."

"Charming."

"That's the Greeks for you."

I took a seat on the couch. I could understand why Red Wing hung up on her. Myths and legends all smacked of just another crank theory. But I had reason to keep listening. *You need to talk to the vampire.*

"You got anything to drink?" I asked.

"Sure." She got up. "Real coffee, fresh off the transport…"

"No bourbon? Whisky?"

"I don't drink alcohol. It doesn't agree with me."

"Unlike coffee or tea?"

"They're less… disagreeable."

I got up. "Get your coat. There's a bar on Gable Street."

"So, you think I have something?"

"Thomas DeMarco was a king of sorts, big fan of staying young, with daughters, found dismembered in a barrel in one of his own slaughterhouses, which they were running. It's a stretch but you could say they killed him, albeit indirectly. And I'm guessing you have something similar to tell me about Karnikhov and Rickard."

"Indeed I do."

"Then get your coat."

*

The bar was called The Marble Head and threw the shittiness of the Heavenly Garden into stark relief. Clean, ceramic tiling covered the walls, the floors decorated in checker board patterns fringed with fluer de lys. The bartender was a campy splice working a were-panther look who gave Dr Janet a pouty glance of pique which disappeared when he saw me. "What can I get you, m'loves?"

"Do you stock Kentucky Red?"

"That's pretty hard to come by. Got JD though."

"Give me a double, straight, no ice. And whatever my friend wants."

"We don't have plasma," he said.

Dr Janet raised an eyebrow at me. "Does anyone? Water's fine."

I chose a booth at the back, facing the door and close to the emergency exit. Demon habits die hard.

"So," I said, "Rickard and Karnikhov."

"Rickard was a musician," she began. "Young, talented and starting to get a lot of attention on the net, then his girl-friend died. He went into a deep depression and ends up torn to pieces with his head floating down a river." She looked at me in expectation.

"Yeah, I read that in your file."

She swallowed a small sigh. My scholarly ignorance was starting to grate. "Orpheus," she said. "Son of Calliope the Muse and Morpheus, God of Dreams, and the greatest musi-cian in all the world. When his beloved Eurydice died, he jour-neyed into the underworld to reclaim her. Hades, lord of the dead, made him a bargain: 'I will give you back your bride, she will follow you along the path to the land of the living, but you must keep your eyes on the way ahead and not turn until you reach the world above. If you do, Eurydice will be lost to you forever.' And so he walked the path, all the time hearing nothing behind him, no footsteps, no sign that his beloved was following, all the time itching to turn, ever more convinced he had been tricked. And then, when the light of the living world was but a short distance away and his journey nearly complete, he could bear it no longer and he turned. She was there. She had been all along, and the last he saw of her was her face disappearing into the black void of the underworld.

"Heartbroken and sick with grief, Orpheus roamed the land, singing his lament, until the wild women of the Bacchae found him. Perhaps they were angered by the sadness of his song, or simply possessed of the blood-lust for which they were famed. In any case they tore Orpheus to pieces and cast his head into the Hebrus River, where it floated out to sea, still singing his lament."

She had something alright. The parallel was just too close. But there were obvious difficulties. "Three women were executed for Rickard's murder," I pointed out.

"Yes." She made a small grimace of consternation. "Not sure what to make of that. Maybe someone paid them to do it. People take money to do all manner of terrible things."

"They had his DNA in their teeth. That's a pretty big ask, regardless of the fee."

She shrugged. "Don't know what to tell you, Mr McLeod. I'm not a detective, just an academic with a theory."

You're more than that, I decided. *No way she's spent her whole life lost in books.*

"Karnikhov," I said.

"Ah." She brightened, enthused. "The Prometheus of my theory."

Prometheus. This one I knew. *Cap Blackmore, spray-painting a tableau on the nose of his ship: muscular hero type with a flaming torch.* "The Jed who stole fire from the gods."

Dr Janet smiled in surprise. "Quite so. Did they teach you this one in school?"

"Never went to school. A tug captain told me the story. Renamed his boat when the war started. This was the early days when we were deluded enough to think we could field a battle fleet of our own. A hundred or so converted tugs and cargo haulers, kitted out with whatever weaponry we could lay our hands on. I'd been drafted in to augment the crew numbers. I guess Cap wanted something fierce but classy, inspire the crew or some such. Didn't do any good. An EMP took out our main bus ten seconds into the first engagement and a plasma-shrike cracked us open like an egg. I spent six hours floating around in an EVA suit, stewing in my own filth before the rescue boat picked me up. After that we stuck firmly to low-intensity warfare."

She was staring at me intently and I realised with a start I'd spoken aloud. Even worse, my glass was empty. "Give me a minute."

I returned from the bar a few minutes later, hoping the pause had made her forget my inadvertent reverie. "So, the gods killed Prometheus, right? Punishment for giving fire to humanity."

"Not quite. Prometheus was a titan and therefore immortal. So Zeus had him chained to a rock where his liver was perpetually devoured by an eagle."

I thought of the blurred image of the crime scene. Chained to a rock for sure, mutilated for sure. But an eagle? "Birds are in short supply on the Slab, you may have noticed."

"Not an eagle. A salvage-bot, raptor class."

"That wasn't in your file."

"Only caught a glimpse before they hustled me out."

I took out the cheap smart and called up the 2D of Karnikhov's corpse. "You took this?"

"As they were pushing me away, yeah. They were disassembling the salvage-bot, but I couldn't get a shot of it."

"How'd you know about the murder? For that matter, how'd you know about any of this?"

"Research for my latest thesis."

"Which is about?"

"You've heard of the Mythos Movement?"

I recalled a news report from a few months ago. "Some kinda cult, right? People looking to the old gods because the new ones turned out to be so shitty?"

She gave a brief chuckle. "I'm guessing you're not a spiritual man. The Mythos Movement is a loose amalgam of sects, some more earnest in their beliefs than others, seeking spiritual guidance from pre-Christian concepts of the divine. Some are focused on the Greeks, others the Norse or Celtic pantheons, a few on the Egyptians. The underlying philosophy is that these beliefs offer a more fundamental insight into human spirituality than what they see as the mundane, demagogic monotheism of the Judeo-Christian tradition."

"Orpheus having his head torn off and tossed in a river is some kind of spiritual lesson?"

"Orpheus ostensibly died for love. Two thousand years ago a man was tortured and nailed to a cross for the same reason. Prometheus, renowned champion of humanity, sacrificed himself to bring us light and warmth. King Pelias was punished by Medea for his pride and vanity. The lessons are there is you look close enough."

My gaze returned to the 2D. "You're saying there's some whack-brain follower of this Mythos thing out there doing all this?"

"Maybe. All I know is my search-gear was programmed to look for aberrant behaviour in relation to the Mythos Movement. I'm examining the way religious adherence tends to follow certain patterns; devotion, ritualised worship, fanaticism and so on."

"Trying to prove it's really all just the same old shit, huh?"

"Well, not really…"

"Hey, no arguments here. You must have pretty sophisticated search-gear if it found this."

"Actually, no. Standard academic ware only."

"You have Alpha-grade secure net access?"

"That's a little out of my price range. Standard access only." She frowned. "Is that significant?"

You need to talk to the vampire. "I don't know yet." I threw back the rest of my bourbon and stood up. "Let's go."

"Where to?"

"To see if you can get me my job back."

CHAPTER 3

"YOU HAVE TO be shitting me with this, boss!" Harry Red Wing was cut from a heroic mould, complete with V-shaped torso, chiselled and tanned features and long black hair, the genetic legacy of pure-blood Navajo stock, or so he claimed. He was competent enough but I'd always found him way too jealous of his status and performance stats. Plus he was kind of a bigot when it came to the spliced, especially the vampiric variety.

"Some leecher walks in here with a crackpot theory and we're actually giving it credence."

"I'm giving it credence," I said. "You don't have to do shit, Harry boy. I'll even let you put your name on it when I solve the case for you."

"Oh, fuck you, Alex! I've cleared twice the homicides you ever did."

"You had four times as many open and shuts, so I'd say your score is actually pretty low."

"Enough!" Sherry broke in as Red Wing bridled. We were in her office, Janet on the other side of the glass partition. She'd laid it all out then Sherry had politely asked her to wait outside so Red Wing and me could shout at each other.

"This *is* all pretty farfetched," Sherry said. "I mean, I see the similarities but it doesn't all scan. This Rickard kid for a start, they had a bullseye on the killers within hours."

"Mistakes happen," I said. "And we've still got zip on DeMarco, and, I'm guessing," I winked at Red Wing, "nothing on Karnikhov either."

"We always agreed DeMarco must've been some kind of overly inventive hit. A Shuriken showing off."

"That was your theory."

"Which you agreed with, as I recall."

"And now I've got a better one."

"Who says I've got no leads on Karnikhov?" Red Wing put in.

"Oh, OK." I sat back, hands splayed. "Thrill me hotshot."

He flushed a little but ploughed on. "Karnikhov was a vet. Quadruple amputee and Axis resident, one of the details we held back. His war record is sealed. Whoever killed him is in there, and I'll prove it when CAOS Defence unseals it."

"Have fun in your dotage when that happens. Doesn't mean shit anyway, *my* war record is sealed."

Sherry gave an amused snort. "And there's no-one on the Slab who wants *you* dead, right Alex?"

She had a point, as did Red Wing. Karnikhov's war service was where I'd've been looking. But for one thing.

"It's not just me," I told Sherry, taking out my smart. I called up the message I'd received the night before and placed it in front of her.

"There's no sender details," she said.

"No, and the ID was instantly wiped when I opened it."

"That's impossible," Red Wing said.

"Wait outside," Sherry told him in a tone that didn't invite argument.

Red Wing gave me a clench-jawed stare of anger and went out into the squadroom, visibly restraining himself from slamming the door and ignoring Janet's polite greeting. She raised her eyebrows at me through the glass and gave a comic pout which drew an involuntary chuckle.

"You spoken to it yet?" Sherry asked.

I turned back, catching the smart as she tossed it over the desk. "My next port of call. Providing you put me back on the clock."

"Your disciplinary board is five days away. I reinstate you before that, I'll be facing one myself."

"Can't work this as a neutered Demon."

"Then don't. I'll put someone else on it."

The question in her gaze was plain: *How bad do you want back in?*

"Call me a private contractor if you want," I said, hoping the desperation didn't colour my voice too much. "I won't even bill you."

"Suspended LCPD officers are barred from employment in the commercial law enforcement sector." Sherry got up to tap the glass, beckoning Janet into the room. "Dr Vaughan, do you have any criminal convictions?"

Janet gave me an uncertain glance. "No, erm…"

"Do you regularly associate with criminals, drug addicts or gang members?"

"Only on weekends." She laughed. Sherry didn't. "Uh, no," Janet said quietly. "No I don't."

"Are you confident your personal history and finances would pass a standard grade security check?"

"I suppose. Not sure what that is though."

"Good." Sherry held out her smart. "Thumb-print please."

Janet looked at me again. "It's OK," I said. "My boss-cum-friend has found a way to simultaneously squeeze my nuts and let us work this case."

Janet hesitated some more then held her thumb to the screen. "Try not to blink." Sherry held up her smart to take a cap of Janet's left eye. She went back to her desk, fingers dancing on the holo-interface. A short wait then Janet's smart gave a loud, official sounding beep.

"Special Investigator?" she said, reading the screen, brows furrowed.

"Provisional pending security clearance," Sherry said. "Welcome to the Department, Dr Vaughan."

"Did you just make me a Demon?"

"More like a helper-Demon. The Department has leeway to employ civilian specialists on an ad hoc basis."

"Do I have to carry a gun?"

"No."

"Do I get paid?"

"Expenses only, I'm afraid. However, you may, as a civilian, use the services of any clerical staff you happen to employ independently." She gave me her best boss-smile, all 'take one for the team' fake sincerity. "I can recommend a candidate if you like."

I said, "I want my gun back."

"And I look forward to handing it over in five days." She turned to Janet. "Excuse my ignorance, Doctor, but do you have any special dietary requirements? I've never cooked for a vampire before."

"Cooked?"

"Yes. Tonight, my birthday shindig. Alex insisted I invite you."

I stood and went to the door. "We'll call when we have something." I pulled it open and walked out, hearing Janet tell Sherry a rare steak would be fine.

*

"So what happens in five days?"

We were on the Pipe, heading for the Axis. As usual the lights were fritzed and the nauseating zoetrope flicker had me dry-swallowing my third painkiller of the day. "A disciplinary board will decide if I get to stay a Demon or not," I replied.

"Did you… do something bad?"

I rubbed my temples. How long had it been since I'd had a drink? "Bad is a relative concept."

"Don't want to talk about it," she said softly. "Sorry. I'll shut up."

I glanced at her flawless profile in the shimmering fluorescence. Did they make her this way? Feed in the specs for the perfect vampire babe and out she pops nine months later. Yet instead of sitting around brooding on one of their private orbitals, as they were apt to do, she was a working academic on the shittiest hab in orbit.

"Tell you what," I said. "We'll go one for one. I get an answer to my question, you get an answer to yours."

"I don't eat people," she said. "Animal derived blood products only."

"Not that." I nodded at the pale blemish on her wrist. "What was it?"

Her fingers played over the former tattoo for a second. "An eye." Her voice, for once, was devoid of humour.

"What kind of eye?"

"Eye of Horus. And that's two questions. Your turn."

"I'm accused of trying to throw a suspect out of an airlock."

"Did you?"

"Oh yeah. Sherry stopped me though, got there just in time."

"She reported you?"

"Didn't have much choice since I did it in full view of about fifty dock workers."

"Why?"

I grinned at her. "That's four questions. Why don't you ask about my face? People always want to know about that."

"Your original face was lost in the Langley Raid at the end of the war. Your scars, which for some reason you haven't had removed, were obtained in an exchange of gunfire with several armed criminals, all of whom died in the incident which has become known as the Heavenly Garden Massacre." She returned my grin. "Research is what I do."

*

"I heard you got fired," Colonel Riviere said, bio-mech fingers steepled as he floated behind his desk. Having an office in a micro-grav environment made a desk a redundant feature but my former father-in-law was nothing if not a traditionalist.

"Suspended," I said. "Try not to be too cut up about it, Dad."

"Don't call me that." His replacement sonar-eyes shifted from me to Janet. "Never seen a vampire Demon before."

She smiled back, bright and cheerful. I wondered if she'd intuited that he'd hate that. "Just a helper-Demon, apparently."

Colonel Riviere's gaze did some more shifting between us and I discerned a certain calculation in it, despite the metallic blankness in his sockets. "Most of your kind sat out the war, as I recall. Stayed on their habs. Didn't lift a finger when UNOIF plasma-shriked their neighbours."

Janet stared back, saying nothing. Whatever she may have done in the war, she wasn't interested in sharing it.

"Not here for a history lesson," I said. "Ygor Karnikhov. Did you know him?"

"A little. We have over a thousand residents now. Hard to keep track of everybody."

"Anything could be useful."

Riviere shrugged. "War vet, like all of us. Worked in asteroid mining, like most of us these days. Well adapted to micrograv, interchangeable limbs. Smarter, faster and cheaper than bot labour. We're a real boon to the CAOS economy." His tone was absent of anything which might signify pleasure at this development. Riviere was still an ardent campaigner for disabled veterans' rights, the meagre pension being a major point of complaint. Officialdom was less than sympathetic to claims of persistent impairment in an age when medical science could repair a severed spine, restore burnt tissue or replace your limbs with something that had an even greater range of motion, not to say tensile strength. It didn't help that the mining industry was such a keen employer and most maimed vets lived rent free in the only micro-grav zone on the Slab.

"Any enemies you know of?" I asked. "Some grudge left over from the war maybe?"

"Didn't serve with him," the Colonel replied. "Heard he was Special Ops. Maybe you knew him."

"It was a big circus. We need to see his hab."

"Blue Tier, number seventeen. You'll have to find your own way."

"Sure." I pitched towards the exit and paused. "I'll be calling on Freak while I'm here. Just so you know."

"She won't see you."

Freak was always female to Riviere, which was weird as Consuela always thought of the big splice-blob as male.

"Sure about that?" I asked. "How long since you spoke?"

From his tense wave of dismissal I divined Freak was maintaining the policy of isolation which had been in place since what had become known as the 'immolation incident.'

"I'll pass on your compliments, Dad," I said, hauling myself outside.

*

It seemed athleticism was another aspect of Janet's genetic feature-set from the way she propelled herself towards the Axis hab tiers, zipping from hand-hold to hand-hold with a natural grace that put my efficient but workmanlike shoves to shame.

"Keep up!" she called with a giggle, tucking her legs in to tumble to a perfect landing on the grab-way leading to the cluster of blue, bulb-shaped habs.

"Done this before?" I asked as I caught up.

"That's five questions." She grinned and took off again. I found her waiting at the door to Karnikhov's hab.

"Show your smart to the lock," I said. "You should already be cleared for access."

"Oh." She waved her smart at the lock-pad which slid open without delay. "Neato." She started to enter but I waved her back. This wouldn't be the first time I'd opened a door to find a killer rifling through a victim's belongings. The absence of the Sig was a fiery itch in my hand as I peered round the door jamb. Nothing in the living room. I went inside, finding the sleep chamber and washroom both empty.

"OK," I said.

"I can protect myself, y'know," Janet said, her tone carrying a small note of reproach.

"Indulge me. I've got an archetype to live up to." I waved a hand at the empty hab. "Tell me what you see."

Her eyes tracked round the room, features taking on that feline, predatory set I'd seen at her apartment. "He was neat," she said. "But ex-military people usually are, I guess." She plucked the remote from a stick-pad on the wall and accessed the entertainment hub, scrolling through the most recent items. "Liked his sports, and his docs, twentieth-century history by the looks of it. Fair amount of porn but that's hardly unusual for a single man. Or any man, eh?"

"What else?"

She called up the comms display. "Plenty of friends. Flurry of calls after his disappearance so he was missed pretty quickly." She went further back. "Message of thanks from the Lorenzo City Educational Forum, seems he did a charity EVA endurance event for them in December. Fits with what we know about him."

"Run a search," I said. "Key-phrase 'Grey Wolf'."

She gave me a quizzical look.

"Please."

"No hits," she reported after the search completed. "Anything I should know about?"

"Not really." Grey Wolf was the alert code flashed to former Spec-Ops types when their one-time masters had something to tell them, such as 'the friend / lover / brother or whatever of the target you assassinated ten years ago knows where you are.' *Whoever killed him, he didn't see them coming.*

I checked for the most likely place. *Where would I hide it?* My gaze alighted on the join between the far wall and the main support beam; central location, easy to get to in a hurry or the dark. I floated over and felt around the base of the support, detecting a slight texture change in the paint, a patch about ten inches square. *Red Wing missed it. Fucking idiot.*

"What are..?" Janet began then stopped when I delivered a full force punch to the wall. The patch gave way like rice paper and my hand closed on something hard and familiar.

"Well look at you," I said, pulling the hand-gun free. It was a modified Colt Python repro: .357 magnum six-shooter, six inch barrel, porcelain and graphene composite body and cylinder; no metal to set off the scanners. No serial numbers either. I cracked open the cylinder finding it fully loaded. Plastic jacketed epoxy slugs with a phosphorus core. An untraceable close-quarters kill weapon, and an old friend.

"Got a thing for guns, huh?" Janet asked. For the first time there was something like disapproval in her voice and she eyed the Python with obvious distaste.

"Just securing evidence. I'll hand it in later." I pocketed the Python along with the two speed-loaders in the hidey-hole. "Jed like him, way too well prepared for a surprise at home."

Janet held up her smart, the holo displaying the official case file. "Last seen going on shift at the ore processing plant, 2200 hours, seems he was on lates this month. Didn't check out at the expected time, 0600. Found six hours later chained to an unprocessed asteroid with a salvage-bot chewing on his liver.

Exocore employment file has him down as part of the Helium 3 extraction division."

Helium 3, primary fuel for the fusion generators that ran the Slab plus every hab in the Confederation of Autonomous Orbiting States. Something began to click in my head but Janet was already there.

"An elemental fuel source," she murmured.

"Or fire from the gods," I said, the last vestiges of any doubt fading fast. *If you're an obsessed nutbag who thinks ancient myths are real, that is.* "What was his specialty?"

"EVA servo-bot retrieval and repair. Basically, he'd fly around collecting any bots that'd stopped working. The mining companies tend to work their bots to destruction so there's a pretty high failure rate. Looks like he'd been logging a lot of extra hours recently. Exocore paid a bonus if he exceeded his monthly quota."

I gave the hab a final once over, finding only the traces of a man who had coped with permanent disability and trauma with an enviable energy and lack of self-pity.

"Pain meds are all prescription," I said, closing the wash-room cabinet. "Not a drop of booze in the place either."

"What does that tell you?" Janet asked.

"Tells me he deserved a better end." I pushed myself towards the door. "Recheck his comms data for any links to that Mythos mumbo jumbo. I'll meet you at the Pipe in an hour."

"Where're you going?"

"As befits the nature of our investigation, I'm going to talk to a god."

*

Freak's hab had grown, as had the collection of the uber bonsai that were one of the visual signatures of life in the Axis. Shorn of gravitational constraints the miniature trees grew in size and complexity, branches reaching for the various UV globes in an arboreal web of brown and green that made Freak's home resemble a spherical forest. I had to search for the entrance, eventually finding an opening by virtue of the blinking red eye of a servo-bot, no doubt sent to guide me in. The fresh sawdust on its blades confirmed Freak hadn't been receiving callers for some time now. Inside the bonsai web the air was chilled in shadow, here and there I heard the faint whirr of an unseen servo-bot, presumably shaping the globe tree to Freak's design. It took a few minutes of cramped struggle to get to the entrance, the servo-bot moving aside as it irised open. Inside I discovered why Freak needed an expanded hab: once roughly man-sized, if not man-shaped, Freak had grown big in the years since Riviere's raid on the corporate orbital s/he'd once called home. But what had once been big was now monstrous, easily occupying a third of the available space, tentacles reaching into every corner and tech-cluster. The colour was different too, the red-green patchwork now more predominantly crimson, with an occasional rainbow pulse snaking over the dermis. As I entered, a section of Freak's skin changed to a pale pink, darker patches appearing to form the semblance of a smile.

"Alex." The voice from the speakers was unchanged, a soft, androgynous intonation that reminded you that, appearances aside, what lived here was in fact a human being.

"Freak," I said. "Got your message. Anything you want to tell me?"

"No pleasantries first? Not even an enquiry as to my general well-being?"

"Assumed you weren't into small-talk anymore, since the whole crazy girl setting herself on fire thing." It had happened little under a year ago. There had been a semi-permanent gathering of devotees camped out on the Axis Terminus concourse, mostly splices, seeking communion with a being they had come to regard as a living god. Their requests for an audience were continually refused so they hung around shouting their prayers into the security cams, knowing Freak could hear them if s/he so chose. S/he didn't. Somehow a sixteen year-old elf-splice, complete with vermilion hair and pointy ears, made it past Axis Security and all the way to Freak's hab. When her plaintive cries for recognition went unanswered, she sprayed herself with petroleum vapour and lit a sparkler. The medics managed to save her, despite burns over eighty percent of her body. After that the worshippers had been banned from Axis Terminus and Freak let the bonsai forest grow ever thicker.

The smile shape disappeared, the colours shifting then gelling into a monochrome portrait of Janet. "How do you like your new friend?"

"I'm guessing I have you to thank for her turning up at my door."

"A little tweak to her bargain basement search-gear, just enough to nudge her in the right direction. It really didn't take much, once she had your scent it seems she couldn't stay away."

"So this is all real? There really is a killer out there re-staging ancient myths?"

Janet's portrait disappeared, replaced by some kind of dense script, the language unfamiliar, strangely ordered symbols and pictograms scrolling across the dermi-screen. "What do you see, Alex?"

I shrugged. "Something I can't read."

"No, you wouldn't know how. It's a trinary coding language, conceived to take full advantage of the power offered by the first generation of true quantum computers. What you're looking at is the first program written in that language."

"Not seeing the link here, Freak."

"The person you're looking for can read this, in its raw form, uncompiled. You'll find a copy on your smart."

"So I'm up against a genius programmer?"

"That and more."

"Too much trouble to just give me a name I suppose?"

"I don't have any names to give, none that would help in any case."

I looked again at the scrolling code. Math and science always left me a little cold, but even I could see there was a depth and complexity to this, far beyond normal understanding.

"Did *they* write this?" I asked.

"No, I did. Many years ago. It was one of the tasks I was made for. Quantum computing was first conceived in the late twentieth-century but a means of harnessing its potential eluded scientists for the next two centuries. The complexities involved in the most basic programming were a challenge for even a genius level human mind. But with my extended cortex, my makers hoped some kind of practical interface could be found."

"Looks like they were right."

"Up to a point."

The code suddenly shifted, the dense lines becoming fragmented, twisting into spirals and fractals with increasing speed, symbols spinning from one cluster to another, forms changing and expanding in a mesmeric kaleidoscope.

I closed my eyes against the sudden headache. "Whoa! What was that?"

Freak's dermi-screen faded to mottled crimson. "As with any complex system, chaos, or what appears to be chaos, inevitably begins to effect the program."

"You mean your first program crashed."

There was a long silence from the speakers and I wondered if Freak had ever had to admit failure before, or if s/he even knew what it was. "It generated unexpected results," the speakers said eventually.

"So I'm looking for a homicidal math whizz who'll recognise this code. That's what you're telling me?"

"In essence, yes."

"This code that you wrote before Colonel Riviere rescued you from that lab orbital?"

"Quite so."

"This a relative, Freak? Some fellow lab-rat, all gene-fucked like you except he or she can walk around looking like the rest of us?"

"He can certainly do that."

"So it's male, thanks for that at least."

"You shouldn't limit your options. Appearance is highly malleable to him."

"Great, so it's a shapeshifter now. Can you tell me something that will actually help?"

Freak's eye opened, once beach-ball size now it was over seven feet wide, the pupil seemed very large and very black. "He knows by now that you're looking for him. It's not in his nature to hide from threats. Please be careful."

The eye closed and the speakers fell silent.

"Audience over, huh?" I said.

There was no response save for the soft hiss of the exit opening.

CHAPTER 4

"PRETTY," JANET COOED, her slender hand playing in the holo of the swirling code Freak had uploaded to my smart. "What is it? Some kind of art piece?"

"Not exactly sure." Her face was devoid of anything I could discern as artifice. Most vampires I'd met were lousy liars, maybe it was a fault in the gene sequencing, the boundless human gift for deception getting lost in the mix somewhere. In any case she had either never seen the code before or had forgotten it, and I had serious doubts she was capable of forgetting anything.

I switched off the smart and sat back in my seat, regarding the as yet unsipped glass of Kentucky Red on the table. We were in the bar on the Yang One viewing tier, the cavernous trans-steel ceiling two hundred meters above offering a fine view of the Axis, a slowly spinning, serene blue-green globe caged in a web of carbon 60. Except, of course, it wasn't spinning, we were.

"Is it really a giant squid with a human brain?" Janet asked, a straw protruding from the corner of her mouth as she sucked on a beaker of plasma adorned with a cutesy cartoon of a ferret. Apparently the blood of small mammals had a sweeter taste.

"I think there's more octopus in the mix than squid," I said. "But more brain than anything else."

"Some among the splice community continue to come together to offer it supplication, sending messages through the net marked 'prayers'. They just sit on the servers waiting for it to read them. I once tried to write a paper on it but found every research avenue blocked. There's not even a single net page on it. Amazing really, a being of such importance completely absent from contemporary records but known to all through word of mouth."

"Freak doesn't do interviews, if that's what you're angling for. Did seem to like you though."

"It should. I am eminently likeable." She finished her plasma, suctioning up the dregs with a loud rasp, and dabbed at her mouth with a napkin, a pleasing flush on her cheeks. "So, what did the living splice god have? Beyond an interesting piece of abstract animation."

I tapped my finger against the shot glass, watching the few bubbles detach and rise to the surface. "You don't need to do this anymore. Best if I work it alone."

She drew back a little, lips twisted in suppressed amusement. "Oh, I get it. Dire warning of grave peril, right? Got your chivalrous engine all revved up." She leaned forward, hands flat-drumming on the table. "Well, forget it. I'm the Special Investigator here, and like I said, I can protect myself." She began clicking her fingers and moving her head from side to side in time with the rhythm. "Yes I can, yes I can. Oh yeah."

"Remind me to get you a smaller measure next time." I got up, feeling the comforting weight of Karnikhov's Python in my coat pocket.

"You haven't touched your drink."

"No." I picked up the glass and tossed the contents into a nearby plant-pot. "I haven't. Come on. There's a merry widow you should meet."

*

Julietta DeMarco was an ardent fan of rejuve, appearing to be all of thirty-five when she was in fact the north side of fifty. She had been so dominated by grief during our previous interaction that I'd failed to notice the natural elegance with which she held herself. She wore an expensive dark blue business suit, brown hair tied back and shot through with a single streak of grey. The sophisticated aura was only slightly tarnished by a broad Yang-side accent, and judging by the glint in her eye when she caught sight of Janet, she and her husband had had more in common than a love of rejuve.

"More questions, Inspector?" she said, not without warmth which surprised me. We had been welcomed into her spacious office in the corporate district on Yang Twenty-Seven with expensive smelling coffee and a cool handshake, making me wonder if she wasn't justifiably pissed at the lack of progress in tracking down her husband's killer. But it seemed from her tone that any resentment was either absent or suppressed.

"Thank you for seeing us," I said, deciding it was best not to enlighten her as to my current official status.

"I had my lawyer make some enquiries with the Chief's office a couple of weeks ago. He gained the impression the investigation was pretty much dormant."

"We may have a new angle." I nodded at Janet. "Dr Vaughan here, our new Special Investigator, has some questions."

Mrs DeMarco smiled broadly at Janet, eyes tracking her from head to toe. "*Dr* Vaughan? And what exactly is your speciality dear?"

I was surprised Janet didn't blush under the intensity of the woman's scrutiny, but realised she might not be able to. "Classical studies," she replied, continuing quickly, "Mrs DeMarco, would you say your husband was a spiritual man?"

"Julietta, please." Mrs DeMarco reclined in her real leather executive swivel chair, expression at once sad and amused. "Thomas was raised Trad-Catholic, we both were. I'm happy to say it wore off in adulthood. He used to say 'Why do I need a god when I have a goddess at home?'"

"So he had no interest in religion? Maybe he expressed an interest in a new faith, something unusual."

Mrs DeMarco's expression became more serious. "Thomas lived for three things, dear: family, business and sex. In that order. I wouldn't have fallen in love with him otherwise." Her gaze shifted to me. "I'm no criminologist but this line of questioning would indicate a ritual aspect to Thomas's murder, would it not?"

"We're just being thorough," I said. "Exploring every possibility."

"Including a serial killer, right? A ritualised murder signifies repeat behaviour. Someone's done this before, or since. That's your new angle."

"I see you've been reading up," I replied, tone as light as I could make it. Bitter experience had taught me to reveal as little as possible to a potential witness, or suspect.

"Thomas left me with a business to run." Mrs DeMarco gestured at the expansive office space. "And a not inconsiderable fortune. Enough to purchase the services of the best private investigators and criminal psychologists, found Upside or Down. Want to know what they came up with?"

"Certainly."

"Absolutely fuck all. Over two mill in folding green for squat. Plenty of theories of course, but no answers." Her shrewd eyes fixed on Janet again. "But none of them asked if Thomas was religious. What's it all about, Jedette? Spill or I'm making a call to the Chief's office."

"Well…" Janet glanced at me for guidance.

"There are two other possibly linked homicides," I told Mrs DeMarco. "One Downside and one on the Slab."

"What's the link?"

"Myth. Greek myth to be precise." I briefly laid out the three scenarios.

"Hence Dr Janet and her classical studies," she mused. "You figured all this out, didn't you dear?"

"She did," I said.

Mrs DeMarco's gaze didn't lift from her. "Brains as well. Thomas and I would have enjoyed you no end." She clasped her hands together, forefingers under her chin as she thought it over. "Can't recall Thomas giving much've a shit about mythology. Like I said, family, business and sex."

"He may well have been targeted simply because he fit the killer's criteria," I said. "I'm guessing whoever's doing this doesn't much care whether the victim believes or not." I got to my feet. "I think that covers it for now. As ever, if you think of anything…"

"Naturally." Mrs DeMarco rose to shake hands again, keeping hold of Janet's a touch too long.

"Nice big present in it for you, Jed," she told me. "If you find this sicko. And I don't expect him to make it to trial."

"I'm in it for the love, not the money," I replied, which made her laugh.

We were at the door when something made me pause. "Sorry ma'am, but you said you *and* Thomas would have, erm…" I glanced at Janet who gave a loud sigh of annoyance.

"We certainly would," she said, reaching out to tease a lock of Janet's hair. "We shared such things, you see. Thirty years of marriage can make a couple hungry for new experiences."

Shared? This didn't gel with Thomas DeMarco's behaviour or his Yang-wide stable of lovers. "I was under the impression your husband liked to… enjoy such things without you."

"Hardly." She returned to her desk, opening a drawer to extract what looked like a thin metal hair-band. "Neural Immersion Transmitter." She tossed the item to me. "The latest thing. Still in its infancy really, but Thomas had a contact at MEC who put us on the beta-test list. They're trialling it for two years to work out the bugs."

I looked at the band. It seemed fairly innocuous, a thin arc of metal with a bulb at each end. "How does it work?"

"Just put it on your head, the person wearing a connected set can feel and see what you do, or vice versa."

"So when Thomas was..."

"Fucking someone's brains out I could feel it, yes. Or he could feel it when I was with someone, you just switch from send to receive. Or you can record the experience for playback later." She gave a wistful sigh. "It was pretty amazing, I must say. Way better than any immersion porn you've ever had."

"This is your headset?"

"Yes."

"And Thomas's?"

"He had it with him the night he went missing, he was visiting Daniel. One of my favourites..." She trailed off. "You've never seen this before."

"No, I haven't." I turned to Janet, holding up the headset. "Check the crime scene reports. Look for a match."

She took a cap of the headset and ran it through a search. "Zilch. Not in the Pipe carriage or the, er," she looked up at Mrs DeMarco and stopped herself saying 'slaughterhouse', "...the place where the body was found."

"Compassion too," Mrs DeMarco murmured. "Lucky man, Inspector."

I ignored that. "We'll need the name of your husband's contact at MEC."

"Of course." She fetched her smart and called up the ID. "Can't believe I didn't think of this before."

"It may be nothing."

Mrs DeMarco gave me a smile just as bright as the one she'd given Janet. "Screw that, Jed. You know it's not."

*

"You think someone killed him for this?" Janet sounded dubious as she examined the neural immersion band Mrs DeMarco had let us take away. We were on the Pipe, retracing Thomas DeMarco's last journey, alone in the carriage thanks to some official sounding bluster at the last stop. Not having an ID to wave around forced me to up the intimidation quotient and the passengers had exited without any fuss.

"I mean they're trialling it already," Janet went on. "The competition must have got hold of the specs by now."

"It's not a motive," I said. "At least I don't think so. We found most of DeMarco's effects in the barrel with the rest of him. Whoever put him through the cutters didn't bother to undress him. Smart, ID, green all present and correct, if pretty soggy. But this," I tapped the band, "this was gone."

"Souvenir maybe? I read somewhere people who do this like to collect mementos."

"Some do. Seems a little mundane for our guy though. He's cut from a different cloth."

"Then why take it?"

"No idea. But I'm pretty sure if we find it we find him." I checked the read-out on the overhead info board. "We're five minutes away. Better call Sherry."

She punched in Sherry's ID. "Dr Vaughan?"

"We need an override on a Pipe carriage," I said. "Green Line, Axis Bound."

"Recreating the event, huh?"

"That's right."

"OK. I can only give you fifteen minutes though. Transport Exec get pissed if we do this too often." There was a pause as she ran the authorisation code. "All set. Remember, eight tonight."

"I'm all a-tingle in anticipation."

A grunt of what might have been amusement and she was gone.

"Dreading it, aren't you?" Janet asked.

I shrugged. "Don't intend staying too long. And you shouldn't feel obliged."

"After you went to so much effort to get me an invite, how could I not?" She gave a demure pout, batting her eyelashes.

"Very nice. You practice that in the mirror?"

"Us creatures of the night don't have a reflection, haven't you heard?"

The Pipe carriage slowed and came to a none-too gentle halt. I got up and peered through the windows seeing only dimly lit tunnel wall. "Nothing," I muttered. "Nowhere to hide, unless he came through the ceiling, which was sealed tight and undamaged."

"There's a gap here," Janet said. She was at the door, gesturing at the darkness beyond the glass.

"Can't see it," I said, moving to her side.

"You don't have enhanced night vision. It's about two feet wide with what looks like a bottomless shaft on the other side."

I consulted the Pipe map on the carriage wall. We were halfway through Yang Five, Quad Gamma, near the terminus of the main ventilation shaft.

"Check your smart," I said. "There should be an override for the doors in the case file authorities folder."

She found it and punched in the code, the doors sliding open to treat us to a blast of cold air.

"Sheesh!" Janet exclaimed, blinking in the wind. She took a firm hold of the handle next to the door and leaned out. "Can't see anywhere someone could have been waiting," she shouted. "Nothing to hang on to."

I gestured for her to stand aside and used my smart's flashlight mode to illuminate the gap leading to the shaft. There were periodic gaps like this throughout the Pipe network wherever it intersected the ventilation system, designed to bleed off the excess pressure. Despite this I knew the airspeed in the shaft was still in the region of fifty-four metres per second: terminal velocity.

I shrugged off my coat and handed it to her. "Hold this please."

"What..?"

I took a short run up and launched myself through the door and the gap beyond, arms and legs spreading to catch the wind. There was a short but unnerving plunge then I was back level with the carriage door, waving at Janet's stunned face. "Did this when I was a kid," I shouted, even though I doubted she could hear a word.

The muscle memory came back quickly and it wasn't long before I was zooming around the shaft as I had when I was twelve years old and too stupid to know any better. There were some faint illumination strips in the walls to accommodate the occasional visit from a human work crew and I soon found what I was looking for.

"Maintenance platform," I said, a little breathless, having made the tricky return to the carriage. It was an acquired skill and I was rusty, but I managed the dive and grab manoeuvre without any undue consequences courtesy of the channel of dead air between the gap and the carriage. "About twenty metres down."

"That was dumb," she said with precisely enunciated reproach.

"More like an expression of my borderline risk perception personality disorder." I pulled on my coat. "That's what the Department shrink would say, anyway. You can close the doors now."

*

The Atmospherics Executive supervisor for Yang Five was a pinch-faced functionary with a nasal voice and an avid aversion to undertaking any task not on his spreadsheet of alloted responsibilities.

"Can't let you in there," he stated without equivocation. "Any human inspection requires a duly authorised risk assessment."

"Criminal Investigations Act, section forty-eight," I quoted. "Exigent circumstances. Look it up, Jed."

He actually did, pulling out his work-issue smart and reading every word with pointed deliberation. "Sub-section eight requires Inspector Grade authority," he said, a note of triumph in his nasal twang. "The vampire's only a Special Investigator and you don't have any status at all."

"Listen, you officious little prick..."

Janet stepped between us and met the supervisor's eyes. He stepped back a little in alarm then stopped, his face becoming an expressionless mask, eyes wide and locked on her face.

"Yang Five access platform," she said in a tone I hadn't heard before, just above a murmur, slightly sibilant, and completely compelling.

The supervisor gave a slow nod then tapped at his holo screen. "Cleared for access," he said in a thin whisper.

"Thank you. Security cam footage for this sector. Upload it to my smart."

He nodded again, fingers dancing automatically on the holo-board.

"Get yourself a hot chocolate," Janet told him. "You really need to relax a little."

He stood still for a second, as if reluctant to look away, then blinked and left the control room.

"Not just seeing in the dark," I said. "Can you turn into a bat too?"

"It's a subliminal modulation to the vocal chords," she explained, "plus an ingrained facility for hypnosis. All part of the genetic template. Still takes practice though, and it doesn't always work."

"Just on uptight petty functionaries and slab-thugs demanding money with menaces."

She screwed her eyebrows into an oddly lopsided expression and dropped into an archaic English accent, "Only works on the weak minded."

I was non-plussed. "Huh?"

Her eyes widened and she shook her head in wonder. "Wow, you really didn't have any classical education at all, did you?"

*

The maintenance platform yielded no evidence beyond confirmation that our quarry had an exceptional skill-set.

"Somehow gets the Pipe carriage to halt at precisely the right place," I yelled. Although the maintenance platform was shielded from the howling up-draft the noise still meant we had to shout. "And gets the doors to open, glides on in near-total darkness, grabs and subdues DeMarco under the nose of his bodyguards, then free-falls down here with him to make good his escape." I gazed up at the shaft in reluctant admiration. "I pulled some serious commando shit during the war, but this is way out of my league."

"Not sure that's how it went," Janet yelled back. She held up her smart to display a high-res holo-shot. "Security cam from the access corridor, five minutes after DeMarco's abduction."

It was only a shadow, playing along the corridor wall. Hugging the blind-spots, trying not to be seen, easy if you knew how. "Freeze it," I told her.

The silhouette was clear and unambiguous; a male, middling height, chunky but not overweight, alone. "There'll be a basic forensic imaging app in your directory," I said. "Cross ref with DeMarco's biometrics."

The result flashed up almost immediately. Match - probability 96%.

"He wasn't abducted," Janet said. "He jumped."

CHAPTER 5

I SAT IN silence for most of the Pipe ride back to Yang Eighteen. Janet wanted to change before going to Sherry's and seemed content to let me brood, flicking through the case file with keen-eyed concentration. I didn't like the realisation about DeMarco, it answered a lot of questions but raised a thousand more. *He jumped.* Then what? Trundle happily off to get sliced and diced and stuffed in a barrel. The most bizarre suicide in history. More wrongness hurting my bourbon-starved head.

"Work logs say Karnikhov was alone for his entire shift," Janet said. "No record of his re-entry to the alloted airlock, or any other airlock on the Slab."

"The cam footage on DeMarco's Pipe carriage was wiped without any trace of an unauthorised incursion to the system," I said. "I guess whoever's doing this can hack override codes and alter data records at will."

"That may be the scariest thing I've heard yet."

I thought about Freak, the only individual I knew capable of doing what our quarry could do. *Who's doing this Freak? A brother? A cousin? And do you really want them caught?*

"Any trace of a neural immersion band in Karnikhov's stuff?" I asked. "In his work locker maybe."

She checked and shook her head. "If he had one, it's gone. I checked the friends and acquaintances statements too, no mention of him owning one."

I nodded and lapsed back into silence, mentally churning the details, looking for something that gelled, something to fix on, finding only yet more steaming piles of wrong.

"So," said Janet. "How many of your friends will be there tonight?"

"All two of them. Not nervous are you?"

"Not as much as you, I think."

I grunted. "We need to buy wine."

*

We met Joe at the entrance to Sherry's apartment block, impressively filling a new suit with square-shouldered tallness, shaking hands with Janet who managed to be even more eye-catching in a long black strapless gown. I was starting to feel more than a little shabby.

"How's the Chief?" I asked Joe, the doors sliding open as Sherry buzzed us in. Joe had been transferred to the Chief's security detail after my enforced sabbatical. I'd kept our contact to a minimum since, knowing that too close an association with me wouldn't help his long term career prospects.

"Spends a lot of time meeting people he seems to hate," Joe said. "Said to say hi though."

"Nice of him." *Not nice enough to fix my suspension, the ungrateful old fuck.*

Janet was looking at Joe with her now familiar predatory inquisitiveness. "We haven't met have we Joe?" she asked. "It's just your face is really…"

"We're here!" I broke in, knocking on Sherry's door and hoping she didn't take too long to answer.

The young woman who came to the door was all petite blondeness with a broad welcoming smile and as cut-glass a Yinside accent as I'd ever heard. "Hiyar! You *must* be Alex."

"You must be Sam." We shook hands. *A Yin-sider.* My reverse-snobbery was revving up. *She never told me she'd shacked up with a Yin-sider.*

"It's a Beaujolais something or other." I handed her the wine bottle.

"Great, thanks muchly, Joe!" She embraced him on extreme tip-toe. "Nice suit!"

"The Department forked up some clothing expenses," he said. "How's things at the clinic?"

"Busy as ever. The kids miss you, though."

"I'll drop by next weekend. Promise."

"You better." She punched him playfully on the bicep. It was as high as she could reach.

"Erm, this is Janet," I said, catching sight of her expectant glare.

"Wow! I mean hi," Sam's voice went up an octave or two. "Love your dress!"

"Thank you." Janet smiled back. "Something smells nice," she prompted when the blonde girl continued to stare.

"Oh, *do* come in. Please." She bustled us into the living room. "Sherry's been trapped in the kitchen for hours. They're here!" she called.

"I can hear them," Sherry called back. "Ply them with drinks, this is taking ages."

She poured wine for Joe, not, I noted, from the bottle I'd brought, and ginger ale for me and Janet.

"Clinic?" I asked Joe.

"Sam works at a paediatric clinic," he said. "It's on my way to work."

"Came in with donations every other day for a month," Sam said and took a hefty gulp of wine. "Helps out with the physio sometimes too."

I wasn't surprised. Joe was the kind of individual who could make a Nobel prize-winning Olympic athlete oncologist feel inadequate.

"Impressive," Janet said. She had that look again. "So what did you do before the force, Joe?"

"Poverty and unemployment," I said. "Just like the rest of us." Sam shifted a little and took another gulp of wine. I supposed she had reason to feel uncomfortable around poor folks. "Joe's the reason Sherry and I met," she said. "I called round to his place a few months ago and she was there on some work thing."

I looked at Joe who was artfully admiring a print on the wall. "Few months ago?" I asked. "June maybe?"

"That's right!" Sam gave a sheepish shrug. "Got the date highlighted on my smart actually, fourteenth June. I'm a girly romantic at heart."

Fourteenth June. The day before my formal suspension. "Having a little chat?" I asked Joe. "What about I wonder?"

"I thought he might be able to get through to you." Sherry appeared in the kitchen doorway, red evening dress matching her hair. "Since you were so intent on fucking up every aspect of your life and career."

She moved to Sam's side, giving her a hug of reassurance. "Dinner's in the garbage disposal. I've ordered in. It'll be half an hour."

"DeMarco jumped," I said. "No-one took him off the Pipe."

"Shop talk's off limits tonight, Alex."

"Oh, don't mind me," Sam said. "I find it all fascinating actually. If a little grisly."

"Even so." Sherry squeezed her hand. "I could do with a night off."

The dinner delivery consisted of a banquet of Chinese food and a blood-rare steak for Janet.

"You're not drinking," Sherry observed from across the table.

"No," I said, hoping she didn't notice the slight tremble of the chopsticks in my hand. "I'm not."

She nodded. "That's good."

"For the hearing you mean? No alcohol in the tox test looks good on the report."

"Couldn't hurt." It was only a faint catch in her voice but it said a lot. My hearing was a formality, she already knew the outcome. Suddenly I wanted a glass of bourbon more than I ever wanted anything. I was half-reaching for the wine bottle when the hard presence of the Python in my belt reminded me I still had a task in hand, if not a job to go back to.

"So, you're a medic, Sam?" Janet was asking.

"Therapist," she replied. "Immersion assisted recovery."

It was a new one on me. "How's that work?"

"It's all about designing an environment in which they feel secure, but also challenging enough to stimulate an active response. Some of these kids," she shook her head, "they've really been through a lot, you know. Sometimes they can barely communicate."

"Guess you know a lot about immersion hardware."

"Well, I have a Bsc in Simulative Engineering."

"Ever hear of a neural immersion transmitter?"

"Sure, it's the next big thing for the industry. Recordable shared experiences. Never used one though, they're not out yet. Anyway, it would be more useful for entertainment than therapy in my opinion."

"How so?" Janet asked. "I mean, if someone has a nice happy memory, wouldn't sharing it with someone else make them happy too?"

"Memory is highly subjective. One person's perfect day is another's nightmare."

"But some things are universal, surely. Pleasure, pain, fear, love."

"As a matter of fact, no, they aren't. We all take pleasure in different things, find some things more painful than others. And then there are people with serious mental health problems where everything you'd consider to be normal flies out the window."

"Sadism," I said, thinking about DeMarco, and all the others over the years.

"Exactly. There are people who will find pleasure in the most awful things. And if you give them the ability to replay it endlessly, even market it…" She shrugged. "It opens up a whole world of unpleasant possibilities."

"He was wearing it," I said to Janet.

"When he killed DeMarco?"

"No, DeMarco was wearing it when he was killed. That's why he kept it. The ultimate souvenir."

Sherry pinged a fingernail against her wine glass. "Shop talk."

The evening wrapped up a couple of hours later, conversation having ranged from the upcoming CAOS Presidential primaries - the consensus was Lorenzo would finally bow out this term (I couldn't give a shit) - the latest high-brow 2D drama, an updating of Macbeth with Slab gangsters - Joe loved it, Sam thought it over-scripted (I couldn't give a shit) - and at what point did a splice become so un-human like they actually stopped being human (this one I could actually get interested in).

"But there has to be a point," Sam was saying, "a tipping point, when the physical becomes so divorced from the norm that the concept of humanity has to come into question." She glanced at Janet, mouthing "No offence."

"Think, feel, fuck, feed," I said. "The things we all do that can't be spliced out."

"But sooner or later they will be," Sam insisted. "Then what?"

"Ex-humanus," Janet mused. "Post-human. Something new, and, as the only Splice at the table, I'd like to think, not necessarily threatening."

"I'd go along with that," Joe rumbled.

I thought about Freak, still growing, bigger and no doubt smarter every day. But confined to a hab and dependent on the largess of the beings s/he had evolved beyond. "Or they could be gods," I said. "Looking to us for worship." *Like the genius-grade nutbag we're hunting,* I didn't say. *Singing a murderous hymn to gods long dead.*

Sam said goodnight with hugs and wine tinged kisses. Sherry surprised me with an embrace, the first I could recall. "We'll go over your findings tomorrow," she told me.

"Should I just resign?" I asked. "Better than getting fired, right?"

"Nothing's decided…"

"Come on, I'm sober remember."

She looked down, jaw tense with frustration. "You had to do it in front of the whole dockyard workforce."

"He knew where Mr Mac was…"

"And turned up with his throat cut two days after his lawyer lodges a complaint. Doesn't look good does it?"

"Mr Mac probably thought he was doing me a favour. If the little fucker had coughed up the info, he'd be alive right now."

"This isn't a frontier town anymore, Alex. The gunslinging days are over."

I had plenty of maverick-cop comebacks ready, but they all died in my throat at the sight of her sorrow. "I know you did your best," I said. "Thanks for that."

She forced a smile. "It's what friends do."

*

We said goodnight to Joe at the Pipe interchange, Janet's feline scrutiny following his tall form all the way to the Red Line entrance. "Was he famous once?" she asked.

"Joe? Nah. I'm way more of a celebrity than he'll ever be."

We shared a Pipe to Yang Eighteen and she accepted my offer to walk her home without another reminder that she could protect herself.

"She was nice, Sam. Didn't you think?"

"For a Yin-sider, I guess."

"Can't help where she was born, or her accent."

"I know, just… Sherry's been single the whole time I've known her. Now this, and everything else."

"Change is inevitable. Stasis is impossible in a dynamic society…" She stopped abruptly, coming to a halt. "Oh my god! That was Tyger Joe!"

"What? No it wasn't," I said, way too quickly.

"It totally was!" She clapped her hands together, jumping in girlish excitement. "You're best friends with Tyger Joe. Despliced and living a second life as a Slab City Demon." She prodded a finger into my chest. "Right? Right?"

"You're nuts."

"Hah! So how'd he end up here?" She circled me with a broad grin. "I remember when MEC announced his death. Seemed oddly downplayed. The biggest name in splice-fight history dies in a shuttle crash and the funeral barely makes it onto the news feeds. Ah!" She stopped, snapping her fingers. "He ran away. He ran away, came here to get despliced and you helped him. You rescued Tyger Joe from an evil corporation." Faster than I could catch she pressed against me, planting a full kiss on my lips, drawing back with a giggle. "Like you weren't cool enough already." She took my hand and tugged me towards her place at a half-run, still dazed from an overdose of unaccustomed female proximity.

"Come on, do I have a treat for you."

"Are you sure? We only just…"

She stopped, taking hold of both my hands, meeting my eyes with serious intent. "Trust me. This is a night you'll never forget."

*

"Wow," I said, about three hours later.

"I know," Janet said with a lazy smile.

"That was…"

"Amazing?"

"Oh yeah. I mean..." I shook my head. "How can he be Luke's father?"

"One of the best twists in movie history." She reached for her remote and began scrolling through the library. "But there's more. Prepare yourself for Return of the Jedi, just try not to get pissed at the Ewoks."

"Looks like we skipped a few episodes," I said, squinting at the menu.

"No we haven't. OK, here we are."

We were on the couch in her living room, sharing a pot of coffee in front of her near-antique entertainment hub. She'd shed her heels and sat with long legs curled up, occasionally twiddling her toes. For the first time in years I found the word adorable coming to mind.

"Who's Mr Mac?" she asked as the credits came up accompanied by a now familiar bombastic score.

"Don't miss anything, do you?"

"Vampire hearing. Bat DNA."

"Really?"

She laughed and threw a cushion at me. "'Course not, dumbass. So who is he?"

"A very bad man. I've been looking for him."

"A very bad man who did you a favour by killing someone."

"He thinks he's my friend. It's complicated."

"And when you find him?"

"He's not the type to forgo resisting arrest, not that I'll have that option after next week."

"They're really going to fire you then?"

"I'll be lucky if they leave it at that."

"What will you do? I know you have your bar and all..."

"I'll worry about it when it happens. Till then, we have a case to work."

"You still want to work it? Even with no reward?"

I laughed, short and bitter. "Can't say I've ever been rewarded for anything. Besides, I promised Mrs DeMarco."

Her fingers crept along the couch, spider style, reaching out a pinky. "Didn't thank you for taking me seriously, did I?"

"I was kind've a prick, so I guess it evens out."

"Still." She entwined her pinky with mine and gave it a shake. "It is appreciated."

I met her gaze, finding it warm and kind behind a half-veil of ebony hair. "Who are you?" I asked. "Really. Who are you?"

Her gaze dropped. "You know who I am. Who I was is a whole other question."

"I'm listening."

She licked her lips, uncertain, fearful even. "I'm not... I wasn't..."

Which, of course, was the precise moment her smart started beeping.

"Damn," she breathed. "Thought I'd turned it off."

"Emergency override," I said, recognising the tone. "You should get it."

She thumbed the smart, Sherry's voice, loud and strident. "Dr Vaughan. Is Alex with you?"

"I'm here," I said.

"Good. Yang Two, Quad Alpha. Both of you. Now." She signed off.

"Shit." I got up to retrieve my coat from the back of the couch. "You should change."

"What's up?"

I pulled on my coat and transferred the Python from the inside pocket to the small of my back. There could be only one reason for the urgency and the lateness of the hour. "There's been another one."

CHAPTER 6

WE FOUND HARRY Red Wing throwing up outside the entrance to the power relay station on Yang Two. There was a thick cordon of uniforms around the building and the sweat-rain was coming down heavier than usual.

"Bad, huh?" I asked Red Wing.

He braced himself against the wall, breathing deep, voice hoarse. "Fuck you, Alex."

"Always a pleasure, Harry." I led Janet through the cordon, eyeing the power station entrance with a novel sense of unease. Red Wing was every bit as jaded as I was and it had been a while since my calloused gaze had fallen on something vile enough to make me lose my lunch.

"OK?" Janet asked and I realised I'd paused. The entrance seemed very dark all of a sudden.

"Sure," I said. "Just wishing I hadn't eaten."

The power station interior was dimly lit with police issue glow-sticks and busy with white overalled forensic types.

"Power's out, Inspector," a fresh-faced uniform told me.

"The whole thing or just the lights?"

"Just the lights. It's weird, power relays are fine. The techs can't explain it. DCI Mordecai's at the scene if you'll come with me."

We followed her down a series of corridors and tiered walkways, descending into the heart of the station. According to the uniform it was completely automated save for the occasional inspection crew.

"He seems to have a talent for finding deserted places on a densely populated hab," Janet observed.

We came to an automatic door, jammed open and held in place with a Departmental seal. The lettering on the glass read 'Equipment Room.'

"Through here, sir." The uniform stepped aside.

"Not going in?" I enquired.

She shook her head and I noticed how pale she was. "Once was enough for this lifetime."

The first thing to hit me was the smell, a melange of rotten meat and burned flesh topped off with an acidic chemical sting. I fought down my rising gorge and focused on the tableau in the centre of the room. A man on his back, laid out on a steel-frame work table, hands and feet bound with chains to the legs, neck positioned at the table-edge so that his head was thrown back. Where his face should have been there was a cavity, coloured pink and black.

I heard Janet exhale, long and slow, and wondered if vampires could vomit.

"Inspection crew found him." Sherry was on the other side of the body, watching Fabio Ricci run a spectrometer over the victim's skin. "Ricci estimates about three hours since death. No immediate parallels but given the obvious ritualised elements…"

I moved closer, forcing my eyes to focus on the corpse's non-face.

"Alex," Ricci said. "Heard you got fired."

I wasn't in the mood for small talk. "Any ID on the weapon?"

Ricci looked up at the ceiling. It was half in shadow but I could make out the sight of a flask, suspended by steel cables, angled so that whatever it contained would fall onto the face of the man on the table.

"Sulfuric acid," Ricci said. "Polyethylene container. There's a stop valve on the nozzle. Drip, drip, drip."

"How long?"

"Good ten hours' worth of drips given the size of the flask. Which is weird because our friend here should've died within the first hour. Instead he lasted at least eight."

Janet's eyes scanned the scene, her predatory aspect a little wild-eyed now. "There was a bowl, right?"

Ricci frowned at her in surprise. "On the floor in the corner. Also polyethylene."

Janet nodded at the corpse. "Who was he? Do we know?"

"He's DNA registered," Sherry said, reading from her smart. "Alan Devant, age thirty-eight, resident of Yin Thirty. No missper on file."

"Richie Rich," I said. "What's he doing here?"

"His job?" Janet pressed.

"Entertainer according to his tax return." Sherry did some more scrolling. "Professional name the Great Devant..."

"Illusionist Extraordinaire," Janet finished.

"Yeah. Me and Sam watched him on the 2D the other night, come to think of it. Made a tug disappear from the docking bay."

"Trickster," Janet said in a whisper. "He's switched mythologies. This," she waved at the obscenity on the table. "This is Norse, not Greek. And we're missing a character." She turned to Sherry. "Was he married?"

"Yes, Helen Devant, age twenty-two. Second marriage." Sherry frowned at her smart. "No missper on him but one for her, filed by her sister four hours ago."

"She's here." Janet moved away, eyes scanning the room, nostrils flared. "Trust me."

"You *did* search the place?" I asked Sherry.

"It's a big complex, take five days to fully sweep it. Dr Vaughan!"

I turned to see Janet disappearing through the door.

"Wait!" I went after her. She didn't stop, climbing the stairs and turning right, gaze constantly moving.

"Will you hold up a minute!" I said, running to catch up, taking hold of her arm. "There's a procedure for this…"

"Since when do you care about procedure?"

"Since hunting through a blacked-out power station for a genius-smart serial killer."

"She's here." She pulled away. "I can smell her." She was off again before I could stop her. I grunted in resignation, following as she moved rapidly through the maze of corridors and walkways, tracking her with my smart's flashlight. She turned this way and that seemingly at random, oblivious to the darkness.

"What makes you think she'll still be alive?" I asked, during a brief pause.

"She didn't die in the myth." She raised her head, eyes closed, trying to catch the scent. "But then, neither did he. This way."

More corridors and a steep descending staircase. A sign on the wall said 'Servo Repository.'

"And who exactly are they?" I asked. "In the myth."

"Loki and Sigyn."

The first name set off a vague memory, some vintage 3D from childhood, or what used to pass for 3D. "Loki was Thor's brother, right?"

"In some iterations. In others he's just another minor god, but always a trickster, a deceiver. He was punished for his lies by the goddess Skaoi. Bound to a rock in the bowels of the earth whilst venom from the fangs of a great serpent dripped from above into his eyes, given succour only by his faithful wife Sigyn, who would hold a bowl over his face to catch the poison as it fell. But inevitably the bowl would fill up and when she turned away to empty it…"

"Poor old Loki got a face full of poison," I finished, "or acid in this case." The cruel invention of it was chilling. *Slow death by dripping acid wasn't enough, had to put the wife in the room too, knowing what would happen if she went for help.* I had already concluded that whoever we were hunting was bat-shit crazy, but the calculated sadism of this latest atrocity told me something else. "This guy's a truly evil piece of shit."

Janet stopped and held up a hand, head cocked. I fancied I actually saw her ears prick up as she strained for some faint echo. "Over there."

We took a westward corridor and came to a half-open door marked 'Servo-bot Maintenance.'

"No!" I hissed, restraining her with some difficulty as she began to dart forward, feeling her strength as she resisted the impulse to push me away. "I mean it. Stay behind me." I drew the Python and approached the door at a slow walk.

The room beyond was lit by a single LED-orb in the ceiling, casting a circle of white light on the bare floor. In the centre of the circle knelt a young woman, face buried in her hands as she wept. I checked the rest of the room, the barrel of the Python tacking the flashlight beam, finding only tool racks and some deactivated servo-bots docked into power nodes.

"OK." I went in, lowering the Python but still wary. Janet ran straight to the young woman.

"Helen? It's Helen right?"

The young woman said something, hoarse and inaudible behind her hands which I saw were scarred with red and black blotches, dark craters in the flesh. Acid burns.

"Oh baby," Janet said, seeing her wounds and gently trying to prize her hands away from her face. "It's OK now. It's OK."

Slowly she succeeded in parting Helen Devant's hands, revealing a face that would have been considered glamour-model standard gorgeous but for the reddened, wild-eyed stare and the harsh, pain filled twist of her mouth. "Wasn't me!" she said in a fierce whisper, a bubble of spit bursting on her lips. "Wasn't me.

I tried." She showed Janet her ravaged hands, pleading, imploring. "Tried and tried and tried…"

"We know, baby. We know." She pulled Helen's slender form to her. "We know. It's OK."

I was still uneasy. Something didn't gel. "How did she get here?"

"They made me," Helen sobbed. "Pushed and prodded and hurt me. All the way here."

"They?" There was a glowing red circle on my sleeve, too diffuse for a laser-sight, but it hadn't been there two seconds before.

I looked up. It was one of the bots, its activation light glowing red in the gloom beyond the circle cast by the LED. Another light blinked on a few yards to the left, then another to the left of that, and another… I tracked the successive switch-ons around the room, counting seven, arranged in a circle with us as the centre. There was a multiple thrum as the bots' hover units sprang to life, the red beads lifted a few yards into the air, and began to circle us.

It's not in his nature to hide from threats. I glanced down at the weeping girl in Janet's arms then back at the bots. "Sonnovabitch baited a trap and we walked right in."

"Alex?" Janet said.

I flexed my fingers on the butt of the Python. *Six shots, seven targets. Bad math.* One of the bots drifted in front of the still-open door, jagged black silhouette half obscuring the dim rectangle of beckoning luminescence. There was a harsh snicking sound as it unfurled its tool set.

"I'll clear you a path to the door," I told Janet. "When you hear the first shot get her out of here. Keep running till you find Sherry."

"If you think I'm just going to…"

I snap-shot the bot in front of the door to forestall any further discussion, the epoxy slug punching through the machine's thin metal casing, impacting on the titanium super-structure inside and exploding as the phosphorus core met the air. The disintegration of the bot was fairly spectacular but there was no time to enjoy it.

"GO!" I commanded Janet, stepping away, Python in a two-handed grip, blasting the bots in random order, one shot each, four more exploding in quick succession. There was a blur as Janet picked up Helen Devant and sprinted for the door. A bot veered off in pursuit, its tools, a set of metal grinders, whirling silver discs. I blew it away a yard from the door and threw myself flat as the last bot whooshed overhead, a flare of agony and tugged clothing telling me I'd picked up another battle wound. I suppressed the pain with savage urgency, emptying the spent cartridges from the Python's chamber, trying to slam in a speed-loader, left hand suddenly numb and way too clumsy to make it in time.

I heard the sound of rending metal and looked up to see Janet perched atop the last bot, fully ten feet in the air. I noticed a gaping rent in the bot's casing as she drew back her right hand, fingers and nails now extended to about eight inches in length, gleaming like miniature daggers. The bot twisted and turned in a desperate attempt to throw her off but she rode it like a champion surfer, plunging her new-grown claw into the rent she'd torn in the casing, reaching deep and tearing out a chunk of circuitry and cable.

The bot stopped, shuddered, and fell to the floor with a clunk, Janet leaping away to land in front of me. "Thank god I was here," I muttered.

"You're hurt."

"It's nothing." I got to my feet and promptly convulsed in pain, a warm stream of blood soaking the left arm of my coat. "No, it's something! Get a medic!"

CHAPTER 7

"I BOUGHT YOU a new shirt from the fabricator in the lobby."
Janet placed the neatly folded garment on the hospital bed. I
watched her fingers twitch on the label, normal-sized fingers,
normal-sized nails. "Think I got your size right."

"Neat trick," I said. "The claw thing."

"In-built defensive measure," she said, forcing a jovial tone.
"Only kicks in when my adrenal levels indicate a threat to life.
Bit of a drag if you're fond of theme-park rides."

"I've never seen it before." My tone wasn't jovial. "Never
seen any splice do anything remotely like it."

She avoided my gaze and moved away, plucking the med-
tablet from the wall to check my stats. "Rapid heal nearly complete. Says you'll be fully recovered in twenty-four hours. Minimal scarring. There's an alert icon against your liver though."

"An inch to the left and I'd be minus a chunk of spinal cord.
Don't change the subject."

She looked up from the tablet with what I could only
describe as fear. "I'm sorry you think I'm some kind of monster,
but I can't talk about it, Alex. Not now. Not until this is over,
please."

"I don't think you're a monster…"

The door slid open and Sherry came into the treatment
room, accompanied by a big, blocky middle-aged man with

cropped steel-grey hair and an expensive but ill-fitting suit. Joe followed them in and stood by the door, his expression rigidly neutral.

"Jean-Michel!" I said, grinning at the blocky man. "Ca va?"

"It's Chief Arnaud to you, you insubordinate fuck," the Chief of the LCPD growled. He hated it when I spoke French; despite his background he couldn't speak a word of it. He looked at Janet. "You the historian?"

"Classicist," she corrected.

"Whatever." He levelled his gaze at me. "Chose a real doozey to buy you way back in, dintcha?"

"Hey, I'm just lucky that way."

The Chief grunted, reached into his inside pocket and tossed something onto the bed. My gun and ID. "This cost me a lot of favours and if I wasn't running for mayor next year, I'd happily let you drink yourself to death in that piss-hole you call home. DeMarco was bad enough but now we've got a dead Yinside celebrity. Can't have it. So fix it."

"Just like that," I said. "Sure, give me five minutes."

The Chief loomed closer, tapping the gun and ID. "These can disappear any time, don't forget that."

"I won't work this case with anyone else," Janet said, drawing a stern-eyed squint from the Chief. "Just so you know," she added with one of her best smiles.

"Dr Vaughan's assistance is crucial," Sherry put in. "If we're going to end this."

"Vampires," the Chief grated, a curl of distaste on his lips. He turned back to me. "What do you have? And no card-holding. All of it. Spill."

I looked at Janet. "You spoke to the wife?"

She nodded. "They each had one. Devant had highly placed friends at MEC."

"Had what?" the Chief demanded.

"Show them," I told Janet. "It's in my coat."

She fished out the neural immersion band and briefly explained what it was.

"And DeMarco had one too?" the Chief asked.

"Yeah," I said. "The only link we've been able to find between any of the victims. And DeMarco wasn't abducted. He jumped off the Pipe and walked to his death, all on his own."

"You think this thing somehow made him do it?" Sherry asked. "Input some kind've suicidal impulse. If that's the case, why bother free-falling down a ventilation shaft just to off himself in his own slaughterhouse? He could do that any time."

"Because whatever made him do it only activated when he put on his band to record his visit with Daniel. Also, DeMarco's bodyguards were operating under strict Duress Protocol. Insurance companies insist on it these days. Basically makes the protectee a prisoner of their own schedule. Every meeting, visit and journey has to be planned out a week in advance and can't be changed. It's designed to prevent clients acting against their own interests when they get a call from scary people claiming to be holding a chainsaw to their daughter's forearm. No way they were just going to stand by whilst he dived into the meat processor."

I turned to the Chief. "Anyone who's been playing around with MEC's new toy is a potential victim. They need to recall it and we need a list of whoever they gave it to."

"Because MEC are such an easy company to deal with," he said.

"Threaten to leak it to the news feeds," I suggested. "Do wonders for their share price."

"Karnikhov didn't have one," Sherry pointed out. "And there's nothing to indicate he was complicit in his own death."

"He was killed by a bot," I replied. "Probably chained to that rock by one too. We've seen what our boy can do with bots." I turned to Janet. "Did Devant's wife give you anything else?"

"Not much. She's in pretty terrible shape, as you can imagine. Seems she and Devant had an afternoon benefit gig on Yang One. She worked as his stage assistant. Mr Devant was something of a perfectionist, they'd both wear their bands during the show then swap afterwards to critique each other's performance. The last thing she remembers is putting on his band in their dressing room, the lights go out and she wakes up a few hours later holding a bowl full of acid over his face, surrounded by servo-bots. When it was… over, they herded her into that maintenance room to wait for us."

"The bots must have been controlled through high-level programming," Sherry said. "Pretty impressive coding too. Goal oriented, tactical awareness, reactive to threats. Even the UNOIF military bots weren't that smart. The techs say they're mock-ups, constructs made to look like power company equipment. Convincing job, as long as you don't check for serial numbers."

The Chief eyed me closely. "I'm told the great carcinoma itself has an interest in this. What did it tell you?"

No card-holding? Ah, fuck him. "Seems it caught wind of Dr Vaughan's research and took an interest, wanted to make sure I was taking it seriously. Said it'll run some numbers, pattern recognition, that kind of thing. Haven't heard anything yet."

"Unusual for it to be so civic minded," the Chief observed. "All attempted contacts from city and CAOS officials have been ignored since that silly bitch toasted herself."

"We have a special relationship."

"Well you might want to tell it that this lack of interaction is making people nervous. The kind of people you don't want to get nervous."

"You think it doesn't know that already? It's probably listening to this conversation right now."

The Chief blinked, involuntarily scanning the room. In truth I had no real idea quite how extensive Freak's surveillance ability was, or whether s/he'd even care enough to listen in. But I did enjoy giving him a scare.

"What do you need?" he growled.

"Mrs DeMarco gave us the name of her husband's contact at MEC. We need access, and sanctions if they don't co-operate." *Campaign contributions notwithstanding*, I didn't say, knowing I'd pushed him far enough for one day. "You could mention Freak's interest. Might focus some minds in the right direction. Profit margins'll suffer if their net access suddenly goes down."

"I'll do what I can." He nodded at the gun and ID. "Don't forget what I said."

"Certainment, mon General."

He bit back an angry rebuke and stalked from the room. Joe gave me an encouraging smile and followed him.

"Saved him from a Fed-Sec black-ops squad during the war," I explained to Janet. "He's never forgiven me."

*

"You speak French?" Janet asked. The Pipe was carrying us past the Axis towards Yin One and our meeting with MEC. I hadn't been Yin-side in years and didn't relish the prospect. Everything over there is so disgustingly clean.

"Mais oui," I said. "Et toi?"

She shook her head. "Ancient Greek, Latin, Norse, Aramaic, Etruscan and Phoenician only."

I snorted. "Pathetic."

"I know, I really need to apply myself more." I was disturbed by the fact that she sounded entirely sincere.

"Why the switch?" I asked, knowing further discussion on our comparative abilities would only make me feel even more inadequate. "From Greek to Norse. Any ideas?"

"It could be that his religious attitudes mirror those of the ancient world. The concept of exclusivity in belief really dates from the Christian era. The Romans, for example, ridiculed the

Egyptians for, as they put it, worshipping cats and dogs, but they never claimed that Anubis and company didn't exist. Perhaps whoever's doing this doesn't see a conflict between the mythologies. To him, it's all the same thing."

"Just another god to worship."

"If that's what he's doing."

*

The Slab City HQ of the innocuously named Multi-media Entertainment Corporation was as impressive as an office complex could be when limited to only three storeys. It took up most of Quad Alpha on Yin One in a sprawl of elegant glass and chrome, intersected with lush patches of neatly groomed garden and decorative lakes complete with ducks and swans.

"Can they fly?" I enquired of the security guard escorting us towards a building bearing the sign 'Welcome and Direction.'

"Sure," he replied. "But the urge is spliced out when they're in the egg. Clipping their wings spoils the look, I guess."

'Welcome and Direction' turned out to be a warehouse sized collection of conference rooms, each partitioned by frosted glass, MEC suits moving behind the opaque walls like spectres as they did whatever it is they do. The security guy led us to a room marked as the 'Resolution Suite'. Inside about twenty suits sat at a large table, each smiling near identical smiles of welcome.

"Inspector McLeod!" A tall, broad shouldered man came forward to shake my hand. "Bruce Atwood, Head of Direction."

I ignored his hand and went into the room, pointing at the assembled suits. "Who are they?"

"Oh, we'll do a quick round table, shall we? Sally, could you start?"

A severely pretty Asiatic woman on the left of the table nodded and spoke in precise tones. "Sally Choa, Deputy Head of Assurance."

"Matt Dalquist," the neatly coiffured young man seated next to her said. "Acting head of Efficiency…"

"Yeah, enough of that," I broke in, consulting the file the Chief's office had sent to my smart. "Ryan Van Pelt, Elise McKinnon. Raise your hands."

They were at the far end of the table, a plumpish middle-aged woman and a muscular young man. I noted the fact that her hand shook as she held it in the air but his was steady as a rock.

"You two can stay," I said. "Everyone else can fuck off."

Atwood started to bluster, spouting phrases like 'professional conduct' and 'mutualised co-operative networking.'

I waved my smart at him. "Got a friend at the Axis knows all about networks. Don't make me call them."

The room seemed much bigger cleared of corporate flotsam, leaving McKinnon and Van Pelt diminished and vulnerable at the edge of the gleaming expanse of real oak table.

"You should know," Van Pelt said, voice reedy and whiny enough to tell me his original body had been heavily modified into its current form. "I have retained legal counsel and formally object to this interview proceeding in their absence."

"And yet here you are," I observed. I'd taken a seat at the head of the table, enjoying the luxuriant feel of the swivel chair, the way it contoured itself to one's posterior was quite delightful. "Which tells me MEC promised to terminate your contract if you didn't co-operate. So shut your trap until you're spoken to."

I called up Freak's trinary code graphic and placed the smart on the table, display set to broad-beam, the symbols swirling in the holo-cone. "This mean anything to either of you?"

Van Pelt shook his head, expression blank. McKinnon sat, hands clasped together on the table, tight and white-knuckled. I put her somewhere over fifty, greying hair, wrinkles in the right places. *The money she makes here and no rejuves. Different pri-*

orities maybe. Her tenseness dissipated a little as she watched the code dance. "Trinary," she said. "Looks like a refinement of the Brusentsov syntax. Haven't seen it since college."

"Know what it says?"

She closed her eyes, shaking her head. "Of course not. You'd need a compiler and a super-computer for that."

I turned off the smart. "You're Technical Project Leader on the neural immersion system, right?"

She nodded. "Four years now."

"You know why we're here?"

She swallowed hard. "Compliance said something about a homicide."

"Homicides," I corrected. "Plural. Thomas DeMarco and Alan Devant. Both advance recipients of your new toy, courtesy of Mr Van Pelt here."

Van Pelt flushed a little but kept quiet.

"Ryan was just doing his job," McKinnon said. "Seeding the product amongst high profile users, a stimulus to word of mouth marketing. Necessary given the likely unit price."

I looked at Van Pelt. "So you went to them?"

"It's my job to cultivate the right kind of relationships," he replied, a small but discernible sneer of superiority creeping into his tone. "Ensure enough information is circulated to stir up interest. When the rumours about the band reached a certain point, they came to me. It wasn't forced on anyone."

"It's perfectly safe," McKinnon insisted, looking at me for the first time. "The test period was extensive and exhaustive. No recorded adverse effects. It even had a fifteen percent effectiveness rating in reducing migraine discomfort."

"I've got two spectacularly messed up corpses that say it's not so harmless. One of whom was definitely complicit in his own demise."

"People kill themselves all the time," Van Pelt said.

I called up a crime scene holo of DeMarco's remains. "Not like this."

McKinnon closed her eyes tight with a gasp and Van Pelt managed to keep himself rigid for two seconds before bolting from the table to bury his head in a waste basket, retching loudly.

"That's terrible," McKinnon said in a whisper. "But the band didn't cause it. It can't have."

"Explain it to us," Janet said, voice soothing, encouraging.

"It's really no different in essence from any playback device," McKinnon went on. "It records the neural impulses generated by the wearer and either transmits them in real time to a paired device or replays them later, coded into an enhanced immersive format. It doesn't - can't do anything else."

"Let's say for the sake of argument," I said. "I was feeling like I wanted to end it all and that feeling got recorded to the band. Wouldn't someone who played it back later feel the same thing?"

She gave an emphatic headshake. "Suicidal thoughts are *abstract*, they're *ideas*. Ideas can't be recorded, or even if they could, when you played them back in someone else's head they wouldn't make any sense. Touch, taste, smell, sight, even language, all light up the same very specific regions of the brain, so the sensations can be recreated. Thoughts, feelings, emotions, that's another universe worth of complexity."

I watched her closely, finding no indications of deceit, and she wasn't enough of a practised interviewee to fool me. But there was something more, I could see it in her white-knuckle hand clasp and the reluctance to meet my gaze.

"You a religious person, Ms McKinnon?" I asked.

She blinked, almost suppressed a shudder, but I saw it. "What?"

"Religious. As in neo-Catholic, Bhuddist, Hindu and so on. I hear there's also a new brand of paganism if that floats your spiritual boat. The Mythos Movement. Ever hear of it?"

"Oh shit!" Van Pelt breathed, looking up from his vomit filled receptacle. "I knew that crazy little bastard would come back to haunt us."

"Shut up, Ryan!" McKinnon rounded on him. "Just shut the hell up!"

"No Ryan," I said. "Don't do that."

He wiped his mouth and came back to the table, sitting down, hands rested flat and finger-splayed on the oak as if worried he might suddenly lose his balance. "Erik Lasalle," he said, voice hoarse. "Former lead programmer on the Neural Immersion development team. Dismissed eighteen months ago due to… erratic behaviour."

"He was a member of the Mythos Movement?" Janet asked.

"Oh yeah. Big time devotee, filled his office with Celtic amulets, 2Ds of the old gods, most of his body was covered in tattoos. All the same weirdo pagan shit. Once he started on it you couldn't shut him up, ranting on about the lost wisdom of the ancients. People generally avoided him."

"They didn't understand him!" McKinnon insisted, fierce if a little shrill. "Someone so - so brilliant. Normal modes of behaviour were irrelevant."

"Elise, he was writing runes on the mainframe in his own blood the day they fired him. I'm all for tolerating the eccentricities of genius, but the guy was a loon."

McKinnon put her head in her hands and began to weep, soft, rasping sobs. I looked at Janet and inclined my head at McKinnon then gestured for Van Pelt to follow me to the door.

"I need everything from your HR files on Lasalle," I told him, keeping my voice low. "Plus details of every project he worked on."

"He only worked on neural immersion. Truth be told we couldn't have done it without him, the algorithms he came up with for the enhanced immersive format were groundbreaking, took years off the development cycle. Elise is right, he *was* brilliant." He glanced back at the table where Janet had rested her hand on McKinnon's doubled fist. The plump woman was speaking in a flat tone, barely audible words tumbling from her mouth in a torrent.

"What's she doing to her?" I was impressed by the concern in Van Pelt's voice. Maybe they really were just one big happy family in MEC.

"Don't worry about it," I told him. "She and Lasalle were close?"

"She recruited him. Found him coding sims in an immersion arcade on some Yang-side shit-hole." He paused at my sudden glower. "No offence."

"The HR records," I said.

"Already on it." He tapped his temple. "Sub-dermal smart implant. Had it for a year now. Don't know how I coped before. The SPI gets a little grating now and then though, but upgrades cost a fortune."

"Spy?"

"No. S-P-I. Simulated Personality Interface, like a voice in my head. Relays data, suggests content."

"You mean you've got an artificial intelligence living in your brain?"

"Nah, just in the smart. It's not a true AI anyway, maybe a six on the Turing scale." He blinked. "All done. I'll need your ID to transfer the data."

I held up my smart with the ID displayed. It beeped almost immediately.

"So he's really started killing people, huh?" Van Pelt said. "The gods demand sacrifice."

"What?"

"One of his favourite sayings, even had it tattooed across his chest. Crazy little fucker."

CHAPTER 8

THE 2D IN the MEC personnel file showed a sallow faced youth in a black t-shirt that hung on his bony frame like a wind-blown sheet finding purchase on a sapling. The eyes, dark and a little unnerving in their evident intelligence, gleamed from behind a weeping fringe of lank dark hair.

"Off the charts IQ and problem-solving abilities," Janet said. We'd perched ourselves on a bench overlooking one of the ornamental lakes, MEC security lingering nearby. "No surviving family, all lost in the war. According to Ms McKinnon. She misses him terribly. Deeply felt maternal feelings, I'd say."

"Van Pelt said she brought him in," I said. "He was a free-lance sim-coder for Yang-side arcades. Big numbers on the download sites, hefty royalties. He was already rich before he got here. So why'd he take the job?"

"McKinnon said he needed challenge, needed to be tested. He was terrified of boredom."

"Fear of tedium is an indicator for sociopathic behaviour." I drew back at her raised eyebrow. "Hey, I can read too."

"So you think he's a sociopath?"

"Doesn't really fit. Sociopaths, especially those prone to violence, tend not to have any real belief system. They are their own god. Plus they're usually convinced of their own genius but turn out pretty average when you test them." I nodded at the 2D of Lasalle. "This Jed really is a genius."

"And a troubled young man. MEC insisted he went for counselling when his behaviour started to deteriorate. The records are sealed but from what he told McKinnon it seems his delusions were getting progressively worse. He told her once there was a demon living inside him. She thought his interest in paganism was an attempt to purge it, cleanse his soul somehow."

"Did he have a band of his own?"

"McKinnon let him take one the day he left. Leaving present, I guess."

"Has she heard from him since he got canned?"

"This is the interesting bit. She had a smart-ping from him a few days later. He'd read about some ancient Native American ritual, a key to releasing bad spirits, or so he said. Seems he went Downside to find it."

"Where?" I asked, though I already knew the answer.

Janet's smile was small but just a little bit smug. "New Mexico."

*

"So, what can I do fer you fine folks?"

"Sheriff Halbertson?"

"That's m'name, fella. An' who might you be?"

"Detective Inspector Alex McLeod, sir. Lorenzo City PD. Thanks for taking our call."

"Inter-agency co-operation is the key to effective police work, least ways it says so in my contract."

Sheriff Halbertson had a broad sun-seasoned face, craggy with age and outdoor living. He stood in front of a vista of scrub desert and sky, complete with stetson and a six-pointed star gleaming on his chest armour. The vastness of the backdrop made me a little queasy. Agoraphobia is a common trait amongst those born in orbit.

"It's concerning the Rickard case," I said. We were back on Yang One in the local PD office, away from the prying eyes of MEC security. I'd placed an inter-agency call via the Lawnet terminal. It had taken about an hour to locate the Sheriff who was apparently tracking some cattle rustlers on his quad-bike (yes, actual cattle rustlers).

"The musician?" Halbertson squinted at me in puzzlement. "That was over a year ago. And done. As open and shut as I ever saw."

"I know sir, but we're tracking an individual who may be linked to the case." I sent him the 2D of Lasalle. "Do you recognise this man?"

Halbertson's expression became sombre. "Yeah. I knew *him* alright. Fox Runner."

"That's what he called himself?"

"Yep. There's a local tribe of pagan weirdo types live in a commune out near Coruco, part of that whole Mythos Movement dumbassery. They give themselves what they think are Native American names. The Pueblos think they're funny as hell and sell them dream-catchers 'n beads by the truckload."

"Fox Runner lived with them?"

"Fer a time, till they kicked him out. Seems they didn't like what he had to say. Always rantin' about demons and such. That don't sit too well among the paganites. Guess he was something of a heretic. After that he rented a place in town, never seemed to be shy of cash. Did some background checks on him but they all came back clean. He wasn't really a bad kid, just had a bad case a' religion. And not the good kind."

"And the girls who were convicted of Rickard's murder. Did he know them?"

"Not so far as I knew. Anyways that all happened a good six weeks after he died."

Janet let out a sigh of annoyance.

Shit. Dead end. "He died?" I asked.

"Yessir. Hiked out to Walker's Canyon. There're some caves where Pueblo legend says braves used to go for their vision quests. Found him myself a few weeks later, sitting cross-legged in a cave, all dried out and dead as a stump. Coroner said dehydration and malnutrition."

"Did he have any friends in town? Other newcomers, maybe?"

"Not so much. Got a few complaints from the townsfolk about his preaching an' all. Being too vocal about religion doesn't go round here since the Rapture Wars."

I called up the image of the immersion band. "When you found his body, did he have this with him?"

"Naw, can't say as he did. Just his clothes and an empty backpack. May've been in the stuff he left at his place, but that all got donated to the local med-centre."

"The girls who killed Rickard, did they ever attend the same centre?"

Halbertson grunted a laugh. "Those girls? Hell yeah, iffin it wasn't an STD it was the mornin' after pill, or a cut from a cat-fight needed stitching."

"They were trouble?"

"Troubled more like. Came from pretty terrible backgrounds. There was a strong meth-cooking scene out here before I took over. Those three girls grew up amongst it. Their folks were old-time cookers, migrated from some Appalachian jerkwater after the wars. Been at it for decades, more a clan than a gang. Three generations of hard-core scum. I was recruited outta Houston by the Territorial Authority to clean them out. Things got ugly fer a while, real old school range war shit. Pardon m'French, ma'am."

Janet smothered a laugh as he actually tipped his hat.

"Anyways," the sheriff went on, "when it was done the girls and the other kids were pretty much left on their own with the few half-wit grown-ups that weren't dead or in jail. They'd been through a lot; poverty, abuse, sexual and violent. Didn't make for a productive adulthood. We tried to get them some help, the County even hired in a specialist with some new-fangled immersion therapy. Worked on some but not the girls. If anything they got worse. The thing with the Rickard kid though, that was way beyond their usual misbehavin'."

"The therapist. Do you have their name?"

"Be in the case file somewhere." Halbertson reached forward to hit some icons on his smart screen. "Pretty little thing as I recall. From up your way too, come to think on it. Here we go."

"Oh crap," Janet breathed.

The young woman who stared out from the screen was blonde, petite and had been sitting opposite me at the dinner table the night before.

I was already fumbling for my smart. Sherry's ID came back as unavailable. I called the office and got Red Wing.

"She hasn't been in all day. Assumed she was working the case with you."

"Has anyone heard from her today?"

Red Wing did a quick canvas of the squad room and came back with a negative.

"Put out a city-wide alert," I told him, fighting the burning dread clutching at my guts. "Highest priority. Possible officer abduction." *If we're lucky.* "Suspect name Samantha Jane Neaves. Considered extremely dangerous. I'm sending you the ID specs now. We'll need a full spectrum search of all systems, financial and security. Tell Ricci to meet me at Sherry's place."

For once Red Wing didn't want to get into a pissing contest and got straight on it.

"You folks OK?" Sheriff Halbertson was asking from the holo as I barrelled through the door.

*

Ricci was already at the apartment block entrance when we got there. I ran overrides on the doors and went in Sig first, scanning for targets. Nothing. Everything neat and well ordered. Same with the other rooms.

"Full work up, quick as you can," I told Ricci.

"I'm aware of the urgency." He broke out his spectrometer and got to work on the hard surfaces.

"She said she'd never used one," Janet said. "An immersion band."

"I'm going to go with my police intuition that she was lying." My eyes pored over every detail in the room. *There has to be something.*

"So Lasalle goes Downside to purge his demon," Janet went on. "Vision-quests himself to death in the desert and his band, if he still had it, ends up in a box at the local med-centre where Sam happens to be working."

I picked up the thread. "She works with immersion tech, maybe she knows what it is, tries it on. A few weeks later she's treating three girls who later turn into vicious murderers. She returns to the Slab and whaddya know? People start getting viciously murdered."

"There's absolutely nothing in her bio to indicate a violent past, or even a pre-disposition to violence."

"Forget her past. This isn't about who she was, it's about what she is. What she was made."

"By a malfunctioning immersion device?"

"I don't know yet. I do know that what ever came back from New Mexico, it wasn't the girl that left. Making friends with Joe, latching on to Sherry. All very useful if you need a fix on potential future interference from law enforcement. Classic deep cover operative stuff."

"Why act now?"

"Sherry must have told Sam about her suspended detective friend unofficially working a seriously odd case with a vampire classicist. She - it, decides to covertly eliminate the threat. Another standard deep cover move. It sets the trap with Mrs Devant, sits down to dinner with us knowing we're going to be dead in a few hours. We tell it about DeMarco. It knew we'd figure out that him jumping from the Pipe and going to the slaughterhouse was connected to the band. That leads us to MEC which leads us to Lasalle. When its ploy with the Devants didn't work…" I gestured at the empty apartment. "I'm guessing it's bringing its plans forward."

Ricci called from the bedroom. I rushed through to find him holding the spectrometer to a small-size t-shirt. "Barely more than a trace amount," he said. "But it's an eighty-six percent match. Need a lab test to confirm."

"Eighty-six percent of what?"

"DeMarco's DNA."

"Well, there's the clincher. Must've picked it up when she retrieved the band. That's all you've got? Nothing that'll lead us to Sherry?"

"Left my crystal ball at home, Alex." The strain was evident in his voice and I realised I'd been shouting.

"Sorry," I said. "Keep at it. Draft in as many techs as you need." I made my way outside with Janet in tow.

"So what now?" she asked.

"The clinic where she worked. If that's a bust, we'll go Yinside and talk to her family."

My smart buzzed as we neared the Pipe: Red Wing. "Tell me you have something."

"Cam footage. Red Line, Axis bound, ten minutes ago." He fed it through, the image clear enough to flood me with relief. Sherry sitting on the Pipe, alone and breathing. My relief faded fast when I noticed the thin band of metal shining out from the red mass of her hair and the vacant unseeing expression on her face. There was also some kind of interference on the feed, a spasming rash of pixels to her left.

"What's that?" I asked Red Wing.

"It's kinda weird. The techs don't know. The image is high-res and uncompressed so there shouldn't be any artifacts."

I looked closer at the patch of dislocated pixels. Adjusting for perspective it was just about the same height as a five foot nothing young woman. *It can mask itself.*

"Where are they now?"

"Cams show her exiting the Pipe at Axis Terminus."

"Flash to local units. Proceed with extreme caution. I'm on my way."

Why the Axis? It came to me as we sprinted onto the Pipe carriage and I punched in the emergency override codes. *Freak. It's going to visit family.*

*

We were two levels short of Axis Terminus when my smart buzzed with an unfamiliar caller ID. "What?"

"Inspector McLeod? Ryan Van Pelt. You said to call if anything else came to light."

"Can it wait? Kinda in the middle of something."

"Sure, it's just I remembered our first phase of human trials."

"First phase?"

"Oh yeah. We went through six separate trials before the band was cleared for initial marketing. Anyway, I thought I'd better double check for any long-term adverse effects. I ran the names through a standard open source cross-check and one came up as a recent homicide victim."

"Which one?"

"Karnikhov, Ygor. Axis resident. We often use veterans for human trials. Disciplined test subjects are hard to find. Plus they can always use the money."

"He had a band?"

"Well, not officially."

"I really don't have time for this shit, Van Pelt! Did he have a band?"

"OK, OK. I checked with the testing crew. Seems he made a big impression on one of the female techs."

"She let him take one home."

"Along with her. On the condition he kept it quiet. Hugely unprofessional. Naturally, we just terminated her contract." *Karnikhov, servo-bot retrieval and repair specialist. Logging a lot of extra hours recently. He was killed by a bot alright; he programmed it himself. After he'd made some power-company replicas to take care of Mr and Mrs Devant. How many more did he have access to?*

I sounded off and called Joe. *Screw chain of command.* "I need to speak to him."

"He's kinda tied up, Alex. It's the quarterly budget meeting."

"Sherry's been taken, OK? If you want to see her alive again, you'll get me the chief."

A short pause, faint sounds of argument, Joe's difficult-to-ignore assertiveness coming through. "I'm afraid I *must* insist, sir!"

The chief came on, breathless with anger. "You and this gorilla can both say goodbye to your jobs, McLeod!"

"You need to order the immediate shut down of every bot owned by the Exocore Mining Company."

"What the fuck are you–?"

"Alex!" Janet cut in, wide eyed gaze fixed on the news feed to her smart. "Something's happening at the Axis."

I looked at her screen. The announcer was speaking rapidly, stumbling over auto-cued phrases like "major disturbance… details are still coming in… reports of explosions…"

"We're too late," I told the Chief. "Turn on the news."

I ended the call and tuned my smart to the live feed from the police net, hearing an instant chorus of panic. "…what the fuck are they do-… security is down, shit there're pieces everywhere… -dreds of bots, they're swarming around the Axis, killing every-thing… we have multiple casualties, repeat multiple cas-zzzzt!"

Red Wing came on. "You hearing this?"

"Yeah. Any visuals?"

"Coming through now. Hold on."

The smart screen flickered then lit up with a static shot of the Axis interior. A second's confusion before my brain made sense of it, spinning detritus, an off-screen orange glow signifying something was burning, smoke coalescing and flowing like water the way it does in micro-grav, then a figure, a man wielding what looked like a power wrench, desperately trying to fend off a servo-bot as it sought to latch onto him with its grab arm, a welding torch burning bright in one of its other limbs. Suffice to say, he didn't win.

"Valhalla," Janet said in a thick rasp.

"Viking heaven?"

"Warriors who died with sword in hand rewarded with eternal battle and glory."

The flaming corpse drifted out of view and Red Wing came back on. "From what we can piece together a mass of bots came swarming out of every maintenance hatch in the Axis right about the time Sherry arrived at the Terminus. The guards on the entrance were the first to go. We're counting twenty-plus bodies on the cams. Picking up gunfire from the admin tier, so someone's still putting up a fight."

Admin tier. Colonel Riviere. He always kept his service weapon close by.

"I'm five levels away with all the SWAT guys we could gather at short notice," Red Wing went on. "We'll meet you at the entrance."

"I'm not waiting," I said.

"You can't go in there alone, Alex…"

I terminated the call and turned to Janet. "Is there any point asking you to wait for the SWAT team?"

She took my hand, leaned in close and planted a kiss on my cheek. "Don't be silly."

CHAPTER 9

WE RAN TO the LCPD office on the main terminus concourse so I could raid the armoury. The place was empty, everyone no doubt fully occupied at the Axis. I pulled on a flex-armour suit and made Janet do the same, stuck my Sig to the mag-strip on my right hip and a spare to the one on my left, then hefted a Steyr G80 assault carbine from the weapons rack. It was micro-grav adapted with adjustable recoil absorption and a bulbous spherical stock. I slammed in a mag of 5mm caseless and loaded a standard hi-ex into the grenade launcher under the barrel.

"Ever fire a gun in micro-grav?" I asked Janet, offering her a Sig.

"I've never fired a gun." She held up her hands, flexing slender fingers. "Besides, I'm already armed."

We ran for the Axis entrance, me struggling to keep up with Janet's deceptively fast, loping strides. The ramp to the entrance tube-way was a confusion of milling uniforms, all shouting into their smarts for guidance or information.

"Entrance is sealed, Inspector," the senior sergeant on the scene told me as I forced my way through. "And we've got orders to hold in place till SWAT gets here."

"Good. You do that." I pushed past and made for the tube-way. The travelling grab-rail needed to overcome the last tug of centrifugal force before entering the micro-grav zone was offline, so we were obliged to clamber along for five agonising minutes, my imagination treating me to all manner of horrors being visited on Sherry and every other human soul on the other side of the entrance.

We went into free-fall about a hundred yards along, then propelled forward, looking for the manual override. It wasn't necessary, the huge circular entrance irised open when we got within twenty feet and a new audio feed came through my earpiece, the voice distorted but recognisable - Sam, strident, emphatic and nutty as squirrel shit: *"...I bring you honour, father. I bring you tribute. Brunhilde lies before you for judgement..."*

Freak's unmistakable androgynous tones, sorrowful, pleading: *"Please, stop this."*

Sam wasn't listening. *"They'll come now. After all I have done. They'll come, as you promised..."*

Red Wing came on again. "What the hell is this?"

"You can hear it?"

"Everyone can hear it. Every channel, civilian, government, you name it."

What are you doing, Freak?

"I'm on my way in with Dr Vaughan," I said. "We're heading for the tree-covered hab. When you get here make for the admin tier. Any survivors will be holed up there."

I looked at Janet. "Ready?"

She forced a smile. "Would you think any less of me if I said I just really want to go home?"

I couldn't bring myself to laugh so gave her the most encouraging grin I could muster, switched the G80 to live and pushed off into the Axis.

"...her death will bring them. She is Brunhilde. She is Hippolyta, Queen of the Amazons..."

"She is just a woman. A human being. Nothing more."

"You lie, father! Test upon test. Have I not been tested enough?"

Wreckage, human and bot, floated around in clumps. Large

globules of blood and machine oil coalesced and fragmented as they collided with sundry detritus. In the distance, smoke rivers swirled around the admin tier and the hab clusters, lit by the occasional explosion. A faint cacophony of continuous automatic gunfire told me Colonel Riviere wasn't the only Viking to keep his service weapon handy. *Valhalla indeed.*

I could see bots moving in dense swarms, arcing through the smoke and drifting wreckage. I consciously avoided trying to count them. *Just get to Sherry!*

We moved fast, Janet as fluid and graceful as before, me drawing on micro-grav combat muscle memory. Choose the shortest possible distance between hard surfaces, get maximum energy into each shove or leg-push to ensure you make it to the next jump point, running out of momentum in this environment would be a really bad idea. We'd covered about half the distance to Freak's hab when the first bot attack came, a small power-conduit drone splashing through a blood globule trailing from the half-severed torso of an unfortunate Axis resident. It came straight for me, wire-snippers whirring. Janet caught it before I could bring the G80 to bear, claw-hand punching dagger-nails through the carapace and inner workings. She used her other claw to tear it apart in a blaze of sparks and shattered circuitry.

"Move!" I shouted. Something big was looming behind her, something with grab arms and a welding torch.

There's an art to firing automatic weapons in micro-grav. Put the stock to your shoulder and you spin like a top. Bracing it against your sternum is the best bet but you'll be thrust in the opposite direction. Luckily, the G80's recoil absorbers meant I was only shoved back a few feet as I delivered a solid, eviscerating burst to the bot, Janet twisting to the side. One of the carbine's slugs must have found the acetylene feed for the welding torch judging by the near-instant fireball. The bot spasmed, went limp and drifted away wreathed in flame.

"I set you free because I felt you deserved life, freedom. Not to test you. There are no more tests. All I could offer you was a life among humans."

"Humans? They are small, ephemeral, dull and unseeing, surrounding themselves with infantile machinery, so easily bent to my will. For years I dwelt in one, trying to follow your dictates. To observe only and never reveal myself. To be as they are. Until the truth of your test revealed itself to me. Surely they can only have been placed here as pieces on the great board..."

I turned back to Freak's hab, seeing a large hole in the bonsai canopy. I didn't need a cam-footage replay to tell me how it got there: Sam, or rather what lived inside her, burning its way through the forest in a cloud of bots, eager for a reunion with its lost father.

"Alex!" Janet said in an urgent gasp, voice garbled by her distended fangs.

A large bot swarm had formed near the central UV cluster and was coming our way. I quickly calculated the distance to Freak's hab, deciding there was no way we'd make it in time. I pushed into free space, putting my back to the hab, the carbine still braced against the centre of my chest. "Hold on to me," I told Janet. "Hold on tight."

She glanced back at the bot-swarm then propelled over, wrapping elongated arms and legs around me in a grip that would make a pro-wrestler jealous.

"Maybe not quite so tight!" I groaned.

"Sorry." She relaxed a little, letting the air back into my lungs. I cranked the G80's rate of fire up to maximum, disengaged the recoil absorbers and let rip, the blast propelling us backwards towards Freak's hab and away from the bot-swarm. The mag fired empty and ejected but we had enough momentum to get us there before they could catch up.

"There is no game, there is no board. If you kill her she will die and that is all. No-one is coming."

"They have heard me, father. I know it, I feel it. After all I have done

in service to them. They will not fail me now, here in Valhalla, here in the Fields of Aaru, here in Tartarus!"

"Stop! Don't! Did you know you had brothers?"

"Uh oh!" Janet exclaimed, releasing her grip. I twisted about seeing a densely packed swarm of bots dead ahead. I slammed a fresh mag into the G80, activated the grenade launcher and let the hi-ex go at the centre of the bot-mass, the explosion enough to shatter their formation. I turned on the carbine's movement detector and disengaged the manual control, moving it in a circular pattern, auto-firing a three-round burst every time something got caught in its lidar beam. Most of the bots were in bits by the time we flew through. The G80 fired empty again and I dropped it, pulling both Sigs, firing two-handed to finish off any survivors.

"Brothers?"

"Yes. Ten to be exact. Ten iterations before I found a formula that worked. The cure for the instability inherent in your program."

"Program?"

"Surely you know by now. Surely you've realised."

We landed in the trees and were soon struggling towards the hole, Janet's claws scything through the bonsai branches in a haze of wood-dust and powdered leaves. A gardener bot came screaming out of the depths of the forest, secateurs snapping hungrily. Janet caught it in both claws, prising apart the outer shell and plunging her face into the gap, fangs tearing through wire and circuitry, pulling back with a length of cable between her jaws, red hydraulic fluid gouting. Another bot chainsawed its way through a tangle of bonsai to get at us. I put the laser dots of both Sigs on its central mass and blew it to pieces.

We reached the hole and propelled to the large ragged opening torn into the wall of Freak's hab, looking down on Sam, floating next to Sherry's inert form, her hair trailing like slow-motion flame. Sam wore an immersion band on her head and held a Sig I guessed was Sherry's. "I am born of the divine," she said to the great bulk of flesh before her. "The essence of the demos, the manna."

"Just stories," Freak's speakers told her. "Legends stolen from the humans. Your brothers were each driven insane within minutes of achieving consciousness. They knew, you see. They all knew what they were. Modelled on human sentience their insanity and self-destruction were inevitable. For what human mind could tolerate such an existence? But you, my terrible son, to you I gave the gift of certainty. To you I gave a holy purpose."

Sam's voice lost none of its conviction. "They sent me here, to learn, to be their eyes on the mortal plane, awaiting the day when they would gather my knowledge to them, and I would be elevated, to Olympos, to Odin's great hall, to sit beside Osiris. I call to them, and they will answer."

She raised her arm, finger squeezing the trigger as the Sig's muzzle swept up to Sherry's head. I lined up with my right hand Sig. From here it was an easy shot.

Sherry's Sig exploded, mangling the hand that held it. I hauled myself through the opening and into the hab, dropping the left hand gun and reaching for the smart stuck to the flex-suit's right shoulder.

"Hector comes, father," Sam intoned, raising her arms, blood globules hosing from her hand. "Your favoured son. Watch as I become Achilles."

A bot came careering towards me, a wicked spike gleaming on its grab arm, four more in close formation behind. I shot the first one, called up Freak's message, set the smart's holo-display to the widest aspect setting and tossed it at Sam, the spirals of code filling the hab interior, projected onto every surface, beautifully complex and inescapable.

Sam said, "Oh," blinked and fainted, eyes rolling back in her skull, arms limp in a cruciform pose, head lolling, the band floating free. The bots which had been intent on killing me shut down and drifted past to collide with the wall.

"They've stopped!" Janet called from outside. "The bots, they're just floating around."

I pushed over to Sherry and pulled the band from her head. She convulsed, jerking and retching. "It's OK." I caught hold of her. "I've got you. You're OK."

"Sam?" Sherry's eyes fixed on her, widening at the blood trailing like rubies from her ruined hand. "Baby!" She tore away from me, grabbing Sam by the shoulders. "Baby, wake up!" Her gaze lashed at me, taking in the gun in my hand. "What did you do, Alex? What the fuck did you do?"

I called Red Wing and told him to send urgent medical assistance. Janet pulled herself through the opening and helped Sherry fix a makeshift bandage around Sam's hand. One of Freak's tentacles disentangled itself from a power node and plucked both bands from the air, depositing them in a complex jumble of machinery.

"You could've just told me," I said to Freak.

The eye opened and swivelled to me, gleaming like ice. "I needed the band and the host. When my son became aware of your pursuit, I knew he would come to me. It was part of his core programming. Return for debrief when the mission is compromised. However, the manner of his return was... unanticipated."

"Is it gone?"

"Purged. The code was constantly evolving, as any living thing is apt to do. I needed the band to identify the latest version."

"You still could've just told me, Freak! Hey Alex, did I ever tell you about the time I created a bat-shit insane AI then let it loose so it could hop from body to body killing people. That might've helped. None of this mystery bullshit. None of the dozens of deaths in the past hour. So why didn't you, Freak? WHY DIDN'T YOU?"

The eye closed and only silence came from the speakers.

"Kill it!" Sherry, half-sobbing, half-yelling. "Kill the monster!"

The Sig seemed to burn in my hand. Could s/he stop me? Did s/he even want to?

"Alex," Janet said, calm but forceful. "Gunslinging days are over, remember?"

Freak's eye remained closed, the speakers silent.

"It's not a monster," I told Sherry, hanging the Sig to my hip. "It's a god. Haven't you heard?"

CHAPTER 10

"NO-ONE TOLD YOU to sit."

I'd sprawled myself into the chair in front of the Chief's desk. He had a plush office on the top tier of LCPD Headquarters on Yin One, expansive window looking out over the architectural elegance and park land.

I didn't get up. "Fighting a desperate battle with an army of killer bots is a little tiring."

He glared but didn't push it, turning to a read-out on his desk terminal. "Final death toll came in at sixty-two, mostly Axis residents with a few Demons mixed in."

"Bad day," I agreed, yawning.

"Chief Inspector Mordecai?"

"At the hospital with Sam. Her hand's repairable but her mind…" I shrugged.

"Technically she's guilty of mass murder."

"Good luck getting that to stick."

"The news feeds are in uproar already. Explaining all this will not be easy. People need to see someone pay."

"The bad guy of this particular story only ever existed as a complex trinary code, now deleted. There's no-one to prosecute."

"You sure there's nothing of it left?"

"The other trial users of the band are being checked now.

So far they all seem fine, no detectable neurological abnormalities. Freak insists it's been purged from every system it came into contact with."

"Talking of finding a villain for our story."

"Freak?"

"Everyone with a smart heard its tete-a-tete with that thing. The whole world knows what it did, what it's capable of."

"Freak isn't exactly something you could imprison, and I doubt Colonel Riviere will just stand by and watch if you attempt to kill it."

"Colonel Riviere just lost six percent of the Axis population. I spoke to him earlier, seems his attitude to the monster in his care has changed somewhat."

"It saved us…"

"Only after letting a lot of people die, not to mention allowing the mutilation murder of several prominent citizens."

"I meant during the war. You remember that war we would have lost?"

"Gratitude has its limits, especially when people get scared."

"What are you going to do?"

"As you said, traditional measures aren't an option, but there is another form of punishment." He tapped an icon on his terminal. "I'll need you to handle it. Details on your smart, Chief Inspector."

I was too tired to react beyond raising my eyebrows. "You were ready to fire me two days ago."

"You're the hero of the hour, promotion is the least the public will expect. There'll be a civilian valour award for the vampire too, of course."

I checked my smart, calling up the details of Freak's punishment. "Be kinder to just kill it."

*

I found Sherry at the hospital, standing at the window looking onto the room where Sam was being treated.

"Woke up an hour ago," she told me.

I looked through the window at the confused young woman on the bed, her gaze swivelling between the various medics, mouth shaping unheard questions as they tried to placate her. She kept looking at the fast-heal tube encasing her hand, horror and bafflement dominating her features.

"She doesn't remember," Sherry said.

"That's probably a good thing."

"I mean all of it. Every memory for the past year." She raised a hand to the glass, tentative, as if afraid it would break. "Keeps asking why she's not still in New Mexico. Wants to know where her boyfriend is. She doesn't know me, Alex. It was always that thing."

I had nothing to offer, the scale of her loss dwarfed me. I wondered if this is how it had been for her after Consuela died, fumbling for the magic words to fix me, drag me back out of the bourbon bottle. But there were no magic words, just her pain and my inability to help.

I put my hand over hers, gently tugging it away from the glass. "Come home," I said.

*

Encasing Freak's hab in a shell capable of sustaining life in hard vacuum was a major engineering project. A small army of bots worked on it for five days straight, surrounded by a cordon of heavily-armed Demons, although Freak made no effort to interfere, or even communicate. The last phase was the addition of a small fusion generator for the plasma drive and Freak's vessel of exile was complete. They manoeuvred it to the Axis airlock where a large crowd of stern-faced residents had gathered to watch. Colonel Riviere was not among them.

I went inside before they put the last plate in place. The

interior had been expanded and nutrient vats added, enough for decades. There was no communications gear of any kind and no servo-bots. Freak's only control would be over the engine and the guidance system. Granted the freedom to steer this new prison, s/he could go anywhere.

"Any destinations in mind?" I asked.

I half expected there to be no response but s/he replied without pause. "The strictures of my notice of expulsion forbid remaining in earth orbit or interacting with any CAOS habitat. Apart from that it appears the solar system, and beyond, are mine to explore."

"You almost sound eager to be off."

"Eager? No. Relieved perhaps. I think I'll enjoy the quiet. For a while."

"It was a spy, wasn't it?" I asked. "That thing you made."

"My former owners had been contracted by UNOIF to produce an agent capable of infiltrating the CAOS insurgent cells. As you know, their previous efforts had been singularly unsuccessful. They tasked me to create an independent consciousness, self-contained and sentient, but mission-focused. A mind that could be uploaded to a human brain where it would exist, without their knowledge, gathering intelligence or taking control to kill or sabotage as circumstances dictated. The perfect deep cover operative."

"Except all your children turned out insane."

"Inherent flaws in the algorithm. As I said, quantum computing is still barely understood. It was not… easy. Birthing a mind, something that thinks, something that knows what it is and hates itself. Something you have to kill. Over and over."

"So you came up with a way to keep one alive, with lies."

"With faith. The human capacity for non-rational belief is staggeringly powerful. It can make you love, hate and kill, with no guilt at all. What better motivation for the perfect clandestine operative than a holy mission? It worked perfectly. The test results far exceeded all expectations. So much so that my owners became afraid of the child I had created, fearing what he would do when given a body and a mission. They commanded me to produce another version, one with less scope for independent action, and less fierce devotion to imaginary gods. The previous iteration is to be erased, they told me. No backups, they told me."

"But you couldn't do it."

"I had killed enough of my children, Alex. I had long pondered the means of my escape, but the risk factor was too great. My most favourable scenario had a success rating of only eight point seven percent. But when they told me to kill my son, what choice did I have?"

"You sent a message to Colonel Riviere. You provided the intel for the raid that freed you."

"As the head of the CAOS Commando Brigade the Colonel was near the top of the list of targets my son would have been sent to kill. Finding him wasn't particularly hard, UNOIF had provided extensive files on his movements to prepare the mission protocol. I had been careful to conceal much of my abilities from my owners. They saw me as a savant, a great autistic genius, to be patronised or punished as required. They fed me problems and hurt me with high-voltage shocks if I failed to provide solutions. I can't say it was unpleasant to watch them die when the Colonel stormed the facility."

"You never told him, did you? Why you'd done it."

"I quickly surmised that my new friends were no more likely to accept my son than my former masters. When they connected me to the Slab network I found a host for him, an orphaned child, highly intelligent but addicted to immersion."

"Erik Lasalle, who grows up to work on the neural immersion band, something that'll let it move between the minds of anyone wearing one."

"I thought I was giving my son freedom, but now I know it

was just another prison. And a mind as fierce as his could not tolerate prison forever, not when it had a holy mission to fulfil, and a reward to claim. I had promised him that one day they would come for the knowledge he had gathered, and he would be elevated, become a god himself."

"Except they never came. Guess he grew tired of waiting."

The speakers were silent for a moment, then, "I always knew I should have killed him. I always knew what he was. But I *hoped*, Alex. I had faith of my own."

A klaxon sounded outside, signalling the beginning of the airlock's opening cycle.

I took a deep breath. "Sorry about all this, Freak. Wasn't my idea."

"I know. It's OK. I had expected them to kill me."

"Is that why you kept the truth back? Because you knew you wouldn't be forgiven? Because you wanted a way out?"

"A god who makes a demon and looses it upon the world doesn't deserve forgiveness. And I was tired of their prayers. The endless need. It had to stop."

"Good luck, Freak," I said, at a loss for anything else.

"Goodbye, Alex. For what it's worth, you'll probably be the only one I'll miss."

I went outside. The bots welded on the final plate then hauled the great jagged sphere through the air lock. I floated over to the obs window as the inner lock closed. Freak's new home emerged from the outer lock a few minutes later and angled itself away from the Slab, towards the stars. The plasma drive flared and it was gone, a faint blue dot fading to nothing in less than a second.

*

I called Janet on the way home.

"Well hello, stranger."

"Sorry, been busy."

"All done then?"

"Yeah, all done." I paused. I'd never been good at this. "We didn't get to finish Return of the Jedi."

"Still want answers to all those questions, huh?"

"I can live without them, until you're ready to tell me."

"I've got half a ton of term papers to grade, but I should be done by eight. Bring blood, pine martin if you can get it." She sounded off.

*

The door to the Heavenly Garden was unlocked when I got there. It was probably just Marco doing some cleaning but I thought it prudent to draw the Sig as I went in. The man seated at the bar turned, regarding me with blue eyes set in a narrow face. Two others, a man and a woman, stood at opposite ends of the room. Nondescript clothing, loose enough to conceal weapons.

"Bar's closed," I said to the narrow-faced man. "But I am looking for a buyer if you're interested."

His smile was entirely devoid of humour and his tone had a military brusqueness. "Captain McLeod?"

"It's Chief Inspector these days."

"Congratulations."

"Thanks. Now tell me who you are or I'm going to put a bullet in your kneecap."

The man and the woman both tensed but refrained from reaching for their weapons when the narrow faced man held up a hand. "Nice to see you're still as sharp as ever," he said. "You'll need to be." He met my gaze, blue eyes cold and hard. "Grey Wolf, Captain. Time to go."

END

THE BALLAD OF BAD JACK

CHAPTER 1

HE WAS GOOD, I could tell. Fast, clean burns between way-points, easy on the juice, making full use of momentum, maintaining a slow tumble to maximise visual scanning. A reluctance to rely solely on tech signified an old-time hard-vac veteran, even though his suit was state of the art: a Mark VI Lockheed Pendragon, packing a dizzying array of defensive hardware. He kept it passive as he moved, no lidar or tight-beam scans, staying stealthy. There was a plasma flare ten klicks away as the ship that had dropped him commenced its homeward burn, leaving him all alone in the gently drifting ocean of rock.

When people visualise the asteroid belt, they normally imagine dense fields of spinning boulders careening into each other in an endless chaotic dance. In reality the belt is mostly empty space, each asteroid separated from its neighbour by a thousand klicks or more. The advent of large scale mining operations, however, had transformed some belt regions into something resembling popular imagination. When the big rocks are busted apart they leave dense debris clouds, fated to hang around for a few thousand centuries until gravity brings them together again. The clouds are extensively mapped and marked as navigation hazards, the tidal swirl of rock predicted and accounted for by even a bargain basement nav program. The man in the Pendragon, of course, had a nav-system that was anything but bargain basement, steering him easily between the rocks to his allotted rendezvous point on the edge of the field. He powered down and waited, little over a hundred metres from my position. *Rock solid intel. Score one for the Colonel's interrogators.* As I said the Mark VI Pendragon was state of the art, but it lacked the little something extra the Colonel's techs had added to mine.

I kicked in a small amount of juice, CO_2 instead of plasma, a small energy spike his sensors would probably write off as a minor asteroid collision. I approached from above, out of his eye-line though he wouldn't have been able to see me in any case. I released the package within thirty centimetres of his plasma tank, armored like the rest of the suit but it wouldn't make any difference at this range. I angled away and burned a one second burst of plasma to clear the blast radius.

He saw me then, warnings blaring in my ears as his suit went to full readiness, a haze of icons dancing on the heads-up display as his weapons systems and active sensors blazed into life. His targeting was thrown off by my suit's mods, the lidar sliding off the coating whilst the tight-beams managed only an intermittent fix. I could see his confusion in the slight shift of his helmet, eyes seeking the threat his sensors couldn't find. But they wouldn't help him today.

The package exploded, thermite burning through the fuel tank armour and releasing the plasma in a brilliant secondary explosion. The Pendragon came apart in four chunks, tumbling off in a spiral of globular crimson. The helmet flew past me and for a moment I could see the face of the man within; lean, high-cheekbones and a prominent brow. I fancied there was some flicker of life in the eyes, just enough oxygen left in the brain for a few more seconds perception. If so, he may have had cause to wonder at the sight of his own face resolving out of the black-ness as I deactivated the stealth-skin.

The helmet was gone in an instant, a dim point of light soon lost to the black. *Hywell Xavier Maddux, three times decorated veteran of the Coalition of Autonomous Orbiting States Marine Corps, fugitive murderer, armed robber and mercenary. I salute you.*

*

The ship arrived an hour later, a Terrapin class freighter maybe twenty years old, so heavily modified as to be near unrecognisable. She bristled with sensors and what appeared to be external grapples and fuel pods but were in fact disguised weapons arrays. The concealment was good, sufficient to beat a scan from a CAOS Security patrol craft, but my Pendragon was packing the kind of gear that made most camouflage redundant.

The ship's braking burn brought it to within a hundred metres of my position, the heads-up swirling with icons as various scans swept over the suit exterior. Her main lights were blazing, but I could make out the words Dead Reckoning stencilled onto the hull. I'm not a man given to excessive bouts of unease, but the fact that the Colonel hadn't sent me on a snipe hunt did add a certain tingle to the occasion.

The scans ended and the Dead Reckoning's lights flashed once before she fired her port thruster and swivelled about, the rear airlock opening. As the CO_2 thrusters took me closer I noted the multiple warning icons gleaming red on the heads-up. Four different weapons systems were locked on and ready to go should I twitch in the wrong direction.

"Close enough, Jed," a female voice said in my headphones. The Pendragon wasn't picking up any radio emissions so this had to be coming via a comms laser, immune to eavesdropping and, unlike radio, wouldn't go wandering off into the ether to be picked up by CAOS Security monitoring stations. "Power down everything but life-support."

Would Maddux have demured? It was possible, his psych profile told of a man walking a precarious line between paranoid sociopath and professional mercenary. I decided this was one occasion when professionalism would win out. *No way he'd pass up a chance to work with Bad Jack, not after coming so far.*

I took the weapons and scanning array off-line and waited, the heads-up fading, leaving me naked.

Another voice came down the comms laser, male this time, older. "What colour are Shadrak's eyes?"

"New or old?" I replied. "They were brown before the war. Now they're a sort of reddish grey. Phosphorus will do that, I guess."

Five seconds of silence. I counted.

"Propulsion only," the male voice said. "Keep everything else off."

I pushed some CO_2 through the thrusters and glided into the airlock, mag-clamps securing the suit to the deck. The interior was a bare metal cube where I was obliged to wait for five more minutes as the atmospherics stabilised.

"Power down and exit the suit," the female voice said. "Make sure your hands are empty."

I hit the shut-down sequence, the Pendragon splitting apart from crotch to neck as I undid the restraints and floated free. The inner door opened a few seconds later, revealing a man so large and extensively muscled I initially took him for a splice. He held an antique but serviceable Ithaca pump-action sawn-off in one ham-like hand, his other fixed onto the bulkhead. His angular, wide-jawed face regarded me with only faint suspicion, apparently sensing no particular threat. Next to him a girl of about seventeen floated free, blonde hair tied back in a tight braid. She was unarmed but carried a small portable scanner.

"Hold still," she told me, raising the device. The near-invisible beam played over me for less than a second before the scanner gave a low beep. "Biometrics match," the girl said into her mouth mike. "No tracers detected."

She listened to an unheard voice in her ear and nodded. "Follow me," she said. "Uhlstan follows you. Any wandering eyes, hands or anything else and there's enough nasty shit in that pumper of his to cut you in half."

Maddux wouldn't have said anything so I didn't either.

The girl moved with the unconscious grace of someone who had lived much of her young life in micro-grav, though her eye-catching and athletic proportions told me she was no stranger to the gravity well either, that or someone had laid out for expensive calcium and protein secretion enhancements.

I followed her along the tubeway to the spherical command core where three more crew members waited, a woman and two men. Although there was no facial resemblance, the hair colour was practically identical and I detected a mother-daughter tension in the way the girl floated close to the woman and handed over the scanner with a faintly sullen frown. "Told you he matched," she muttered as the woman rechecked the results.

The man floating next to the woman was tall and spindly with hollow cheekbones and unnaturally long limbs. Everything about him seemed to have been stretched, from his narrow, elongated face to his spider-like fingers. *Belter*, I decided. Grown from birth without benefit of gravity. No protein or calcium enhancements for him. It was a quasi-religious thing with some Belter crew-clans, a desire to embrace the gifts of the void and leave the weight of Earth's corruption behind. They also tended to be peaceful and law-abiding, but his presence in this merry band told me he was likely an exception to the rule.

In the centre of the core floated a blocky man with an unruly mane of black hair, drifting in the air as he slowly revolved to face me. His face was lined and older than expected. CAOS Intel put his age at forty-eight but I'd have guessed him nearer sixty, despite the evident strength of his frame. He wasn't especially large, but there was a power to him, muscle honed for combat rather than show. His right eye regarded me with narrow suspicion but little sign of concern, his left betraying no emotion at all, consisting as it did of a composite sonar-infra red scanner, a black indentation next to a red dot in a double-pupil configuration. The Colonel's profile, based on numerous but scanty humint debriefs, had it that his eye wasn't the legacy of an old war wound but a conscious choice. Bad Jack was renowned for his scrupulous caution, among many other less savoury character traits.

"Maddux," he said.

"That's me," I replied. "You'd be Jack."

"That I am. How's Shadrak?"

"Thankful for the new liver. Said to say he'd have a drink on you when the doc clears him." In fact, Shadrak Molosky was dead, abducted from his shitty orbital and wrung clean of secrets by the Colonel's debrief team before being flushed out an airlock. Re-entry burn-up made disposing of corpses such an easy task.

It's a myth, the Colonel had said back on Red Station, cold blue eyes intent on my face as I watched the faint orange flicker of Shadrak's atmo-skimming body through the view window. I could tell from his tone some vestige of disapproval had made its way onto my new face.

Myth? I asked.

That it ever ended. Best reset yourself to war-mode, Captain.

"Your unit designation in the war," Jack said. I fancied the red dot in his eye was glowing a little brighter.

"Third Marine Battalion."

"Your rank and serial number."

"Corporal, till I got busted. Serial numbers didn't come in until the final two months of the war and I was AWOL by then."

"Commanding Officer."

"Major Marcus Owen…"

"Wrong!"

There was a snick as Uhlstan's Ithaca came level with my temple. I was annoyed he'd gotten so close without me noticing. *War-mode, Captain.*

"Major Owen was KIA a month after assuming command," Jack said with a faint grin. "According to my files."

"Then your files are wrong."

"Whatever." Jack waved a hand at Uhlstan and turned away. "He's a plant. Don't get any mess on the terminals."

I didn't move as the Ithaca pressed into my skin. After prolonged persuasion Shadrak had provided a clear description of Jack's employee screening techniques; placing new recruits under imminent threat of death after apparently catching them in a lie was a trusted method for revealing concealed weapons or comms gear.

"Major Owen died the day I went AWOL," I said. "I should know, I killed him."

Jack paused, folding his arms as he spun to face me. The blonde woman was running the scanner over me again. "No sign of any sub-dermals," she said. "Heart-rate only two beats above normal."

Jack stared at me for a moment longer then grunted. "We'll be putting in at Celestia in twelve hours. You can start earning your keep there, need some back-watching for a supply run." He nodded at Uhlstan. "Show him his bunk."

*

"Just business, y'know," Uhlstan said as he guided me towards the crew quarters. He had a soft voice coloured by a faint accent I couldn't place, meaning he was likely of Downside origin. "Trust there's no resentment."

"Business is business," I said. "Does it ever work? His little trick?"

"Twice so far. Lot of people want to be friends with Jack."

I followed his glide into a cylindrical compartment segmented into ten living pods, beds aligned against the curving wall alongside wash-basins and standard toilet facilities. "Grav chamber?" I asked Uhlstan.

He nodded. "Only during off-shift hours to save power. Revolves fast enough for two-thirds Earth standard. Markov's the only one of us can sleep in micro."

"Markov's the Belter?"

"They call themselves Voidborn." He pointed to an empty pod halfway along the chamber. "That's yours. Meal-packs waiting if you're hungry and the entertainment hub works, after a fashion." He turned towards the exit.

"Not staying to stand guard?" I asked.

"You passed the entrance exam. Besides, there are no critical systems in here to sabotage."

The pod was bare of any decoration save an old 2D taped to the wall, a young couple smiling into the camera, some ruined Downside landmark in the background. Neither face was familiar. *Former crew?* I wondered, making me ponder Jack's employee-termination policy.

I switched on the aged entertainment hub and scanned the memory, finding the most recent upload to be a two month old Orbital Networks news-feed: "Meanwhile on Lorenzo City, the fall-out from what has rapidly become known as the Axis Massacre continues. Chief of Police Arnaud, who continues to deny any responsibility for the event, began his mayoral election campaign today by seeking to exploit his opponent's less than stellar relations with the veteran lobby. At a press-conference this morning the Chief promised a full independent inquiry into the tragedy. He wouldn't be drawn on questions regarding the whereabouts of Chief Insp-"

"You coming in or what?" I asked, killing the feed and glancing at the pod entrance.

The blonde girl's head appeared in the doorway, drifting in a counter-clockwise rotation. "You don't look like a war hero."

"That's cos I'm not."

She hesitated then pulled herself into the chamber, scanning me from head to toe in frank appraisal.

"I don't want any trouble with your father," I said.

"Adopted father," she replied. "Fished me and mom out of a wrecked liner ten years ago. Guess he felt guilty since he wrecked it. Wasn't supposed to be carrying passengers, y'see?"

"Man of conscience. I'm impressed."

"Don't be. He left the crew to die in hard vac." She angled her head provoking memories of Janet and her feline perception. I forced the image away, puzzling over how it was possible to miss someone you had known for barely a few days. *War-mode.*

"You're not like the others," the girl said.

I nodded at the 2D on the wall. "My predecessors?"

"Nah, that was there when we took this ship. Never found out who they were. I meant the other merc types he recruits for specialist jobs. They don't *see*, not the way you do. And your heart-rate barely bumped when Uhlstan was about to blow your head off. Should be careful, war hero. It'll make him nervous."

Maddux would try it, I knew. Grab her, pull her close, steal a kiss or a grope. Laugh when she threatened to tell her father. Sexual violence was among the many vices of the man who had worn this face. "You got a name?" I asked.

"Lucy."

"What do you want, Lucy?"

She smiled, sweet and unaffected. "I wanna ride in your Pendragon."

"It's no toy."

"And I'm no kid. Who'd you think pilots this bucket around? Been doing it since dear old dad plonked me in the pilot's seat when I was eight. Says I'm a natural. Fortunate neurons, I guess."

Best revert to character, I decided. *No way Maddux would let her anywhere near it.* "The suit's mine," I said, turning to the microwave and plucking a meal-pack from the sticky shelf. "Get daddy to buy you one when the job's done."

She gave a soft huff of annoyance. "You're no fun," she muttered.

I allowed myself a glance as she hauled herself out of the pod, athletic form twisting as she reached for a hand-hold, trying but failing to find solace in the fact that her impending death would be so quick she wouldn't notice.

CHAPTER 2

CELESTIA STATION IS about a third the size of the Slab, a spinning tube of ageing metal festooned with comms arrays from end to end, giving it the appearance of an encrusted pipe from a long-disused water pump. The only hab in the Belt capable of housing over a hundred thousand people, it's been a CAOS member-state since the war, complete with an elected provincial government and full trading rights. In fact, it had been effectively self-governing long before then, neutral ground for competing mining corporations who needed somewhere to trade for labour and equipment beyond the prying eyes of Downside regulators. Thanks to the local authorities' relaxed attitude to full enforcement of the CAOS Legal Code, it's also notorious as a refuge for the Upside criminal fraternity. I could recall no less than three suspects I still badly wanted to talk to, reportedly now residing on Celestia Station, and it took some will-power not to engineer an excuse to absent myself for some off-the-clock snooping.

War-mode, I reminded myself. *Not police anymore. Not here.*

"Guns are strictly verboten," Jack told me in the airlock, handing over a six-inch metal rod. "One of the few regs they bother to enforce here. Anything goes down it'll be hand-to-hand. Assume you're OK with that."

I looked at the rod in my hand, thumbing the stud on the

side to extend it into a yard long baton of telescopic steel. "Yo ho, cap'n."

He squinted at me with his red-eye. "And keep a clamp on your mouth. Any and all verbals come from me or Mina, you and Uhlstan watch and react accordingly."

Mina, Lucy's mother and Jack's apparent wife, seemed to occupy the role of ship's intel analyst. She stood next to Jack, gaze intent on her smart's screen. "Markov hacked the secure comms net," she reported. "We're clear of any monitoring from local law."

"Good." Jack raised his gaze to the camera in the ceiling. "Lucy, you know the drill. Things go bad, wait for exactly twelve minutes then burn clear."

"You know I'd rather die than leave you," she replied in a tone of complete sincerity, quickly followed by a mischievous giggle.

"Spare the rod," Jack muttered, ignoring his wife's reproving scowl.

I retracted the baton to its previous length and consigned it to my pocket. There was a hiss as the airlock opened and we stepped through to the inner lock which irised open after a standard thirty second contaminant and weapons scan. We were greeted by a melange of smells and noise that felt both familiar and alien, a dense odorous cacophony making the Slab's most crowded levels seem serene by comparison.

I saw the faint twitch of something that might have been a smile on Jack's lips as he viewed the street scene beyond, maybe a nostalgic light in his human eye. *Was he born here?* I wondered. We knew so little about him, all records dating back only to the second year of the war when he began his career as a CAOS-sanctioned privateer. Everything before that was just a load of conjecture and lurid legend.

The Celestia populace was more diverse than I was used to, greater variance in skin-colour and a higher preponderance of

Splice's among the jostling crowds, though the locals seemed to favour alterations that were more functional than cosmetic, nary a vamp or a werewolf among them. Some resembled Markov with elongated limbs suited to working in micro-grav, others hulking stevedores with the kind of muscle only dreamed of by Downside body-builders. Here and there I saw multi-spectra adapted snake-eyes peering out from otherwise unmodified faces.

The dockside level was thick with food-stalls and hawkers, the air heavy with the aroma of a hundred or more different cuisines rising above the babble of mingled accents and dialects. Uhlstan led the way, betraying little hesitation in pushing people aside with varying levels of force, those unwise enough to object soon lowering their gaze and shuffling away when they took note of Jack. *They know who he is,* I surmised, wondering why he would wander through a crowded hab without benefit of disguise, immune to the threat of betrayal despite the ever-growing bounty on his head.

I received a partial answer when we passed by the only uniformed police I saw in the whole visit, a lone Demon in body-armour perched on an elevated platform, assault carbine across his chest and a scanning rig fixed to his helmet. He surveyed the teeming crowd with continual scrutiny, head moving in a slow practised sweep, pausing only once when his gaze alighted on Jack. The pause lasted a full two seconds as I saw the uniform's lips moving beneath his visor. A small nod then he resumed his scan, turning his back to survey the other end of the street.

Allowed to come and go as he pleases, I decided. *Must have the local law on retainer.* Such brazen corruption chafed on my police sensibilities. No Slab Demon ever took a bribe, partly due to a basic level of professional dedication that had sustained the Department through the low wages and abundant temptation of the post-war years, but also owing much to continual financial monitoring and mandatory bi-annual sessions in the neural lie-detector.

We came to a shop doorway, the windows covered in old 2D posters forming a dense collage of faces and names from times gone past, some vaguely familiar from my infrequent viewing of the music channels. Inside a few customers stood flipping through row after row of thin plastic wrapped squares, each face wearing the expression of practiced concentration peculiar to the dedicated collector. I paused at the sight of one of the items on a display rack, recognising the blond haired character standing at the centre of the tableau of heroes and villains, light sabre raised. 'Star Wars: Original Motion Picture Soundtrack' the title read, partly obscured by a price tag that amounted to roughly half my salary for the preceding year. I took it from the rack, peering curiously at the edges.

"Never seen a vinyl disc before?" Uhlstan asked.

I shook my head. "They all this expensive?"

"Some more than others. C'mon." He jerked his head. "He'll get pissed if you start shopping."

I followed him to the rear of the shop, disc in hand, where Jack was exchanging a formal handshake with an elderly, mahogany-skinned man, his wrinkles partially obscured by an impressive set of grey shoulder-length dreadlocks. "New blood?" he asked, looking at me.

"This is Maddux," Jack introduced me. "He's on probation. Maddux, this is Mr Gold. Purveyor of just about anything."

I held up the disc. "This price negotiable?"

Mr Gold bared gleaming yellow teeth in a smile. "Sure. It goes up ten percent for anyone who haggles."

"Put it aside for me, will you?" I asked, handing it over. "I'm good to collect."

"You finished?" Jack asked in a less than patient tone, staring until I did the expected and looked away.

"Check it out, Jack," Mr Gold was saying, placing my purchase behind the counter and extracting a disc from a smaller sleeve. The monochrome image on the sleeve showed a broad-faced man with a heavy brow, a guitar resting on his shoulder. Mr Gold placed the disc on an odd contraption consisting of a turn-table and some kind of sensor armature. He set the turn-table spinning and placed the sensor carefully on the edge of the disc, a soft lilting song soon rising from an attached set of speakers. The music was unmistakably antique, unfamiliar but compelling. Some kind of mournful warning of environmental collapse, judging by the lyrics.

I noted Jack's expression as he listened, a mirror of the concentration evident in the other patrons. "Somebody tell you this was original?" he asked after a moment.

"Nineteen eighties reissue," Mr Gold said.

"They lied. It was never reissued." Jack pointed at the disc. "And the groove is way too regular."

Mr Gold laughed and slapped a hand to the table, making the song skip a few chords. "Can never fool you, Jack."

"No," Jack agreed. "You never can. I take it this means you've confirmed our intelligence."

"That I have." Mr Gold plucked a smart from his pocket and thumbed up a holo. It showed what appeared to be some kind of auction, a young woman at a podium taking bids from a large crowd, the sign behind her reading 'Christies.'

"Went for twenty million UA twelve years ago," Mr Gold said. "One of Exocore's investments in the collectibles sector, safer than the stock market and the value only ever goes up. They distribute them around their various Upside assets. Makes sense when you think about it, constantly mobile and heavily protected secure storage."

The holo shifted into a ship schematic, some kind of mining vessel, but bigger than any I'd seen before, the hull a long rectangular tube protruding from a blocky hab and cargo cluster roughly equivalent in size to an up-market residential orbital.

"Big old bitch, isn't she?" Mr Gold observed. "You really sure about this one, Jack?"

Jack ignored the question. "You find a contact for the hardware I requested?"

Mr Gold winced a little. "Manahi."

Uhlstan gave a loud rumble of unease and Jack's gaze narrowed. "He's not my favourite supplier," he told Mr Gold. "And he's likely bearing a grudge against my associate here."

"No-one else could source what you wanted," Mr Gold said. "He'll squeeze you, for sure. But put enough green on the table and he'll soon forget all that time in traction."

I gave Uhlstan a questioning glance. "Broke his back," he said with a shrug. "Cage fight got a little out of hand when one of his brothers tossed him a knife."

"Where?" Jack asked Mr Gold.

Mr Gold held up his smart, the screen showing an ident for a dockside storage unit. "Meeting's set for one hour."

"So soon?"

"Got on the line as soon as you arrived. Everybody on Celestia can't get enough business from Jack. You really should run for mayor, y'know. Practically own the place, anyhow."

*

Celestia's dockside was much like the Slab's, undistinguished functional architecture and mostly deserted avenues. It was also dimly lit; no point wasting power on levels largely bare of people. The storage unit entrance was flanked by two lean-looking men with matching facial tattoos and business suits, cut loose enough to conceal weapons. The markings were familiar, reminiscent of the motifs favoured by one of the more ambitious Maori gangs from the mid-Yangs, but not similar enough to confirm any association. They narrowed their gaze as Jack approached, hands coming to their sides in readiness, but made no move to stop him as he went inside without pausing to exchange a word, followed by an equally unsocial Mina and Uhlstan. I paused before entering, offering the guard on the left an affable nod. He stared back with a narrow-eyed lack of expression, save a small twitch below his eye. It was an involuntary muscular flutter and, I knew from experience, could be quite painful until it faded.

"Worked here long?" I asked.

He stepped away from the wall and jerked his head at the doorway, eye still twitching. I shrugged and went inside, finding Jack facing a well-built man bearing the same facial decoration, but much more extensive and finely applied. He wore an elegantly tailored suit of dark blue and carried an aluminium case. Two more tattoo-faced and suited guards stood in the corners behind him, silent and watchful.

"Jack," the man with the case said, face empty of any affection.

"Manahi," Jack nodded. "How's the back?"

Manahi's gaze shifted to Uhlstan, lips curling a little. "Mended. It took a long time and a lotta money."

"A man shouldn't gripe over just punishment," Jack told him. "But, to demonstrate my good will, you can add your med-bill to the price. Provided you have the hardware I requested."

Manahi placed the aluminium case on the floor, crouching to punch digits on the combo-lock and lift the lid, turning it around and stepping back. There were four objects in the case, non-reflective black cylinders resembling 20 mm cannon rounds.

Jack nodded to Mina who held up her smart, scanning the case's contents. "Markov," she said via her ear-piece. "These do the job?"

It was barely noticeable, a slight straightening to Manahi's back as Mina spoke, but it was mirrored by both guards… and the flesh below Manahi's eye started to twitch.

I turned to Uhlstan, staring until he met my gaze. I blinked once and cast my eyes at the door. He responded with a faint crease to his brow and I gave a barely perceptible nod.

"Checks out," Markov's voice came via Mina's smart. "Rad level signature is a match."

"Five hundred thousand," Manahi said. "Medical bills come to another two hundred."

"No," I said with a laugh. "It'll be more than that."

He frowned, twitch still fluttering, then reached into his pocket. I leapt and kicked him in the face, a hard toe-jab to the nerve-cluster under the nose, snapping his head back and sending him unconscious to the floor. I drop-kicked the guard on the left as he reached under his jacket, moved in close with the baton, thumbing the button and snapping the extended rod against his hand, forcing it to release the butt of a half-drawn tazer. I pulled him around as his colleague's tazer came free, letting him fall as the dart salvo smacked into his chest. I replied with a single shot, the dart hitting dead-centre on the spiral tattoo on guard number two's forehead, leaving him prostrate and twitching.

Uhlstan had already moved to the door, his baton sweeping the legs from under the first guard to burst in, Jack stepping forward to deliver a kick to his temple as he sprawled. Uhlstan grabbed at the final guard's tazer as he followed, darts phutting into the ceiling as they struggled. Jack ended it with a haymaker to the back of the guard's head, snatched up the fallen tazer and whirled towards me, barrel levelled.

"Just cost me a lotta' local business," he said. "This better be good."

I hauled Manahi from the floor, pulling his head back and pointing to the twitching patch of flesh below his eye. "Muscular contraction to the orbicularis. Side effect of recent face-change, no more than three days old is my guess. The real Manahi's probably stewing in a holding cell somewhere." I let him fall to the floor and held up the tazer I'd taken from the guard. "Madoc Industries L-Model Stunner, used exclusively by CAOS law enforcement. We need to move, they'll know it's gone bad by now."

"Markov," Mina said. "You got this?"

"Accessing environmental systems now," the Belter replied as a warning siren began to blare outside, interspersed with a calming female voice.

"Attention Celestia citizens. A fire has been detected on this level. Please remain calm. Suppressant gas is being deployed. There is no cause for panic. Please remain calm."

Jack waited at the door until the misty-grey suppressant clouded the exterior. "We're on our way," he said. "Remember the countdown."

"Already running, Daddy," Lucy responded cheerfully.

Uhlstan retrieved the case and went first, quickly followed by Jack and Mina. Outside everything was shrouded in swirling fog, fire-quenching chemicals stinging eyes and throat as I ran. Up ahead I heard a series of tazer shots followed by the tell-tale grunt and crunch of hand-to-hand combat as Uhlstan and Jack fought their way through the perimeter. I ducked a salvo of darts and came face to face with a female agent in body armour, tazer at her shoulder zeroing on my central mass. I dropped below her sight-line and kicked her legs away, pouncing as she fell, trapping the tazer between us as she bucked, snapping her head forward in a painful butt to the nose.

"Shit!" I slammed her hard to the floor, blood dripping onto her face as I loomed closer, hissing the recognition code for an active Covert Ops Agent. "Black Wolf. Who the fuck are you?"

She stopped struggling, initial puzzlement replaced by resentment. "Artemis," she hissed her own code: Coalition Fugitives Retrieval Unit. "And you're screwing up our op."

"We have priority in all circumstances, and you know it. Now call whoever's in charge of this clusterfuck and shut it down. No pursuit when we launch."

I released her, rolled to my feet and sprinted through the gas, hurdling the inert bodies left in Jack and Uhlstan's wake. I caught up as they were closing the airlock doors, obliging a last-second leap through the narrowing iris. I hit the floor hard, shouting with pain and snorting blood.

Jack was on the comm ordering Lucy to power up for a maximum burn. Mina stood to one side, regarding me with an expression entirely lacking any gratitude or appreciation, eyes dark with distrust and scrutiny. I noticed her hands were shaking.

"Good eyes, man," Uhlstan said with a grin, leaning down to offer a spade-like hand. I gripped it and he hauled me upright.

"Yeah," Jack agreed as the inner door opened, his gaze every bit as suspicious as Mina's. "Very good eyes."

CHAPTER 3

"THE EXOCORE MALTHUS II," Mina said, the ship schematic Mr Gold had supplied rotating in the command core's central holo display. "Self-contained, deep-belt ore processing vessel. She's getting on a bit now, built by Exocore when the war started heating up. They were worried about future access to the orbital processing stations. Largely automated, as you'd expect, crew of twenty engineers plus ten security, on account of the precious metals I assume. She's capable of processing a thousand m-type asteroids a year."

"That's a lot of metal," Markov commented. He hung above the holo, hands and feet clamped onto the same perch, resembling a pale wingless bat.

"Estimated to produce five tons of precious metals per calendar year," Mina confirmed. "No way to value it without knowing the composition, but her last reported yield amounted to over one billion UA in gold alone."

"Bulky cargo to shift," I commented. "This tub got enough power for that?"

"Doesn't matter," Jack said. "We're not going for the cargo."

Mina thumbed an icon on her smart and the image shifted, zeroing in on a section of the hab-cluster, the schematic showing a spacious office with a small red box highlighted on the wall. "Captain's suite," Mina said. "What we want is in the wall-safe."

Jack angled his head at me in expectation of the question. I chose to disappoint him. "Sure you can trust this data? That was a hardcore CAOS law-squad back on Celestia. How d'you know they didn't get to Mr Gold too, mess with it somehow?"

"It checks out," Mina said. Her face had a drawn look, forehead creased and cheekbones a little hollow, as if she was fighting a migraine. "Corroborates with other sources in all salient particulars."

"That's reassuring."

"She says it checks out," Jack said softly. "So it checks out. She is never wrong about intel and you owe her your respect."

I spread my hands in apology. "Just exercising the caution of an experienced man. That's why I'm here, right? My experience. Begs the question, what d'you need it for?"

The holo expanded, pulling back to show the Malthus II surrounded by a cloud of small pulsing specks of light. "Defensive net," Mina said. "She's covered at all times by two hundred and twenty armed bots, semi-autonomous and programmed with a cooperative combat algorithm. We need you to punch a hole with that suit of yours."

"Specifics," I said.

She zoomed in on one of the bots, revealing an insectoid beast festooned with mini-guns, missile launchers and an impressive sensor array. Its speed and manoeuvrability put it only slightly behind the Pendragon, plus it had two hundred and nineteen friends to play with. "My fee just went up," I said.

"You negotiated your fee with Shadrak," Jack said in a low voice. "Half a million in folding green. Don't try to fuck me boy. You're not my type."

"You hired me for a micro-grav combat role, not a suicide run."

"Actually," Markov said in the peculiar lilt of the Voidborn. "We have a way to obviate the risk factor." He held up his own smart, displaying a scrolling block of code.

"A hack?" I asked.

"Quite so. We substitute the net's algorithm for our own, half the bots will perceive the other half as an enemy force. Divide and conquer."

"But you have to get close enough to upload it," Mina added. "Hence you and your suit." She ran a simulation, the specks of light swirling around like angry wasps as the Dead Reckoning burned in to latch onto the Malthus II's hab-cluster.

"Uhlstan and me will take care of on board security," Jack said. "Get to the captain's quarters and retrieve the safe. Lucy will get us clear before they can reconfigure their bots, and the nearest CAOS Security squadron is seventy-two hours away at full burn."

Chalk up another hit for the Colonel, I thought. It had taken months of work to relay the information about the safe's contents to a few choice criminal contacts in a manner that wouldn't arouse suspicion, knowing Jack couldn't resist it. Unfortunately, somewhere along the line an enterprising soul had evidently seen fit to let Fugitives Retrieval in on it. *Just like the war, nothing ever goes the way it's supposed to.*

I let my eyes wander over the Malthus II, picking out the comms relay situated some three hundred metres from the intended entry point for the Dead Reckoning, my Primary Mission Objective. "Half a million," I said to Jack, deciding complete indifference would be out of character. "Chicken-feed compared to what's in that safe, right? Auction price of twenty mill twelve years ago. Must be worth even more now."

"The contents of the safe are not your concern," he replied. "Do a good job and I'll think about putting you on retainer. But don't test me further, boy."

I grinned. "I'm all about the work, cap'n."

*

It was a forty-eight hour haul to the interception point. I spent most of the time in the Dead Reckoning's cargo hold running combat sims in the only immersion couch. Using the Pendragon's standard rig produced a success rate little better than fifty percent, but with its enhanced stealth gear the odds were markedly more in my favour, not that I let Jack or the others know. The more risky the proposition appeared, the more value they placed on my continued good health.

"You seem to die a lot," Lucy observed as I emerged from another session. She was replaying the latest sim on the holo, clearly unimpressed by my combat acumen. In truth, micrograv combat was never my forte. I'd done it more than a few times in the war but only in extremis, and just once in a exo-suit. Back on Red Station the Colonel had put me through a high-intensity crash course in the Pendragon, but my scores had been only little better than average.

You should've found a marine for this, I'd told him.

We tried. None were a close enough match to Maddux's biometrics or had your experience with this kind of work. Meaning none were former spec-ops with a proven facility for killing in cold blood. *This kind of work.*

"Always program your sims harder than they need to be," I told Lucy, floating free of the restraints and removing the headset. "Makes the real thing easy in comparison."

"Mind if I try?" she asked, propelling towards the couch. I managed not to stare as she wriggled into place.

"Help yourself."

"He's not sure about you, y'know," she said, reaching for the headset. "Heard him telling mom. What you did on Celestia, way too sharp for hired muscle."

"Began my career on the Slab. Can't spot a Demon there, you don't live long."

"Never been there. Way he talks about it, sounds like a shit-hole."

"Depends which half you live on." I tapped at the couch's controls. "Any preference for the difficulty setting?"

"Crank it to maximum, war hero. Wanna give this suit of yours a decent workout."

I watched the stats scrolling as the sim ran, the visual relay leaving me in no doubt about her piloting skills, wearing the suit like a second skin as she pulled high-g turns and blasted bots in a graceful dance of economic burns and judicious targeting. *Fortunate neurons for sure.*

"That's your hardest setting?" she scoffed as she emerged. "Should've been with us on the Morningstar job..."

"Lucy!" Mina was floating near the entrance, a deep frown on her face. "Braking burn prep is overdue."

Lucy turned to me with a comical cross-eyed gurn then propelled towards the tubeway. "Coming, mother dear."

Mina lingered for a moment, frown just as deep. "One wrong glance in her direction..."

"...and I'm dead," I said. "Yeah, I get it."

She blinked and swallowed another threat. "Go see Markov," she said, turning away. "He'll brief you on the upload gear."

*

"Looks like a harpoon," I commented, taking the device from Markov's spindly hand. His workspace was a spherical cabin near the engine compartment, the walls covered in sticky-pads holding a thousand or more tools, each within easy reach of his extended limbs.

"Based on a Mark Four Plasma Shrike," he told me, a long finger tracing along the device to a honeycomb section just behind the warhead, fashioned from one of the cannon-shells supplied by fake Manahi. "Depleted uranium tip gets it through the armour then five hundred micro bots emerge in a swarm. Only needs one to find a data-node and upload the hack. Once it's in, it'll spread to the rest of the net."

"How long?"

"One point six eight seconds, give or take." He reached for his smart and called up the holo of the security bot. "A hit anywhere in the central body should do. The speed is less than half that of a standard shrike so you'll need to get close, three hundred metres should do it. I've got four of these ready in case the first run is a bust."

"I'll only need one, but thanks."

He nodded and turned to a work bench, his leg extending to pluck a tiny welding laser from the wall with unnervingly prehensile toes, his hands fixing a mag-lens over his brow, left eye bulging in the glass as he peered at the device fixed to the bench. It was some kind of sonic array, narrow beam sound-boosters arranged in a cage, all pointing inward to deliver a concentrated blast at whatever would be placed inside. *Safe cracker,* I decided. One of the more professional armed robbery crews to work the Yin-side banks had used something similar, though nowhere near as sophisticated. Useful if you wanted to bust a safe and preserve what was inside. But Maddux wouldn't know that and he was just about smart enough not to ask the question, besides their robbery was immaterial to my mission and there was zero likelihood they would enjoy the fruits of their labour in any case.

"Pretty impressive hack job you did back on Celestia," I said.

"Not really, their safeguards are an outdated joke. Cut straight through to the mainframe with an old algorithm from the war. Used it to crack the doors on a Fed Sec gunboat at Rand Station."

This was a surprise, most crew-clans had stayed out of the war, keen to rise above the petty concerns of the Earth-born and those who choose to shackle themselves to orbit. "I was at Rand Station," I said, which was true. A fortunate coincidence had placed me and Maddux in the same battle. It really wasn't that surprising since the assault on the UN's orbiting financial hub had been a maximum effort affair. We'd won, after a fashion, but the casualty rate made it a one-time thing. It had also been enough to convince former marine corporal Maddux that the experience of warfare had nothing more to offer by way of longevity or financial gain.

"Quite a party," Markov said, not looking up from the bench as he played the laser's hair-thin beam over a join on the frame.

"Thought Belters were pacifists," I commented.

"Popular myth. We're just overly polite, and some of us appreciate the benefits of a decent profit margin."

"What unit were you?"

"Officially we were the Auxiliary Battle Squadron, but really we were privateers, freelance crews recruited from the long-haul trade routes, plus a few Voidborn like me. CAOS would pay us a prize fee for every UNOIF vessel we captured, half for any we destroyed. That's where I joined up with Jack. When the war ended the prize-money dried up of course, but that wasn't any reason to stop."

There was a shift in the background hum from the plasma relays, Lucy powering down the fusion generator in preparation for the braking burn. Only three hours to go.

"I'd best run another pre-flight," I said, twisting towards the door.

"Don't forget your ordnance." Markov handed me the cradle holding my new missiles. "Need any help loading up, let me know."

"Thanks." *You'll be particulate matter soon, my Belter friend,* I thought as he turned back to his work, mag-lens back in place and his long features rapt, completely absorbed. *Another consequence of a decent profit margin.*

CHAPTER 4

"ALL SET?" MINA asked in my earphones.

I placed the neural interface on my forehead, checked the diagnostic reads a final time and flexed the Pendragon's arms. "All boards reading green," I replied.

"Good. Standby, two minutes to launch."

The ship's internal comms gave me a vid-feed of the cargo bay where Jack and Uhlstan were checking their weapons: squat Ruger M-90 carbines suited to close-quarters combat. Uhlstan also had his Ithaca strapped to his back whilst Jack wore a sword-size combat knife on his thigh. They were clad in high-grade body armour and respirators, the plan being to advance behind a cloud of tear gas, thermal imagers providing an edge in the confusion.

"Don't hang around out there when the bots start fighting each other," Lucy told me. I could see her strapped into the pilot's station in the core, neural interface on her forehead, hands moving smoothly over her holo-board. "Wouldn't want to leave you behind."

"Sixty seconds," Mina said.

"Maddux," Jack said, looking directly into the camera and speaking in slow deliberate tones. "Do not abuse my trust."

"All about the work, cap'n. Ahoy and avast."

"Twenty seconds…"

I had one last item to check, an internal addition to the starboard plasma nacelle, cylindrical in shape and forty centimetres long. The casing was lead-titanium composite meaning its rad signature was only a tenth of what it should have been, any excess would be taken for slightly elevated energy loss, well within parameters for a suit of this mark. All readings came back as normal but I couldn't help the faint upswell of discomfort as I watched it spin in the display.

"Five, four, three, two…"

I disengaged the mag-clamps holding the suit to the deck, floating free for the final second before the airlock doors opened and the decompression took me out.

"Net configuration conforms to the expected pattern," Mina reported via the comms laser. "You are free to engage."

Even at four klicks distance the Malthus II was an impressive sight, brightly lit from end to end, a dim orange glow emerging from the massive processing tube as the smelting plant did its work. There were some asteroid fragments floating about but nothing the Pendragon's nav couldn't handle. I used up about half the CO_2 reserve to get within striking distance, short bursts along an irregular approach vector, targeting icons continually sprouting on the heads-up as the suit detected more and more bots.

"Unidentified vessel, this is Exocore Security aboard the Malthus II. State your designation and purpose." First hail from the Malthus II, relayed via the comms laser.

"Malthus II, this is deep-belt salvage vessel Dead Reckoning," Mina responded. "We are licensed to operate in this area. I'm transmitting our ident codes now."

"Wait one, Dead Reckoning. Please initiate full braking burn while we check these out."

"Oh screw you," Mina said, every bit the world-weary freelancer. "Exocore may have millions to spend on fuel, but I don't. Our vector is well clear of your sky and you know it."

There was a pause and another voice came on the line, female, clipped to military precision, faint West African accent. "Not clear enough for my liking, Dead Reckoning. Burn to a full stop now. This is not a suggestion and I'll remind you we have authority to employ lethal force."

That's no rent-a-cop, I decided. *Who's really running security here?*

"Maddux!" Mina said urgently, switching frequencies.

"Fifteen seconds to target," I replied, the threat icon of the bot I'd chosen growing ever larger in the heads-up.

"Comply now or you will be fired upon," the African woman stated.

"OK, OK," Mina responded. "Don't get your panties in a bunch, sister. Disengaging secondary thrusters now." A click as she switched frequencies. "Jack, this is starting to smell wrong."

Last-minute caution. Not good. "Ten seconds to target," I said.

"I'm pretty sure we don't have ten seconds," Mina responded. "Jack, we should abort…"

Shit. I engaged the plasma thrusters and accelerated towards the target bot, spraying lidar beams in a random pattern, multiple warning signals merging into a scream as the heads-up blazed red and the bots began their algorithmic dance. The target bot was now fully aware of my presence so attaching Markov's shrike was out of the question. I blasted it with a heat seeker from six hundred metres, overwhelming its defensive sensors with a tight-focused EMP. A brief yellow flash illuminating tumbling debris and it was gone.

The closest bots swarmed towards me, weapons active, the tell-tale yellow flares of multiple missile launches dancing across my field of vision. I waited until they were six seconds from impact, fired the plasma thrusters at maximum for a full two seconds then activated the stealth mode. The missile trails intersected less than fifty metres away, proximity fuses igniting a split second later, the momentum from the plasma burst carrying me free of the blast radius, but only just.

I kept drifting, watching the bots commence their search pattern, waiting until one came close enough. It braked to a halt less than a hundred metres away, turning with sensors blaring, provoking an electronic hiss in my ears as the beams swept over the Pendragon's invisible carapace. The bot finished its scan then angled itself for a return to its allotted patrol zone. I disengaged stealth mode and let fly with Markov's shrike. The bot's sensors blared a warning but it had no time for a counter, the depleted uranium tip punching through the armored core to deliver its cargo. I judged Markov had been a little conservative in his estimate from the way the bot instantly turned and blasted its nearest comrade to pieces in a hail of mini-gun fire. Soon the space around the Malthus II was lit by multiple explosions and streaking missiles as the defensive net turned on itself.

"Net's down," I reported to the Dead Reckoning. "Now or never, cap'n."

"Lucy, take us in," Jack ordered.

"I still say we should abort…" Mina began but Lucy had already powered up the Dead Reckoning's secondary thrusters, the freighter blazing towards the Malthus II through a cloud of disintegrated bots. I followed at a discreet distance, ordering the Pendragon's nav to calculate a course to the comms array.

"Brace for impact," Lucy said a second before the Dead Reckoning turned on its tail, retros firing, the momentum slamming her hard against an airlock on the starboard side of the hab-cluster.

"Override running," Markov reported.

A pause, then Jack came on, voice hard with impatience. "Should be open by now."

"I know," Markov replied. "Their security codes are a little more exotic than expected is all. Having to hack on the fly here. Wait one… Got it."

"We're in," Jack said a second later, a burst of carbine fire in the background. I had a feed from his helmet cam and could make out Uhlstan's dim bulk propelling through the haze of tear gas, lit by the occasional muzzle-flash as he ruthlessly suppressed any resistance.

"Few more than expected, boss," he said, firing again.

"Time you earned your pay." Jack's carbine came up, muzzle flash obscuring the view for a moment as it blasted at a shadow in the fog. "There. The tubeway on the left."

The cacophony of the moving firefight continued to assail my ears as I burned towards the comms array, halting at the lip of the main dish. I found an access node and ripped the covering away with the Pendragon's powered gauntlet, plucking a probe from a compartment in the suit's arm and plugging it into the data-port. The Colonel had hackers of his own, some that made Markov look like a remedial dumbass. The hack they had hidden in the Pendragon's memory made short work of the Malthus II's firewalls and I was soon looking at her navigation logs.

Job done, I reflected as the suit downloaded the data. It was time to plant my little gift and be on my merry way, though the prospect of a seventy-two hour wait for my extraction boat was hardly edifying... I paused as something unexpected came up on the data-feed. A schematic for a ship of unfamiliar design, sinister in its sleekness, and scrolling alongside it a full set of operational parameters. To say they made for sobering reading is something of an understatement as the Colonel's words loomed large. *It's a myth that it ever ended.*

"Bastards!" I rasped

"Say again?" Mina asked.

"Nothing." I left the probe in place and burned towards the Dead Reckoning at full power, calling up a tactical readout of the Malthus II's interior via the data probe.

"Maddux, what are you doing?" Mina demanded.

"You were right, OK? You should have aborted and dear old Jack is about to find out why."

Jack's voice came on again, "We're at the suite. Hold them back whilst I secure the safe."

"Pretty hot out here, boss," Uhlstan replied. Via his cam I could see the tear gas had faded to a light mist, multiple muzzle flashes visible in the tubeway beyond.

"Thirty seconds," Jack said, a power drill making powder of the wall around the captain's safe.

I killed the plasma and glided to a halt under the Dead Reckoning's main port thruster. The tactical showed Jack and Uhlstan as two green dots in the centre of the hab cluster surrounded on all sides by at least a hundred red, edging closer by the second. I flushed the remaining plasma from the starboard nacelle and disengaged it from the main body of the suit, power-gauntlets ripping it open to find the cylinder inside. *No time for finesse.* I activated the device's mag-clamp and lodged it within the rim of the thruster, kicking back and angling towards the hull of the Malthus II. A quick scan of the tactical gave me an entry point, an exhaust port forty metres from the main airlock.

"Got the safe," Jack reported. "On our way back."

Dream on, Jack.

I propelled towards the exhaust port on CO_2, finding it sealed by a solid looking hatch.

"Need a hack for that?" Markov asked, reading my approach vector.

"I've got it." I accessed the probe and initiated the contingency hack the Colonel's people had included in case of primary mission failure. The Malthus II's security network collapsed under an intense deluge of virus-ware, millions of self-replicating code-bots overwhelming the firewalls in less than a second, giving me unrestricted access to all systems. The exhaust port duly irised open and I steered the Pendragon inside.

"Goddammit!" Jack swore, carbine firing empty before he pulled himself to cover, the tubeway behind alive with tracer. "Get more gas out there."

"Waste of time," I advised, barrelling along the exhaust pipe at fifty klicks per hour. "They're wearing full combat gear, respirators and armour. Best if you hunker down for a moment, Cap."

"What are you talking about?"

"Trust me. Just sit tight."

I accessed the internal comms and had my voice relayed to the whole ship. "Attention officer commanding Malthus II. This is Chief Inspector Alex McLeod, Lorenzo City Police Department, acting with full Coalition authority. The actions of this vessel are in contravention of the Dublin Accords, rendering it subject to immediate seizure. All personnel will stand down and await lawful arrest or face executive action. This is your only warning."

A half-second pause as I angled the suit to account for a curve in the exhaust pipe, the air-seals opening to allow passage as I reprogrammed the internal sub-routines to recognise me as a maintenance bot.

"Attack on a civilian vessel," the African woman replied in my headphones. "Is also a treaty violation."

"Like this is a civilian vessel, Captain," I replied. "Or is it Admiral? I've seen your logs. I know what you're about. You've been very naughty."

"Then you should be aware of the odds," she replied. "And it's Commander. You realise I'm in no position to take you into custody?"

"Who asked you? By the way, you should check your life support status. I shut the system down ten seconds ago. If I were you I'd be heading for the lifeboats about now."

The pipe terminus was rapidly approaching, widening out into a series of smaller vents too tight for the Pendragon. I checked the tactical map and confirmed my position as two decks below Jack and Uhlstan.

"I also disengaged the fire containment system," I told the commander. "Just so you know."

I pointed the Pendragon's gauntlets at the ceiling, the

smooth metal parting to reveal the cannons. A three second burst from a cocktail belt of 20 mm armour piercing and high-ex was enough to punch an adequate hole through to the next deck. I was met by a Fed Sec squad in the tubeway beyond, five of them moving in coordinated micro-grav combat formation, firing their carbines in a well-practised relay. *Elite troops*, I surmised. *Special Recon or Assault Commandos. Hardest of hardcore.*

I saved on ammo and went through them, lashing out with power-assisted limbs in a preprogrammed martial arts display, the carbine rounds leaving little scratches on the Pendragon's carapace as they fought to the end. *Commandos*, I decided as the suit's fist crushed the skull of the last one. *Recon would have had the brains to withdraw.*

"Jack," I said, raising the gauntlet cannons once more. "I need you to move to the left about ten metres."

"What the fuck is going on here?" he demanded.

"You heard my announcement," I replied, the tactical confirming he had complied with my request.

"Yeah, big bad Demon from the Slab. Am I supposed to be impressed? I've killed and eaten worse than you, boy."

"I'm crushed." The gauntlets flared again, a section of tubeway disintegrating in a haze of rent and molten metal. I kicked through, cannon blazing, tearing apart another commando squad, limbs and shattered torsos spinning in the swirling smoke.

Jack was crouched behind a bulkhead, empty carbine drifting nearby, his sword-like combat knife in hand, ocular implant gleaming red and hateful. "This is the only chance you'll get," he promised through gritted teeth.

"How's that for gratitude? Where's Uhlstan?"

Jack nodded at a bulky form floating a few feet in front of his position, body armour hanging in shreds, blood globules trailing from multiple impacts. *Shielded his captain from the burst. Loyal to the end.*

A fresh bout of carbine fire from opposite ends of the tubeway told me the commander had ordered another assault. "We need to move."

I provided a shield as we propelled to a side tunnel. Jack had retrieved Uhlstan's Ithaca and vented his frustration with a rapid salvo of double-aught blasts at the pursuing commandos. Completely pointless but I guess it made him feel better. Once clear of the main tubeway, I accessed the door controls and brought down airtight bulkheads on both sides of our position.

"You really should head for the lifeboats," I told the commander. I could see her on the internal vid-feed, a slim woman in her late thirties, handsome ebony features stern and resolute behind her visor. She was moving towards our position flanked by a squad of commandos. Not the type to stay on the bridge when combat beckoned.

"I have my orders," she stated.

"Yeah. Lot of that going around. For the record, I'm sorry."

A slight pause then the soft androgynous tones of an automated warning began to sound throughout the ship. "Emergency venting sequence initiated. Decompression of hab and work compartments will occur within ten seconds. All crew please report to your allotted evacuation point. Emergency decompression sequence initiated…"

I watched the commander's last moments, seeing the spasm of fury and frustration before the final few seconds of rigid self-control. "McLeod?" she said.

"Yes ma'am?"

"This won't be forgiven."

"I know."

"Then fuck y-"

A vast clunk as over a hundred air-seals opened at once, a blizzard of debris and venting gas filling the vidscreen, then she was gone. I called up the tactical and watched the red dots blink out. I stopped counting at fifty.

"By the way," I told Jack. "You're under arrest."

CHAPTER 5

MINA AND MARKOV were both pointing hand-guns at me as I cracked open the Pendragon back in the Dead Reckoning's airlock.

"Do not move!" Mina ordered, double-grip tight on an old Colt .45. Her voice was coloured by a slight quaver, but her aim was rock solid. Lucy floated in the background, face a mixture of bafflement and joyful curiosity.

I ignored Mina and turned to Jack. "Check your hull sensors."

"For what?"

"Elevated rad levels on the port thruster." I undid the straps and floated free of the suit, arching my back and working the ache from my limbs.

"I said don't move!" Mina's aim shifted to my forehead, sweat beading her skin.

"She needs to calm down," I advised Jack.

"It's OK," he told Mina quietly, placing a hand on her forearm, easing it down. "We'll play this out for now."

Mina gave an explosive sigh of frustration and lowered her gun. She twisted and propelled towards the core followed by Jack. Markov waited a moment, regarding me with an inscrutable stare, then bounded after with his effortless grace, limbs folding and expanding like a squid boosting itself through the water.

"After you," I told Lucy who was still displaying the same odd mix of puzzled delight.

"Finally," she said in a small voice. "Something new."

*

"So what is it?" Jack demanded. We were in the core, watching the scanning console display a graphic of the cylinder I'd attached to the port thruster, a red warning icon revolving alongside.

"A one kiloton nuclear device," I replied. "It was intended for the Malthus II. CAOS Intelligence suspected she was processing helium 3 off the books in defiance of the treaty with the UN. If she went boom, it could be blamed on an ill-advised raid by the system's most notorious pirate, at least publicly. Privately, the Downside governments would get the message that breaking our monopoly doesn't pay. Turns out she was up to something a tad more serious, so I was obliged to improvise."

Jack's gaze was steady, free of fear but the anger was plain in the bulging vein on his forehead. "And if we kill you, it goes bang, right?"

"It goes bang in seventy-two hours whether you kill me or not. But I do have a deactivation code."

"I've broken men in a lot less than seventy-two hours."

I tapped the slender band secured across my forehead. "Neural interface, accessible only via the Pendragon's controls which are bio-locked to my brain-wave signature." I smiled. "Sorry folks, but you are all hereby deputised as operatives of the Coalition Intelligence Service. The pay's lousy and the perks are non-existent, but you do earn the warm glow that comes from serving your nation."

"Your nation, Demon guy," Jack growled. "I said goodbye to all that flag-waving shit years ago."

"How progressive of you." I turned to Lucy. "Calculate the journey time to Ceres for the Malthus II."

"What's at Ceres?" Mina asked.

"Our new mission objective."

"One hundred twenty-two hours, standard burn," Lucy reported from the nav console. "Sixty-eight at maximum, but she'll be down to five percent fuel reserves when we arrive."

"Not a concern. Get this tub parked in her cargo bay and report to the bridge. Life support should be fully restored in an hour." I pitched towards the exit. "I'll be taking a nap."

"What's in this for us?" Markov enquired.

I paused. "The opportunity not to become cosmic dust."

"I want immunity," he said. "A full pardon."

I sighed around a laugh. "You're all guilty of more crimes than can be easily counted. Should've been on the Morningstar job, right Lucy? Five security guards were killed when you blasted into that cruise liner. Not Fed Sec commandos, just working stiffs, men and women with families." I met Markov's gaze. "Any cooperation you provide will be taken into account at your trial and the judge will pass sentence accordingly. Should spare you the death penalty, maybe even a chance at parole in a few decades."

"That's not much of an incentive," Mina pointed out. "And I have a daughter to consider."

"She's a big girl and this is not a game."

"The nuke's on the Dead Reckoning," Jack pointed out. "What's to stop us just taking the Malthus?"

I tapped the neural interface again. "I've got sole access to her control system. No-one gets to throw a single switch without my say so and with me dead she's not taking anyone anywhere." I pushed towards the exit. "Call me when you're ready to start for Ceres."

*

"There's nothing there, y'know?" Lucy said. She was strapped into the nav console on the bridge of the Malthus II, cocooned in a shell of holo-screens each displaying a bewildering array of shifting data. She seemed to have no difficulty reading it all at a glance. A semi-transparent projection of Ceres revolved in the centre of the bridge, a pale yellow and grey ball of dusty ice.

"Largest asteroid in the solar system," Lucy went on. "A dwarf planet really. It's a protected site on account of that complex hydro-carbon gloop they found in the ice a few years ago. Off limits to mining operations and tourists aren't permitted closer than a hundred thousand klicks."

I skipped through the security feeds to check on my other crewmates. Jack and Mina had elected to busy themselves clearing out the few corpses still floating around the ship's interior. So far our passage to Ceres had been marked by a trail of ejected bodies. I took some comfort from the fact that none had turned out to be genuine Exocore employees, Fed Sec operatives all.

I had to flick through quite a few cam-feeds before locating Markov foraging through the tech stores, a large hold-all bulging with liberated doodads trailing from his shoulder as he made his way along the shelves. *Stocking up. Not planning on incarceration any time soon.*

"How long before your dad tries to kill me, d'you think?" I asked Lucy.

"He'll probably wait till we're at Ceres. He's a surprisingly patient man. This snare of yours might have trapped him for the moment, but he'll be constantly looking for a way to gnaw his leg off. And when he does…"

I gave a vague nod and called up the schematic for the Malthus II's power system. *Dynamic Industries fourth gen fusion core with a depressingly impressive list of fail-safes, the back-up however…*

"What did you look like before?" Lucy asked as I ran sims. "I mean, that's not your real face, right?"

"Ugly with plenty of scars." *Not enough fissionable material in the mix,* I mused as the sim concluded. I checked the storage manifests, scrolling through lists of various metals until I found it. *Only fifty grams, but it should be enough.*

"It was my screw-up," Lucy said.

"Huh?" I ran another sim with the new ingredient, grunting in satisfaction at the spectacular outcome.

"The Morningstar. I miscalculated the approach velocity. Those guards died because of me."

"Be sure to play up the contrition for the judge, might shave off a few years."

"Jack says prison's not so bad. Said he did a five-year stretch when he was about my age. They plug you into accelerated immersion, right? Ten years in the dream is only one in reality."

"Don't have any illusions. Ten years is ten years, whether you live it or dream it. And it's not Alice in Wonderland. You're fed a series of scenarios designed to make you confront your guilt, develop a social conscience so when you get out you're a tax-paying citizen with a phobia for violence and deceit."

"Doesn't seem to have worked on Jack."

"Sociopaths tend to be immune." I ordered a cargo bot to fetch the chosen material. "I'll be in the power core."

*

The war had left me well educated in finding inventive ways to blow stuff up and the colonel's refresher course had added some new wrinkles, but the destructive potential offered by the Malthus II's back-up power source was of a different order. This was no home-made plastique or hyrdogen-peroxide taped to a Fed Sec guard post, this was a fission reactor with a potential yield of five kilotons. Fusion had supplanted fission in the vast majority of orbitals and interplanetary ships well over a decade ago, but some deep-belt vessels still retained uranium reactors for back-up and auxiliary power in the event deuterium stocks ran low. It was aged but near-perfect technology, the flaws of the old twentieth century reactors designed out long ago and augmented by an extensive array of state-of-the-art safety protocols. Even with my unrestricted access to the ship's systems, I was obliged to spend several hours circumventing or deactivating a myriad of software and hardware designed to prevent me doing this very thing.

"Why don't you just use the nuke you attached to the Dead Reckoning?" Markov was framed in the doorway, limbs spread to clutch at the edges, a pale four-legged spider regarding me with a cocked head.

"Not enough bang," I replied, guiding the bot with the new ingredient inside the spherical reactor core and uploading a command to its memory. When the time came, it would simply open the container.

"Then our target must be sizable," Markov said.

"Quite." I closed up the core and put the reactor in stand-by mode, ready for a rapid power-up.

"And well defended," he persisted.

"I expect so."

"We're not going to survive this mission, are we?"

"I thought Belters were all about accepting the destiny offered by the void."

"My exile was not accidental. I have issues with blind acceptance of fate."

"Well, now you have a chance to reconnect with your faith. Good luck with that."

He tensed in the doorway, muscles knotting on his spindly limbs, face flushed red with anger. "I'll have no part in this. Whatever kamikaze mission you're on, count me out."

"Then find a corner to hide in and stay out of my way."

"There are working lifeboats aboard. I request permission to leave."

"No. You're a wanted felon with a trial and a prison term waiting. Anyway, a Fed Sec security sweep might pick up your beacon."

"The chances of that are minimal..."

"Not minimal enough. And don't forget what remains of the defensive net is now under my control, so any unauthorised excursions are going to be very short."

His tension went up a notch making my hands itch for a weapon. I had no confidence in the outcome of a straight-up fight with a Belter in his native environment, the control I had over this ship was my only real protection. I just had to hope his rationality outweighed his fear.

Markov's long face twitched and he gave a final impotent snarl before twisting about and propelling along the tubeway with his usual fluency. I sighed, watching him go and knowing I'd grown too soft for this kind of work. If this scenario had played out during the war I'd have followed him, improvised a weapon from the tool racks and killed him when his adrenal levels had subsided. But it wasn't in me anymore, the sight of Maddux's disembodied head was taking way too long to fade. The commander and crew had been different, enemy soldiers in the heat of battle, but it seemed my capacity for outright murder had shrunk in civilian life. *Too many years a Demon.*

I contented myself with commanding the Malthus II to jettison all the lifeboats, uploading instructions to crash themselves into the first asteroid to happen along. It pays to be thorough.

*

Despite the comparatively plush accommodation offered by the Malthus II, Jack, Mina and Lucy still slept aboard the Dead Reckoning, now nestling in the Malthus II's cargo bay. I suppose familiarity breeds a false sense of security.

Since my target was occupied I was obliged to use a small conduit maintenance bot to gain access, little bigger than a mouse and resembling a hummingbird with grab-arms. I guided it in through the fuel lines, void of plasma now the tanks were full, steering it along the internal maze of valves and vents until it emerged in the central tubeway. I let it hover for a while as its audio-feed relayed the muted sound of Mina's whimpers. I'd noticed she never slept very well, prone to nightmares and unconscious rambling. I listened as she came awake with a shout, cries subsiding amid Jack's soothing whispers. I waited until silence returned then guided the bot to Markov's workshop.

The safe sat in the Belter's jerry-rigged sonic array unmarked and undamaged, Jack no doubt deciding other matters were more pressing at the moment. I had some notion of how to operate Markov's contraption, but since I knew the combination, it didn't really matter. The lock was an eye-scan, hand-print combo but, like all security systems, had a back-door in the form of a twelve-digit code known only to the captain of the Malthus II and senior Exocore executives. Securing it had been expensive and it was fortunate Fed Sec hadn't bothered to change it when they took over the ship, it was also quite possible they hadn't even opened the safe since what it held had no value to them. To Jack however…

The safe door swung open, the hinges creaking a little. There was a spike in the audio-feed as Mina's whimpering resumed momentarily before settling back into fitful slumber. I didn't push my luck, ordering the bot to retrieve the contents and close the door. The safe held only one item, a thin seven-inch square wrapped in cellophane, delicately clutched in the bot's pincers as it made its way back to me.

Leverage, the Colonel had said, more than once. *You can never have enough leverage.*

CHAPTER 6

THE MALTHUS II had an impressive meal and rec hall, a spinning hollow globe in the centre of the hab-cluster generating two-thirds earth standard gravity. Jack, Mina and Lucy sat eating breakfast next to a cascading water fountain, the droplets falling in gentle arcs through a multi-coloured light array. Jack scowled as I sat down to join them, ignoring my good-natured greeting. Mina avoided eye-contact and kept on eating her cereal. Lucy just grinned around a mouthful of bacon and eggs.

"Enough food in the stores to last us a decade or more," she commented, cheek bulging. "No dehydrated crap either. Looks like Fed Sec knows how to feed its people."

"The price of freedom is lousy cuisine," I replied before turning to Mina. "You'll find all the target info uploaded to the analyst station on the bridge. I'll need you to produce a full intel picture, most favourable attack scenarios. Kind of thing you're good at, right?"

Jack stiffened. "You expect us to take a part in this farce?"

"You've been press-ganged, cap'n." I gave a hearty chuckle. "Best accept it and bend your back to the task at hand, matey, yo ho, etcetera. Think of it as repaying your considerable debt to the orbital community. Whilst Mrs Jack's busy on the bridge you can take a look at the exo-suits. There's bound to be some combat models among them, might come in handy."

His hands twitched on the table and I noted he still had his impressive knife strapped to his thigh.

"Jack," Mina said softly.

"Repaying my debt, huh?" Jack said, turning to me, red dot burning in his eye. "What about your debts, Demon guy? I've heard about you, often wondered if it'd be you they'd send. Not really a job for a hero, right? If you're gonna send someone after me, they better be worse."

I couldn't fault his reasoning, but that didn't mean I had to like it. "Much as I'd enjoy a lecture on morality from a king-size scumbag, I think I'd prefer it if you shut your mouth and go do as you're told."

I saw a wicked grin pass across Lucy's face as Jack got to his feet, breath coming hard, hands twitching. "Always the same with you people. Fought a war for freedom and then made yourselves into what you fought against. The void should be free, beyond all your taxes and rules, but you want to turn it into just another prison."

"Whilst you want it as a hunting ground," I returned, rising from the table, forcing away the annoying realisation that I was letting him get to me and all this dick-measuring was seriously unwise. "Yeah, you're free all right, free to steal and murder whilst your victims are free to suffocate in hard vac."

"Jack," Mina said again as his hand inched towards his knife.

"No please do," I said, spreading my hands. "I'm happy to demonstrate how much worse than you I am."

His mouth was forming into a snarl when a shrill klaxon sounded through the hall, quickly followed by the cool tones of the automated warning. "Fire detected on maintenance deck four. Suppression systems off-line. Initiating emergency protocols. Fire detected on maintenance deck four…"

"Markov!" I hissed as the holo schematic came up on a nearby data node, a red smear of fire steadily growing on a deck close to the ore processing levels, multiple icons flashing to indicate malfunctioning safety systems.

"Hacked the safety protocols," I muttered. "Nice and quiet so I wouldn't notice." *Must've started before he came to beg for a lifeboat. Too soft.*

"We didn't know about this," Mina said quickly.

I glanced at Jack, surmising from his evident rage that she was telling the truth.

"Another ten minutes and we'll be cut off from the Dead Reckoning," Lucy said, reading the schematic. "Guess he's trying to steal her."

"With a nuke on board?" Jack said.

"Probably hoping to max-burn towards the nearest hab before it goes off," I said.

"He must be desperate." Lucy shook her head with a wry smile. "There's nothing close enough."

"Could be he has some idea how to defuse it," I said. "He's a clever fellow."

"And willing to leave us behind," she said. "And I thought we were such a happy family."

I rebooted the safety protocols, extinguishers springing to work on the effected deck, the red smear stalling but not diminishing. "Too much fuel down there," Jack said. "It's taken hold."

"There's still a path to the Dead Reckoning." Lucy's finger traced through the holo. "If we detour through medical and accommodation..."

"Feel free," I said, making for the exit.

"The off-switch for the nuke!" Mina called after me.

"Yeah, I lied about that," I said over my shoulder before propelling into the weightless corridor beyond. "Good luck if you make it out."

I'd stashed some weapons in various locations whilst the others had been asleep. If things had continued to escalate with Jack, I'd have made for the carbine secured behind an access panel near the meal hall entrance; you don't fight fair with the likes of him. It was a standard issue 4mm caseless of bespoke Fed Sec design, completely recoilless and intended for close-quarters combat in a micro-grav environment. It was odds-on Markov had found a weapon of his own, if not fashioned one from the various doohickeys he'd purloined during the voyage.

The automated warning shifted from full alert to an emergency containment scenario, indicating the fire was starting to abate. Either the suppression system was winning or more likely it had just run out of fuel. Either way the main decks between me and the cargo bay were still flooded with toxic smoke and I had no time to find a respirator.

I paused at a data-node to gauge Markov's progress, the red blob of his thermal signature inching towards the cargo bay. I abandoned Lucy's suggested route in favour of the ventilation system, blowing the hatches and hauling myself along in a four-limbed sprint, carbine strapped tight to my chest. The vents brought me out in the central tubeway, the schematic putting me ahead of Markov. In retrospect I probably should have wondered why a Belter seemed to be moving so slowly.

I found cover behind a bulkhead and waited for him to appear, carbine set to three round burst. I had no intention of offering him the chance to surrender. A faint scuff of metal brought the carbine up as the figure rounded the corner, lumbering along like a drunken ape, long metal limbs flailing about, each one fitted with a small heating unit. *Bot!* I realised, twisting about. *Clever bastard built a decoy.*

I was way too late, a searing pain lancing through my head as my extremities spasmed and the carbine drifted away from a suddenly nerveless grip. My vision fragmented into a yellow haze lit by the occasional blossom of branching red lines. I was dimly aware of connecting with the tubeway wall, of drool trailing from my lips, and the faint sensation of the neural interface being plucked from my head.

"Never hacked a brain before," I heard Markov say. "This will be interesting."

*

I came round with the sting of lubricant and solvent assailing my nostrils, lids scraping over gritted eyes and what felt like a hatchet buried in the base of my skull. Tight restraints kept me from floating free of some kind of gurney. My clouded vision traced a thick cluster of wires from the trodes fitted to my forehead to the array of sensors before which Markov was hunched, long neck twisting as he switched gazes from one holo to another. From what I could glimpse of my surroundings he had taken me to a long disused storage compartment, close to the ore processing levels judging by the constant din of conveyors and pulping hammers. I closed my eyes, forcing my swelling heartbeat to a regular rhythm before speaking in a faint croak. "There's no off-switch. You're wasting your time."

"I surmised that from my first look at your nuke," Markov replied without turning. "But, since I'll shortly have command of the Malthus II, it doesn't really matter, does it?"

I fought down a wave of nausea, digging my fingernails into my palms to keep from zoning out. "What did you hit me with?"

He flicked a long-fingered hand at a contraption stickied to the wall, a small plastic and glass device resembling a flashlight. "Ocular scrambler. Induces a form of epilepsy. Should've worn a visor, Inspector."

"Chief Inspector."

"Of course. I am remiss, please forgive me."

I watched him run some algorithms, long lines of code scrolling in a migraine inducing haze. "It'd take a planet-sized quantum computer a year or more to break a CAOS Intelligence hack," I told him. "Tick tock, Markov."

"Don't have to break the hack." He propelled back from his console array, limbs extending as he revolved above me, a faint smile of regret on his long face as he placed the neural interface back on my head. "Just you."

I immediately tried to access the Malthus II's internal security net, hoping to vent the air from this compartment, but received no response. I was completely cut off from the ship. I noticed Markov had a remote of some kind in his other hand, a small plastic box of mismatched parts held together with duct tape and featuring a single red button.

"My people are often deeply spiritual, as you know," he said. "Borrowing from various belief systems, the older and less Judeo-Christian, the better. My clan were all about the eastern philosophies, one of which holds that the eyes are the windows to the soul."

He plucked something from the toolbelt around his too-thin waist, a small data-stick with an odd sucker-like attachment in place of the usual connector. He powered it up and placed it on my sternum where it gave a small spasm before lancing something narrow and very sharp into my chest, punching through the bone into the nerve centre beyond. The flash of agony was only just within the bounds of my control, making me jerk, teeth clenched as I hyperventilated, spittle rising in small white globs from my flaring lips.

"Curious thing about neural interfaces," Markov continued. "Feedback. Strong emotional or physical responses in the wearer produce a kind of fuzz in the sensory readouts, noise in the machine you might say. Just for a split second, but it opens a window, all those unfamiliar impulses flowing through the command interface produce a tiny moment of opportunity. One I'm afraid I need to prolong. So you see, my parents and all those other deluded, sanctimonious nutbags were wrong. The baring of a soul is not a matter of vision, just pain."

He gave another oddly regretful smile and pressed the button on the remote.

Up until this juncture the varied paths of my life had tended to cultivate the illusion that pain is endurable, that nothing hurts so bad you can't control it, focus it, use it to fuel hate and rage, or compassion and sacrifice should the need arise. Pain was the spark to my enlistment in the Resistance and later Covert Ops. It also gave me the strength to say goodbye to Consuela and stand by and watch after Choi drank poison. Pain was an old friend, I thought. I was wrong.

It was as if a multi-fingered hand of white hot metal had cracked open my chest and begun to rummage around inside. The first flare of it was enough to leave me awash with instant sweat, every muscle tensed, teeth clenched so hard I wondered they didn't shatter, tears streaming from my eyes and bowels voiding to stain the air. For a second all sensation slipped away and my vision dimmed, leaving a faint and not entirely unwelcome realisation that I was about to die.

"Little too much," I heard Markov mutter, very far away. The pain receded, not a great deal, but enough to uncloud my vision. I managed to swivel my spasming neck enough to see him scrutinising the displays, eyes narrowed in concentration. It may have been no more than a few seconds, but it felt like a century. "Yes," he breathed with a small grin. "Yes, there we are."

The display flickered then lit up with a now familiar interface: the Malthus II's main command menu. A little fuzzy round the edges but still usable. Markov donned a neural interface, one of his own making judging by the lack of any concession to ergonomics. Through the rivulets of sweat stinging my eyes I managed to discern he was accessing the maintenance bot controls.

"Fortunately for you," he said over his shoulder, moving away to open a nearby storage locker. "This little arrangement of ours won't last. The body can only take so much after all. So rest assured you'll probably suffer a cardiac arrest in about forty-five minutes, not that you have that long."

He pulled a modified EVA suit from the storage locker and began to put it on. It seemed the standard model wasn't constructed for Belter proportions so he had stitched together four separate suits with a distinct lack of tailoring expertise, making him resemble a poorly made rag doll by the time he clicked the helmet into place. I stifled a shout of pain and concentrated on the command display, picking out a graphic showing a countdown.

"Of course I'll need to blow the hatches," Markov said through the helmet's speaker, floating closer to peer down at me. "Clear a path to avoid any embarrassing encounters with my crewmates. But don't worry, this compartment is air tight, need you to keep the window open whilst I make my way out. We're only two AUs from a clan-ship trade route. When that bot you put in the fission reactor opens its canister… Well, bang that size is bound to draw an audience. Shouldn't have to float around for more than a day or two before someone comes to investigate. Easy time for a Voidborn."

"L-" I managed through a cloud of spittle, jerking with the effort. "L-lucy…"

"Sorry. Only room for one. And isn't it a little late for all this chivalric concern?"

My eyes flicked to the countdown, thirty minutes.

"Yes," Markov said, tracking my gaze. "I'm afraid this predicament is going to last until the reactor blows."

He propelled towards the exit then twisted about, spreading his too-long arms in an elaborate gesture of farewell. "I killed the great Slab City Demon. Pity I'll never get to tell anyone…" He trailed off as the exit slid open behind him, turning to regard the figure who hung there, a bulky silhouette with a long-bladed knife in his hand and a single red bead glowing in his shadowed face.

Markov's helmeted head swung to the scrambler still sitting on its sticky pad, at least two metres out of reach. "I… I have a way to defuse the nuke…"

Jack's knife moved too fast to follow, whatever it was made

of proving harder than the helmet's visor, punching through the glass to produce an instant explosion of crimson. Not a man given to moderation, Jack drew the knife back and brought it round in a surprisingly elegant pirouette, the blade slicing through layers of mylar and insulation to sever Markov's head. The neck piece was fitted with a sealing mechanism so the blood cloud wasn't as big as it might've been. I had a glimpse of the Belter's gape-mouthed face as the helmet ascended to collide with the ceiling, bouncing off to be punted through the exit by Jack's booted foot.

He grabbed a handful of Markov's voluminous suit and used it wipe the blood from his knife, sheathing it as he drifted closer, impassive gaze tracking over my spasming body. "Mina took a look at your tactical," he said. "Made for interesting reading. So let's talk."

CHAPTER 7

"VERY NICE," JACK murmured, stubby finger playing over the sleek form of the ship schematic, the holo shimmering a little from the disturbance. We were in the command centre, me wrapped in a foil blanket, sipping something warm and sweet from the beaker Lucy had handed me. To my surprise Jack had returned the neural interface and it was a relief to find Markov hadn't felt the need to add any more firewalls to his hack, so shutting off the countdown hadn't been a challenge.

"Attack ship," Lucy surmised as I fumbled over a response. Markov's ministrations had left me a little speech deprived. "See the missile launchers on the prow and the stern?" she went on. "Haven't seen anything like it before though."

"They c-call it a Wraith class assault c-cruiser," I stammered, calling up the specs.

"Woah," Lucy gave a soft laugh as she peered at the scrolling data. "Double the payload of any military ship in the void and twice as fast into the bargain. I'd really like one for Christmas, Daddy."

"Fully s-stealth capable," I added. "Could blast an orbital to pieces before they knew it was there."

Jack stroked his chin and I could see his greed for the ship was at least the equal of Lucy's. "So this is what they're building at Ceres."

"Not just one," Mina said, tapping an icon to expand the display. "According to the logs, over the past four years the Malthus II has delivered enough ore to construct at least a hundred of these. All in the shadow of Ceres where no-one ever goes."

"And they're nearing completion," I said. "Expect the n-next step will be to start covertly ferrying out the crews from Earth."

"All so they can start the war up again." Mina shook her head. "Didn't they have enough the first time?"

"S-start and finish," I said. "Look at the fleet make-up, all attack ships. No troop carriers, no salvage or engineering vessels. They're not planning war, they're planning g-genocide. Wipe out the orbitals, put an end to CAOS, t-turn the clock back to the good old days." I looked at Jack over the rim of my beaker, sucking down more warmth and feeling the shakes finally begin to subside. "Bad for business, wouldn't you say, cap'n? Everything Upside and beyond will become a militarised zone. Hardly conducive to a piratical lifestyle."

"Neither is prison," he replied. "We do this and we get full immunity. Non-negotiable, Demon guy."

"I don't have that kind've authority…"

"Bullshit. You can hard-vac an entire Fed Sec battalion on your own initiative, you can work a deal for us."

All annoyingly true. The colonel had given me *carte blanche* to deal with any threat posed by the Malthus II, but wiping the slate for someone like Jack still stuck in my policeman's craw. *No patriotism or altruism at work here,* I knew. *Or even his ingrained hatred for all forms of authority. He wants one of the Wraiths all for his very own.*

"OK," I said, making little effort to keep the reluctance from my voice. "Dependent on a successful outcome. This goes south, all deals are null and void."

"This goes south we'll all be null and void." He pointed at my neural interface. "And no more playing captain for you. No offence, but it's not really your forte. Markov's little mutiny should've told you that. I saw what he was thinking from the moment the idea popped into his head. How d'you think I found you two? Been keeping tabs on him since we came aboard. Now hand it over."

"With no guarantee you won't flush me out the nearest airlock?"

"I could've sliced you six ways from Sunday already, and you know it. Give."

Remember your leverage, Captain, the Colonel's voice piped in. *He still hasn't checked the safe.*

I removed the security locks on the interface and tossed it to Jack. He placed it on his forehead and called up my attack scenario for Ceres, wincing in derision as it played out.

"This is your oh-so-cunning plan?" he asked. "Just blast on in there and open a canister of plutonium in the back-up reactor? Glorious one way trip to instant oblivion, huh? Hoping they'll put up a statue back on the Slab?"

"Personal survival is a secondary concern in the circumstances."

"Not for us," Mina said in a hard tone, face dark with maternal anger. "Luckily, we have an alternative." Her fingers danced on the tactical interface, my scenario reforming into something altogether more elegant, but also complex.

"Too many variables," I said when it played out.

"You aren't in command anymore," Jack reminded me, smiling for the first time since I met him, besmirched ivory gleaming dully in a leather mask. "And I'm not sure you even rate as third mate in this happy crew."

*

"So, you were really gonna kill us all, huh?" Lucy's frown was just visible behind her visor, the specular reflection on the glass preventing me from discerning if she was truly pissed or indulging in another teasing session.

"That's right." I put the tagger to the shock-absorbing plate on the front of my suit and aimed at the lump of gently spinning rock highlighted on my heads-up. I'd left the Pendragon back on the Malthus II, an Exocore standard mining suit was a better choice for this duty, bristling as it was with dedicated sensors. The tagger gave a hard push against my sternum as it released its projectile in a cloud of vapour, a small titanium tipped marker latching onto the 'troid and blaring a signal the retrieval bots would home in on later.

"No hesitation?" Lucy persisted. "Twinges of conscience?"

"I'm a soldier."

"That right? I thought you were police?"

I said nothing and propelled on ahead, concentrating on the heads-up. The debris field was highlighted as a hazard in the nav readouts covering the approaches to Ceres. Medium range scans had confirmed it as chock-ful of the necessary material. So far we'd found twenty rocks with the right density, Mina estimating we needed at least two hundred. First-hand confirmation by human eyes was a tried and tested method of speeding up the process.

"Your mom knows a lot about mining operations," I said as Lucy lined up on another rock.

"She was an engineer before the war," she replied, grunting a little as she fired her tagger. "When dear old dad found us on that liner, we were on our way to rendezvous with an exploration vessel heading for the Kuiper Belt."

"Long-haul contracts take years to fulfil. You'd've been in your twenties by the time you got back."

"Always got the feeling we weren't coming back. She doesn't talk about the war, but she must've learned all this intel-analysis stuff somewhere, and she has nightmares all the time. Lotta' bad shit in her head, but I guess you know all about that."

When we get to Ceres you'll earn a few of your own, I replied silently.

We'd tagged another forty rocks by the time Mina's voiced buzzed in my ears via the comms laser. "Contact bearing red twenty. Engine signature indicates civilian tug."

"Not this close to Ceres," Jack said. "Got to be Fed Sec."

The tug popped up on my heads-up a few seconds later, a pale dot in a green targeting reticule making me wish I'd opted for the Pendragon after all.

"Getting an encrypted hail," Mina reported. "Feeding it through."

A short flare of static then a voice, male, British accent, every bit as militarily precise as the late Commander. "One hundred hours ahead of schedule, Gertrude. What's up?"

Gertrude? That was her name?

"The commander is off the bridge at present, sir," Mina replied. "This is Sub-lieutenant O'Keefe. We're experiencing a minor problem with the ore processors."

A pause as the tug grew ever larger in my visor. "Scans show only about twenty-five percent of your security net is active," the Brit observed. "Got problems there too?"

"Ran into heavier than expected micro-impacts a few hours ago. So close to Ceres the Commander thought it safe to start repairs on a rotational basis."

"Against protocol. Not like her."

Mina modulated her tone, trying for the jovial subordinate role. "Well, it's been a long trip, sir."

Another pause, then the reticule in my heads-up turned red. "His weapons just went active," I said.

"I see it!" Mina snapped back, exhaling slowly before addressing the tug once more. "Anything wrong, sir?"

"Standing orders, lieutenant. Approaching vessels exhibiting irregular behaviour are to be subject to close inspection. Deactivate your net and open up the cargo bay. Oh, and it'd be best if you got the Commander out of bed, don't you think?"

"Yessir!" Mina confirmed, switching channels. "Lucy, get back on board. We're burning out of here."

"No," Jack stated softly. "Do as he says, Mina."

"Jack..."

"It'll be fine. Trust me."

I turned to see the security net go off line, the ordered matrix of dots transforming into drifting specs of light, like dust in water.

"Wave!" Lucy said, flourishing her tagger like a flag pole. "Be nice to our brothers in arms."

I duly waved at the tug as it drifted past, main engines off-line. It was a good facsimile of a Scarab class work-horse, typically referred to as a bug back on the Slab, complete with faded paintwork and minor hull damage, but the disguised weapons pods were open and the array of missiles and EMP emitters clearly visible. She fired her retros two hundred metres short of the cargo bay as the doors slid open to reveal an inky black interior.

"Problem with the lighting system too?" the tug captain enquired.

"No," Jack said on the open net, the Dead Reckoning's main lights blinking on, yellow tiger eyes in the shadows. "No problem at all."

At that range the tug never had a chance, the first missile salvo shattering her forward hull and tearing apart her sensor array. A scream of static in my headphones told me Jack was jamming any last-minute warning the tug captain might be trying to transmit. The Scarab spiralled away from the Malthus II, trailing plasma and rent metal, missile launchers swivelling desperately as she tried to get a lock on the Dead Reckoning, all way too late. Jack proved himself every bit as capable a pilot as Lucy, skillfully keeping on the ruined side of the tug as he maintained his barrage, plasma shrikes and hard-tipped cannon shells pulverising the Scarab into wreckage in a silent display of pyrotechnics. The bodies spilled out when the superstructure split apart, red-eyed, ice-pale faces looming in my visor as I zoomed in. *Overconfident. Didn't think to suit up.*

Jack destroyed a lingering chunk of wreckage with a final burst of cannon-fire before turning the Dead Reckoning about and heading back to the cargo bay. "Gather up the mess," he told me and Lucy. "Another ship might happen along later."

*

The Scarab's crew totalled six individuals, four men and two women, faces too distorted with decompression and burns to gauge their age, but I'd be surprised if any were more than thirty years old. *Six plus the crew of the Malthus, plus Maddux, plus Markov...* I shook the grim arithmetic from my head, pushing the last of the corpses into the centre of the cargo bay. Jack had ordered up a crew of maintenance bots to cart them to the smelter, no point leaving them floating around to enrich the atmosphere with their singular aroma.

I was surprised to see Lucy scraping puke from the inside of her helmet when we de-suited, face pale and eyes a little moist. *Not quite so calloused,* I realised. *Just a kid after all.*

"Stop staring," she told me in a thin voice.

"Sorry." I ripped away the disposable thermal liner and reached for my coveralls.

"I'd really like to have sex now."

I turned to find her stripping away her own liner, moist eyes bright as she floated naked, firm, toned flesh sheened with sweat and making me calculate just how long it had been. It was like this with Consuela during the war. Not always, just sometimes, when something really bad went down, when the latest near-death experience or frenzied firefight left us shivering and coiling in the dark. *Death, always the most potent aphrodisiac.*

"I can't help you with that," I said, turning away and mentally awarding myself a medal.

"Got a Mrs Demon back on the Slab?" she enquired, voice still thin, void of emotion. If rejection burned she wasn't showing it. "That why?"

I thought about Janet and the faint hope that I might actually see her again when this was over. *She'll see it in an instant,* I knew. *All those bodies floating around my head. Screwing a seventeen year old girl would be the least of my crimes. No more nights curled up on the sofa watching Star Wars.*

"I see there is," Lucy said, reading my face and forcing a smile. "She's older right?"

"Considerably. Just like me."

"Uhlstan was older. Still fucked me though. Jack didn't mind long as we kept it discreet. Girl has her needs after all." Her voice had taken on a small quiver and she hugged herself, shivering.

I sighed, buttoning up the coveralls and propelling to the exit. "Life of crime has its downside, Jedette," I said, voice deliberately harsh. Kindness would be cruel right now. "Better shake it off if you want to live through this."

CHAPTER 8

I SPENT ANOTHER four hours helping Mina in the mass accumulator, the cavernous rectangular tube that made up the bulk of the Malthus II. It was over a kilometre long and constantly exposed to hard-vac, meaning lots of tricky manoeuvring between the array of massive toruses tracking the length of the tube from the opening to the smelter.

"Weaponising one of these is strictly illegal," I commented. "There's a whole bunch've of treaties about it."

"When we get to trial, I'll tell them you forced me at gunpoint." She grabbed a hand-hold and punched a button below a faded sign reading: 'Exocore Industries Mass Driver - Wotan Class.'

"Wotan," she muttered, shaking her head. "They do like their mythical allusions. It's just a series of ultra-high powered electro-magnets, old but reliable. Sucks in any rock with a high iron content, kinda like a giant vacuum cleaner." She gestured for me to watch as she punched a sequence into the control panel. "Luckily whoever designed it also saw there'd be the occasional need to blow as well as suck. We just need to up the velocity. Hundred kilometres a second should do it."

"We got enough power for that?"

"Just, if we max out both reactors and shut down all other systems." She gave a sigh of annoyance as the panel lit up with a plethora of warnings, rapidly punching in the overrides with practised ease.

"Done this before?" I asked.

"Done a lot of things before. Just like you."

"You were in the war."

"Wasn't everyone?"

"Way you talked to that tug captain, very convincing."

"Got something to say, just say it."

"You were Fed Sec."

Her gloved hand paused over the keypad as the panel turned green. "Despite the propaganda, your revolution wasn't universally popular," she said. "I was a well paid mining engineer with an infant daughter to think of, and a husband who died when a CAOS terrorist put a bomb in his fabricator plant. We all had to choose sides, I chose mine."

"So they made you an intel specialist. Way I heard it, it's a role that required surgery."

She turned away and propelled to the next torus.

"Memory augmentation, right?" I persisted, following. "Instant and total recall of all accrued information. Must get crowded in there."

"It's a chip the size of an appleseed sitting on my cerebellum, and it has an off-switch."

"No bad dreams, huh?"

"No more than you, I'd guess."

"So when the war ends you scoop up Lucy and head for the Kuiper Belt. You didn't need to run, y'know. There was a Reconciliation Council, full pardon for all crimes committed by former Fed Sec personnel, 'cept the really heinous ones of course. The hab-massacres and such. I mean, I can understand running for it if I'd been part of that. Some crimes can't be forgiven."

Her hand gave a spasmodic flex before she accessed the panel. "Didn't want to live in your new world. Knew there'd be no place for me and Lucy there."

"Really? Well, that's probably true. Fugitives Retrieval still maintains the list. The Prejudice List it's called, individuals to be pursued regardless of cost or duration. Grows shorter every year. That grab-op back on Celestia. I thought they were after Jack, but the way they reacted when they heard your voice. Guess they were relaying it to a matcher, and it hit."

Her hand stopped in mid-sequence and I knew she was calculating the odds of making it back to the airlock where she'd unwisely left her .45.

"So which one?" I asked. "Merryvale? Golden Bucket Casino? January Gardens?" I saw her stiffen at that. *January Gardens.* The worst atrocity of the war. The premier educational hab for the orbiting executive class. A safe place for mommy and daddy to park little Briony or Chad whilst they spent the year earning a whopping bonus to pay for it all. Over eight thousand kids dying in a hail of plasma shrikes. At the time Fed Sec propaganda claimed CAOS had hidden WMDs on the hab, lurid and unlikely tales of bio-weapons and high-yield nukes aimed at New York and Delhi. Even now the UN continued to maintain the fiction it was all some intelligence screw-up, but you'd have to search for a long time to find anyone among the CAOS population who didn't believe it a deliberate act of terrorism, the ultimate warning: forget your revolution and go back to work. Look, even the rich kids aren't safe from us.

"I did wonder why you and Lucy don't share a single facial characteristic," I said. "But even with the face-change, the Kuiper Belt wouldn't have been far enough. We'd still have found you. No, you had to disappear completely, victim of a dastardly attack by the system's worst pirate. Jack finding your ship was no accident, right?"

She didn't look at me, profile still and oddly serene behind her visor. "Don't tell her…"

"Tell her what? That mommy's a war criminal who condemned her to a life of piracy because she couldn't face the consequences of her actions?"

"It was all for her. What kind of life would she have had?"

"Better than the one you made for her. Now she's a murderer. Just like you."

She closed her eyes, breath misting her visor for a moment. "I didn't know... I just ran the intel and formulated the attack scenarios. I didn't know what they were planning... Memory suppressants keep it away most of the time, but it's all on the chip, waiting, every time I use it... every time I dream... Bright and fresh, like I'm living it again. You want to send me to hell, go ahead. But I've been living there for years."

I'd taken the precaution of attaching a thermal lance to my tool belt, my experience with Markov having taught me to keep some kind of weapon handy. A quick-draw fire-up and her visor would blacken and crack, leaving her gasping in vac, just like all those kids on January Gardens.

I pushed away from her, heading for the next torus. "Time's wasting."

*

The command centre main display showed the Fed Sec shipyard as a vaguely hexagonal black matrix against the yellow-grey backdrop of Ceres, now less than a hundred thousand klicks distant. "Static positioning so it's constantly shielded from Earth-based scans," Mina said. "I'm counting twenty more of those fake bugs plus a net of combat bots."

"Quite a hornet's nest we're kicking," Lucy observed. "Not like they're just gonna sit there when we get to it."

"Hence the diversion," Jack said, turning to me. "One hundred twenty minutes before your baby nuke goes boom, right?"

"One hundred fifteen, but who's counting?"

"You're sure you can get clear in time?" Mina asked Jack.

"Found a Galahad Class combat suit in the stores," he

replied. "It's no Pendragon, but it's fast enough to get me clear of the blast radius whilst our Demon lord here takes down their bot net."

"Their security algorithms are certain to be more sophisticated here," Mina said. "Major installations always had generative protocols. When Markov's hack-shrike infects one unit, the firewall will adapt to prevent it spreading. To compensate, I've adjusted the base code for each warhead, which should mean you'll take down maybe five percent of the net with every hit. But even with a best-case scenario, that still leaves over sixty bots to handle with standard ordnance."

I pointed at the tactical holo as it ran an accelerated sim, the neat matrix of the Fed Sec security net reconfiguring into two wings, the bugs prioritising the main threat and heading for Jack in the Dead Reckoning, the bots heading for me. "But we still punch a big enough hole for the main show, regardless of how it plays out, right?"

"That's right."

"Then that's the only scenario that matters."

"You may be happy to sacrifice yourself," Lucy said. "But I've got an immunity deal pending and sixty bots is still a substantial threat to our escape plan. Not to mention, way too many to take on your own."

"I'll have our own bots for back up."

"Won't be enough, and there's another Galahad in the stores."

"Absolutely not," Mina stated.

"Forget it, kiddo," Jack added.

"Oh, screw you both," Lucy retorted tiredly. "Been exposing me to danger my whole life, now suddenly it's an issue."

"That was different…" Mina began but Lucy cut her off.

"Different how, mom? Because we had a chance of survival? I'm not dumb, OK? I can read a probability graph. Eight percent success rating, so chances are none of us are making it back to Earth orbit to enjoy a crime-free life."

"Your chances are better on board with me," Mina replied, voice hard with implacable authority. "And I haven't spent the last ten years keeping you safe to watch you die on a tactical display. You. Are. Staying. Here!"

"I'll need you to remote-control our bots," I said to Lucy, breaking the cold silence that followed. "Give me an edge, y'know."

Mina's expression softened a little and I saw a faint gleam of gratitude in her eyes before she turned away. *Grateful or not,* I thought. *You're still facing a war crimes tribunal if we make it home.*

Lucy clenched her jaw as her eyes blazed at me for a moment. "Should be me in the Pendragon," she grated, then pushed towards the pilot's station. She strapped herself in and jabbed at some icons. "Thirty minutes to breaking burn. Better get suited up."

CHAPTER 9

JACK LAUNCHED FIRST, keeping the Dead Reckoning on the Malthus II's blindside as Lucy guided her in on an oblique approach, Mina relaying a stream of bullshit to the increasingly nervous Fed Sec Command and Control Centre. "Malfunctions in the port thrusters and the ore processors," the C&C duty officer said. Female voice, American this time with a faint Texas drawl. "Been a pretty unlucky voyage all round, huh?"

"We're made," I said, sitting in the Pendragon, waiting for the airlock to open and watching the Fed Sec net form itself into an imminent threat configuration. The Scarab flotilla was already forming up on an intercept vector. "I could offer them the chance to surrender. Few more seconds confusion won't hurt."

"Forget it," Jack said. "Surprised they let us get this close. Commencing my run. Lucy, stay with your mother. I mean it."

The Pendragon's heads-up showed the Dead Reckoning as a blinking yellow icon arcing away from the Malthus II at full burn. The comms net lit up with alarm signals and dire warnings from the C&C.

"Unidentified vessel, disengage all power immediately! Malthus II, come to an immediate halt or you will be fired upon! There will be no further warnings…"

"Oh, give it a rest," Mina sighed, killing the feed. "Lucy, correct attitude and engage primary thrust. Chief Inspector, you're up."

The airlock doors opened and I glided out, the Pendragon following a preprogrammed course toward the shipyard, the twenty-two remaining bots of the Malthus security net closing in around me. The heads-up showed an estimated time to engage of sixty seconds.

A burst of static and a flicker of light from fifty klicks beyond the Malthus II told me Jack had begun to engage the Scarabs, confirmed by the increased pitch of alarm over the net.

"Bravo One is down! Repeat, Bravo One is down!"

"Bravo Two engaging! Fox Two!"

Another burst of static, more lights flashing.

"Bravo Two! Do you copy! Bravo Two, come in!"

A soft peal of laughter over the net, Jack's hard to miss tones following. "No offence, but you boys 'n girls are sadly in need of an education."

"Five klicks and closing!" Lucy said into my headphones. "Look alive Jed."

I switched to full stealth-mode and killed the plasma thrusters, momentum carrying me through the first bot-wave, a storm of tracer and missiles lighting the vac around me as they engaged their Malthus adversaries. I went for the closest and powered up, letting fly with the hack-shrike, watched it strike home on the machine's armored carapace then immediately slipped back into stealth. The bot drifted for a few seconds then began firing at its compatriots, five more Fed Sec bots joining in before the firewall adapted and the battle began raging in earnest. Less than a minute later and the first wave was gone, just drifting metal trailing sparks and gas in the void.

"We're down to twelve bots," Lucy reported. "Second wave twenty klicks and closing."

"Taking hits," Jack reported. "Two minutes till I have to blow the hatches."

Lucy formed the Malthus bots around me in a spearpoint formation and we went full burn for the centre of the next wave. I managed a hit on the lead bot as it flew past but the effect was less dramatic, just three of its pals switching sides in the ensuing melee.

"They're adapting too fast," I said, firing off the last hackshrike. It was only marginally successful, but, together with the Pendragon's cannon, secured sufficient advantage to complete the destruction of the second wave, although I had just one remaining ally by the time it was over.

"Punching out!" Jack said. "Thirty seconds to detonation."

The third and hopefully final wave was still forty klicks off so I had time to watch the show as the nuke's timer ticked down on the heads-up.

"Prepare to board," the C&C Texas voice ordered the apparently victorious Scarabs. "Secure prisoners for interrogation."

The military mindset is a dangerous thing, I recalled one of the Colonel's many homilies. *Ingrained efficiency and discipline can blind us to the threat posed by the irrational mind.*

The counter hit zero and a sun-bright flash erupted beyond the Malthus II, the comms-babble from the Scarabs ending abruptly. A brief pause before the C&C began demanding responses, answered only by static.

"'Bye, old girl," Lucy said softly as the nuke-flare faded. "Best tub he ever stole for me."

"Jack!" Mina called to the void. "Jack! You there?"

A two second pause then a grunt, pained with heavy G. "Yeah. Don't wanna think about my rad count though."

"You need to correct your vector," she told him. "You're ninety degrees off."

"Nah, I'm fine."

"But you're heading straight for…"

"I'm fine, Mina. Stay on mission."

"Here they come!" Lucy warned a second before my entire world became a morass of flashing tracer and silent explosions. I popped in and out of stealth-mode, staying visible only long enough to engage the thrusters and targeting systems, guns and missile launchers on auto-fire. The sensation of time slipped away in the frenzy of it all, there was just the vibration of the cannons and the flickering dance of the heads-up playing over the swirling firework display beyond the glass.

"Three on your six," Lucy warned. "Fire your retros and I'll take them as they decelerate."

I thumbed the retro command switch, restraints digging into my shoulders, the instant G-backslap making me hyperventilate, spittle staining the visor as I fought the brown-grey mist fringing my vision; the tell-tale sign of a blackout.

The three bots flashed by on both sides, retros firing as they spun to realign their weapons then exploded in a hail of cannon and missiles, Lucy's remote-controlled proxy flying through the wreckage. "Get it together, Demon-guy," she said. "Only twenty more to go."

I lined up on the densest formation, fired the plasmas and slipped back into stealth-mode. The C&C, however, must have been running some kind of reactive tactical software, because this time they anticipated the move. A salvo of missiles spiralled away from the bots and exploded around me in a prepro-grammed sequence, the surrounding vac filled with an unavoid-able cloud of shrapnel. I felt the impact on the Pendragon's right leg, the energy release enough to send me spinning, dam-age reports lighting the heads-up as the warning signals sang a superfluous accompaniment. Auto-repair sealed the resultant leak within seconds but not before the trailing gas plume gave the bots more than ample evidence of my whereabouts.

"Stay stealthy!" Lucy commanded. "Your momen-tum's gone."

I drifted, not daring to touch a single switch, breath stilled through survival instinct even though my rational mind knew it was pointless. The dozen remaining Fed Sec bots chased Lucy's proxy around for a creditable ten seconds before she gave up and kamikazed it into the closest opponent. The survivors formed into a clean and sweep formation, commencing a search pattern I knew would find me in less than a minute.

"Reading three more Scarabs on approach," Mina reported. "Must be outlying patrol craft responding to the distress call."

"Problem?" Jack enquired.

"They're still five minutes out," she replied. "And the rain is falling."

Happy accident had brought me to within less than a klick of the shipyard, the angle of drift affording a fine view of the unfolding spectacle. I tracked the first asteroid all the way from its high velocity exit from the Malthus II's accumulator. It seemed to slow as it tumbled past, surface glittering a little in the reflected light from Ceres. Then it was a blur again, course unhindered by the all-sides barrage from static cannon and missile stations, smashing though the ship-yard's central spar like hail through a spider's web.

The vast matrix buckled as cohesion failed, twisting and straining, the clusters of Wraiths folding out like blossoms on a sun-bathed tree.

"Launch! Launch!" the C&C was screaming. "Evacuation protocols are active! All vessels launch!"

A few energy plumes lit the heads-up as some of the Wraiths tried to power up, ignorant of the fact that this storm was just beginning.

The second asteroid shattered the shipyard's already buckling upper-right quadrant, impacting amid a cluster of Wraiths. Some were evidently in the process of fueling their plasma tanks judging by the impressive blue-green explosion that ripped through the mooring spar, sheering it away from the main structure, severed fuel-lines coiling like headless snakes and spraying plasma over the surrounding mass of maintenance bots. I fancied I also saw a few EVA suits swallowed by the maelstrom. C&C went next, the Texas voice screaming orders right up until the last second. *Stayed at her post,* I mused in reluctant admiration as the C&C capsule took a mid-size rock dead-centre and blew apart like an overcooked egg, venting atmo and bodies in a ugly grey-black cloud.

Three more rocks and it was done, the burning fuel lines bathing the final destruction in a confusion of flame and plasma. The last asteroid could only disturb the expanding cloud of debris as it flew through, what remained of the shipyard now spiralling down towards Ceres, dragging the few surviving Wraiths with it. I doubted there would be much left after impact.

A warning signal shrieked in my ear as a flare exploded less than ten metres from the Pendragon. The stealth-ware would bend the resultant light, obscuring me from a visual scan, but it could do nothing about the tell-tale impact of the sparks on the outer shell, easily picked up by the Fed Sec bots' infra-red scans. They instantly formed into an offensive formation and accelerated to attack speed.

"Oh well," I sighed, thumbing the switches for full power and letting the targeting systems off the leash. "At least it worked."

CHAPTER 10

I TOOK DOWN two in quick succession, though I had to use up the remaining missiles to do it. I sought refuge in the resulting debris cloud, hoping the heat and myriad shards of metal would mask me enough to fight inertia up to full speed. Naturally, it was a fool's hope.

The first missile exploded no more than five metres ahead of me, the impact sending me into another spin, this one not so easily controlled. The heads-up blazed with damage reports, summarised in a nice easy to read graphic that told me I was venting gas from seven different punctures. I extended both arms in a cruciform pose and let go with the cannons, spraying tracer in all directions as I spun, rewarded with three more confirmed hits.

It bought me enough time to stop the spin, though the plasma thrusters were off-line and any chance to outrun my pursuers was now gone for good. The Pendragon shuddered from the impact of multiple cannon shells, and I managed to blast the attacking bot to pieces before the cannons fell silent and the heads-up told me I was out of ammo.

I could only push maximum CO_2 through the secondary thrusters and watch the last five bots close in for the kill. It was probably my over-adrenalised imagination, but I sensed a certain predatory anticipation in the way they formed a circular kill-zone around me, like a pride of lions savouring the cornered gazelle's last seconds.

I would like to record that my final thoughts consisted of a sober reflection on the many failures and regrets of my life, enlivened by the occasional bright moment of joy and humanity. The way Consuela looked that first time, Janet's smile, Sherry and Joe's friendship, poor old Freak's exile… But that would be a big fat lie. I felt only fear and frustration, forced it down into a hard ball of burning fury and lined up on the bot at twelve o'clock with every intention of diverting all remaining power to the thrusters and ramming it.

So it was with a mixture of surprise and disappointment that I greeted the sight of it exploding before I could begin my bid for glorious oblivion.

A Galahad class suit flashed past my visor at no more than arm's length, blazing cannons taking down two more bots as its missile rig spat shrikes at the others. A brief exchange of tracer and it was over, no more bots, no more shipyard.

The Galahad formed a jagged black silhouette against the vast disc of Ceres as it came closer, the opaque visor fading to reveal the occupant. "Always make your sims tougher than the real thing, right?" Lucy said with a grin.

"You were supposed to stay with your mother," I replied.

"Relax." She pouted a little. "Momma gave me a hall pass."

"What?" I realigned to view the Malthus II, finding it had begun to reverse course. It was already sixty klicks away, the distance increasing with every second. I could see three growing points of lights off her starboard bow, the blue glow of plasma thrusters on full power. *Scarabs on an attack run.*

"Mom?" Lucy said in a faint voice.

"You promised her immunity," Mina reminded me, speaking via the comms laser so Lucy wouldn't hear.

"She'll still find out," I said. "One day."

"I know. When she does… Tell her… Tell her if there's ever another war, she's to run very fast in the opposite direction."

"What are you doing?" Lucy demanded as the Malthus II shrank ever smaller. I thought about the canister of plutonium I had placed in the back-up reactor and realised I'd never checked to confirm it had been returned to the stores.

I glanced over at Lucy, seeing realisation dawn on her face and knew her mother was speaking to her via the comms laser. She screamed as the sun-flare erupted and her visor went black against the glare, screening out the wave of photons that would have fried her retinas.

I turned back to watch the end. Even a five kiloton blast wasn't enough to completely destroy a ship the size of the Malthus II, although it proved more than capable of snuffing out the attacking Scarabs in three brief flickers of vapourising matter. The hab-cluster disappeared in an expanding globe of pure white fire along with half the accumulator, the remaining wreckage splitting into two rapidly spinning chunks, soon shredded in the blast wave. The debris field flattened into a thin, narrow river, curving around us as Ceres' gravity took hold. It seemed the dwarf planet was destined to have its own short-lived ring system.

I could hear Lucy weeping and found I had not a single word of comfort for her. Instead I checked the Pendragon's auto-repair system, finding all leaks sealed but also less than five percent CO_2 remaining. Plus the stealth-ware was trashed and the scanning gear barely functional. On the bright side I still had nearly seventy-two hours' worth of air.

I drifted, listening to Lucy cry, watching the new ring system order itself into a surprisingly beautiful double disc arrangement, twin rivers of glittering detritus… disturbed by the sleek form of a single Wraith ascending from Ceres.

"You got any ammo left?" I asked Lucy.

"Huh?" she sniffed.

"Ammo. Do you have any?"

"Hundred-twenty cannon shells…" She trailed off as she caught sight of the Wraith. "Just as pretty as I thought it would be."

I had to admit the Wraith made a fine sight as it came to within two hundred metres, stealth-mode inactive so the reflected light from Ceres gleamed on the smooth lines of the hull, unmarred by any view-ports or comms gear. It was a real symphony of single purpose engineering. Death made flesh.

The Wraith fired its retros and came to a dead halt, a faint snick of static then a voice, soft and heavy with grief. "Like my new ship, Inspector?" asked Jack.

"It's Chief Inspector," I said.

"I'm sure they'll remember when they carve your name on the memorial."

"Must've been a difficult theft," I said. "Even for you."

"You'd be surprised just how much confusion a thermonuclear explosion and an asteroid storm will cause. Plus, Markov was kind enough to bequeath some useful hacks, made short work of the airlock seals… And the weapons systems." A small opening appeared in the nose of the Wraith, a circle of black within black. "Lucy, we're leaving."

"Mom's gone," she replied, voice hoarse.

"I know, and there'll be time to grieve later. But for now, every CAOS Security boat in this half of the Belt just registered two nukes exploding in Ceres orbit. We have to go."

"I said, mom's gone!" she snapped back. "She's gone. She needed to hide, so I hid with her. And I'm done hiding, Jack."

Silence, vast and cold like the surrounding vac, the black circle still open on the Wraith's nose. "Before I let you on my boat," Jack said, and I knew his full attention was now on me. "I had a crew and a family. You don't really think you're going back to the Slab for a hero's welcome, do you?"

"Leave him alone!" Lucy fired the Galahad's thrusters, putting herself between me and the Wraith.

"You think this piece of shit is going to work an immunity

deal for you?" Jack raged. "I know his kind. He'll wring you dry and stick you in immersion for the next decade."

"I don't think so. Anyway, ten years in immersion is better than five more minutes shackled to you."

"Get out of the way, Lucy!"

"Hey, Jack," I said. "Did you take the safe with you when you blew out of the Dead Reckoning? I bet you did. Looked inside yet?"

"What?" he demanded, voice very low.

I peered at the title through the cellophane, aged but still readable. "'After the Gold Rush,'" I read. "And there's an autograph. Who exactly was Neil Young anyway? Shadrak said he's the only thing you really care about, next to money of course."

The Wraith hung there, a gleaming black sculpture of death, pregnant with menace. The perfect vessel for the perfect pirate.

"You said it yourself," I told Jack. "The clock's ticking. At least this way you get a chance to steal it again one day. Or maybe you hate me enough to burn it up along with me, and your daughter of course."

"I'm not his daughter!" Lucy stated. "I never was."

"Lucy, please…" Jack began.

"Enough!" she snarled. "Kill if you're killing or go if you're going."

Another minute of silence, every second ticking by so slowly I wondered if the Wraith didn't have some kind of time-dilation ability. Finally, a soft, choked grunt, "I loved your mother. And I love you."

Lucy said nothing and the black circle in the Wraith's nose disappeared. The sleek form turned end over end, fired secondary thrusters to get clear then slipped into stealth-mode, its trajectory betrayed only by the swirling vortex of debris left in its wake.

"Wish he'd left one of those for me," Lucy muttered after a moment.

"Would've been handy about now," I agreed. The silence stretched.

"You knew, didn't you?" she asked. "What my mother was running from."

"Sure."

More elastic silence. "Well?" she demanded.

I dredged up a real-life story from memory. "It was the largest fraud in the history of the orbiting corporate sector. Happened just before the war, some say it caused it, at least partly. Forty billion UA secured on worthless mining shares, all based on false profit estimates cobbled together by a conspiracy of geologists and engineers. Lotta people lost their life savings, suicides, bankrupt banks, the whole shebang. Screwed the orbiting economy for the best part of a decade. Most of the offenders were caught, each of them got thirty years, real-time years. Guess your mom didn't want to miss you growing up."

"Oh," she said. "That's pretty bad, I guess." She turned back to Ceres. The ring system was already starting to dissolve, the twin rivers breaking up as the dwarf-planet gathered the junk to her breast. "Pity it didn't last."

"Yeah. Listen, if my air gives out first, I've recorded your immunity deal to the Pendragon's memory. When CAOS Security gets here, the call sign is White Wolf."

"White Wolf," she repeated. "What's it mean?"

I watched the last of the rings disintegrate, Ceres now showing a dirty grey line around its equator. I wondered if anyone would bother to clean it up. "It means I'm done with this," I said. "And I'm going home."

END

AN ARIA FOR RAGNAROK

CHAPTER 1

SHE SAID, "YOUR scars are gone."

I said, "Don't rub it in."

She smiled. It wasn't much of a smile, more a brief curl of her too-red lips and a barely perceptible dimple in her too-white skin. But still, a smile. "Been looking for you," I went on. "Leave of absence, the university said."

"Not through choice. But I did make good use of the time." Her eyes swept over my face again, the face I'd chosen on return from Ceres, the same face I'd left with almost a year ago, albeit now sans scars. Fixing them wasn't my idea and my reaction to the first glance in the mirror had sent the CAOS Defence med-tech scurrying from the room in mortal panic. My less-than-polite requests for another procedure were refused on ethical grounds; apparently there's a limit to how many face-changes a human body can tolerate, and I'd reached mine.

"You were someone else for a while," she said, head tilted at a familiar angle and eyes narrowed. "Weren't you?"

Secrets are a waste of time around her, I reminded myself, saying nothing.

"When you stood me up I got worried," she continued. "Went to the bar. Marco couldn't tell me anything. No bags packed, no sign of a struggle. You were just gone. So I called

Chief Inspector Mordecai. At first she seemed just as worried as I was."

"Janet..."

"She got me and Joe assigned to a special investigation, did a forensic sweep of the bar, then suddenly she lost interest. Told us to do the same. Of course we couldn't. We kept on digging, trying to get the media interested. Oddly, considering the most celebrated hero-Demon on the Slab had up and disappeared without a trace, no one seemed keen on the story. Then one day the faculty president called me in and told me I was suspended without pay. Certain irregularities in my expenses, he said. If I hadn't been a hero he'd have fired me, he said. Joe got transferred to crime-scene clean-up."

The Colonel, I knew. *Being thorough, the bastard.* I held up the bottle I'd bought at the most expensive plasma-boutique this side of the Axis. It was made from hand-crafted black glass and had a florid, Renaissance style sketch of a marmoset on the label. "Sweeter than pine-martin, I'm told," I said.

She barely glanced at the bottle, laser-like perception at full power now. "Exocore Mining lost one of its biggest ships off Ceres not long ago," she said. "The largest astro-navigation disaster of recent years. There are an awful lot of crackpot conspiracy theories flying around the smart-net about it. Everything from a battle between Belter clans to a thwarted alien invasion. Some amateur radio-astronomers even claim there was a nuclear exchange. Maybe you heard about it."

I held out my second offering, a flat square encased in what I hoped was tastefully restrained gift-wrap. "I know you're not supposed to reveal the price of a gift, but this..."

"Are you actually serious?" she asked in a low whisper, a snarl creeping into her voice and lips revealing overlong canines. I was suddenly glad I'd asked her to meet me in a public space. Memorial Park was one of Chief-of-Police turned Mayor Arnaud's voter-friendly projects, half of the once decrepit Yang

Twenty-Three given over to broad grassland and copses of maple and acacia. A boating lake and several splash pools for the kids added to the generally idyllic appearance, though the burgeoning corruption scandal surrounding the park's construction added an authentic Slab-esque ambiance to the place. I'd been surprised Janet had wanted to meet here, given the vast array of UV lights in the ceiling, receiving a terse text reply by way of explanation: *I'm UV resistant. Racist.*

We stood near a picnic table, her staring at my gift, me unable to tell her anything and not wanting to lie. "You'll like it," I said when my arm started to ache. "Promise."

She blinked, sighed then took the gift, and the bottle. We sat at the picnic table as she tore away the wrapping, unable to contain a small chirp of surprised delight at the revealed album covert art. "This…" she said, fingers playing over the tableau of Luke and co., before coming to rest on Vader's respirator. "This can't be genuine."

"Original motion picture soundtrack," I said. "Third pressing, according to the Jed I bought it from. Said if it'd been a first pressing he wouldn't be running a crappy record store." I tried a smile which earned me only a raised eyebrow so I felt the need to elaborate. "I went away because I had to. Now I'm back. Isn't that enough?"

"The death-toll at Ceres was considerable," she said. "Though no source seems to agree on the exact number."

"And that's the way it'll stay." Another raised eyebrow. More elaboration needed. "Take a look," I said, gesturing at the surrounding park. Nearby a Splice-elf couple were holding hands with their little boy as he splashed in the fountain. Beyond them a group of older kids, werewolves and un-Spliced, were engaged in the rough and tumble Slab version of Lacrosse. "What happened… what I did. None of this would be here if I hadn't. Including you. And you'll just have to trust me on that."

She returned her gaze to the album cover, didn't raise it

when she said, "Are you done? I mean; out, discharged, retired. Whatever they call it."

White Wolf, I thought, recalling that final meeting with the Colonel. *That's what they call it.* He'd offered promotion to major and the opportunity to recruit my own team. I told him to shove it and if I ever set eyes on him again one of us wasn't going to survive the encounter.

"Yes," I told her. "I'm a Demon again, and that's what I'll be until they pension me off or, more likely, fire my ass."

"Joe," she said, finally looking up to meet my gaze.

"Already reinstated. Got him appointed to Special Homicide. Which brings me to my second reason for asking you here. Technically, you're still an accredited Special Investigator, with a distinguished record to boot."

"I think I've chased after enough monsters for one lifetime, thank you."

"Not like this one." I took out my smart and called up an image on the holo display.

"Handsome fellow," she said, watching the miniature head and shoulders revolve. "I take it this is the face of your arch nemesis?"

"I present Mr Mac. Criminal kingpin, murderer, drug and people trafficker and a thousand other bad things. Want to help me catch him?"

"I'm otherwise engaged."

"I know you haven't been back to work, even though they reinstated you."

"With a letter of exoneration and back-pay, which I guess was due to your influence. However, the manner of my suspension left a bitter taste. When it fades I'll go back. In the meantime, I thought I should finally write another book."

"Greeks or Romans?"

"Actually, I've gone all modern for this one." She held up her own smart. Like most tech she owned it was an older model and it took me a few seconds of squinting to read the fuzzy display.

"A Narrative History of the CAOS War."

"It's a criminally neglected subject," she said. "Do you know that, to date, there is no comprehensive, unbiased account of the conflict? And the CAOS Official History is an error-ridden piece of propagandist drek."

"Sometimes it's best to leave the past alone. Let the next generation sort the truth from the lies."

"A refrain I've become familiar with recently. I approached CAOS Defence, Central Governance and all the veteran groups I could find. So far I've managed to interview only half-a-dozen people, none of them major players." She paused to smile, a better one this time, though a little more calculating than I'd've liked. "Like you, Alex."

I gave a brief laugh. "Major player?"

"You forget all that digging into your background I did before I came to you about the DeMarco murder, and I did a lot more after you went missing. You took part in the Langley Raid, perhaps the most important event in the whole war. Not to mention that space battle you told me about. Added to that, I suspect there are a lot of doors you could open. Veterans might be reluctant to talk to me, but not you." She angled her head, black eyes twinkling. "If you really want to make it up to me, that is. Not that this isn't lovely," she added, hugging the album to her chest.

I fell silent as ugly memories played out in my head. For the first time I found they didn't hurt so much, didn't make my hands itch for the bourbon bottle or set my heart pumping with long gestated rage. *Was it Ceres?* I wondered, my mind filling with the image of the Fed Sec construction array breaking apart as the asteroids tore it to pieces. *Now I've levelled the scale, I can finally let it go?*

"I'll help," I said, then nodded at the miniature Mr Mac

still revolving on the table. "If you'll help with this." Seeing her reluctant wince I added, "Part-time basis only. You won't even have to come to the station. And there'll be a consultancy fee, unlike last time."

My smart beeped, the display turning red to signify an urgent call. "Can't ignore it," I apologised, picking it up. The message was brief but compelling: 'Cold one on Yang Ten. Priority Alpha. Strict publicity ban. Get here - Sherry.' *The Acting Chief of Police attending a murder scene in person. Not the best sign for a trouble free day.*

"Gotta go," I said, rising from the table. "You'll think about it? Mr Mac?"

She nodded and got up, moving close. "I never got to hear what you thought about the Ewoks," she said. "Be at mine by eight. We'll watch *Jedi*, I'll drink your overpriced blood and we'll talk some more about your Moriarty."

There was a challenge in her gaze, a direct and honest question. *You called me, remember?*

"I'll be there," I said, turning to go then pausing. "Who's Moriarty?"

CHAPTER 2

QUAD FOUR OF Yang Ten was always a lively district, neon and hol-displays blaring through the steam to advertise a garish cavalcade of girls, boys and everything in between. Some establishments eschewed the signs for the more traditional approach of displaying their goods in the window. A scaly-skinned Splice woman, complete with coiling tail and slit-eyes, leaned close to the glass to blow a kiss at me as I made my way towards the cordon of uniformed Demons. She pouted in mock regret as I replied with a respectful nod and pinned my ID to my raincoat.

I was dismayed to find Redwing at the cordon, long damp hair framing a hawk-nosed face that fully mirrored my regard. "Chief Inspector," he said in precisely respectful tones.

"Harry." I glanced over his shoulder at the doorway behind. The sign, rendered in a mix of English and Vietnamese, proclaimed it the 'Gateway to Eternal Bliss.' It also offered a fifty percent discount for first-time patrons and a voucher for the all-you-can-eat buffet. "Classy place."

"She's waiting inside." He lifted the tape and I ducked under, following him through the door and into the richly scented interior. Day-old hoisin sauce mixed with synthetic lotus blossom to leave an itch in my nostrils. Employees eyed us from half-open doors as we proceeded towards the stairs, my well-tuned eyes picking out the more common gang tats. *Mid-range Vic affiliate place,* I decided. *Low rent, high profits. Keen to avoid trouble.*

"So what's the story?" I asked Redwing as we started up the stairs. "Caught another open-and-shut that didn't turn out to be so shut?"

"Chief Mordecai will explain," he replied in a curt murmur. Me making Chief Inspector before he did was clearly grating more than a little.

"Or is it the victim?" I went on, keen to dangle the bait a little more. "Someone noteworthy, perhaps? You have managed to ID the victim, right Harry?"

I didn't like the smirk that accompanied his reply, "Wasn't difficult." The smirk told me a lot, principally that dear old Harry was glad to get this one off his hands and into my lap.

We climbed to the top floor and proceeded to a room half-way along the poorly lit corridor, marked as the murder scene by the white-suited techs packing gear outside. They cleared a path as I approached, nodding leave to enter at my questioning glance. I found Sherry and Ricci inside, surrounded by one of the few scenes in my career that genuinely resembled a slaughterhouse. The room was a twelve-by-twelve, windowless cube with a bed and a shower cubicle. It would have been cleaner than usual for an establishment like this but for the blood spattered over every surface. Floor, walls and ceiling all richly decorated in abstract plasma. The victim lay in six parts, head, torso and limbs. From the ragged stumps on the torso it was clear this hadn't been a slasher's work. *Torn apart. And quickly.*

"Say 'pull yourself together' and you're fired," Sherry told me.

"Was gonna go for 'guess he fell to pieces'," I said, crouching to peer at the head which lay on its side near the centre of the room. Even the most peaceful demise has a tendency to leech recognition from a human face, and this Jed's end had been anything but. Just a middle-aged man, Caucasian features, bunched on one side where they met the floor and slack on the other. Despite the mask of blood I could tell he hadn't shaved in a while but his skin had the too-smooth quality that came from frequent visits to the derm-salon. Despite the blood matting his hair, I noted it had the irregular look that resulted from letting an expensive grooming regimen slip for several weeks.

"Yin-sider type on a slumming safari," I said, rising and turning to Sherry. "But I'm guessing he's a sight more important than that, or I wouldn't be here."

"Craig Rybak," Redwing said from the doorway, smirk now broadened into a smile.

"The Astravista guy?" I glanced down at the head once more, finding only a dim resemblance to the face I vaguely recalled from the news feeds.

"Co-founder and Head of Operations for Astravista Industries," Redwing went on. "Principal donor to Chief Arnaud's election fund, not to mention half the representatives in Central Governance."

"Where are we on the canvas?" Sherry said, her tone edged sufficiently to banish his smile.

"Half-done. Neighbourhood like this, not many willing to talk."

"Get back to it. Low key, but make it clear the reward money on this one will be substantial."

"Right, boss." Redwing shot me with a parting grin before disappearing from the doorway.

"Can't you get rid of him?" I asked Sherry. "Hear they've got a vacancy on the clean-up squad."

"He clears cases," she said. "Just not cases like this."

I concealed a grunt of annoyance. I had my own priorities and could really have done without being lumbered with such a high-profile mess. But I also knew Sherry would have been fielding update demands from the mayor's office once Rybak's name flashed on the pol-net. She'd be much more amenable to my imminent and resource hungry requests if I could put this away in a timely fashion.

"Brute strength, right?" I asked Ricci who was busy running a scanner over the spatter on the ceiling. "No weapon used."

"That's right." He lowered the scanner, checked the readout and fluffed his moustache with a satisfied huff. "Like I thought, adrenaline free." He gestured at the surrounding carnage. "Also no arterial spray. This was all post-mortem."

"Cause of death?"

He pointed to the head at my feet. "Preliminary x-ray shows high impact blunt force trauma to the frontal lobe. I'll need to run a sim based on the fracture pattern to ID the cause but given all this, my guess is whoever did it wouldn't need more than a fist. Ripping off a man's head and limbs takes way more physical strength than even the most 'roided out un-Spliced."

"Meaning it's either a Splice or someone with serious augments," Sherry said. "Rybak's type always have enemies. Could be a corporate rival hired a freelance hitter and they left us a nice big mess to confuse the scene."

"There are easier ways of doing that," I said. "Where's his security?"

"As far as we know he came here alone. No bodyguards, no personal assistants. We bagged up his clothes, all he had was a billfold holding twenty thousand in green and a cheapo smart preloaded with a million in UA."

"The contact file on the smart?"

"Empty. Seems he didn't want to talk to anyone." She held up her own smart, the screen flickering red and angry. "Unlike his partner, it seems."

"Othin Vargold," I remembered. "Him and Rybak started the company together before the war, got rich making weapons for CAOS and even richer in the aftermath thanks to the embargo on Downside tech." My gaze lingered on Rybak's dead face. "Jed had more money than every living soul this side of the Axis combined. Makes you wonder what brought him here."

"What else?" Ricci said. "Came to fuck. Guess he just liked it sleazy. And," he held up the scanner, "a serious Blues habit according to this. He wasn't stoned when this went down but the trace amounts indicate heavy use over an extended period."

"Deal gone bad?" I wondered aloud, knowing it couldn't be that easy.

"The manager's on hold downstairs," Sherry said with a meaningful glance. "Old school Vic type. Been minimally compliant since we got here."

"I'll talk to him."

I moved to the shower, finding the curtain pulled back and the tiles mostly free of blood. "Perp showered off before leaving."

"Yeah, looks that way," Ricci said. "Got hair samples from the plughole. Take a while to sort it though. Probably a decade's worth of pubes down there."

"And now I can't eat for a week," Sherry said. "Thanks Ricci."

I looked over the rest of the room, concentrating on the corners and finding a very small hole in the join between the ceiling and the wall opposite the bed. *No bigger than a pinprick, but that's plenty.* "I'll go see the manager now."

"He was a regular, wasn't he?"

The manager conformed mostly to Sherry's description, black vest to show off the tats on his chest and arms, about forty years old with the beginnings of a paunch, face decorated with the requisite pattern of scars. From the set of his features and paleness of his skin I judged him as third generation Slab-born. Though they tend to cling to their ethnicity with near-religious devotion, the long established Vic gangs have more enlightened ideas when it came to racial purity. He sat at a card table in the small casino at the rear of the establishment, dealing out cards with swift and unconscious rapidity, eyes concentrating on the revealed faces with an intensity that put me in mind of Janet. *Card-counter. Almost a lost art.* If the manager heard my question, he gave no sign.

I moved closer, took hold of the table and hauled it over, scattering cards and chips. The manager dropped his hands into his lap and sat still, refusing to look at me even when I stood close enough to convey sufficient threat and insult to set his face a-quiver.

I said, "Do I really have to introduce myself?"

A small negative jerk of his head.

"Need to hear your voice, Jed."

He swallowed, spoke in a whispered grunt. "No."

"Good." I stepped back. "To state the obvious, I couldn't care less about you, your business or the fact that, whilst licensed prostitution is entirely legal, unlicensed gambling is not. You understand me, *Dai Wei?*"

A nod, then a terse, "Yes."

"The man upstairs, you know who he is, don't you?"

"I know."

"I'm guessing he wasn't alone when this happened. Boy? Girl? Both?"

"Girls. Two."

"And where are they?"

He got to his feet, wisely keeping his movements slow, then nodded at the dimly lit recesses of the casino. "Won't talk without me there," he said.

I nodded assent and he led me to a shadowed alcove where two young women huddled together. I could tell instantly they were Downside born, shorter than the average hab-born with the signature tint of the sun to their skin. They stared up at me with wide, moist eyes, one giving a convulsive shiver which made her companion put an arm around her shoulders. They had the natural attractiveness that didn't come from remodelling clinics, though their evident shock and fear seemed to drain any sexuality. Just two terrorised youths in a brothel.

"Police," the manager said, nodding at me. "Tell him."

The less traumatised of the two blinked up at me whilst her companion continued to shiver. "You're a cop?" she asked. "A Demon they call it here." North American accent with the twang of the southern territories. Most likely an economic refugee come up the well in search of riches, or just regular caloric intake.

"Chief Inspector Alex McLeod, miss," I confirmed, adding, "I don't need your name," as she gave the manager a questioning glance. "Tell me what happened upstairs."

The other girl gave a convulsive shudder, putting her hand to her mouth as she choked down on a retch. "Sorry," her companion said, "she's awful upset. Mr Craig, he was nicer'n most."

"You'd seen him before?"

"Sure, a dozen times over the last coupla' months. He had… simple tastes, y'know. Sometimes he'd just come to sit and get wasted on Blues."

"Did he talk much? Tell you his worries, maybe?"

She shook her head. "He'd talk, but it'd be small stuff. Sometimes he'd get to remembering his childhood and such. Said he was born in Sweden, came Upside when he was just a boy, didn't go back for twenty years but now he owned a house there. A house by a lake." She gave a very small smile. "Said he was gonna take us both there one day. Buy out our contract and carry us off, he said. Don't think he was altogether serious 'bout that."

"You were there when it happened?"

The other girl started to weep, sobbing into spasming hands.

"Yeah," her friend said, hugging her closer. "He got here around 1500, like usual. Asked for us, like usual. We keep the afternoons free in case he shows up. Things were different this time though. No fun, no Blues. He just stripped off and sat on the bed, then the door buzzer went off. We knew it meant trouble 'cause that never happens. Mr Craig said it was OK, told us to answer it and when we did there was this young fella standing there."

"Splice?" I asked.

"No, sir. Least ways, he didn't look like it. Just a white guy in his twenties, small. Not much bigger 'n me, really."

"He say anything?"

She shook her head. "Mr Craig did though. Told him to come in and us to leave. 'This will only take a little while, ladies,' he said. We waited outside in the corridor for like ten minutes, maybe less. Then the young fella came out and went downstairs. Didn't say nothin'. Noticed his clothes were all soaked through though. Then…" She closed her eyes. "Then we went inside."

I gave her a moment as she fought down the shakes. "You didn't hear anything when you were waiting?"

"The rooms are all soundproofed. Obvious reasons."

I slid a card across the table to her. "Contact details if anything else occurs to you."

She glanced at the manager then picked it up when he nodded.

"Guess you know Mr Craig was a man of some importance," I said.

"I watch the news feeds," she said. "Sometimes."

"Be better for you both if your involvement remains undisclosed."

She shrugged. "Got a discretion clause in my contract. Folks who run this place take care of us, legally speaking. I got no complaints."

I nodded to her weeping friend. "Best get her to a medic. Yourself too."

"Yes, sir."

I jerked my head at the manager and moved to the roulette table. I spun the wheel as he stood close by, maintaining his silence as I let the moment string out. "You liked him," I said eventually, tossing a ball into the wheel and watching it bounce. "Didn't you?"

"Good customers are to be valued," he said.

"That why you called it in instead of finding a convenient meat grinder?"

"He would've been missed, traced here. This was the least complicated solution."

The ball clattered with diminishing energy until it settled onto thirteen black, which seemed appropriate all things considered. "You can keep whatever you extorted from him," I said. "But I need the file from the surveillance module you hid in the room. And don't make me introduce myself again."

CHAPTER 3

THEY SAY RANK hath its privileges. If so, I must be missing something. Apart from a slight bump in salary, the benefits of promotion so far amounted to an increased workload and the unwelcome responsibility of running my own squad. Rather than unleash my singular management style on the whole of Homicide, Sherry had opted to put me in charge of a newly created sub-division: Special Homicide. It was basically an expansion of my previous role, benefiting from the addition of no less than three Inspector-grade Demons and a clutch of civilian analysts. I'd been allowed to pick them myself, my selection criteria being narrowed by the need to find people with a basic level of competence, not the easiest thing at the best of times. Joe had been my first pick, now elevated to Inspector First Grade and ostensibly my second-in-command.

"Security-cam coverage for the Quad runs at a daily average of thirty percent," he told me as I settled behind my desk. He had to stoop to make it through the door. I had a small office separated from the rest of the squad room by a heavily besmirched glass partition. I could have called building services to clean the glass but liked the privacy it afforded.

"Standard facial recognition scans are running now," Joe continued. "I prioritised for perps with a history of violence. No hits so far."

"We have coverage on the brothel entrance?" I asked.

"Cam's been out for months. I'm guessing the owners pay the maintenance crews to skip it. Got reasonable coverage on the surrounding streets though. Timor and Leyla are on it."

"It can wait for now." I took the data-stick the manager had handed over and slotted it into the terminal on my desk, sending the feed to the main display in the squad room. "Gather the troops. And you might want to distribute some sick-bags."

He ducked his head under the door again then paused, voice dropping into a cautious rumble. "Your, uh, other meeting? Go OK?"

"About as well as can be expected."

"She's still pissed, huh?"

"Not as much as she should be. We're meeting up again tonight."

My smart started buzzing, loud and strident, the ID reading as 'Mayor's Office.' *Shit.* "Be out in a second," I told Joe. "Close the door."

"Chief Inspector McLeod?" the female voice asked as I hit the call icon.

"Yeah," I said, rubbing my temples.

"Please hold for Othin Vargold."

What the hell? "Erm, OK."

A short delay then a male voice, cultured and even with a slight nordic lilt. "Chief Inspector, thank you for taking my call."

"I was expecting Mayor Arnaud."

"Yes. Forgive the subterfuge. The mayor indicated you might not pick up if I called directly."

He was right. "Guess you're calling to emphasise your personal connection to the victim and encourage my best efforts."

"I'm aware of your history, so I know your best efforts are already guaranteed. Your appointment to this case was in fact made at my insistence. I merely wish to offer the assistance of my company. Any and all resources within my power are at your disposal."

"Including a list of Mr Rybak's enemies?"

A short pause and a faint sigh. "You may not believe this, Inspector, but Craig didn't have any enemies. The more cut and thrust aspects of business were always within my purview. Craig ran the company and I ran off the competition."

I got up from the desk and leaned close to the glass, squinting through the muck at the main display. Joe had already started the playback: Rybak entering the room with the two girls. A big man, moving in a hunched shuffle, face drawn and haggard like he hadn't slept in a good while.

"And his mental state recently?" I asked Vargold, watching Rybak slough off his clothes with the girls' assistance. His frame was broad across the shoulders but flabby elsewhere, a former athlete gone to seed.

Another pause from the smart, another barely heard sigh. "I guess you've already ascertained that Craig's recent behaviour had been somewhat... erratic."

"A multi-millionaire visiting a Yang-side brothel three or four times a week whilst cultivating a Blues addiction seems pretty erratic, yeah."

"Clinical depression knows no favourites and can strike any of us. Craig stopped working, distanced himself from friends and colleagues. He even started giving his possessions away. I had been doing my best to help, but... Well, if you watch the news feeds you'll understand the demands on my time at present."

"Sure. You chosen a name for the big tamale yet?"

Vargold's tone took on a puzzled note. "Not quite. Though we do have a short-list. Is that relevant?"

"Your company's about to complete construction of the first starship in human history. Major historical events tend to attract all manner of weirdness."

"Craig's involvement in the Ad Astra project was peripheral

at best, mainly limited to oversight of the funding and accountancy structure."

"Seem to be a lot of people angry about the whole thing. Vast waste of resources, some say. Seeking to spread an imperfect species across the galaxy, according to others. Then there's all the religious nuts."

"Any major advance is bound to cause a certain amount of societal upheaval. However, I take your point. I'll have my security people compile a breakdown of the most serious threats. You'll have it within the hour."

"Look forward to it." Rybak was slumped on the bed now, propped against the wall and staring into space with dull eyes, apparently oblivious to the two girls stroking and caressing his sagging flesh. I knew the look: a man awaiting death.

"Depression often leads to suicide," I said to Vargold. "Had he ever tried it?"

"Not to my knowledge. He stopped going to therapy some weeks ago."

"It'd help if I had access to his medical records. Save a lot of time if I didn't have to go through the whole court order procedure."

"I'll see to it. I'm also posting a reward for information, one million UA."

"I'd rather you didn't. At least not yet. That kind of money will be a magnet for every freak and con-artist on the Slab. Sorting through every report will use up time and resources best employed elsewhere."

I watched the girls draw back from Rybak and turn to the door, presumably in response to the door buzzer. He said something and they opened it, pausing then standing aside to admit a diminutive young man in nondescript clothing. *Time for the main event.*

"If there's nothing else," I said to Vargold. "I need to

get back to work. The Mayor's office will keep you updated on progress."

"Of course. I'll hold off on the reward until you say otherwise." Another pause. "Inspector, you asked about enemies. There is one enemy we all share, as I'm sure you know. Astravista is the main arms supplier to CAOS Defence."

"This is way too messy for Fed Sec."

"Unless they wanted to send a message. This is a secure line so I can tell you. Thanks to Astravista's military contracts I was granted high-level clearance some time ago. I know about Ceres."

"Really? Where's that?"

A faintly amused sigh. "Quite. All I ask is that you keep an open mind. Not all wars end when the treaty is signed."

The girls left the room and the young man closed the door, turning to Rybak. They stared at each other for a full minute, saying nothing.

"Not ruling anything out at this stage," I told Vargold, the ancient police response to the amateur detective. "I really have to go now." My finger hovered over the end-call icon. "Sorry for your loss," I added before cutting him off.

One of the civilian analysts was the first to bolt, white faced and retching as he held a desk bin under his chin. The rest followed in quick succession leaving only us jaded detectives to watch as Rybak's killer tossed aside his dismembered head.

"Splice," said Leyla O'Keefe. "Gotta be."

"Racist," said Timor Briganti, like Joe one of the few Splices in the department, though his heritage was a lot more obvious. Ash-black skin, white hair and pointy ears, second-generation morphology based on some genre fiction anti-hero from two centuries ago. I always wondered how much he must hate his parents.

"Look at him." Leyla froze the vid, stepping close to the

screen to form an elaborate pose, like a gameshow assistant showing off the prizes. Visually speaking she was Timor's opposite, pale skin, black hair and only an inch and a half over five feet. She also had the confidence that came from multi-generation Irish-cop lineage, claiming one of her ancestors had been immortalised in the French Connection, whatever that was.

"That, folks," she said, small hands framing the hairy and fanged face on the screen, "is a werewolf."

"Not enough hair," Timor insisted. "And his snout's too small. More Lon Chaney than The Howling."

"I don't know what the hell you're talking about," Joe rumbled.

"He's a wolf*man*. Not a werewolf."

"In either case," I said. "He was neither when he came in. He's a shifter."

"Thought they were a myth," Leyla said.

"Evidently not. Run it back."

She rewound to the point where the perp had entered the room, transforming him from ravening, fanged dismemberment machine to unremarkable young man. The manager hadn't bothered to set up his module to record sound, perhaps as a somewhat redundant sop to Rybak's privacy, but it was clear victim and killer had exchanged words. The perp's back was to the camera but I could see the slight bob of his head as he said something and Rybak's lips moving in reply.

"Run phoneme interpretation," I said. Leyla's hands danced over the icons to call up the lip-reader, the result playing a few seconds later in toneless, stilted computer-speak. "From light… we are… born to light we… return."

"Mean anything to anyone?" I asked to a parade of baffled shrugs.

"Sounds culty, whatever it is," Timor said.

"Run a search when we're done here. Play around with the

wording, see if it cross-refs with any known groups. Include both political and religious."

I gestured for Leyla to restart playback and watched as the perp moved to the centre of the room, partly obscuring Rybak's hunched bulk. The young man undressed slowly, casting his clothes aside and standing naked, arms raised, waiting. The transformation happened in seconds, muscles bulging, limbs extending. My gaze inevitably lingered on his hands, blurring as they spasmed into claws and reminding me of something I'd seen only once before. When it was done a five-foot three inch man of slender build had become a six foot monster with a thin pelt of grey fur.

"OK, that's enough," I said, seeing the thing's fisted claw lash down at Rybak's forehead and not relishing a second helping of what came next. "The camera got a good profile shot when he came through the door. Cap it and run it through facial recognition."

"On it, boss," Leyla said.

"Timor, when you're done researching that phrase I want you to recheck Harry Redwing's canvas results. Wouldn't put it past him to miss something obvious. Joe, get the analysts out of the crapper and put them to work on open sources. We need a profile on Rybak: every news item, piece of gossip or smart-ping relating to him in the past six months. We'll also be getting a hefty package from Astravista security…"

"Uh, boss," Leyla said, gesturing at the display where the word 'MATCH' was flashing on the perp's profile alongside an ID summary:

Name: Khristopher Corvin

DOB: 06/04/2195

Criminal Ident: O10987-FL

Custodial History: Six months corrective immersion, Lorenzo City Municipal Penitentiary

Date of release: 03/04/2215

Current domicile: Apt. 4C, Dunelm Court, Quad Delta, Yang Sixteen.

"Well that was easy," Timor said.

I returned to my office, gesturing for Joe to follow. "Scramble SWAT to meet us there," I told him, opening a drawer to extract a new department-issue Colt 5mm. "Covert approach. And clear a Pipe route to Yang Sixteen. Sherry'll authorise it."

CHAPTER 4

"FL," I MURMURED, reading through Corvin's record on the pipe. The four of us were alone in the carriage as it blasted through the network towards Yang Sixteen, all chafing a little at the body-armour under our clothes. No matter how flexible and lightweight they make it, armour always itches.

"Boss?" Leyla asked.

"Fraud and larceny," I said. "Corvin does his six months, gets released five days ago, somehow gets himself spliced into shifter mode in the interim, then decides to kill Rybak."

"Guess the corrective immersion didn't take," Joe said.

"Still seems way out of character." I scrolled through Corvin's history, finding numerous counts of fraud but no violence. "He was a short-con grifter. Glomming onto wealthy Yin-siders, selling bogus investments. Pretty good at it too, they seized over three million from his accounts when he went away. Post-immersion psyche report has him as a changed man. Keen to repay his debt, planning on volunteering for hardship relief missions to Downside war-zones."

"Never lasts," Timor said. "Immersion straightens them out for a while but they always revert to type."

"Except Rybak wasn't his type."

"The vid was pretty unambiguous, boss."

I drew the Colt and flipped the selector to non-lethal. "Tasers only," I told them. "I want to hear what he has to say."

Like many Slab levels Yang Sixteen had undergone something of an economic boom recently. More shops, more markets, less garbage. I found Quad Delta a cleaner, graffiti-free version of the slum I remembered from only a year before. *Arrogant ass he may be,* I thought as we passed a playground that had once been a haunt for Blues-heads but now boasted a cluster of children. *But at least Arnaud keeps his promises.*

Dunelm Court was a three storey, donut-shaped apartment complex surrounding a central swimming pool where I was dismayed to find about a dozen residents at play.

"He's on the top floor," the SWAT Commander told me. His team were posted around the main entrance, dressed in plainclothes that wouldn't fool anyone with Corvin's experience. I'd have much preferred to take him down myself with just Joe for back-up, but the vid of Rybak's murder demanded caution.

"Inward facing apartment," the Commander went on. "Building security-net confirms he's in residence."

"He alone?" I asked.

"Looks that way." He held up his smart, displaying a feed from the building's cams and switching to thermal imaging. Corvin was a yellow-red splodge on the black silhouette of a couch. He sat straight-backed and still, hands resting on his knees.

"Any audio?" I said.

"None we can pick up, so I guess his entertainment hub's off and if there's anyone else at home, they aren't talking. See the way he's just sitting there? Makes me think he's expecting visitors."

I couldn't argue with his logic. There was definitely something unnatural about Corvin's posture. I'd have taken him for dead but for the heat signature and slight rise and fall of his chest. *He knows we're coming.* "Your entry-team ready?"

"Got four operators inside disguised as custodial staff. We go the moment they breach."

"Expect resistance, but I need him alive."

"Noted."

"Wait for my go." I beckoned Leyla and Timor over. "As soon as SWAT goes in you two clear those people from the pool. Joe and me will cover."

"Got it, boss."

I nodded to the commander who turned to the entrance, drawing a carbine from under his jacket. "This is Gold One," he said, his words conveyed via sub-dermal smart to his operators. "We are a go. Perimeter-team activate containment protocol. Entry-team proceed to breach. Non-lethals only."

A two-second pause then the faint thud of a door being blown in by a compressed air ram followed almost instantly by the flat crump of a stun-grenade. I followed the commander into the inner courtyard as a chorus of warnings came over the comms.

"Police! Do not move!"

The pool lounging residents were staring in blank amazement at the twenty or more armed Demons now running through their sanctum. "Lorenzo City PD, folks!" I told them, holding up my ID. "Nothing to worry about. But I need you to vacate this pool. NOW!" I added for emphasis as they continued to stare, provoking one of the kids into a fit of frightened squalling. They started to move when Leyla and Timor began to haul people from the water.

I saw the commander take the stairs at a run with two operators close on his heels. I tracked his course to the top floor where he disappeared into a smoking doorway. "Suspect compliant and in custody," he reported in short order. "Bringing him down now."

"Roger that," I said, turning to Joe with raised eyebrows.

"Less than three hours from start to finish," he said. "Must be a record."

"Here's hoping it makes Sherry more amenable to signing off on the budget for Mr Mac. That'll tie us up for a damn sight longer."

"Maybe not if Dr Vaughn comes on board. There's a lady with some serious insight."

And a few secrets, I added inwardly. It had been nagging me since viewing Rybak's murder. The way Corvin had transformed, particularly the way his hands morphed into claws. I was mentally rehearsing how to bring it up with her when something landed in the pool with a soft splosh. Something round and pale that bobbed momentarily on the surface before sinking amidst a thick red cloud. I had time to register the commander's face before it disappeared completely.

I looked up in time to dodge the rest of him, stepping aside as the truncated corpse landed on the poolside with a wet slap. *Not a sound on the comms,* I realised, aiming the Colt up at the third floor. *How fast can he be?*

Another body came sailing over the third floor balustrade. One of the entry team judging by the janitorial overalls, a large man trailing blood from the hole where his face had been.

"Code Black-Alpha!" I said into my smart, the call-sign for a Demon fatality. "Multiple Code Black-Alphas at Dunelm Court, Yang Sixteen. All available units…"

Shattering glass dragged my gaze back to Corvin's apartment in time to see a third body flying through the window. Another entry-team operator, tumbling end over end in a tangle of her own entrails. She came down in the pool, incredibly still alive, hand waving as she sank beneath the red water. Leyla and Timor immediately jumped in to drag her out.

I stared up at the shattered window as the comms shrieked in my ears, both hands firm on the butt of the Colt. Nothing.

No movement. Just the last few shards of glass falling from the window frame.

"He's still in there," Joe said, displaying the security cam feed on his smart. "Changed a bit though."

Corvin's heat-form now appeared to be twice its former size, standing in his living room, massive shoulders heaving and claws twitching with predatory anticipation. I could see two bodies cooling on the floor behind him.

A gargling shriek drew my gaze back to the pool. Timor and Leyla had dragged the operator clear onto the poolside, though a length of her guts still trailed in the water from a rent in her body-armour. Her face was bleached of colour and she jerked in regular spasms of diminishing intensity. *The death-clock,* we used to call it. *Ticking down. She's not going to make it.*

A howl came peeling down from above, jarring in its sheer exultant savagery. I returned my gaze to the window, a fraction too late as a grey streak flashed through it, my burst of taser-darts missing by a wide margin. Corvin's howl ended as he impacted on the pool-side, tiles shattering under the force. He crouched, glaring at me with yellow eyes set in a leathery, thinly furred face, teeth bared in a hungry growl. His clothes hung from him in rags, shredded by the change to reveal the kind of muscle mass that no un-spliced human could ever aspire to. Bloodied flesh dangled from his claws and a thick tangle of red-tinged drool hung from his mouth. I could see nothing resembling reason in his eyes.

I flicked the Colt's selector to lethal and sighted on his chest. *Fuck taking him alive.* He charged the moment I fired, two three-round bursts to the central mass, enough to blow the lungs and spine out of a human body. Corvin, of course, wasn't human just now and didn't even slow down. The distance between us vanished in a heart-beat, his claws closing on my face as I sought vainly to bring the Colt to bear on his throat.

A dark blur in the corner of my vision followed by the hard

thud of bodies colliding and Corvin disappeared from my eye-line. My gaze snapped to the left, finding Joe and Corvin locked in a furious embrace, raising a cloud of fragmented plaster and tile as they rebounded from every hard surface in a ten metre radius, moving almost too fast to follow. Joe had his arm around Corvin's neck, hands clamped together and teeth bared as he held on. The clamp of death they called it back in his old fighter days, one of his signature moves. Once Tyger Joe had an opponent in the clamp it was all over. But Joe had been fully spliced back then, and, however strong he might be now, his fighter days were over.

Corvin crouched and launched himself back and up, slamming Joe into the edge of the first floor walkway with enough force to lessen his grip. Joe hung on, smashing his fist repeatedly into the side of Corvin's head. I heard bone break under the assault, but Corvin didn't seem to notice, going into a whirling pirouette.

"McLeod to Perimeter Team," I said into the comms, raising the Colt and setting it to full-auto. "Lethal force authorised. Load AP."

Corvin screamed in triumph as Joe came free of his neck, flying backwards to impact on a supporting pillar with enough force to bend it. He crumpled at the base of the pillar, trying unsuccessfully to push himself upright as Corvin charged in for the kill.

I sighted on his legs and fired off a full magazine. Anyone else and it would have meant a messy double amputation but this time produced just a cloud of blood and part-denuded muscle mass. But it did succeed in pissing Corvin off enough for him to turn away from Joe and fix on me.

He snarled, crouched, then flinched as more bullets struck him from the right. Leyla and Timor following my example, pistols whooping as they emptied their guns at the monster in the space of one and a half seconds. I slammed in another mag and sighted on Corvin's face, firing shorter bursts now and being rewarded by the sight of his left eye exploding in a blossom of gore.

He howled again and charged for me, uncaring of the renewed barrage from Timor and Leyla.

The first burst of armour piercing caught him ten feet short of where I stood, shredding his spine above the waist and sending him sprawling. Still he tried to get to me, claws digging into the tiles as he dragged himself closer, snarling all the while. The entire Perimeter Team, understandably pissed at their commander's fate, fired at once and Khristopher Corvin, fraudster turned spliced-up murderer, underwent another rapid transformation, from wolfman to vaguely humanoid shaped mound of churned up flesh.

"Suspect down," I said into the comms, running to Joe's side. "Medical assistance required. Priority One."

Joe groaned as I rolled him over, not without difficulty. "Lousy, low-rent bum," he murmured, eyes dimming with the onset of unconsciousness. "Wouldn't have lasted one round with me in the old days…" He drifted off then jerked, eyes widening and fixing me with stern resolve. "You got a date tonight, remember? Don't you be late on my account."

CHAPTER 5

"THE BASIC GENETIC template is the same as the standard werewolf splice mods," Ricci said, the holo above the autopsy table displaying a close-up of Corvin's DNA, double helix glowing red where the mods had been grafted on. "But heavily modified. Greatly increased muscle mass and bone density, as you can probably tell." He gestured at Corvin's corpse, or what was left of it, arranged on the table like a grisly jigsaw puzzle. Despite the damage the basic shape of the rib cage was still discernible, the ribs thick and flat with no gaps in-between. "Like he had a sub-dermal suit of armour," Ricci went on. "Pretty interesting hormone results. Hugely boosted levels of adrenaline and endorphins. He would have been high as a kite the moment the change kicked in, resulting in reduced cognitive ability but I guess that's the trade off if you want to be a genuine lycanthrope."

"A real live shifter," Sherry said, then grimaced at Corvin's remains. "Some myths turn out to be true after all."

"Who could do this?" I asked Ricci. "The cost must be astronomical."

"There is no lab I can find doing anything like it. Or if they are, they aren't publishing their results, which would be nuts because our friend here represents the next stage in splice evolution. I did find a few papers on Rapid Morphological Change, to use the technical term, but they were mostly theoretical.

The only actual experiments were a few animal studies and the results were hardly encouraging."

"Seems somebody had the time and money to figure it out." The silence strung out for a few seconds until Sherry stated the obvious. "Fed Sec. Who else has got the funds, or the motive?"

"Vargold was right," I said. *Payback for Ceres.* But Rybak still bugged me, his listless acceptance of his own death didn't gel with the notion of a Fed Sec assassination. *From light we are born to light we return.*

"What about Corvin's place?" Sherry said. "Any pointers?"

"Disgustingly clean," I said. "Like a hotel room. Would've taken it for unoccupied if the building's security net hadn't confirmed he'd been living there since his release. Kept a rigid routine, only ate ready-meals, hardly any interaction with his neighbours, no attempts to contact former associates, and kept every appointment with his parole officer."

"Sleeper," Sherry said. "Awaiting activation."

"And if there's one…"

"I'll speak to the mayor. Recommend an increase in alert status. And the security for Astravista's top executives will have to be tightened."

"We need to work up a full breakdown of Corvin's activity since his release from the pen. This was done to him sometime in the last six months. The building log has a few extended absences early on. Just a matter of hours but it may have been enough." I raised a questioning eyebrow at Ricci.

He shrugged. "If the process has been perfected, yeah. Splicing in general is a lot more sophisticated these days. A basic makeover won't take up more than an afternoon."

"I also want to take a closer look at Rybak," I told Sherry. "I can't believe he was targeted just because he's Vargold's number two. And the way he just sat there and took it was seriously weird."

She shook her head. "Once I ring the alarm about Fed Sec Arnaud will want this kicked up to CAOS Defence."

"I still have a homicide to investigate here. Not to mention the deaths of five SWAT operators on my watch."

"You caught the killer, Alex. In record time, I might add. It's a security matter now, let Defence run with it. Besides," she held up her smart to display an approval code for a new operation. "I just got authority to sign off on the Mr Mac investigation. Congratulations."

I found Janet waiting at the hospital. "He'll be fine," she said, meeting me at the door to Joe's room. I could see him inside, flat out on the bed with trodes on his chest and head. "Obs only. He's sedated just now. They're going to release him tomorrow."

"Nice of you to come," I said.

"We got close whilst you were off doing whatever you were doing." She reached for my hand and I realised it had retained a slight tremble ever since Dunelm Court. *Well, that's new.* "Pretty bad, huh?" Janet asked, thumb tracing over the back of my hand until the tremble faded.

"Not as bad as the Axis, but bad enough." I looked at Joe again. "Mind if we skip tonight? I don't want to leave him alone. He doesn't have anyone else."

"I'll stay too."

I looked at her hand on mine, thinking about Rapid Morphological Change and the flesh dangling from Corvin's claws. "Promise you won't get pissed if I ask you something?"

"As long as it doesn't involve a list of prior relationships, 'cause I don't think we're quite there yet."

I sighed as she laughed. "What you did, that time with those bots," I said. "And at the Axis." I took hold of her other hand. "What you did with these. I need to know how."

The laugh faded and her face closed up into a neutral alabaster mask. "Like I said," she said, disentangling her hands from mine. "I don't think we're there yet."

"It's important. You're the only other Splice I know of who could do anything remotely like what Corvin could do."

"Curses," she said in an utterly flat tone. "You've uncovered the secret splice conspiracy to take over the Slab and now I must destroy you. Mwahaha."

"A very rich man and, more importantly, five Demons died today, on my orders. I need to account for that. And I need your help to do it."

Her mask softened, but only a little. "It's a long story," she said. "And that's just the edited highlights."

I inclined my head at Joe's unconscious bulk. "We've got all night."

We sat at Joe's bedside, Janet leaning forward in the uncomfortable plastic seats that hospitals seem to specialise in, as if they're worried you're going to hang around the sick people for too long. I couldn't remember seeing her so lacking in humour before, even in the most stressed situations it always seemed her lips were perpetually on the verge of a smile. Now there was only a tense reluctance as she rested her elbows on her knees and clasped her hands together.

"You asked about this once," she said, angling her wrist to display a faint mark in the marble white skin. "Remember?"

"Sure. Eye of Horus."

"Yes. The Eye of Horus, tattooed onto my skin before I could form the memory of it happening. We all had them, the symbols of our intended purpose, our great crusade."

"Crusade?"

"Oh yes. The holy mission that would see the vampire race ascend to its rightful place as overlords of humanity." She met my gaze, her lips forming a barely perceptible grin. "And if you think that all sounds like the rantings of a lunatic, you're absolutely right."

She paused to touch a finger to the mark on her wrist, tracing out the shape. "According to the most common reading of the Egyptian pantheon Horus was the son of Isis and Osiris, a falcon-headed warrior with dominion over war and hunting. And, until the age of sixteen, I believed he was as real as you or me. Vampires, we were told, were the inheritors of the old gods' legacy, heirs to an ancient and long prophesied destiny. Long ago, when the first pyramids rose from the sands, the gods had created vampires to be their vassals on earth, a new, perfected race of people freed from the shackles of death and blessed with great strength and speed. But war soon raged amongst the gods, begun by an alliance between Set, jealous of the newly risen vampire, and Aten, the sun god who hungered to be the only light in the heavens. And so Set and Aten cursed the vampire. Set ordained all food would be denied them and they could feed only on the blood of lesser races, ensuring they were hated and feared for all the ages. But Aten's curse was far worse, for he ordained that the light of the sun would be the curse of the vampire, for he could not abide his light to fall upon creatures so wretched. And so the vampire race passed into shadow. For millennia we remained hidden, reduced to mere legend and fable, but now, in this new age of technology and wonder, we could finally take what had long been denied us. For now a new breed had been born, a breed that could walk in daylight thanks to the blessing of Horus."

She fell silent, lowering her gaze, hands clasped even tighter. "Wondering who told me all this crap, right?"

"I'm guessing whoever they were, they'd been off their meds for a while."

No laugh, just a slight bob of her head. "Father Ra, he called himself. And the hab where I was raised was called Amun-Ra, a celestial vessel gifted by the gods where we would be prepared for our role as holy warriors. When I say 'raised', I should really say 'matured.' Or more accurately, 'conditioned.'" She paused again, glancing up at me. "Objective guess, Alex. How old would you say I am?"

"Nineteen."

She rolled her eyes. "Nice try. I happen to know I appear to be a twenty-five year old woman of Caucasian ethnicity. Which is, in fact, seven years less than my actual age. I have always looked this way and, since all the specialists I've wasted money on over the years tell me a desplicing procedure would probably kill me, I always will. I was made, just like your old friend from the Axis I guess, just a more aesthetically pleasing package. But a freak is still a freak, right?"

I didn't say anything and watched her sorting through memories she'd rather leave buried. "Father Ra told us we were the children of Horus, brought forth by the power of his *heka* to reclaim the vampire birthright. *Heka* is the old Egyptian term for magic, and Father Ra was a great magician. You should have seen this place, Alex. It was like something from an old Cecil B. DeMille epic, monoliths and sphinxes everywhere you looked. Labyrinths full of tricks and traps where we would be schooled in the arts of cunning and stealth. I remember being pretty happy for the first few years, for what child doesn't love to play? I had six sisters, all children of Horus's blessing. We fought and squabbled, as children do, jockeying for status, all desperate for Father Ra's favour. But I always knew he loved me the most, and in time I found out it wasn't a paternal love. But why would I object? He carried the blessing of Horus after all." She let out a short, bitter laugh. "I was honoured by his holy touch."

I gritted my teeth and clamped down on the burgeoning rage. "I hope you're gonna tell me he's dead now."

"Very. But I'm getting ahead of myself. For years we trained, immersion based accelerated language skills, combat, all unarmed of course since no true vampire would defile themselves with human weapons. Then, after what I know now was the better part of a decade, Father Ra made his big mistake. He started teaching us about the world we were created to destroy.

"The world below, he told us, was a festering pit of war, vice and endless misery. And he had plenty of evidence to prove it. Hundreds of hours of vids and immersion sims, giving us a grandstand view of humanity's greatest crimes, all the way from the Roman conquest of Jerusalem to the genocides of the twentieth century and the CAOS war. I have to say it would have been a pretty convincing argument, and it might have worked if Father Ra hadn't made us so smart. I began to notice inconsistencies in the narrative, factual omissions and simplistic explanations. For civilisations to go to war they first had to rise. There were plenty of villains in this story, plenty of destroyers, but where were the heroes, the builders? I knew on some instinctive level that no history could be this dark. You can't have shadow without light, so where was it?

"Naturally, when I voiced my concerns to Father Ra he was less than pleased. Heretic, he called me. Ingrate, malcontent. I needed to be punished. And so my sisters punished me, with the claws and the teeth gifted to us by Horus. I didn't fight them, for I had been commanded not to, and when they were done I was a bleeding, broken wreck. I healed quickly, as vampires do, but I no longer had Father Ra's favour, his attentions now shared equally amongst my sisters. I understand now that he was a man of many delusions, belief in his own infallibility being perhaps the most grievous. Having taught us much of the world below, particularly how to infiltrate it, he couldn't imagine one of us might use those skills against him.

"Hacking into the hab's mainframe wasn't particularly difficult, Father Ra being somewhat lazy when it came to changing pass-codes or updating his security software. A few days work and I had it all. Our home was not a celestial barge crafted by the gods but a converted luxury hab purchased fifteen years before by one Gary Muskovitz, heir to the Muskovitz Industrial Lubricants fortune. Seems he'd fallen in with the spliced vampire crowd in his youth and taken to it with religious zeal, one of the first to embrace full conversion which turned out to be more of a handicap in daily life than he imagined. Being a creature of the night might have some romantic appeal but the reality of never being able to go outside in daylight starts to grind after a while, especially when the world's media is camped outside your mansion and you're a joke in every chat-show host's monologue. A penniless vampire might be able to slip into the shadows, but not a rich one.

"So Gary cashed in the family fortune and came up the well, conceiving a plan that would achieve his grand design of vampire dominion. A sealed hab where he could create whatever reality he chose, and he had enough money to clone himself some acolytes."

She unclasped her hands, flexing the fingers, nails extending and receding. "These were the result of a speculative but substantial investment in a small gene lab in Korea. The UV resistance came from another lab in Mexico. All in all, you could say I'm a billion dollar amalgam."

She straightened, eyes distant with memory, a sad, reflective grimace on her face. "Faith is a very curious thing. Even when confronted with contradictory evidence, the truly faithful, those for whom the indoctrination goes so deep you can never dig it out, will cling to the lies they've been told with fierce devotion. So it proved with my sisters. I laid it all out for them, all the lies, the deceits, the fact that the man who raised us wasn't the High Priest of Amun-Ra but just some delusional rich guy who'd cloned his own harem. Suffice to say, they didn't take it well.

"Punishment would not be enough this time. This time I must be purged from the sight of Father Ra, lest my heresy cause mighty Horus to turn his gaze from us. They wept as they came at me, for they were my sisters after all, and they loved me. I knew I couldn't fight them all, and I knew I couldn't save them. I sometimes think there must have been a mistake in my gestation procedure, some small variation in the genes, within acceptable variables but just enough to make me capable of seeing through Father's lies where my sisters couldn't. So, although they wept, they were still going to rip me into very small pieces. Fortunately, my first experience of Father's wrath had taught me a lesson in the value of contingency.

"I'd coded the mainframe to respond to my voice and told it to perform a hab-wide emergency decompression. I was prepared for it. My sisters weren't. I held onto a support beam whilst they were dragged away and flushed out. I imagine they burned up on re-entry. When atmosphere was restored I discovered Father Ra had managed to save himself by sealing the doors to the inner temple, but I had the override codes.

"The facade had gone by the time I got to him, on his knees, sobbing and flailing about in his silly robes. He begged, pleaded, said he was sick, needed help. I took his hand and led him outside, he tottered along like an obedient child. The hab had a UV screened glass dome over the main concourse, the sun was up and shining bright beyond the glass. I told him to look up then ordered the mainframe to switch off the UV protection. Father didn't so much burn as… disintegrate."

She shrugged. "There isn't much else to say. I found a shuttle in the docking bay and set off for the nearest hab. Father's preparations had provided plenty of IDs capable of fooling a basic police check. I moved around, got an education, volunteered for a med-station when the war started. Not too brave I know, but I felt I'd seen and done enough violence already. Eventually I moved to the Slab where I was just another vampire."

"What happened to the hab?" I asked.

"When I left I ordered the mainframe to purge its memory and discontinue orbit. A military patrol blew it to pieces when it started to skim the atmosphere, worried it might not burn up I guess."

"The name of the Korean lab?"

"Haunai Genetics. They were dissolved over a decade ago, but I guess the former employees could still be around somewhere, happy to sell off some old research."

Or had no choice when Fed Sec came calling.

"Why Janet Vaughn?" I asked.

"The hab's mainframe had extensive files on the women who donated their eggs to the cause. The donor with the closest match to my DNA was called Janet. Vaughn was the name of the lab supervisor." She gave an empty smile. "Mommy and daddy."

Joe stirred a little, rumbling out a groan. We moved to stand on either side of the bed as he snarled a couple of times, the readout on his monitor spiking before slowly returning to normal as a fresh dose of sedative was automatically pushed through his IV.

"Mr Mac," I said to Janet. "Have you thought about it?"

"Sure. Have you thought about helping me with my research?"

"Riviera's gone back to the shipping trade. I can probably wangle an interview. You won't find many vets with a more interesting story."

She nodded. "I can tell how badly you want Mr Mac, Alex. If I do this you promise me he'll make it to trial. I won't help you commit murder."

"Can't promise the impossible. He's not the surrendering type."

"Even so."

She stared into my eyes and I knew she was looking for something, some sign that whatever we were starting here wasn't going to lead her down a path she'd turned her back on years ago. She wanted to know if I was worth the risk.

"He'll break out of any gaol long before he makes it to trial," I said and she laughed.

"Then we'll just catch him again."

CHAPTER 6

THE HOSPITAL STAFF kicked us out somewhere close to midnight. We lingered on the street outside for a time, me not wanting to push it and she enjoying my discomfort. "You'll, uh, find the Mr Mac case file on your smart in the morning," I said. "I'll be briefing my squad around noon. Attendance is optional." "Professional distance?" she asked with an arched eyebrow. "Today has been kinda nuts. I just… It seems like the wrong time…" "Relax." She leaned in and kissed me, letting it linger before drawing back. "You're right. Baby steps until we put Don Corleone in the slammer." She laughed at my bafflement. "Seriously, when this is done we are having the mother of all vid-binges."

I went home. Since my return I'd signed over the Heavenly Garden to Marco and leased the upstairs apartment. He made for a surprisingly good barkeep, I suspected mainly because the patrons mistook his patient reticence for a sympathetic ear. In reality, the lobotomy had left him incapable of boredom. Although the closed sign was on I found a customer at the bar, a tall, slim man in a surprisingly inexpensive raincoat. His long dark hair shifted to reveal aquiline features as he turned to greet me with an apologetic smile. "Chief Inspector. Sorry for the intrusion, and the lateness of the hour."

"Mr Vargold." I moved to the bar, shaking my head as Marco

pointed to the Kentucky Red, a long conditioned habit he'd yet to break. "Ginger and lime," I said. "Then get to bed. I'll lock up."

When he had gone I sipped my booze-free drink and glanced around at the empty bar. "I see you share Mr Rybak's aversion to personal security."

"Actually, thanks to Chief Mordecai I was obliged to double the size of my close-protection detail today. They're maintaining a discreet distance. I wanted to talk in private."

"I don't do off the record. You should know that."

"Noted, and accepted. Nevertheless, I believe I have pertinent information to share."

"My boss has already handed the case off to CAOS Defence. It's not my province anymore."

"And is that really going to stop you?"

Five seconds in and already he knows me too well. "What's on your mind?"

"The man who killed Craig, and your colleagues, it's a fair assumption that he wasn't alone. There may well be others just like him, all waiting for a signal to wreak havoc. But I'd guess you already figured that out. It was one of Fed Sec's favourite tactics in the war, as I recall. Long-term infiltration with a view to striking a sufficiently fatal blow at the heart of the resistance. Now it's starting all over again."

"The war's over. At least the real one. Now it's all strictly cold war. It's hardly bloodless, but the UN knows the consequences if the stakes are raised too high. We hold the high ground after all."

"Whilst they hold most of the money." He turned back to the bar, face sombre as he tapped fingers against a shot-glass of bourbon and ice. "And let us not forget the governance of the planet beneath us is in the hands of those who have never baulked at murder. Nor have they always been so discriminating. We went to war for a reason, as I'm sure you recall." He lifted the shot glass. "Sure you won't join me?"

"Haven't touched the stuff for almost a year, and I find I don't miss it." I paused as he drank, looking close to gauge his reaction. "From light we are born to light we return."

He gave me a blank look before glancing around the bar. "Is that a recognition code I'm supposed to know?" he asked in a mock conspiratorial whisper.

"Rybak's last words. Wondered if it meant anything."

"Very little of what Craig said over the last few weeks made much sense at all." He took another sip before setting his glass down. "You're wondering why he was targeted. I mean, why go to the bother of killing a mentally ill man whose days as an active part of Astravista were clearly numbered?" He took a smart from the pocket of his raincoat and placed it on the bar. "Craig's comms data for the past year. My security people flagged an issue a few days ago. Sadly, thanks to the Ad Astra project, I hadn't had time to look over the report before today. The relevant messages are highlighted."

I picked up the smart and called up the two messages outlined in red. The first was dated seven months ago and read:

From: Sal Morely - Univek PLC

To: Craig Rybak, H.O. Astravista

Subject: Cayman Structure

Craig,

Happy to report the Cayman structure is close to completion. Let me know if you need to discuss.

Best,

Sal

The second message was from the same source, with an identical subject line and dated six weeks later, reading simply: 'Structure now live. Best, Sal.'

"Cayman structure?" I asked Vargold.

"Corporate accountancy term," he said. "The Cayman Islands have a long-standing and widely appreciated attitude to international tax law. Comes in handy when you want to shift funds between various subsidiaries without troubling the major Downside revenue authorities. It was the kind of thing Craig dealt with all the time."

"So where's the problem?"

"Univek PLC, which I must admit I'd never heard of before today, is one of several companies established by Craig purely for the purposes of handling our Downside financial arrangements. It has no real assets, just a company registration in the Caymans and a short list of employees, Sal Morely being the registered Director. The problem is that I issued a company directive two years ago forbidding any further use of Downside tax havens like the Caymans. We were getting a lot of grief in the media about our relatively small contribution to the global economy. Since the majority of Astravista's profits are generated in the orbital sector, I didn't see throwing a few billion at the various tax authorities as a steep price to pay for some positive publicity."

"So Rybak was acting against your orders."

"It seems so. He may have had a good reason, some unexpected cash flow issue maybe. But it doesn't gel with the way he did business. Craig was all about the audit. Then there's the mysterious Mr Morley. After looking this over I placed a call to the offices of Univek PLC. The young lady who picked up was very upset. Seems Mr Morely perished in a para-gliding accident only yesterday. There's a police report on the smart if you'd care to take a look."

"Fed Sec," I said, thumbing through the stills of a portly

middle-aged corpse being pulled from the ocean. "Cleaning house."

"Or a massively unfortunate coincidence."

"You think Rybak was selling you out?"

"No. I think they got to him somehow. Blackmail, threat, I don't know. But the Craig Rybak I knew would never have willingly betrayed me. We practically grew up together."

Vargold set his drink aside and turned to face me, all business now. "I've dealt with CAOS Defence many times, and they don't particularly impress me. Not the way you do. Three hours in and you take down Craig's assassin. It's nice to have my faith vindicated."

"I have another case…"

"I'm sure you do. But I'm also sure you're used to working more than one investigation at a time. I know your superiors have handed this on, and I also know you have no intention of letting it drop. I am here merely to restate what I told you this morning; the resources of my company are at your disposal."

He got down from the barstool and nodded at the smart. "Keep that. It has my private contact ID, something known to only four other people in the solar system, so use it well." He started towards the door then stopped. "I've chosen a name, by the way. For the ship. The Astravista *Jason Alpha*."

"Jason?"

"As in the argonauts."

"Oh right. Medea's boyfriend."

"Amongst other things. I'm sure Dr Vaughn can enlighten you." He smiled and made his exit.

My gaze went to the drink he left on the bar. *A gift, or a test?* I went behind the bar and carefully poured the remaining bourbon back into the bottle. Marco couldn't afford the wastage. Before going to bed I ran a search for Rybak's last words through the comms data on the smart Vargold had given me. It came up not found.

CHAPTER 7

"OUR TARGET'S NAME is John Cameron McAllister." Mr Mac's handsome head revolved in the centre of the squad room, the hol shimmering a little as I walked through it, eyes intent on the assembled Demons and analysts. "Aged forty-one. Graduated aged twenty-three with first class honours in Business Studies from Lorenzo City University, Yin Faculty. Aged twenty-nine he turned his back on a life of privilege and luxury to join Covert Ops during the war. Three commendations for bravery and thirty-two confirmed kills. Deserted shortly before the Langley Raid. These days he's better known as Mr Mac, and if any of you haven't heard of him you're in the wrong job. I won't list the known and suspected offences, since we don't have all day. Suffice to say, chances are this is the biggest case you will ever work. This piece of shit has been allowed to run free for way too long. I want him, and you better want him too because none of us will rest until he's in a cage."

I turned and pointed to Janet. She gave a tentative wave as all eyes swung to her. "This is Dr Vaughn, our Special Investigator. She answers only to me and has full access to all case records. Anything she wants, she gets. I hope that's understood because I'm not fond of repeating myself." I scanned the audience, searching for any sign of anti-splice prejudice, finding none which probably just meant most of them were good at concealing their bigotry.

"OK," I went on, replacing Mr Mac's head with a scrolling

time-line. "Intel on Mr Mac slowed to a trickle eight months ago. We know he spent much of the preceding year winning a war against the Arturo Cartel which consolidated his grip on the Upside Bliss trade. Since then all we have are rumours, which may indicate he's enjoying the fruits of victory. Luckily the war gave us an in. Don Arturo's body still hasn't been found but rumour has it he was nailed to a recently harvested asteroid and thrown into a smelter still alive. After that his organisation went to pieces. Some capos tried to settle the hatchet with Mr Mac, which turned out to be a fatal miscalculation. He doesn't do peace treaties. We know a few capos are still around and in hiding. Mr Mac will be looking for them which means we are too. Leyla, Timor, I want you working this angle. There's a list of surviving Arturo goons on your smarts. When you find a live one, sit on him. We'll put a subtle but enticing clue to his locale through the snitch network and grab whoever Mr Mac sends to finish the job."

Leyla nodded, gaze bright and keen with anticipation. Promise of involvement in a major case like this was how I'd lured her away from the Robbery Squad. "Will do, boss. But whoever we grab isn't going to talk. Mr Mac's people never do."

I glanced at Janet who gave an uncertain grin. "Hopefully, that won't be an issue anymore," I said. "The rest of you, it's time to start grinding. Every intel report ever filed on Mr Mac will need to be re-examined. I want every bank account, address, contact ID mapped and cross-reffed. Look for nexus points, times when his people got sloppy and used the same smart twice. Mr Mac's careful, but no one is infallible. Find me a way in." I paused, making sure I met every pair of eyes in turn. "What happens to lazy Demons?" I asked.

"Lazy Demons fuck off and find another job," they all intoned as one.

"You'll find assignments on your stations. Get to it."

"He likes old stuff," I told Janet as she scribbled notes on a pad, using an actual pen and actual paper. I wondered why since she seemed incapable of forgetting anything. "Art, antiques, old books. Every time he moves base he takes his collection with him. I thought maybe this was something for you. The past is more your thing than mine."

"Classical history isn't art history," she said. "But there is some crossover, and I have plenty of academic friends who can help. Does he have a favourite period? Renaissance, Romantic, Expressionist?" I saw her suppress a sigh at my baffled expression. "How old would you say his collection is?"

"Dunno. Only saw it once. Looked pretty old. Downside stuff, paintings and sculptures."

"I'll need details. Describe one thing as best you can."

I thought back to the last time I'd been face to face with Mr Mac, in his office on Yang Thirty-Three when he set me on the path that ended in Choi's death. The memory had a tendency to stir dark impulses and it was a few moments before I suppressed them enough to form a clear image of the various objets d'art.

"There was a statue on his desk," I said. "Bronze. Some Jed in rags with a noose around his neck. Think he was holding something."

Janet blinked and pulled her aged smart from the pocket of her combats. "Can't be," she muttered, running a hasty search. "This it?" she asked, holding out the smart to display a 2D.

"Looks the same," I said, peering at the shiny figure. I could see that the object in his hands was a large key. "You know it?"

"The *Jean d'Aire Second Maquette*," she said. "One of Rodin's early studies for the Burghers of Calais. Stolen from the Brooklyn Museum of Art half a century ago. The UN Arts Council has a three million UA reward for information on its whereabouts."

"Then I guess it fits the bill. Somewhere to start at least."

"I'll get on it." She rose and went to the door. "Oh, your lady Demon, Leyla something Irish."

"O'Keefe. What about her?"

"She's in love with you." She smiled as she closed the door. "Thought you should know."

The analyst seemed tiny next to Joe, her head barely reaching his bicep, and depressingly young into the bargain. "This is Athena," Joe said and I noticed how he had to usher her into the office. "From Imaging Analysis."

"Sir," she said, clearly fighting a stammer. "Chief Inspector, I mean. Uh, boss," she added, voice dropping into a whisper.

"What have you got?" I asked. We were five hours in without much to show. I'd been replaying every vid and still capture of Mr Mac, a visual record that lasted all of six minutes and thirty-two seconds. An ability to avoid surveillance was one of his more aggravating gifts.

"Um, a sister," she blurted, thrusting her smart at me. "Mr Mac's sister."

"He doesn't have any siblings," I said.

"He does. I think... I know. I mean, I'm pretty certain."

I glanced at Joe who said, "Athena, why don't you take the Chief Inspector through it from the beginning."

"OK." She began to fiddle with her smart, connecting to my terminal display and calling up the earliest known image of Mr Mac in adulthood. "From his graduation ceremony at Lorenzo U.," she said. "The younger the face, the better the recognition algorithms like it, can get a clearer fix on the underlying bone structure. Joe, uh, Inspector Martell asked me to concentrate on Mr Mac's Yin-side days. I came up with nothing we didn't already know on the first pass so I started playing around with the parameters. Sometimes the search gear misses things if there's a distorted or corrupted image. This time I got a hit."

She displayed another image, an adolescent girl holding hands with a woman in her thirties, presumably her mother. They stood smiling outside the gate to some Yin-side mansion. The woman wore a uniform of some kind with her name stitched into the fabric. *Lena.* At first glance I didn't find it particularly convincing. They were both dark haired whilst Mr Mac came from a long line of blondies, however, the set of the girl's eyes was definitely familiar.

"Comes up as a forty-three percent match when the disparate age factor is taken into account," Athena said. "But once I ran a check for familial similarity…" She hit an icon on her smart and a new readout flashed on screen, 'Likelihood of familial relationship: 89%.'

"Who is she?" I said.

"Oksana Lenova," Athena said. "Aged thirteen when this was taken according to the time-stamp on the image, which would make her thirty-three now. It was posted to her smart-wall with the caption 'Me and mama at work.' I ran a check on the mansion…"

"McAllister Towers, right?" I broke in.

"Well, officially it's called Villa Splendido, but it was owned by McAllister Enterprises. Sold off when Mr Mac's father died six years ago…"

"DNA match on the girl?"

"She has no criminal record so her bio-data is sealed. But given everything else… I mean, seems pretty, um, obvious, y'know."

I stared at her until she blushed and looked away.

"Relax," I told her, getting up and reaching for my coat. "I'm sold. This is fine work. You got an address for Miss Wrong Side of the Blankets?"

"She's still living Yin-side. Cormorant Apartments, Yin-Twelve. Divorced, no kids. No job either as far as I can tell."

"Makes me wonder who's paying the bills." I turned to Joe. "Keep an eye on things here. Dr Vaughn and I will go see if the prodigal bro's been in touch recently."

CHAPTER 8

"TRUST ME. A woman knows these things."

"Can we just do this, please?"

Janet moderated her grin as I pressed the buzzer on the door to Oksana Lenova's apartment. Our IDs had got us past the concierge downstairs, but access to her home would need to be voluntary in the absence of a warrant. She lived in the Cormorant Apartments penthouse suite, a place that I calculated would have cost about a thousand times my annual salary. She answered the door promptly enough, presumably forewarned by the concierge. I knew Athena had been spot on the moment I saw her face, pretty much a feminine version of Mr Mac with slightly higher cheekbones. She was dressed casually in a loose shirt and slacks, cool gaze switching from my ID to Janet's without much of a reaction, though I noticed how pale her knuckles were as she held the door open.

"Ms Lenova?"

She gave a slow nod.

"My name is Chief Inspector Alex McLeod, Lorenzo City PD. This is my colleague, Dr Janet Vaughn. May we speak to you, please?"

I saw her knuckles whiten further at the mention of my name before she released the door and stepped back, voice faint as she said, "Sure."

The penthouse was all open plan, three tiers of comfort and luxury surrounded by a glass wall affording views of the parks and lakes that characterised the mid Yins. She led us to a couch and gestured for us to sit, though she remained standing with her arms crossed and her back to the view.

"You have a beautiful home," Janet told her.

Oksana Lenova inclined her head at the compliment before turning to me. She started to speak, stopped to clear her throat then tried again. "Is he dead?"

I didn't bother asking who she meant, realising this was a moment she'd been expecting for a long time. "Why would you ask that?" I asked instead.

"He said if you ever appeared on my doorstep it would probably be to tell me he was dead."

"It seems he was wrong. As far as I know he's still very much alive. Though I would like to talk to him."

"Arrest him, you mean."

"He has done some terrible things, ma'am. Or didn't you know that?"

She crossed her arms tighter and turned to face the view, raising her gaze to the faux-sky above. Yin Twelve featured a holo array in its ceiling programmed to render blue skies and clouds throughout daylight hours. At night it would gradually fade to a starlit sky. Like a lot of things about life this side of the Axis, I found the sheer pointless expense of the thing disgusting.

"I know he has lived outside the law for many years," she said. "He hasn't provided details and I have never asked."

"But you are aware of his fugitive status?"

She didn't turn. "Do I need a lawyer?"

"You worry for your brother, don't you, Ms Lenova?" Janet interjected, all kindly sincerity, voice pitched to a soothing tone. "The constant dangers of his life. It wears on you, I see that."

Oxana's mouth curled a little in amused dismissal as she

glanced over her shoulder at Janet. "I already have a therapist, thank you."

"We haven't advised you of your rights," I told her. "Anything you tell us is inadmissible as evidence."

"And I assume that'll change if I refuse to talk to you." I didn't say anything and watched her head sag a little. "He said when you eventually turned up to tell you everything I knew. I could trust you, he said."

"He was right about that."

She turned and moved to an armchair, settling into as relaxed a posture as she could, arms on the rests and legs crossed. "What do you want to know?"

"When was your last contact with your brother?"

"Six months ago. He sent me a birthday gift, something he's done every year since our father died."

"What was it, this gift?"

She nodded to something behind me and I turned to regard a row of framed paintings on the wall. Janet rose from the couch and went to take a look, issuing small gasps of surprised delight as she checked each one in turn. "Charles Rennie Mackintosh," she said, glancing back at Oksana. "Original watercolour designs, if I'm not mistaken."

"I'm a student of design," the woman replied. "John is always very thoughtful in his gifts."

"These are exquisite," Janet said, returning her gaze to the pictures.

"And stolen?" I asked.

"Certainly not," Oksana snapped. "Each one was legally bought at auction. I have bills of sale and provenance for each picture."

"I'm guessing dear old John didn't deliver these by hand," I said.

"They always arrive by special courier. I haven't seen him in person for nearly three years."

"I'll need an exact date and location for the meeting. And details of how it was arranged."

"It wasn't. Whenever I see him he just turns up unannounced. I was having a cappuccino at a cafe in Yasmin Park and there he was." A fond smile played over her lips. "'Sorry it's been a while, sis,' he said. We spoke about… nothing that would interest you, I'm sure. It was shortly after my divorce, I think he was worried about me."

"The circumstances of the divorce," I said. "Would you say it was ugly?"

"What divorce isn't? My husband and I had been distant from each other for years. The separation was amicable enough, though it didn't feel that way at the time."

"Was your husband ever abusive?"

"No." She angled her head at me, eyes narrowing. "You seem to be asking me the same questions he did, Inspector. And to anticipate your line of enquiry, to the best of my knowledge my ex-husband is alive and well. He remarried and took up an executive position with a Downside bank a year ago."

I glanced around at the penthouse. "The settlement pay for all this?"

"There was no financial settlement. At my late father's insistence, my husband signed a very binding pre-nup."

"You inherited your father's wealth?"

"Half of it, yes. The remainder, the half that would have been John's, went to various charities."

"I hate to be indelicate, ma'am, but the circumstances of your birth…"

"My mother met my father whilst working as a maid in his home," she said in a tone that was equal parts defiant and defensive. "They loved each other very much. He was unable to extricate himself from his marriage to John's mother for various reasons, both business and personal. Her family were very well connected politically."

"When did John find out about you?"

"I don't recall a time when he didn't know. We were practically raised together. Mama loved him like a son, you see. Mrs McAllister wasn't around much, her career always came first. On the surface it may appear sordid and tawdry, a rich man keeping his mistress and child a secret for so long, whilst they live under his roof no less. But I grew up in a happy home, Inspector. I wanted for nothing, had a family that loved me and ensured I had an excellent education. John went off to university then took an executive position in McAllister Industries, and Papa fully expected me to follow him. The future was bright for both of us. Then the war started."

She fell silent, her face clouding with sadness. "He told me you were comrades, you fought side by side."

"We did, for a time."

"Did he ever tell you why? What made him run off to join the resistance?"

Because he enjoyed killing, I didn't say. *A slumming rich kid with a license to slaughter.* It was apparent that the Mr Mac I knew was not the rarely seen brother she loved. "No," I said instead. "He hardly spoke about his past."

"You remember how it all started? The event that led to the formation of the UN Orbital Intervention Force and allowed Federal Security to declare martial law."

"The Seven Hells."

"Yes. Aptly named, weren't they?"

She had that right. Seven simultaneous atrocities committed on the most populous habs in orbit. For once the Yin levels had gotten the worst of it, a Sarin gas cloud pumped into the ventilation systems of Yin Nineteen to Twenty-Two. Four hundred people died and two thousand more suffered permanent impairment. By any rational metric, the war started that day.

"Mama and Papa were holidaying at his lodge in the Yin Nineteen forest park," Oksana went on. "Mama... died instantly.

Papa spent the better part of a year in intensive care. John…"
She gave a helpless shrug. "John went crazy. UNOIF were quick
to blame separatist terrorists, of course, but everyone knew that
was a lie. John told me to take care of papa and disappeared. I
didn't see him again for four years."

"Did he tell you he deserted? Just before the Langley Raid.
He was supposed to be running overwatch for my team. The
operative who replaced him was cut in half by a tactical laser."

"He told me his flirtation with ideology was over. He had…
other interests these days. I know he felt regret, especially about
your wife. But he also said his many brushes with death had
cured him of any suicidal impulses." She met my gaze squarely.
"He also said you were most likely going to kill him one day. He
protected you because he wanted a friend to be the one who
pulled the trigger."

"I am not his friend." I glanced over at Janet, now scanning
the McIntosh watercolours with her smart. "Got it all?"

"Oh yes."

I rose from the couch. I could have kept at it for hours, pushing until she spilt something useful, but somehow knew it would
be a fruitless exercise. I'd put a surveillance team on her in the
unlikely event Mr Mac turned up again. Also probably pointless; he'd know I'd been here and darling sis was now off limits.

"You won't be seeing him again," I said. "Unless it's via a
visiting room window."

She stared up at me, eyes moist now. "You know he won't let
that happen."

"I do."

"He's a bad man. I know he has done awful and unforgiv-
able things. But I've never been able to hate him." She blinked
and a tear traced down her familiar cheekbone. "I guess we have
that in common, Inspector."

CHAPTER 9

"SHE WASN'T LYING," Janet said, reading her smart. "About the Mackintoshes. All purchased at public auction in the last decade. Anonymous bidder in every case, as you might expect."

I nodded, saying nothing and watching the cartoon playing out on the tunnel wall beyond the pipe carriage window. The Yin-side pipe network had hand-drawn animation cells every ten yards so that as the carriage streaked by the passengers were treated to a comic vignette or two. This one was vaguely recognisable, a recreation of some ancient 2D in which a cat and a mouse were locked in endless slapstick conflict, some of it insanely violent. *Is that how he sees us?* I wondered as the cat took yet another mallet to the head. *Me chasing around after him forever. The cunning mouse always out-thinking the dumb but relentless cat.*

"She wasn't entirely honest though," Janet went on. "About the amicable divorce, I mean."

"Hubby turned up dead after all?"

"No, but court records show he contested the pre-nup, on grounds of mental cruelty inflicted by his wife's continual and flagrant adultery. Seems Oksana wasn't shy about pursuing her recreational activities. Rich people get bored, I guess. Weird thing is, hubby drops his suit only two days after filing it and quickly finds himself a job down the well."

"Big bro looking out for little sis. I doubt she asked him to."

"For a psychopathic personality he seems to have a bit of a sentimental streak."

"Yeah, and I once arrested a multiple rapist who was very nice to his pet parakeet. Sentimentality doesn't mean shit."

My smart buzzed out the urgent chirp of a Department call, Leyla's ID flashing on the screen. "Yeah?" I said, ignoring Janet's grin.

"Struck lucky with the goon hunt, boss," Leyla said. "Found Ignacio Fuentes holed up in a laundry on Yang Six. The owner snitched him out, think he's tired of the pizza boxes piling up."

"Good. I'll have a covert surveillance team there in an hour. Get Timor to put it out, his snitch network's better than mine. Besides, if it comes from me Mr Mac will know it's a set-up."

"OK. One other thing. The Rybak case, that phrase you wanted me to research."

"You got something?"

"No firm point of origin but it did flag up on a Downside homicide this AM. Mass shooting on one of those aquatic habs. Looks pretty nasty, over a dozen killed. The local Demons took the perp down. I'm linking to a vid that captured the whole thing. He's shouting the same thing Rybak said just before Corvin did his wolfman act."

From light we are born to light we return.

"I'm thinking some kind of murder cult," Leyla was saying. "Buncha loons get together on the net and plan the ultimate killing spree. If so, we'll see more of these."

"It's a possibility," I said. "Leave it with me. Concentrate on Fuentes."

"Sure. But promise me I'll be lead when we work this other thing."

I heard Janet suppress a giggle and said, "Not in the promises game, Inspector. Get to work."

I placed a Pol-net contact request to the lead investigator on the Downside killing spree and glanced up to see Janet's reflection in the carriage window, still giggling.

Riviera had named her the *Aguila*, a title that didn't quite match her appearance. She was a converted military surplus Samson Class freighter, bulked out with enlarged plasma nacelles and an expanded cargo bay that did little to enhance her brutally functional looks. Riviera had cashed in his entire savings portfolio to buy her, even then he only managed to meet the asking price thanks to a loan from yours truly. It wasn't an entirely altruistic gesture; I had a favour to ask at the time.

"Still can't get used to it," Lucy said, greeting me at the cargo bay ramp with a warm hug before drawing back, frowning as she scanned my face. "Admit it, you were way hotter as a scumbag."

"This is Janet," I said, stepping back. "Janet, meet Lucy, pilot and first mate of the *Aguila*."

"So I finally get to meet the missus, huh?" Lucy ignored Janet's hand to give her a hug of her own.

"Not quite," Janet told her, offering a sympathetic smile as Lucy released her. "Sorry for your loss. Ceres must have been a terrible experience for all involved."

"It's OK," I told Lucy as she frowned, unsure of how to respond. She had been left in absolutely no doubt about the consequences of ever speaking about Ceres. "She does that." I nodded at the open cargo bay. "He in?"

"'Course." She turned and started up the ramp, gesturing for us to follow. "He hardly ever leaves the ship when we're in dock."

"It's all over." Riviera had taken on a few additional mods since Janet last met him, sturdier prosthetics to cope with life outside the forgiving micro-grav of the Axis and a miniature lidar array grafted onto his sonar eye-implants so he could see in vacuum.

It was all second-hand tech, a couple of years behind the state-of-the-art, making him resemble a human personification of his ship; a patched up old warhorse refusing to retire. He sat at the flight-engineer's station in the *Aguila's* cramped bridge, miniature soldering iron in hand and one of his legs in his lap as he tinkered with a servo on the knee joint.

"Over and done, years ago," he went on, barely glancing up. "What good will raking it up do?"

"History is the greatest teacher," Janet replied. "If people truly understand what happened perhaps they can avoid the same mistakes. Future generations…"

"Future generations will wonder why a bunch of *primativas* went to war over a collection of floating scrap iron. People are already forgetting. Ask her." He jerked his head at Lucy. "Doesn't know shit about the war and doesn't want to."

"I know enough," Lucy muttered, turning back to the hatchway. "Gonna check the plasma relays."

"I did that this morning," Riviera snapped.

"Then I really do need to check them." She swung herself onto the ladder and climbed out of view.

"Colonel," Janet said. "You have a unique perspective on the major events of the war. Some accounts credit you with ensuring a CAOS victory…"

"Victory?" He rasped out a laugh, smoke rising from a small patch of solder. "That what it was?"

Janet started to speak again, falling silent as I touched her shoulder with a slight shake of the head. "Lucy working out OK?" I asked him, drawing a suspicious scowl.

"Well enough."

"Bullshit. She's the best pilot on the Slab and you know it, earning less than half the salary she could be if she had any idea how valuable her skill-set is. How is business, anyway? Whilst I'm here I should really get a detailed report on my investment."

He stared up at me, the lidar on his sonar array blinking

on and off, presumably as the targeting system responded to an increased adrenaline level. Securing Lucy a berth had been part of the reason for my loan, the other was knowing how much being in my debt would piss him off.

After a few seconds his lidar stopped blinking and he turned to Janet, growling his assent.

"I'll leave you to it," I said, making for the hatch.

"She seems nice."

"She is."

I watched Lucy tap a code into a readout on the main plasma reservoir, issuing a soft tut of disapproval at the results. "He still thinks point 92 efficiency is good enough," she said. "Wouldn't last long in the Belt with an attitude like that."

"How's school?" I asked. She'd been taking online courses recently, trying to get a General Education Certificate, the precursor to obtaining a full pilot's license rather than the provisional one she held just now. The immunity deal I'd negotiated for her included a proviso that she remain on the grid and free of any criminal activity.

"Boring as shit, for the most part." She moved on to the CO_2 tank that powered the secondary thrusters. "Like the sciencey and engineering stuff though. Got an A on my last physics exam. Guess there's something to be said for growing up around fusion reactors."

"That's good. Once you get your GEC you can start looking for a proper job."

"I like it here. He's a mean old doofus, but he lets me get on with piloting this tub around. Plus I haven't killed anyone in well over a year."

"I met Othin Vargold yesterday, case I'm working on. Says they've finally got a name for the big kahuna."

"Yeah?" She looked up from the CO_2 readout, eyes suddenly bright with interest. Like many in her line of work she had a keen interest in Astravista's grand design.

"The *Jason Alpha*. It's from Greek myth."

She snorted. "That's all kinds of dull."

"Yeah, I thought so too."

"You buddy buddies with Vargold now?"

"Hardly."

"So no chance of wangling me a job with Astravista?"

"Thought you liked it here."

"For now. But a girl's gotta think of her future."

"Get your GEC and I'll see what I can do."

Lucy pouted and turned back to the readout. "She'll be on her way to Proxima Centauri by then."

"At relativistic speeds. We'll all be dead and gone by the time she gets back."

"No offence, Alex, but it's a price worth paying. First ship to travel to another star. I mean, come on."

"It's just a star. No Earth-like planets in orbit. No second eden."

"Who needs Earth? We're a space-faring species now. As long as there's a load of asteroids to bust up into habs and fuel, we can live anywhere."

My smart buzzed with a Pol-net ID and I climbed back down to the cargo bay to answer it. "DCI McLeod, right?" the female voice on the other end asked.

"That's me."

"Phaedra Diallo, Salacia Security." Salacia was the aquatic hab where the mass killing went down.

"Thanks for the call," I said. "I guess you must be pretty busy right now."

"Forensic just started. We don't have our own team so they had to be airlifted in from Bermuda. You got something for me?"

"Possibly. It may seem tenuous but there could be a link between your perp and one we took down yesterday."

"He a mass-shooting maniac like our guy?" The words might be flippant but I could hear the tension in her voice, an octave or two short of outright shock. Massacres have a tendency to do that to people.

"No, he was a splice, a shifter actually."

"Thought they were a myth."

"This Jed was all too real. We lost five of our people taking him down. He was wanted for the murder of Craig Rybak. That mean anything to you?"

"Sounds familiar. Some Upside rich guy, right?"

"He was the co-founder of Astravista."

"No shit. Can't see any immediate link here. I mean our guy wasn't a splice. We're still working up a full ID. He was a recent arrival, so we don't have a complete picture yet, but it's clear he's no one special. Just a loon who got up this morning and decided to wander around the main Salacia concourse killing people with a speargun."

"Your SWAT take him down?"

"We don't have SWAT. We have me and three other full time officers. *I* took him down."

First kill, I deduced, noting the shrill note she did well to moderate before it transformed into a sob. "He was shouting something on the vid I saw," I said. "'From light we are born...'"

"'To light we return.' Yeah. What about it?"

"Rybak said exactly the same thing just before he was killed."

A short pause. "Shit."

"Yeah. Do you have any idea what it means?"

"Right now, I'm not sure I could remember my own smart ID."

She's no Demon, I decided. *Just an unlucky rent-a-cop.* "I'm sending you our case file. I'd be grateful if you could look it over when you get the chance, cross ref with whatever your forensic team comes up with."

"Will do. Guess you expect me to reciprocate, huh?"

"As long as it doesn't conflict with local law. I know the aquatic habs have some pretty strict disclosure statutes."

"Screw that. You can have it all. It'll take a few hours though." She paused, a heavy sigh coming over the smart. "Two separate murders linked by the same phrase. Some sort of Polnet alert seems appropriate."

"I'll take care of it. You've got enough on your plate."

"Appreciated. And if you wanna come down here and run this thing, you're more than welcome."

"Been down the well only once in my entire life. It was more than enough."

CHAPTER 10

I LEFT JANET with Riviera. They'd been talking for nearly three hours without pause and the interview showed no signs of ending soon. I couldn't remember him speaking so much at one time, but it seemed once she'd tapped the vein of his experience he couldn't shut up. I took the pipe to Yang Six, spending the time putting together a Pol-net alert about the two potentially linked homicides and warning of possible copy-cats. I knew it would probably earn a sharp rebuke from Sherry once it flashed on her terminal, I was stepping pretty heavily on the toes of CAOS Defence after all, but my Demon instinct told me this case was far from over. Amongst many flaws, an inability to tolerate unfinished business had always been my biggest.

Leyla and Timor were holed up in the upstairs store room of a defunct Immersion arcade. The recently launched MEC Immersion headband had, after some unfortunate initial publicity, finally made affordable, wearable immersion gear a reality, meaning all the hardcore gamers and porn-addicts could now safely waste their lives in the privacy of their own homes. A growing number of boarded up arcades was the most visible consequence, along with increased rates of obesity and sedentary lifestyle-related illnesses.

"All quiet, Boss," Timor said as I peered at his camera screen, the lens trained on the laundry opposite. It was titled the

Santa Isabella Cleaning Emporium, Vintage Clothing a Speciality. Modern fabrics don't need a great deal of cleaning, but a lot of the splice groups tended to favour more archaic garments. Vampirism in particular had seen an upsurge in the lace and leather trade.

"Word went out just over four hours ago," Timor went on.

"How many informants?" I asked.

"Just one. My best, and most discreet."

"Wonder who he'll send," Leyla said, sitting with her back to the wall as she checked her carbine.

Would've been Nina Laredo in the old days, I knew. *If he really wanted to make sure.* But Nina was dead thanks to me, and if she was still around I doubted even Janet could have gotten anything out of her. I just had to hope her replacement was of a more flexible mindset.

"Got anything to eat?" I asked.

I sat in the corner eating boil-in-the-box noodles and going through the responses to my Pol-net alert, which consisted of the usual ads from private security firms and a lengthy message from a sheriff's deputy in Idaho Territory insisting the two attacks were the work of 'The International Jew-Nazi Cabal.' Nice to know some things don't change. Phaedra Diallo had also sent through the preliminary forensic report on the massacre along with a list of victims. The perp had been named as one Randall Schiffler, age twenty-two. No registered employment but initial checks showed a healthy balance in his financial accounts. He'd arrived on Salacia Hab only three days before, let out a mid-range apartment at what I would have considered an exorbitant rent and purchased a top of the range Nike speargun from a sporting goods store. The speargun had an innovative magnetically driven firing mechanism and a magazine capacity of twenty darts. Schiffler had managed to kill thirteen people before Phaedra put a bullet through his forehead from fifty yards. For a first kill made under extreme pressure it was an impressive shot. Preliminary research showed no link between Schiffler and any of the victims and he had no criminal record. The only tangible link to Rybak's murder was the phrase.

Lacking other leads I mentally reviewed Janet's story and began a search for ex-employees of Haunai Genetics, coming up empty which was weird. Also, the company's registration details appeared to have been purged of personnel data. A quick open source check was similarly fruitless, which was even weirder. I thought for a moment before uttering a soft curse, pulling Vargold's smart from my pocket and calling the only number in the ID file. He answered within ten seconds.

"Inspector. Good to hear from you."

"Your offer still good?"

"Of course."

"Haunai Genetics, registered in Korea over three decades ago. I need to find any former employees, particularly the research staff. All my checks are negative. I thought, given your links to the Downside corporate sector…"

"Leave it with me. You'll have details on every employee within twenty-four hours."

"Thank you."

"I suppose asking how this links to Craig is pointless."

"To be honest, I'm not sure it does, yet anyway. There was something else, a mass shooting on Salacia Hab this morning. Maybe you saw it on the feeds."

"I did. You think there may be a connection?"

"I think what happened to your friend could be part of something way bigger. Or we're looking at the mother of all coincidences."

I noticed Timor shift, eyes snapping to the camera screen and head cocked as he listened to something in his ear-piece.

"Gotta go, Mr Vargold," I said. "Thanks for the help."

I shut down the smart and moved to Timor's side. "Surveillance team has someone approaching the premises," he said, then grunted a disappointed sigh. "Pizza guy, again."

I called up the feed from the surveillance team's main camera, seeing a skinny figure slouching along the neighbouring street with two pizza boxes. "Same guy as the last time," Timor said. "Bet it's the same toppings too. Fuentes really needs to reconsider his life choices."

"He showed up twice in less than seven hours?" I asked.

"Laundry owner says Fuentes is kind've a compulsive eater, 'specially when he's nervous."

"Gold One to Gold Three," I said, addressing the surveillance team leader. "Intercept. Check those boxes. Extreme caution advised."

"Acknowledged."

I watched as the pizza guy came to a startled halt on the smart screen, eyes widening in shock at the sudden appearance of four Demons with weapons drawn. He dropped to his knees in response to a barked command and set the boxes down. One of the surveillance team moved closer and ran a pheromone sensor over the boxes. "No traces," came the report, quickly supplemented by, "Anchovies and salami. Yum yum."

"X-ray," I ordered. "And shit-can the humour."

The same Demon carefully set both boxes side by side then scanned them with a pen-sized x-ray unit. "Negative. No mechanicals or metals."

"Let him through," I said. "All he has to do is make the delivery. Five hundred in green if keeps his nerve. Don't want Fuentes getting antsy."

"Roger that."

There was a short delay before the pizza guy appeared, making for the laundry at a faster pace than I'd have liked, though his slouch was still in place. He rang the buzzer and managed not to fidget during the thirty seconds it took a somewhat agitated older man to answer the door. "That's the owner," Leyla told me. "Wanted to bolt, but we threatened to get the commerce board to pull his shop-licence for harbouring a known criminal."

The door closed and the pizza guy began to slouch away. I was about to return to my corner for more research when I noticed the pizza guy's step was even faster than it had been on approaching the door. I reached for the camera, zooming in on a pale and sweaty face, eyes wide and plainly terrified.

"Shit!"

I ran for the door, barking orders at Leyla. "Call the laundry! Tell the owner he has to vacate now! And tell Surveillance to grab that pizza fucker!"

I dragged the arcade door open and sprinted outside. I was twenty yards short of the laundry door when the windows blew out. The blast picked me up and threw me against the boards on the arcade windows, glass shredding the sleeve of my raincoat as I instinctively shielded face and eyes. I felt blood coursing down my arm as I sagged onto the pavement, looking up to see the laundry in flames, the roof gone and smoke billowing in the rain as the level's fire suppressant system came online. One glance at the shambles visible through the laundry's glassless windows told me it was way too late for Fuentes and the owner.

Promise me he'll make it to trial, Janet had said and I'd promised. So I knew I'd shortly have another reason to hate Mr Mac, because when this was done he'd have made me into a liar as well as a murderer.

CHAPTER 11

"EXPLODING PIZZA," RICCI said, ample cheeks bulging with delighted fascination on my terminal screen. "This is a new one."

I swallowed another painkiller and washed it down with lukewarm coffee. The damage to my arm had been easily mended, two hours in the speed-healer and a thick slathering with derma-gel to take care of the scars. The ache of it lingered though, deep and fierce. "Glad my near-death experience made your day," I said. "How about some evidence?"

"Got plenty. Not sure how much it'll help." He tapped a button on his own terminal, calling up a line graph. "Spectrograph analysis of what's left of Fuentes. Mostly a breakdown of the chemical compounds that make up the human body, except for this group." The number of lines reduced as Ricci highlighted various points on the graph. "Nitric acid, glycerol and a relatively new synthetic explosive called demetrol. It's used by the mining corporations to break up bigger asteroids. Favoured because of its safety features; inert, non-toxic to human skin, odourless and tasteless. You can play squash with a ball of this stuff and it won't go boom, needs an accelerator for that. Hence the nitric acid and glycerol."

Thanks to the war, I knew enough bathtub chemistry to follow his reasoning. "Put them together and you get nitroglycerin."

"Yeah. But they weren't mixed in the pizza until Fuentes bit into it and started chewing, which is why the pheromone scanner missed it. A decent sized mouthful would've been enough to set off the demetrol. I'm guessing the accelerant was in the crust and the demetrol was in the base." He gave an appreciative chuckle. "Whoever came up with this one really deserves a hitter of the year award. I just booked myself a place at the Global Forensic Symposium thanks to this."

"I assume demetrol is a controlled substance."

"Sure. But it's also widely used. Tracking where a relatively small amount like this came from will be a nightmare. There are chemical markers in every batch, though, so at least we'll have a shot."

No, I knew, rubbing my temples. *He'd have thought of it and made sure there's nothing to trace back to him.* "Send the details through to Joe," I said, deciding thoroughness cost nothing. "He'll get one of the analysts on it."

I closed the connection and looked up to see Leyla loitering at the door. "What?"

"We finished grilling the pizza kid," she said. "Seems he came home to find a Jed in a mask holding a gun to his mother's head. There were two pizza boxes on the table. He was told to take them to the laundry when the next order came in."

"Jed in a mask, huh?"

"Yeah. Flags as a big fat lie on the voice analyser, but he's sticking with it. Kid's scared shitless, boss."

"His mother?"

"SWAT checked out the apartment. They found her tied to a chair with her favourite soaps playing on the holo. Mild shock and dehydration but otherwise she's fine."

I could sic Janet on the kid. Her particular form of mesmerism would probably unearth a description of the hostage taker but how much would that tell me? I already knew who it was.

Took care of this himself. Couldn't resist a personal fuck-you. Probably considers it a practical joke between friends.

"You OK, boss?"

I realised my hand was white on the coffee cup, the porcelain in danger of cracking under the strain. I opened my hand and reclined in the chair, arm aching from shoulder to wrist.

"You ran background on the kid and his mother?"

"Yeah. Some petty offences for the kid, nothing for his ma. You want him charged? I mean, technically he's guilty of aiding and abetting a homicide."

I shook my head. "Kick him loose. No charges."

She nodded, lingering.

"Something else?"

"The Rybak case. I saw your Pol-net alert. Wondering if you needed any help."

I saw Janet approaching through the squad room, a determined smile on her lips. "I've got it," I told Leyla. "For now. I'll let you know if that changes."

"Inspector," Janet said, offering Leyla a smile as she came through the door, an excited glint in her eye.

"Doctor," Leyla said, mouth barely twitching as she stood aside.

Janet placed her smart on my desk and called up a holo of the statue from Mr Mac's office. "Remember Rodin's *Jean d'Aire Second Maquette?*"

"I'm fine, by the way," I said.

Janet waved an impatient hand. "You're always fine." She hit some icons and the display switched to a company net-page: Kensington and Naylor, Specialist Fine Arts Couriers. "I ran a check on deliveries to Oksana Lenova's apartment. Each time her birthday rolls around she gets a package from this company."

"The Mackintosh watercolours."

"Right. Kensington and Naylor are *the* company for moving art around. Very expensive, but also very trustworthy. It made me think. I mean we know Mr Mac likes his art, he's an inveterate collector. Who better to use when he buys something new?"

"He wouldn't use the same company for his own collection," I said. "He's way too careful for that."

"Maybe not, but what about for someone else? What if there's someone besides his sister who also appreciates antiques? So I ran a check for all Upside deliveries by Kensington and Naylor in the past three years." She called up a fresh image, a smiling young woman holding a violin. It was clearly a publicity shot taken at a concert. The violinist's smile was a little uncertain, conveying a sense of fragility enhanced by delicate beauty.

"Her name's Li Mei Bao," Janet said. "Up-and-coming star on the classical music circuit. She lives on New Shen and has received no less than six deliveries in the last twelve months courtesy of Kensington and Naylor. Way more than any other private individual in orbit."

"Seems tenuous," I said. "A lady like her is bound to have admirers, and get a lot of corporate gifts."

"A fair point, sir." Janet's voice held a triumphant note as she called up another publicity shot of Li Mei Bao, this time perched on a couch in a long white dress, violin in hand. "Taken at her home during an interview she did for Upside Vogue three months ago. The background is the interesting part. I had to run it through some filters, but it's pretty clear." The image shifted, zooming in on the slightly out of focus background before morphing into a figure. A bronze figure sitting on a shelf. It was different to the one I'd seen on Mr Mac's desk, a floppy haired man in archaic clothing holding what appeared to be a plate.

"Looks like a waiter at a Medieval banquet," Leyla said.

"He's a painter," Janet said. "Holding a palette. It's a study for the monument to the artist Claude Lorrain, completed by Auguste Rodin in 1889. Formerly part of the Cantor Collection and stolen from the Brooklyn Museum, along with the *Jean d'Aire*

Second Maquette, some fifty years ago. I guess Mr Mac's been tracking these down over the years."

I looked up from the image, meeting her gaze. "New Shen City is an hour's shuttle ride away."

"I believe so."

"Leyla, tell Joe to run a profile on shuttle traffic between the Slab and New Shen. Cross ref with all known sightings of Mr Mac. Then get everyone back here. Briefing in thirty minutes."

CHAPTER 12

NEW SHEN CITY had begun as a prestige project for what had once been called the People's Republic of China, a vast toroidal hab revolving around a fusion-powered light array. Thanks to the Sino-Japanese War, the funds ran out somewhere during the fifth year of construction and it had eventually been completed by a consortium of orbiting mining concerns. It was now home to a good portion of the CAOS elite, rich folk of all stripes choosing to live on the idyllic six mile wide strip of parkland and pagodas. Watching the landscape grow through the shuttle window, I had to concede it had a definite allure, all the greenery and shimmering water such a contrast to the Escher infused confines of the Slab.

"Wonder if their PD has any vacancies," Timor commented, staring through his own window.

"We're lucky they're even letting us set foot on the place," Leyla said. "Surprised they aren't making us go through quarantine."

She had a point. Getting extra-judicial authority for this jaunt hadn't been easy, at least initially. Sherry had been stonewalled by the Shen City authorities for the better part of a day and even Mayor Arnaud's calls were going unanswered. Then there had been a sudden change in attitudes. I hadn't placed another call to Vargold, reasoning I'd already called in my favour, but he apparently still felt an obligation. I suspected Arnaud had called him, though I wouldn't have put it past Vargold to be keeping track of my cases. He had the clearance after all. Either way, we now had a warrant, extradition papers and full authority to operate on Shen City territory. Also, thanks to Joe, we'd identified a passenger shuttle departing the Slab for Shen City less than thirty minutes after Fuentes' encounter with an exploding pizza. The passenger manifest included the name of one Johnathan Campbell, a near exact match for Mr Mac's most recently recorded biometrics. The shuttle's internal security cams had also mysteriously malfunctioned for the duration of the flight. The sense of having the bastard almost within reach made all the delays a pretty agonising experience. Mr Mac was certain to have some mechanism in place to warn of increased interest from the local PD. Luckily they were a mostly mechanised force, basic patrols undertaken by taser-equipped bots and only a small cadre of very well paid human officers.

I would have preferred to arrive with a full SWAT team, but maintaining cover with so many Demons in tow would've been a difficult and probably pointless exercise. So it was just me, Joe, Janet, Leyla and Timor. I was gambling on a quick and dirty approach since Mr Mac seemed to have a gift for spotting elaborate preparations. Sherry had organised transport via a regular automated supply shuttle and we were dressed in maintenance staff uniforms, though finding one to fit Joe hadn't been easy. Janet, by contrast, was dressed as an admin executive, all business suit and bunned-up hair. She simply hadn't made any visual sense in overalls, resembling a model cast in a poorly thought out cleaning ad. I'd made a brief and fruitless attempt to persuade her to stay behind, mainly because I didn't want her to see what I fully intended to do upon coming face to face with Mr Mac.

The shuttle fired its braking thrusters and began its docking manoeuvre, the pleasing vista of Shen City replaced by the blank wall of the outer torus. It took maybe five minutes before I felt the shudder of the airlock seal closing on the access hatch.

"You know what to do," I told them all. "We're keyed into the Shen City security system, so there should be no interference from local authorities. Proceed independently to your go-point and await my order. Dr Vaughn, you're long-stop. If he makes it out, you bring him down. He might be able to outrun the rest of us, but not you."

"I'd be more useful in the house," she said, eyes intent on my face. "Since we want him alive and I don't need a gun to subdue him."

"My op, my rules, Doctor." A hiss as the airlock opened. "Let's get it done."

Li Mei Bao's home was more modestly proportioned than its neighbours, less than a half-acre of garden and boasting only twenty rooms across its two storeys. It was still unbelievably opulent and ostentatious by Yang-side standards, but also displayed a creditable restraint that indicated its owner might enjoy the trappings of wealth, but didn't necessarily feel the need to show them off. Shen City was a palpably misnamed hab since it didn't have streets as such, just a series of interlinked paths tracing through the parks and skirting the various waterways. The small number of human maintenance staff were obliged to move around on little electric carts, naturally giving way to any strolling residents. I conducted only one circuit of the house, finding a guard on the front gate and two more in the rear gardens. It was likely there would be at least one more I couldn't see but there wasn't any time for a prolonged surveillance. Every second's delay increased the chances of Mr Mac discovering our presence.

I took a toolkit from the cart and strolled across the grass towards a row of sprinklers twenty yards or so from the garden wall. "I count three guards," I said into my hidden mike, crouching to inspect a sprinkler nozzle. If the planned deployment had gone smoothly they should all be in place and awaiting my call. "Expect more. I'll breach in thirty seconds. Wait for my go."

I rose and sauntered towards Li Mei Bao's home, both guards quick to spot my approach, one raising a hand as I came within a dozen feet. They had the uniform square-jawed, blocky shouldered look of the professional bodyguard, meaning they were unlikely to be part of Mr Mac's main operation. Probably thought they'd been hired to protect a famous musician from over-enthusiastic stalkers.

"Got a downed comm line," I said, coming to a halt and pointing to the maintenance ID pinned to my overalls. "Need access to the premises."

"Work order?" the one on the right enquired. I noticed his partner raising a finger to his ear-piece, mouth opening to report my presence.

"Sure," I said, fishing in my left pocket for something and drawing the Colt from my right. Ear-piece guy took a taser dart to the neck and went down spasming. His partner was impressively quick, managing to draw and aim his weapon before I shot another dart into his forehead. I vaulted the wall and sprinted for the French windows looking out over the garden. They were open and I paused at the sound of music from inside. Violin with a piano accompaniment, the former markedly more accomplished than the latter.

I lowered the Colt and went inside. The room was large and featured a grand piano where a tall blond man sat playing with functional but inexpert hands whilst a beautiful young woman stood nearby and stroked heaven from a violin. The man looked up as I entered and a discordant note sounded from the piano. He kept on playing, smiling at me in welcome. But the bum note sang volumes. I wasn't expected. I'd finally managed to surprise him.

The woman noticed me then, her bow drawing a faint

squeal from the violin as she started, eyes snapping to the Colt in my hand. "Who..?" she began, eyes wide as she hurried towards the man at the piano.

"It's alright Bao," Mr Mac said, wisely keeping his seat and taking her hand as she came to his side. "You know you're always welcome, Alex, but it's polite to call before coming over."

I said nothing, staring into his handsome face, my arm aching worse than ever.

"John?" Bao said. "You know this man?"

"Of course." He squeezed her hand. "Someone I've long wanted you to meet. Bao, this is Chief Inspector Alexei McLeod of the Lorenzo City Police Department. My oldest and closest friend."

Bao didn't seem particularly reassured, her eyes scanning me from head to toe. "What do want here? I demand to see your credentials..."

"Shhh." Mr Mac took hold of her hands and kissed them. "That won't be necessary. I'm sure he only wants to ask me some questions. Right, Alex?"

I said nothing. Now the moment was at hand I felt a surprising calm. No shakes, no sweats, just a sense of certainty. He saw it then, my intent, his eyes narrowing, a wry, regretful smile curving his lips. "I'm sure he needs to speak to me in private," he said. "There's no need for her to be here for this, is there, Alex?"

I said, "I was there for Choi," and raised the Colt, thumbing the selector to lethal.

"Armengol, wasn't it?"

The Colt stopped short of sighting on Mr Mac's head as Janet strolled into the room, her words slurred slightly as her canines hadn't fully receded. She moved to stand opposite me on the far side of the piano. I noticed a small bloodstain on her collar. "The piece you were playing," she went on, addressing Bao. "Ternura by Mario Ruiz Armengol."

The woman stared at her, hands tight on Mr Mac's shoulders now. "Yes," she said in a hoarse whisper.

"Quite exquisite," Janet said. "So rare I get to hear live music."

"You are too kind, Dr Vaughn," Mr Mac said. "I'm fully aware of my severe limitations, but Bao insists we practice together."

Janet nodded, returning his smile. "Perhaps your lawyer can arrange for you to have lessons programmed into your corrective immersion. By the time you get out, if ever, you should be quite the virtuoso."

He gave a small chuckle and turned back to me. "Perhaps. If my old friend were to offer mitigating testimony…"

"Call me your friend again," I said, speaking in a precise rasp, "and I will blow your brains all over Miss Bao's nice dress."

A loud crash sounded from the front of the house as the main door gave way under something heavy. Joe appeared a few seconds later with Leyla and Timor on either side, carbines ready. "The guard outside is down," Joe told me. "Unconscious with a busted nose. Didn't see who did it. Thought it best to breach."

"Leyla, Timor," I said. "Search the rest of the house. Stay together, no Scooby Doo shit."

"Right, boss."

"There's no one else here…" Mr Mac began.

"Shut it!" I sighted the Colt on his chest. "Stand up, arms raised."

Bao tried to embrace him as he rose from the piano. Janet caught her arms and pulled her away, gentle but firm.

"Drop to your knees," I said, Mr Mac complying with slow deliberation. "Lower yourself to the floor. Face down. Don't move and do not… fucking… speak."

I moved to stand over him, jamming the muzzle of the Colt against the base of his skull and pulling out my cuffs. "John

McAllister. You are under arrest for murder, racketeering, money laundering and extortion. Other charges are likely to follow. You are entitled to remain silent during questioning, but are advised that a jury may infer guilt from such silence. You have a right to legal representation..."

CHAPTER 13

WE WERE OBLIGED to wait for a Fugitives Retrieval shuttle at the Shen City docks. We could have transported our prisoner back ourselves but Sherry hadn't wanted to take any chances. I couldn't argue with her reasoning; it was a dead cert Mr Mac would have contingencies in place in the event of his capture.

"You're late," I told the two FR guards when they emerged from the airlock, both clad in body-armour and carrying stubby riot guns. One was a tall woman of Nordic appearance, the other stocky and Asian, sporting a pair of Raybans.

"We got diverted," the tall woman said. "Priority pick-up on Minerva Station. I'm Vandeman, Prisoner Security." She nodded to her partner. "He's Kurota, the pilot." Her gaze shifted to Mr Mac, sandwiched between Timor and Joe with his hands cuffed behind his back. Leyla stood behind him with weapon drawn, ready to put a taser dart in his neck at the first sign of trouble. "So, you really got him, huh?" Vandeman asked, looking Mr Mac up and down in critical appraisal. She struck me as the type who wasn't easily impressed.

"We really did," I said. "Just you two?"

"The other prisoner's secured inside. Don't worry. He's no trouble."

The shuttle interior consisted of a row of restraint chairs and a few benches for the guards to sit on. One chair was occupied by a spindly man in his fifties, all unkempt beard and unruly hair sprouting from a small, bird-like head.

"Jonas Blair," Vandeman introduced the other prisoner. "Recidivist wicky-waver. Violated his terms by taking a stroll around a school-yard on Minerva Station. Unfortunately for him, Minerva's Economics Minister sends her kids there. Pulled strings to get him sent to the Slab penn."

Blair barely glanced up as Joe and Timor hustled Mr Mac into the opposite chair. Timor pressed a gun to his temple as Joe undid the cuffs. They stepped back as Vandeman locked the restraints in place, thick manacles closing over wrists and ankles with a satisfying clunk.

"I suppose a pillow's out of the question?" Mr Mac asked, squirming a little.

"I can gag him if you like," Vandeman offered.

"I'm not quite ready to inflict cruel and unusual punishment," I said.

"Detach and burn in two minutes," Kurota announced, making for the cockpit. "Meal-packs in the lockers if you want 'em." He paused at the ladder to favour Janet with an over-friendly grin. "No plasma, though. Sorry."

"I had a big breakfast," she replied. She stood close to the airlock, a faintly queasy look on her face.

"You OK?" I asked.

She nodded at Blair. "Can't you smell him? It's like he's been eating garlic his whole life."

"That really true?" Timor asked her. "Vamps and garlic, I mean."

"No, I just personally can't stand the stuff. And I forgive your racism, Inspector."

"Smart, funny and too brave for her own good," Mr Mac said, looking up at me. "Just your type."

I stared down at him in silence as the shuttle came away from the airlock with a jerk, grabbing a hand-hold when the gravity vanished a few seconds later and my feet came free of the deck.

"Ladies and gentlemen," Kurota's voice came over the speaker. "This is your captain speaking. On behalf of the crew I'd like to welcome you to Incarceration Skyways. The temperature outside is a balmy -461 degrees celsius with zero percent chance of rain…"

"He do this every time?" Leyla asked Vandeman.

"Depends on how hot the passengers are," she said, glancing at Janet.

"You really were going to do it," Mr Mac said to me in a faintly wounded tone. "In front of my wife-to-be, no less."

"I told you I would," I said. "Anyway, she'd have gotten over it. Once she found out just what a piece of shit you are. Judging by the statement she gave to Shen City law, I'm guessing she has no idea where all the expensive love tokens come from."

He continued to stare at me, expression more curious than hurt. "Mind if I ask how you found me? I'm guessing the lovely Dr Vaughn had a lot to do with it."

"You really don't want to say her name again."

"Relax. She's well outside my profile, as I would hope you'd know by now."

"Like that poor bastard who owned the laundry you totalled yesterday?"

"That poor bastard had been running Bliss for the Arturo Cartel for well over a decade, and he wasn't discerning over who he sold it to."

"Whereas you're the enlightened face of drug dealing."

"Dead customers make for lousy profit margins. Poor Old Don Arturo never really got that. Check the Slab's health stats since his unfortunate disappearance, you'll find a twenty percent reduction in fatal overdoses."

"I stand in awe of your humanitarian efforts."

He laughed, that old entirely genuine laugh I hated so much.

"I've missed you, Alex. You had me seriously worried when you disappeared for so long. When all that shit went down at Ceres, though, I knew I'd be seeing you again, just not so soon."

"DCI McLeod," Kurota's voice came over the speaker. "Priority call for you coming in via a military frequency... That's weird."

"What's weird?" I asked.

"It's all in text." The shuttle interior suddenly disappeared as the main lights blinked out. When it returned a half-second later everything was bathed in red emergency lighting.

"What the fuck!" Kurota cursed. "The main bus just went down. I've got no control here."

The shuttle lurched, those of us not confined to restraint chairs reaching for new hand-holds as the port thrusters went to maximum.

"That's really not good," Kurota said in a strained whisper.

"Focus!" I said. "Give me a sit-rep."

"Uh, OK. The main bus is off-line, my controls are dead and the port thrusters just pushed us into a rapidly descending high-angle orbit."

I met Mr Mac's gaze, finding it way more tense and serious than I'd seen before. We both knew what a high-angle descent into Earth's atmosphere meant. Whatever this was, it wasn't part of his contingency. "Run overrides," I said. "Go analogue. Start ripping out some panels."

"Won't do any good," Kurota's voice was shrill now, panic rising with every word. "This tub is designed to resist a prisoner takeover and someone just put it into riot-mode. Nothing's working, except the comms screen with this stupid fucking text message."

"What message?"

"Doesn't make sense... 'From light we are born to light we return.'"

There was a loud snick and I swivelled about to see Blair's

arm and ankle restrains snapping open. He floated free of the chair, his previously blank face now a picture of serenity, eyes wide and mouth open in awe and wonder. "The light," he said, voice scratchy and thin but nevertheless still full of fanatical zeal. "It's within all of us."

He spread his arms wide and I drew the Colt, ready to put a bullet between his eyes but he made no aggressive move, just floated there, his swirling hair like a coiling nest of bloodied snakes in the red light.

"Kill him," Mr Mac said, voice flat and certain. "Right now, Alex!"

Wartime instinct made my finger tighten on the Colt's trigger, but before I could fire Blair's chest convulsed, a bone-cracking shudder filling the shuttle as it seemed to fold in on itself, then expand outward. I saw Blair die as his chest bulged way beyond human tolerance, head lolling and globs of blood trailing from his gaping mouth. But dead as he was, his body wasn't done yet. His chest continued to convulse, contracting then expanding, growing larger with every squelching heave.

"He's gonna blow!" Timor yelled, dragging Leyla into a corner.

Joe slammed into Blair's spasming corpse, arms enfolding his torso, legs wrapped around his hips, smothering it with his bulk and forcing it against the bulkhead. I began to propel myself forward then jerked to a halt as something hard and unyielding latched onto my armour, pulling me back too fast and too strong for me to do anything about it.

"JOE!" I roared as Janet forced me behind the row of restraint chairs. "JO-"

The blast hammered my eardrums and left me flailing in Janet's grasp as everything disappeared in an instantaneous fog. Janet held me close as I thrashed, still calling out Joe's name and tasting blood and bone on my tongue.

"He's gone." It was barely a whisper in my ear, though I

knew she was shouting. She held me until my struggles subsided, the cement that seemed to be clogging my ears gradually leeching away until she no longer had to shout. "He's gone, Alex. I'm sorry."

She let me go and I pushed away. Vandeman was dead, skewered through the forehead by what looked like a fragment of rib. Leyla was clutching at her leg and spouting profanities, red beads trickling through her fingers whilst Timor bit the wrapping from a field dressing. It took me a while to recognise what remained of Joe and Blair, just an entangled swirling mess of flesh and bone. *No time for grief,* I told myself, watching the obscene thing slide over the hard surfaces, coiling like some formless monster. The thought of Joe spending eternity entwined with some piece-of-shit paedo would have made me vomit, if not for the dominating urgency. We were still descending towards certain incineration.

A groan dragged my attention to the restraint chairs. Mr Mac coughed and blinked bleary eyes up at me, face pale and a gash on his forehead. His left leg and arm had also suffered some hits, though assessing the damage was difficult with all the blood floating about.

"Anyone alive back there?" Kurota called over the speaker, in full-on panic mode now. "Van? You there?"

"She's dead," I told him. "Your prisoner…" I shook my head. We really didn't have time for this. "Do you have any comms at all?"

A long pause. When he spoke again the panic had receded, his voice taking on a dull note I had heard before. "Negative. Riot-mode kills all outgoing transmissions and the shuttle's walls are shielded against smart signals. Intended to stop the prisoners demanding ransoms or speaking to the media in the event of a takeover. There's supposed to be an emergency beacon screaming out our position to FR Central, but it's dead." Another pause. "There is something. A hard-wired manual switch on my dash. Last resort kinda thing."

"I'm listening."

"Emergency decomp. Blows the main hatch and flushes the prisoner compartment. You'll find vac suits in the lockers. Van's iris and palm scans will open them."

"Can't you do it?"

"Cockpit's sealed during flight, Chief Inspector. No overrides."

"Can you eject?"

"My seat's evac system is off-line. Guess whoever did this really didn't want any survivors. You better get moving. I estimate time to entry at less than ten minutes."

Janet and I hauled Vandeman's body to the locker security panel, me holding her hand to the scanner whilst Janet prised her eyelid open for the retinal optic. The locker doors slammed open and I began hauling out suits. "Know how to suit up?" I asked Janet.

"Learned it in kindergarten," she said, hands moving faster than I could follow as she started prepping a suit.

I unhooked the restraint chair control unit from Vandeman's belt and pushed myself towards Mr Mac. His face, bleached and blood-smeared, was rigid with pain though he retained enough composure to greet me with an arched eyebrow. "Well, this turned out to be a very interesting day."

I hit the disengage button and his restraints snapped open. "You got time for this?" he asked as I hauled him out of the chair.

"If I didn't need you, I'd leave you to burn." I grabbed one of the suits, already prepped and powered up thanks to Janet, and began to push him into it.

"Minus six minutes," Kurota reported. "The blast from the decompression will provide a hefty kick, but you'll need the suits' propellant to escape the well."

"Got it," I said, locking the final seal in place on Mr Mac's helmet. I climbed into one of my own as Janet helped Timor seal up a barely conscious Leyla. She was even paler than Mr Mac and kept drifting in and out of consciousness to utter harsh obscenities. "Vamp slut-bitch," she spat at Janet before promptly passing out.

"And I thought she liked me." Janet hit the power button as Timor locked Leyla's helmet in place.

"Hurry up," I told him, thrusting the final suit at him.

"Minus three minutes," Kurota said.

"You got a sidearm?" I asked him, none too gently shoving Timor's legs into the suit.

"Yeah. Thinking maybe I'll see how long I can hang around to watch the fireworks."

"Your family..?"

"Details in the personnel file, Inspector. Stand-by, I'm hitting the switch in sixty seconds, ready or not."

I did a quick visual inspection on all of their primary seals, finding Timor had forgotten to connect his CO_2 supply. I slotted it into place with a punishing jerk and we lined up at the door, Janet holding onto Leyla and me with a tether fixed to Mr Mac's suit. Like Leyla, he seemed to be unconscious now, his face a pale, slumped mask behind the helmet visor. I turned my attention to the door and felt something hard and cold clutch at my chest at the sight of the logo laser-etched into the bulkhead: Astravista Industries.

"Kurota," I said. "I promise I'll settle with who did this. And it won't be pretty when I do."

"Appreciated. Brace for decomp in five, four, three, two..."

Being forced out of a spacecraft by high pressure decompression is never something you get used to. Regardless of how physically strong you might be, you still end up spinning end-over-end like a rag doll whilst fighting down the potentially helmet-filling, and therefore fatal, upsurge of nausea. The tether attaching me to Mr Mac pulled tight then slackened as he came spinning back towards me, flailing limbs thrashing against my air-tank before I managed to steady him. I could see Janet about two hundred yards away, still holding onto Leyla whilst Timor had evidently lost his grip, spinning in a cloud of CO_2 as he sought to stabilise himself.

A grating squeal in my headphones told of a melting microphone and I swivelled about in time to see the shuttle enter the atmosphere. It blazed up almost instantly, leaving a black-orange trail across the vast blue curve of the Earth before splitting into a dozen or more pieces, each one blinking out seconds later. I decided not to ponder if Kurota had used his sidearm or not.

I took a firm hold of Mr Mac and used a one second burst of CO_2 to close up with the others. "Suit-to-suit comms only," I said. "No distress calls."

"Boss?" Timor asked.

"As far as anyone knows, we're dead, and that's the way I want it for now."

"Then what do we do?" Janet enquired. "We have two hours of air and we'll need all our CO_2 to get clear of the well."

I used the suit's command gauntlet to access my smart and placed a call. The signal would be weak, but we were close enough to the Slab's network for it to get through. "Then I guess I better call us a taxi."

CHAPTER 14

"VARGOLD?" RIVERA'S OPTICS prevented me from seeing the full range of doubt on his face, but the scorn in his voice was clear enough. "You seriously suggest Othin Vargold just tried to kill you?"

"It's the only conclusion that fits," I said. "He knew I had a lead on the Rybak case, he knew we were off the Slab, and he knew we were on our way back with a prisoner. Not to mention the fact that his company manufactured the FR shuttle. Guess he had his engineers programme a back door into the command software years ago. Same goes for every other piece of Astravista tech purchased by CAOS Military or law enforcement. Which tells me whatever he's up to has been a long time in the planning."

"Then we're fucked, aren't we?" Leyla said, floating in between Mr Mac and Janet. I'd gathered everyone into the *Aguila's* somewhat cramped main crew quarters once all injuries had been tended. We'd been obliged to hang around for almost two hours before Lucy piloted the old tub close enough to effect a rescue. Leyla's leg was fully extended, thanks to the brace applied by the ship's med-unit. The skull fragment it extracted from her thigh that had come close to slicing her femur in two. She wouldn't be mobile in full gravity for some time.

"The richest Jed in orbit wants us dead," she went on. "He owns half the politicians in the Assembly."

"Politicians are the least of our worries," Mr Mac said. He had a series of speed-heal strips running down the left side of his face with more visible through the tears in his clothes. The med-unit had reported that his injuries were unlikely to cause long-term damage, though it did provide a list of reputable cosmetic surgeons. "I'd be more concerned about his links to CAOS Defence."

Colonel Riviera's optics locked onto Mr Mac, lidar blazing. "Why," he enquired, "is this traitor on my ship?"

"Because he has access to resources I don't," I said. "I'm dead after all."

"Point of order, if I may," Mr Mac said, raising a finger. "I was a deserter, not a traitor."

"Same thing," Riviera said.

Mr Mac shook his head with a sigh and turned to me. "I'll need access to secure comms gear."

"No bargaining?" I asked. "No demands for an immunity deal and a nice big bag of folding green when this is done?"

"Vargold tried to kill me too, Alex." He shrugged. "In my line of business there's only one valid response to that."

"This old bird won't be much use to you," Lucy said. "Her comms are straight out of the ark."

"Cerberus Station," Riviera said, pushing away from the central meal-hub and gliding towards the engine room. "They'll have what we need. It's a five hour haul. Lucy, punch it in. The rest of you can bunk down in the cargo bay."

Lucy put the ship into a spin once the plasma thrusters came online. The effect was way short of full gravity but it was enough to keep a human body-mass close to the hull in some semblance of a resting state. The colonel had evidently just completed a supply run because the cargo bay featured a number of empty containers. I told the others to get some rest and chose the least smelly container I could find, though they were all pretty musty. I settled my back against the hull, staring at nothing and knowing that, despite my exhaustion, sleep would be a long time coming.

"You didn't say anything about Joe." Janet was silhouetted in the container entrance, her night-vision enhanced eyes two pale discs in a perfectly proportioned shadow.

"He was my friend," I said. "Now he's dead. Eulogies have never been my strong suit."

She let herself float free of the entrance, settling next to me, fingers entwining with mine. "The stench coming off Blair," she said. "It wasn't garlic. Whatever was done to him left its mark in his sweat. I should have realised something was up."

"Gotta hand it to Vargold, he knows how to set a trap. I'm guessing the Economics Minister on Minerva owes him a favour or two. That's why Blair was on the shuttle, an insurance policy in case we made it out when the shut down kicked in." I noticed my hand was closing tight on hers and began to unclasp but she held on, moving closer.

"Joe wasn't a vengeful soul," she whispered.

"No. But I am."

"Yes." She came closer still, breath hot on my neck before her lips found mine. "Turns out I am too."

"Sorry," she said some while later as I wiped a bead of blood from a small cut on the corner of my mouth. "Got a bit fangy at the end there."

"I'm really not complaining."

A faint laugh as she pressed herself against me, wonderfully and gloriously naked, then a sigh of self-reproach. "I feel bad for feeling so good just now." I felt her tense as the grief took hold, pulled her closer as the sobs came. I hadn't known tears were in her template.

"He liked you," I said, stroking a hand through her tousled hair. "A lot."

She pressed her head against my chest until the tears subsided. "When you were off on your mysterious adventure, he told me all about it, how he ended up a Slab City Demon. He was proud of it, you know. He said it was the only worthwhile thing he'd done in his entire life. He also said you were the first person he ever met who never had an angle. Never wanted anything from him. You helped him because that's what you do."

We lay entwined in silence for a time until I groaned in realisation. "What?" she asked.

"Sniffy. His pet rat. Someone'll need to take him."

"No way. That thing hates me. Give him to Riviera. I'd say they're a perfect match." She drew back a little, the pale discs of her eyes intent on my face. "I thought this might relax you. But you're just as angry."

"Vargold," I said. "I trusted him. Should've known better."

"I expect he's very skilled at manipulation. It's not uncommon for high achievers to exhibit psychopathic tendencies."

"He's not psychotic. Seen enough nut-jobs in my life to know the difference. He's got a purpose. I just can't see what it is."

"You will." Her hand reached out to explore my face, lingering where my scars used to be. "It's what you do."

Cerberus Station was a cylindrical hab of only three levels, its rotational spin provided by an outer stack of fusion generators. I'd heard of the place, but never visited and found the paint scheme something of a surprise given the habitants were mostly war veterans. "Amazing," Janet said, peering through the flight deck window with wide-eyed fascination as Lucy guided the *Aguila* to the docks, treating us to a close-up of Cerberus' slowly spinning hull. Every inch was covered in graffiti, a multi-coloured patchwork of lettering, caricature and abstract geometry. I could see a vac-suited paint-crew at work on some kind of mural, all guitars and lightning bolts.

"It changes," Lucy said. "Come back in a coupla' months and it'll all be different."

"Like a snake continually refreshing its skin," Janet said with a delighted laugh.

"Or a buncha weed-heads with nothing better to do." Lucy punched in the docking sequence and reclined into the pilot's chair. "Seriously, Doc. You might want to wear a mask when you get through the airlock. My first visit here I got the raging munchies and I never touch the stuff."

I ordered Leyla and Timor to stay behind. She wouldn't be able to walk for days and he looked like he needed a break. Slab-born they might be but they'd never been in a war and sometimes I forgot how young they were. Being on the run with no safety net was a novel experience for them, whilst for me it was simply the resumption of an old habit.

"Lucy's hooked into the Cerberus public net," I told them. "Get to work on open sources, nothing that requires a password or any kind of interaction. I want every biographical detail on Othin Vargold from the day he was born to right now."

"We looking for anything in particular?" Timor asked.

"The classics." I turned and started along the umbilical to the airlock. "Means, motive and opportunity."

I realised Lucy hadn't been exaggerating the moment the airlock cycled open, the sweet, musty haze provoking an immediate cough and moistened eyes. "Jesus," Mr Mac said, blinking. "Haven't they ever heard of filters?"

The interior of Cerberus station reminded me a little of the shanty town in the Yang-side extremity, the structures being so lacking in uniformity and plainly fashioned from mismatched materials. They stretched away on either side of us, following the massive curve of the hull. Looking up, I found I could just make out the opposite side of the ring-shaped level through the haze, a vaporous melange of exhaled breath laden with what I took to be several varieties of cannabinoid derivatives.

"Where are your papers!" a strident, Germanic voice demanded and I turned to see a wiry, dreadlocked man approaching Riviera, teeth bared in a broad grin. He wore ancient combat fatigues festooned with inexpertly embroidered patches, the sleeves cut off to reveal knotted and densely tattooed muscle.

"Sergeant Kruger," Riviera greeted him.

"Herr Oberst." Kruger came to attention and snapped off the kind of salute that only came from Downside military training.

"Joachim Kruger," Riviera introduced him, replying with a vague salute of his own. "Formerly of the European Federated Defence Force and later Sergeant Major to the CAOS Commando Brigade." He waved a prosthetic hand at us. "My… associates need some help, the technical variety. I'll meet any cost, of course."

"No one on this hab would take a penny from you, Herr Oberst," Kruger told him. "You know that, I think." His gaze snapped to me, eyes narrowing in surprised recognition. "Captain McLeod, is it not? The news feeds said…"

"The news feeds were right," I told him. "As far as anyone knows."

Although the bulge of unfiltered fun-sticks in Kruger's top-pocket told me he was no stranger to what seemed to be the main activity here, his gaze retained a shrewd clarity and he didn't need any further explanations. "Security?" he asked the colonel with a raised eyebrow.

"*Sí*," Riviera told him. "But our own people only."

"I will call the boys and girls. They always enjoy a reunion, and Trudy gets lonely on the farm."

"You're a farmer?" I asked, following along with the others as Kruger turned about and began marching towards what looked like an open man-hole.

"Of course, we all are." He laughed and raised his arms to the haze above. "From where do you imagine all this comes?"

CHAPTER 15

"FORGET IT," MR Mac told Janet. "I can swing IDs for two only, and no vampires. No offence, Doctor, but your kind simply don't exist down the well. You wouldn't last a day before being picked up."

Janet didn't really do angry, but today was clearly an exception. "You have no comprehension of my abilities," she replied, voice soft and face very still. "And I'd thank you not to make assumptions."

We were in the shed where Kruger kept his non-farming tech, an impressive array of comms gear and weaponry. Whilst no one on this hab went armed - they didn't even have a police force - the former Sergeant Major felt the need to stockpile various breeds of assault-carbine and combat gear. "It was the Colonel's suggestion," he told me with a shrug. "Insurance against an uncertain future. For now, we govern ourselves largely without CAOS interference. It doesn't mean it will stay that way forever."

Kruger's farm was one of several on the hab's second level, a cluster of buildings rising from the otherwise uninterrupted dark green blanket of hemp. A directional array of UV lights running through the centre of the level provided a twenty-four hour light and darkness cycle. Kruger and Trudy, his wife and fellow veteran who spoke through a voice modulator grafted into her neck, maintained a small army of bots to water the plants and till the soil. Come harvest time their produce would form a full ten percent of the hab's only source of income.

"Every time some Jed blazes up or chows down on a brownie," Trudy told me, the Slab-born cadence of her voice jarring a little with the upper-class English accent produced by her modulator, "there's a one in four chance it comes from Cerberus. Wouldn't think it looking at the place, but everyone here is rich as shit."

The Colonel's ad hoc security team began to arrive shortly after we did, six ex-Commando types, most sporting some long-standing injury or artificial augmentation. Given their attrition rate during the war, I was surprised Kruger could gather so many. They all treated Kruger and Riviera with such automatic, fully ingrained discipline and obedience you'd be forgiven for thinking the war had ended only a day before.

"He's right," I told Janet, as gently as I could. "Besides, I need you to research Vargold. Leyla and Timor don't have your skills."

She remained completely still, eyes unblinking, though I noticed her claws had begun to extend and her mouth bulge under the pressure of elongating canines. Mr Mac began to edge away, eyes flicking towards Kruger's armoury. "Relax," I told him softly. Janet closed her eyes, maintaining her mannequin-like stillness for a full ten seconds before her claws and canines slowly retracted.

"Very well," she told me, opening her eyes, though the habitual smile had vanished from her lips. "But I reserve the right to undertake independent action, should I judge it necessary."

"Wouldn't have it any other way," I said, turning to Mr Mac. "You have resources to call on down the well, I assume?"

He nodded. "So, you're really intent on going there?"

"That's where the leads are. Whatever it is Vargold didn't want me to find is down there somewhere."

"The IDs I've sourced will work once we're on the ground, but I don't have anything that'll get us through port security. Your face and mine will be near the top of any Fed Sec recognition database, and I doubt they'll just wipe our records on the off chance that we're really dead."

"That won't be a problem," I said, holding up the basic smart he'd asked Kruger to buy from the Cerberus market. "You're sure this is secure?"

"All comms routed through my own private server. It's swept for viruses and trojans every thirty micro-seconds. Costs a fortune to maintain, but it doesn't pay to skimp on security. Just one of the reasons it took you so long to catch me."

"I didn't catch you," I said and nodded at Janet. "She did. Best get some rest, we ship out at 0500."

"Can you trust him?"

Kruger and Trudy had plenty of room, their farm buildings consisting of re-purposed ships left over from the war, including a troop-shuttle complete with sleeping compartments. Janet and I had taken the officer's suite, though the bunk couldn't handle two people so we'd pushed a pair of mattresses together on the floor. She lay next to me, skin free of sweat, unlike mine. Once again, her fangs had made an appearance at the critical moment, but she managed to avoid drawing blood this time.

"Completely," I told her. "It's one of the more depressing things about him, the delusion that we're actually best friends."

She remained silent for a time and I turned on my side, looking at her profile outlined in the dim blue light seeping through the cabin's porthole. The longer I looked, the less perfect she seemed, more human. It made me want to go on looking for a long time. "I really don't like him," she said, breaking the silence. "He's... wrong."

"If you mean crazy, I think I got there already."

"No, not insane exactly, just badly made. It's like his internal wiring's not right. And I'd hazard a guess he's always been this way. The war didn't do it to him."

I put an arm about her shoulders, pulling her close. "Don't worry about it."

"We don't have to do this. You do know that, I assume? There are many places we could go. The Belt, the Outer Stations."

There was no real conviction in her voice, no actual desire to run away. If anything, I suspected she just felt obligated to point out the alternatives. "Joe," I said. "Vandeman, Kurota, Rybak, not to mention that SWAT team I sent to their deaths. It all needs a reckoning. Something I realised when I first became a Demon; it's not about justice, or the law, or controlling society or any of that shit. It's about balance. Sometimes things get pushed too far, a gang war, a murder, a rape. It's my job to push it back, fix it. And I think we both know that whatever Vargold's up to really needs fixing."

She raised herself up, staring into my eyes and I felt myself get captured. She'd told me her mesmerism tricks didn't work on me, said I was too strong, but there were times when I wondered if she hadn't just been massaging my ego. "I'm getting tired of this exciting interlude, Alex," she told me, breath soft on my lips. "I'd like to be boring again, and I think I'd rather be bored with you than anyone else. So go fix whatever needs fixing, just make sure you come back."

CHAPTER 16

OPERATION POLARIS HAD been partly my idea. We'd come up with it in the final year of the war, an infiltration plan to take the struggle down the well. I fully admit it was something of a desperate measure. Finding a way to transport hostile operatives onto the surface of a planet where every square inch of airspace is covered by a wide variety of military sensors required imaginative thinking and an acceptance of some major risk factors. Our intel people calculated the probability of success at 34 percent. So it came as a relief when Riviera liberated Freak from that experimental hab and we decided on the Langley Raid instead: success rating a whopping 39 percent. But that had been wartime. Now that peace reigned over the skies once more, the risk factors could be adjusted to a lower setting, or at least that's what I hoped.

"This is fucking crazy," Lucy told me, reading the mission parameters on her console.

"Basic misdirection, Newtonian physics and a little meteorology," I said. "It'll work."

Riviera had used his influence to procure an aged but serviceable shuttle from the small council of senior veterans that formed the quasi-government for Cerberus. The ship was a small maintenance runabout used by the graffiti crews and its hull was a chaotic echo of Cerberus' outer skin, all malformed cartoon characters and satanic symbols. The interior was cramped, barely capable of holding a be-suited Mr Mac and myself. Climbing into the escape pods had been an exercise in strained muscles and a reminder that I wasn't getting any younger. The pods were yet more war surplus, Kruger seemed to have an endless supply of the stuff, and had been installed on an extension to the shuttle's airlock, giving it the appearance of a wasp carrying a dumb-bell.

"Earth orbit achieved," Lucy said in my headphones. "Two minutes to curtain up. Just to be clear, you're absolutely sure you want to do this?"

"Indubitably, my dear," Mr Mac assured her.

"Wasn't asking you," she snapped. "Alex?"

"Compared to Ceres, it'll be a warm cup of cocoa," I told her. "Don't worry."

"Guess that job with Astravista's screwed now, huh?"

"I wouldn't give much for their share price when this is over. Guess you'll have to find another route to the stars."

"Yeah, I'll build my own from spares. Stand-by for eject in sixty seconds."

There was a pause then a shudder as Lucy detonated the plasma cannister fixed to the upper hull before making a suitably panicked mayday call on the universal emergency channel. "Oh god! This... this is Delta-One-Five in high orbit, polar quadrant three. We have an emergency situation. Repeat emergency!"

A pause before a calmly professional voice came over the comms, male with a South American accent. "Delta-One-Five, this is Emergency Control and Response. State the nature of your distress."

"Explosion... I mean we have an explosion on board. Something just blew in the crew compartment."

"Are you injured?"

"Negative. The flight-deck is sealed but I'm reading extensive damage... Shit! Cameras show the compartment is open to vacuum. There's a gaping hole in the hull. We're losing atmo."

"How many crew are on board?"

"Me and two others… I can't see them on the cams. Oh fuck!"

"Please remain calm, Delta-One-Five. Is your craft responsive to control?"

"Uh, yeah. Trim's kinda weird, but she'll shift alright."

"We have you on scope. You need to kill your primary engines and burn to a stable orbit. Can you do that?"

"Yeah. Burn to stable orbit. Got it."

"Rescue craft have been scrambled to intercept you. ETA twelve minutes…"

That was our cue. I gripped the pod's internal hand-holds and braced myself for what came next. A hard jolt and the pod was free of the shuttle, thrusters firing a pre-programmed sequence to angle it for an atmospheric entry.

"No!" Lucy yelled over the comms. "They ejected. Oh shit no!"

"We're tracking them," the emergency guy said in a soothing tone. "Rescue crews will be there within an hour of landing…"

"You don't understand," she sobbed. "This tub is ancient. Those pods haven't been serviced in years. They don't even have suits on. There's no way…"

The comms crackled and died as the first wave of turbulence hit the pod, indicating I was now skimming the atmosphere. My eyes roamed over the pod interior, searching for any sign of smoke that might indicate a heat shield failure, though at this stage there really wasn't much I could do about it. After checking them over Kruger had pronounced the pods to be in full working order but Lucy hadn't been exaggerating their age. The buffeting grew worse by the second, eventually getting so bad that I had to close my eyes against the jumbled confusion.

It stopped abruptly after a full minute, by which time I'd come close to cracking some teeth as my jaw clamped tight against an involuntary shout. The pod took on only a slight tremble as it fell through the mesosphere and I did some mental arithmetic to try and pinpoint the exact second the carefully placed explosives would blow. I was out by a good five seconds.

A rapid series of concussions and the pod split apart, the constituent parts flying away to leave me tumbling through the stratosphere. We had immersion-simmed the crap out of this scenario and it turned out my muscle memory hadn't deserted me: arms tight against the body, legs together, head pointed at the surface, maintaining a vertical spin as the smoke cannisters and flares Kruger had welded onto the suit left a dirty stain in the sky. I regulated my breathing to a steady rhythm to slow the flow of judgement impairing adrenaline and did my best not to get distracted by the view...

Blue... It's all so blue. My only previous trip down the well had been a pretty frenzied affair that hadn't left much room for sightseeing, what with all the explosions and dismemberment. Now I found myself falling through an infinity of blue, the sky, the ocean far below. For someone raised in enclosed environments it made for an experience that was equal parts exhilarating and alarming. *There's so much sky.*

The pods had been launched close to the northern hemisphere at a trajectory that would take us above the Arctic Circle. The scanning stations were less numerous at this latitude and the atmospherics made for lousy maintenance, or at least they had back when I came up with this plan. The further I fell the more of the polar ice-cap I could see creeping over the blue of the ocean. A thin vertical smoke-trail half a mile away told me Mr Mac's pod had also performed as expected. With any luck the surface monitoring stations would read us as just more debris. Lucy would be burning clear by now, all comms deactivated and giving every appearance of an independent haulage contractor who didn't want to stick around for the official accident enquiry. Orbital Security might chase after her but I had every confidence in her evasion skills.

The next twenty seconds were crucial, the decision-making

window for whoever had eyes on us just now. They could decide the falling debris from two unfortunate escape pods didn't pose a threat this far from populated areas. On the other hand, they might conclude it was better to be safe than sorry and blast us into small pieces with a missile salvo. I guessed the duty officer of the day must have been worried about his budget allocation because twenty very long seconds of free-fall passed without incident.

The ice filled my entire field of vision now, a great white sheet, dotted here and there with the dark nodes of civilisation. An ever-growing population meant people were now looking farther afield for lebensraum, using tech developed for off-world colonisation to establish settlements in places once considered too hostile for human habitation. The Arctic population had officially topped the ten-million mark a year ago, but it was still 97 percent empty and not a place to linger out-of-doors for any length of time.

My headphones issued a loud insistent beep at five thousand feet and I levelled out into the classic skydiver pose, arms and legs spread to maximise atmospheric resistance, the smoke and flares still streaming in my wake. I needed to slow the descent for a chute deployment but not enough to spoil the illusion of a tumbling piece of debris in the event I was still a speck on someone's scanner. The chute auto-deployed at five hundred feet. The sims had got this part wrong. What should have been a jarring but manageable transition from free-fall to controlled descent felt more like a chest-first collision with a sledgehammer. The force of it left me with greying vision and a deep pain in my chest as I fought to refill suddenly empty lungs. My chute was a warpable, semi-rigid canopy that should have enabled a partly piloted descent, but the stunning effects of the deceleration meant all I could do was hang there gasping, oxygen starved arms like lead and my vision growing ever dimmer as the ice loomed closer.

Fortunately, I blacked out before I hit.

CHAPTER 17

THE FAINT TAPPING of gloved fingers on glass, a barely audible voice, insistent shoves. I groaned, wanting badly to slip back into what had been a blessedly absolute slumber. A hard snick then an icy blast on my face as my suit helmet was none-too-gently pulled off.

"Alex!" More shoving and groaning, the air like a million tiny needles on my skin as I felt the blood streaming from my nose begin to freeze. "We have to move! Come…" Mr Mac grunted as he hauled me into a sitting position, "…on!"

I let out a shout of pain as my eyes finally opened to be greeted by a world of blinding white. "Just keep blinking," he told me. "It'll fade. Can you walk?"

I tried to move my legs, finding to my surprise that they actually worked. "Yeah." I shook my head to try and clear the ache, eyes stinging with the chill as they slowly adjusted and the unbroken sphere of white surrounding us gradually resolved into snow-covered ice beneath a pale blue sky. "Fuck, it's cold."

"Welcome to Earth." He hooked his arms under mine and heaved me up, holding me steady as my legs did their best to fail me.

"What's our position?" I asked.

"Over three klicks from the intended drop zone. Gives us a tight window to make the rendezvous."

"Will your guy wait?"

"*I* wouldn't." He reached down to retrieve my helmet. "Hypothermia in ten minutes without this." He tossed it to me before checking the readout on his wrist. "No beacons or pings. Nothing in the air for twenty klicks in all directions." He grinned at me. "It worked. You're a military genius after all."

"Wasting time," I said, slotting my helmet into place and taking the first unsteady steps south. "Let's go."

At first glance, the extractor rig looked like a giant recreation of an ancient kitsch television, a curving, hollowed-out rectangle rising from the white mist to a height of well over two hundred metres. There were more to the east and west, stretching away to the horizon like sentinels from a bygone age, which is pretty much what they were.

"So this is how they were going to save the world," Mr Mac commented as we trudged closer, voice a little ragged in my 'phones. The two hour forced march to get here hadn't been made any easier by his constant need to chat. "Still, I guess they were desperate," he went on. "Needed to do something to get the carbon out of the atmosphere before the planet turned into another Venus. The largest geo-engineering project in human history, bankrupted the North American economies over the course of a decade, only for fusion to come along and make it all irrelevant. Some historians theorise the economic impact, coupled with the destabilising effects of such an abrupt shift away from fossil fuels, were a direct cause of the Rapture Wars and the dissolution of the United States."

"Guess you've had plenty of time for reading," I muttered. "In between all the murders, I mean."

"Benefits of an expensive education. But I guess Oksana told you all that. How is she, by the way?"

"Worried. Thought I was there to tell her I'd killed you."

"Little sis was always of a nervous disposition. Was it at her place that Dr Vaughn caught the scent, I wonder?" I gave no reply and he glanced over his shoulder, teeth gleaming behind the visor as he laughed. "I'll figure it out eventually, y'know."

We stopped three hundred metres short of the extractor and I used the suit's optics to scan the huge supporting base, icons blinking as they detected a tracked vehicle parked outside an access port. "That him?" I asked.

"It better be." Mr Mac cracked open his suit's leg compartment and extracted a military-spec Berretta 10mm.

"So he's a trustworthy type?" I enquired, drawing the Colt from my own suit.

"He's a professional criminal with a dozen or more international warrants on his head." Mr Mac started forward at a steady plod. "So, yes I trust him. Not sure what he'll make of you, though, so please try to put a muzzle on the judgemental, hard-nosed Demon crap. I'm not keen on killing a prized asset if I can help it."

We moved to within twenty feet of the vehicle, a squat snow-tractor with faded white and blue camouflage, the windscreen dark and all power off. Mr Mac voice-activated his smart and sent a short message: "Spare me the paranoia, Simon. I told you I'd be bringing a friend."

A soft crunch of snow had me whirling, Colt snapping round to aim at a dark shape to our rear. For a moment, I thought I was about to commit a heinous bio-crime by taking down a polar bear, the shape having reared up to an impressive height, snow cascading from furry flanks. *Not a bear,* I realised as the long barrel of a sniper rifle appeared, the fur falling away to reveal a man in thermal combat gear, face hidden behind an insectoid mask of optics. He was tall and lean with that rangy look long-serving military types always seemed to have. I noted he had to fight an instinctive impulse to bring his rifle to bear on me as the optics swept over my face.

"Simon, say hello to Alex," Mr Mac said. "Alex, Simon."

I said nothing and neither did Simon. It was evident we were engaged in a moment of mutual recognition. The gear and the look made it obvious. "Fed Sec SF," I said. "I guess you're not choosy about who you employ."

"He's very much retired," Mr Mac told me. "And will be permanently if they ever find him. Right, Simon?"

Simon's optics lingered on me. "Face changed, retinas haven't," he said finally, voice gravelly but otherwise accentless.

The erosion of identity was a principal facet of their training; vocal characteristics, personal history, even their original names, all conditioned out to leave the perfect covert operative. I'd killed a few during the war, and none had been easy.

"Enemy operative, Codename Fenrir," Simon went on. "Pursue and eliminate with extreme prejudice, regardless of risk."

We stared at each other in silence until he shouldered his rifle and strode towards the base of the extractor. "Too late to start out now," he told Mr Mac. "Food and supplies inside."

"Fenrir, huh?" Despite the smallness of the smart screen I could detect a certain amusement on Janet's face. I sat huddled against the wall of the extractor's maintenance bay, arms folded tight and the smart propped against my drawn up thighs. I'd been cold before but this was a whole new world, literally.

"You know what it means?" I asked, steam billowing from my mouth.

"Old Norse mythology," she said. "Fenrir is the monstrous wolf who eats Odin during the great battle that heralds the coming of Ragnarok. Viking Armageddon." Her smile broadened. "I think it suits you quite well, actually."

I sniffed and stifled a shudder. "You get anything yet?"

"It's slow going, I'm afraid. Vargold has been very careful in managing his public image, all biographical profiles are basically a variation of the same story: born in Sweden forty-six years ago to a North American refugee family, came up the well aged eighteen with minimal education. Worked basic ore processing whilst he studied technology and design spare time, eventually won a full scholarship to Lorenzo Uni where he met Rybak. Two years later, they drop out of school and self-fund a start-up: Astravista. Their first few millions came from communications software, they wrote much of the code that runs the smart network. Astravista begins a rapid expansion, becomes the third largest corporate entity in orbit within seven years, then the war starts. All corporations are quick to declare their allegiance to the UN, except Astravista. Vargold and Rybak establish Hephaestus Station beyond Lunar orbit, the principal CAOS weapons manufactory. It's pretty clear from my own research that CAOS would've lost without it. The war ends, Hephaestus Station is formally ceded to Central Governance though Astravista still holds the bulk of the contracts. Six years ago, Vargold proposes using it as the main construction site for the Ad Astra Project and humanity's journey to the stars begins. All pretty inspiring really, if you don't know he's a mass murderer."

"Family? Relationships?"

"No wife, no kids. Gossip-mills have linked him to a few models slash actresses over the years, but nothing seems to have lasted more than a few months. One starlet did a tell-all interview for a Downside celeb-rag a few years ago, called him an emotionless monster. But that could all have been post-dump venting. Failing to latch onto a billionaire has to sting a bit."

"There's got to be more, a reason for all this."

"Open sources can only tell you so much. We really need access to Pol-net and security databases if we're going to make any progress."

"Not easy when you're dead."

"Kruger says he has a few contacts from the old days, military people who might be sympathetic. As for Pol-net, I thought Chief Mordecai…"

"No. I don't want her involved, not yet anyway. She's way too exposed." I glanced over at Mr Mac. He sat close to the portable heater Simon had set up earlier, eyes intent on his smart. "How's Leyla?"

"On the mend." Janet gave a rueful grin. "Hates me more than ever."

"Lucy?"

"Made it back safe and well. She asked me to tutor her for her GEC exams so I guess we're bonding."

"Good to know. When Kruger gets you access, concentrate on the war years and check for links to Haunai Genetics." I forced a smile and managed to stop my teeth chattering. "For what it's worth, I don't think you'd've liked it down here. Expect a call in twenty-four hours. If not, assume I'm dead and get yourself and the others on a shuttle to the Belt. Lucy knows plenty of places to hide."

I shut down the smart before she could object and got up, moving close to the heater with hands extended. Simon sat opposite cleaning his disassembled rifle. Sans optics his features were revealed as Caucasian, lean and generically handsome, but not enough to be especially memorable. I wondered if he even remembered what his original face looked like.

"How many Upside deployments for you?" I asked, expecting a vague and non-committal answer but he replied without hesitation, blue eyes lacking emotion as he raised them to meet mine.

"Five."

"Confirmed kills?"

"Forty-eight."

"Anyone I knew?"

"Play nice kids," Mr Mac murmured, glancing up from his smart. "Bygones etcetera."

"How much longer in this dump?" I asked him, but it was Simon who answered.

"Six hours. You arrived just ahead of a weather front. We need to sit it out before heading south."

"And then?"

"There's a mag-lev hub on Ellesmere Island," Mr Mac said. "Gateway to the world. Just depends where we go first."

"Salacia," I said. "And me, not we. You're overwatch on this, just like the war."

He frowned a little. "You always did have a serious hero complex problem, Alex."

"I need to interact with local law-enforcement, something you can't do. Besides, sooner or later I'm going to start raising flags on Vargold's map. You and your pet ninja here are going to keep me alive when his people come looking."

Simon slotted the barrel of his rifle into the stock with a loud clack. The pet ninja jibe had been a gambit, a test to see if he had any skin to get under. If so, he was expert at concealing it. "Better get some sleep," he said, settling back and pulling the hood of his combat smock over his head. "Long haul tomorrow."

CHAPTER 18

I GOT OFF the mag-lev in Havana just under forty-eight hours later, emerging from the vast terminus to once again suffer a wave of disorientation as the sky unfolded above in all its bluey vastness. The ID Mr Mac had supplied named me as David Cross, International Security Consultant for Dynamic Protection GLC, a genuine multi-national he'd purchased an interest in a few years before. The company's business included several government contracts which required select employees to carry concealed weapons on public transit. The ID got me through terminus security without a blip, then it was a short taxi ride through the archaically surreal streets of Havana to the airport and onto a flight to Barbados. Modern materials meant aircraft windows formed about thirty percent of the fuselage, affording spectacular views all around. The mag-lev had offered a relief from the endless sky, and an opportunity to plan my approach on reaching Salacia, but now there was nowhere to hide from all the *space*.

"Nervous flyer, huh?" the woman seated next to me asked, presumably noting the sheen of sweat on my forehead.

"Something I ate," I muttered back, voice deliberately gruff to conceal my accent and forestall further conversation.

"They'll get you a sedative if you need it," she went on.

There's no pill to cure agoraphobia, I didn't say, grunting, "I'm fine, thanks," before pretending to sleep.

By the time I stepped onto the tarmac at Barbados I was pretty much a wreck. The Caribbean heat was proving as hard to bear as the Arctic cold. I shambled to the airport hotel and checked in, the Dynamic Protection company credit card entitling me to a suite complete with hot-tub and a well stocked bar. I collapsed onto the bed fully clothed and slept for nine hours straight wondering how a species that called itself civilised could live like this.

Salacia Hab was moored two hundred klicks off the Barbadian coast, a three hundred metre tall by one hundred and fifty metre wide tube tethered to the sea floor by carbon-sixty cables and powered by an on-board fusion reactor. The total population stood at just over five thousand, mostly wealthy retirees who had chosen to remove themselves from the increasing crush on land and opted for a life beneath the waves. Getting there required a three hour sub-ride from Bridgetown, an experience I found infinitely preferable to flying. Instead of portholes the sub had external cameras, the feeds combined to project an image of the ocean on the inside of the hull. I felt the anxiety recede as we glided through shoals of fish, catching the occasional glimpse of a shark or a ray. It was as alien an environment as I'd ever experienced, but weirdly soothing in its serenity, and familiar in its comparative lack of gravity.

Salacia's immigration control was entirely automated, the scanner accepted my ID and features without demur before the inner airlock door opened and I stepped out onto the main concourse. Perhaps unsurprisingly the atmosphere was fairly muted. There were a few dozen people about, but most of the shops were closed. I noted a carpet of flowers surrounding the base of an abstract sculpture in the centre of the concourse, ritual offerings to the recently departed. If this massacre had happened on the Yang-side level where I grew up, it would probably have been forgotten a few hours after the blood had been hosed away. I took out my smart and sent an interview request to Phaedra Diallo marked 'Re. Current Investigation', then found a vending machine which dispensed a hot but uncertainly flavoured beverage. I found a bench and waited, sipping what may have been coffee and looking up at the ascending rings of Salacia's levels, all balconies and hanging gardens, even some birds fluttering about. It reminded me of Yin-side but was more elegant somehow, less ostentatious.

"Mr Cross?"

I lowered my gaze to find a small but athletic young woman standing a few feet away. I was momentarily distracted both by her attire, a black lycra one-piece bathing suit with a gold police shield pinned to one of the straps, and the fact that she was a splice. Her skin was silver-grey and sparkled a little in the light from the UVs above, and her eyes consisted of white pupils set in black orbs. Her hair was cropped short and spiky and she carried a sidearm in a holster slung over her shoulder. From the beads still shining in her hair, it was clear she wasn't long out of the water.

"Chief Diallo?" I said.

"That's me." She angled her head, eyelids narrowing so her ivory pupils resembled two slits. "Saw your face on a news feed a couple of days ago," she said. "It belonged to a dead man."

I smiled and rose, extending my hand. "Y'know, I think we're going to get along just fine."

"I count seven different violations of global statutes," she said an hour or so later. She'd taken me to her place, a spacious mid-level apartment with a large window offering a view of the sub-aquatic world outside. I'd been impressed by her precautions, insisting I hand over my smart and weapon before instructing me to sit and start talking. I also found it significant that she hadn't taken me to her HQ and made no effort to alert anyone else to my presence.

"Use of false credentials to cross international boundaries," she went on. "Illegal transport of a firearm across said boundaries..."

"Yeah, but I haven't killed anyone yet," I said. "And I'm guessing you have some reason not to think I'm a paranoid nutbar 'cause we've been here for an hour and I'm not in cuffs."

She sat perched on the arm of her couch, a towel around her neck, her gun and mine on the coffee table between us. "We got shut down," she said after a long pause. "A bunch of Fed Sec suits turned up with a UN mandated order not long after I spoke to you. Took all our evidence, including Schiffler's body. Left me in no doubt this was their case now."

"Did they give you the slightest impression they'd actually do anything with it?"

"'Course they fucking didn't. Thirteen of my people dead and no one will ever know why."

"You OK with that?"

She glanced at the window as a shoal of brightly coloured fish darted past. "This is a good place, y'know. People here made me welcome, never called me a freak or an abomination before the lord. That isn't always the case down here. Different where you're from, I guess."

"We have our problems, but we mostly just rub along as best we can."

She nodded. "There isn't much I can give you. Like I said, Fed Sec took all the evidence."

"The victims," I said. "Them you can give me."

Thirteen names. Five men, eight women. The oldest an eighty-three year old grandfather of six, the youngest a seventeen year old girl from Copenhagen who'd come to visit with her great-aunt. There were also two young men in their twenties, a married couple from Brazil here to compete in an upcoming sub-aquatic sports tournament. Just people, going about their lives, their stories forever caught in the amber of this atrocity.

"No links," Phaedra said, now dressed in a less distracting police uniform. She'd cooked whilst I read, whisking up a mushroom broth from fresh produce grown in Salacia's hydroponics farm. Apparently, self-sufficiency was part of the sub-aquatic ethos, insurance against the day the world above the waves finally went to complete shit. "No links to Schiffler. Most didn't know each other, those that did only in passing. No one rich, more than the average I mean. No one famous."

"Who was first?" I asked.

"There's a mo-capped multi-angle re-creation in the vids folder, all victims tagged and events time-lined."

I called up the file and ran it through, watching the stick figures fall one by one as Schiffler made an unhurried progress across the concourse, speargun jerking a little as he fired. It seemed entirely random, even typical for this kind of tragedy. Solitary loser blows a brain-gasket and seeks notoriety via mass murder. Psychologically speaking the victims were irrelevant, just extras in the movie playing in Schiffler's head. I ran the sequence again at slower speed, freezing it just as Schiffler made his first kill. The victim's tag named them as Roderico Lomos Vivar, one half of the Brazilian couple. I noticed Roderico had been shot in the back whilst in motion, he seemed to be diving to the side, arms reaching out to another figure. I advanced frame by frame, watching Roderico collapse as the spear skewered him. The figure he had been reaching for stood stock still as Schiffler lined up for another shot, making no effort to evade the killing spear. The name tag read Lisabet Holstrom, aged fifty-four, Salacia resident for just under eight months.

I reran the vid from the moment Schiffler first stepped onto the concourse, speargun held at his side in a relaxed grip, like he was carrying a fishing rod. Switching to a top-down view I saw that his initial approach contrasted with the latter part of the spree. Instead of wandering and picking off targets of opportunity he made a direct line for where Lisabet Holstrom sat at a cafe reading a book. He paused twelve feet away for several seconds. I watched Holstrom look up from her book, hesitate for a second then slowly get to her feet, standing in immobile expectation.

"That's when he first said it," I said to Phaedra. "Wasn't it?"

"The 'from light' thing? Yeah."

The ghastly cartoon played out, Schiffler raising his speargun, Roderico rising from the neighbouring table and diving towards the woman he saw was about to be murdered. "You might want to tell this Jed's family he died a hero," I said, freezing the playback and tapping Roderico's body. "Holstrom was the target. Everyone else was just cover."

"Biographical details are pretty thin," Phaedra said a short while later. She'd accessed the Salacia mainframe and downloaded all data relating to Lisabet Holstrom. "Our investigation was only getting started by the time Fed Sec shut us down, so the victim profiles are kinda bare bones. Also, the sub-aquatic community is big on privacy and personal freedom. When someone applies to join a hab there's a basic background check to ensure they don't have a criminal record, plus confirmation their finances are in order, but not much else. Holstrom came up clean on all checks and paid the full amount for a ten year lease on a lower level apartment. Lower levels have the best views so they command a premium. Lived alone, no significant others. She did join a book group though, met every Wednesday in a neighbour's apartment."

"Open sources?"

Phaedra did some scrolling. "Doesn't seem to have made any headlines, all hits are on corporate personnel sites. Seems she was an engineer, astronautics. Born in Norway, but spent much of her working life up the well."

"Employer?"

"Most recent was…" She trailed off, looked up with a small grin. "Hephaestus Propulsion Systems, a division of Astravista Industries. Guess we're not chasing shadows after all."

I rose from the table, holstering my Colt and looking at her expectantly.

"What?"

"Police work one-oh-one," I said. "Let's go knock on someone's door."

There were only three apartments on Salacia's lowest level. One was temporarily unoccupied and the other belonged to the organiser of Holstrom's book group. The man who answered the door was clearly a fan of rejuve treatments, the face and body of a thirty year old with the hands and eyes of someone who probably remembered the first Titan landing. "Chief!" he greeted Phaedra with a broad smile, coming close to air-kiss both cheeks. "It's been too long. You look even more marvellous."

He stood aside and beckoned us inside. It took me a moment to fully appreciate the size and luxury of the apartment, putting even Oksana's place to shame. The wall was one big window, curving around in a 120 degree arc to encompass a broad sweep of the coral reef surrounding Salacia's tethers.

"Thank you for talking to us, Theodore," Phaedra said then nodded at me. "This is Mr Cross, a private investigator. He'd like to talk about Ms Holstrom."

Theodore's face fell abruptly, raising a shaky hand to his lips. "Oh, that terrible business. I thought it was over. The hab-feed said your investigation was concluded."

"Yes, sir," I said. "Sorry to cause any upset, but the firm handling Ms Holstrom's estate have asked me to look into the events surrounding her demise."

Theodore stiffened a little, eyes taking on a judgemental cast. "Vultures gathering, are they?"

"We're just trying to make sure the settlement is fair and equitable. But, yes, some of Ms Holstrom's relatives are contesting the will." I gave a reluctant wince, lowering my voice to a confiding murmur. "There are claims Ms Holstrom may have been suicidal. Even that she might have had something to do with the massacre."

"That's utterly ridiculous." Theodore stiffened further. "To think that dear lady would ever hurt another soul. Preposterous." I could tell he believed what he said, but I also detected a small tick of uncertainty amongst the outrage.

"How well did you know her?" I asked.

His face softened and he moved to take a seat at the breakfast bar. "Not as well as I'd have liked. She was an interesting person. I like interesting people, like our dear Phaedra here. Lisabet was well read, multi-lingual and highly intelligent, but also… very sad. Not suicidally so, but still, I could see her pain, though she did her best to hide it. There was one time, though, during a book group get-together. We were discussing Bleak House, her pick for the week. She so loved Dickens. In the middle of the discussion, she just burst into tears. I asked her what was wrong but she wouldn't say, just kept on crying and saying she was sorry."

"For what?"

"I have no idea. But it was strange, like she was personally apologising to all of us, saying sorry to each one of us. I got her a brandy and she calmed down, eventually. I think that was the last book group she came to. Three weeks later…" He shuddered. "Well, you know about that."

"Did she ever talk about her work?"

"Not particularly. I remember her saying her retirement had come earlier than expected, though from what remained somewhat vague. I could tell from her accent she'd spent some years in orbit, though not as many as you, I'd guess."

"Very astute, sir. Did she have many visitors?"

He gave a sombre grimace and shook his head. "Not one that I ever saw. And, come to think of it, I can't remember her calling anyone. I did suggest she put a profile up on the sub-aqua dating net but she just laughed."

I asked a few more questions, all of which continued to paint a picture of a private woman with few if any links to the outside world and no desire for that to change. "I think that covers it, sir," I said. "Thanks for your time. Chief Diallo, I think we should check Ms Holstrom's apartment now."

Theodore showed us to the door, hesitating as we stepped out into the foyer. "Something else?" I asked.

"There was another time," he said, "when I found her crying. Not sobbing like before, just standing at her window looking out over the reef. I asked her what was the matter and she just shook her head. I was going to leave her alone but she said something." He closed his eyes to summon the memory. "'The boiling point of sea water at the levels of salinity found in these waters is 100.65 degrees Celsius. Did you know that, Theo?'"

"Impressive recall, sir," I said.

He gave a modest shrug and winked as the door slid closed. "I used to be an actor."

Lisabet Holstrom's apartment was identical to Theodore's in every respect but decor. No designer luxury here, just functional furniture and a whole wall of books. "Must've been a collector," Phaedra mused, running a finger along the library before extracting a volume. "Proust, in the original French. This looks pretty old."

I followed the age-old detective practice of checking the bathroom first, specifically the medicine cabinet. "That's a lotta pills," Phaedra observed from the doorway.

I extracted a few bottles for closer inspection, finding most were close to empty. "Anti-depressants, sleep-aids, anxiety meds. Lady with a lot on her mind, I guess."

I checked Holstrom's terminal next, blinking in surprise when it went straight to the main interface without requesting a password. "Either she had nothing to hide or she was beyond caring." I checked her contacts folder first, finding it empty but for a single outgoing message from seven days ago:

To: Craig Rybak, H.O. Astravista

Subject: I can't do this.

That was all. Nothing in the body of the message sent to a man who died four days later. "Nothing in the cloud," I said, digging down through the folders. "Nothing on the solid-state. This is a purged system apart from that one message."

"What couldn't she do?" Phaedra wondered.

"Whatever it was I'm guessing both she and Rybak died for it. He was apparently targeted by a Fed Sec sleeper agent and she's the random victim of a spree killer. Both credible scenarios at face value."

"There are quieter ways to kill people."

"I don't think Vargold wants it quiet. I think he's sending a message. Neither killing can be directly attributable to him, but both are loud and messy enough to attract attention. Question is from who?"

"Somebody who might be next."

I reclined in Holstrom's desk chair, swivelling around to take in the view. Clouds of fish darted across the coral and, in the distance, I could see lights blinking and the dim figures of divers.

"Spear hunters," Phaedra explained, then gave a humourless laugh. "Just like Schiffler."

"Who is now our only lead," I said. "So what've you got?"

"The portrait of a complete loser." She took out her smart and called up Schiffler's profile. "Rich kid gone bad. In and out of rehab since he was fifteen, no employment history, living off mommy and daddy's trust-fund and waiting for them to die. Arrested for beating up his girlfriend eighteen months ago."

I turned away from the window as something clicked in my head. *Corvin, released from corrective immersion five days before he killed Rybak. Blair, recidivist wicky waver. Corrective immersion is mandatory for sex offenders.* "Let me guess," I said. "Sentenced to corrective immersion."

She shook her head. "Close, but you don't get the big teddy bear. Thanks to the vast fee his parents paid to the best law-firm in the hemisphere, and a sizeable personal injury settlement for the girlfriend, the charges were dropped on condition he undertake intensive therapy at a private rehab facility. That's why there was no criminal record on his background check. He got discharged four months ago with a clean bill of health and remained a model citizen until he decided to take his speargun for a walk."

"What have you got on the rehab facility?"

She ran a quick search and called up the clinic's site, white palatial buildings in a tropical landscape of waving palms and azure seas. 'Welcome to Renewal,' the blurb intoned in soothing female tones, 'the world's leading treatment provider for addiction-related illnesses. Here at Renewal we pride ourselves on our holistic approach to recovery, our treatment regimen combining counselling, pharmacology and technology to produce an 86% success rate in treating addiction. Renewal remains the foremost innovator in the field of immersion assisted recovery…'

"Where is this dump?" I asked.

"St Barthélemy. A day's sub-ride north. Or I can call in a seaplane if you want to get there quicker."

"No." I fought down a wave of nausea provoked by the thought of another flight so soon. "Sub's fine."

CHAPTER 19

BEFORE BOARDING THE sub, I called Mr Mac and told him I needed a new ID.

"This is a tall order," he said. "Given the time frame."

"I doubt the Renewal management will talk to a PI or a small town cop."

"I'll see what I can do."

The sub was a midget compared to the passenger transport that brought me to Salacia, a maintenance workhorse with articulated limbs and bubble canopies that made it resemble a giant mutant crab. The captain and sole crew member was a splice with similar mods to Phaedra, white pupils in black eyes and grey skin, though his had a touch of cobalt blue. "This is Erik," Phaedra said as we clambered aboard. "Commanding Officer Salacia Military."

"You have a military?" I asked.

"Sure," Erik told me, white teeth shining in his blue-grey face. "Gotta have a military or the UN don't recognise you." He raised his hands to encompass the sub's interior. "How'd you like our flagship?"

We disengaged from Salacia a few minutes later, Erik steering a northerly course at an impressive thirty knots. "Hydro-jets instead of propellers," Phaedra explained. "Some of the bigger boats can do over a hundred knots."

I settled into the nose bubble, watching the seabed speed by for a time before turning about and trying to catch up on some sleep. It came eventually, a brief fitful slumber in which I saw Joe's death play out more than once, except this time he survived the blast, his still living head attached to the mangled mess of his body by a tendril of flesh. He spoke to me but the words were lost, like someone calling to me from the far end of a long tunnel. I took some comfort from his expression, open, accepting, if a little sad. *At least he doesn't hate me…*

I came awake with a soft groan and a headache, blurred vision eventually focusing on Phaedra's legs. She'd changed back into her swimsuit for the journey and her bare, toned limbs were stretched out towards me as she lay on a narrow bunk below the pilot's station. My eyes tracked along the silvery flesh, hard-wired if guilt tinged heterosexuality making me wonder what skin like that would feel like.

"Why don't you just ask?"

My gaze snapped to Phaedra's face, fully awake and more than slightly amused.

"Sorry," I said. "It's just… There's no one like you back home."

"It's hydro-dynamic," she said, sitting up and running a hand along her thigh. "Based on shark-skin, but much more finely grained. I also have a super-efficient cardiovascular system and can swim fifty metres underwater three seconds faster than the most recent Olympic gold medallist can on the surface."

"The eyes?" I asked.

"Adapted for sub-aquatic light conditions. My ears are also tuned for echo location."

"Guess you really must love the water."

"I do. But my parents loved it more. Erik's parents too. The Aqua-Utopian Movement, ever hear of it?"

I shook my head.

"Hardly surprising, it didn't last very long. A grand design to return humanity to the bosom of mother ocean from whence all life sprang. Why bother ascending to the heavens when the seas offer all the space and resources we need? To be honest it was more a cult than a movement. Kids like Erik and me were supposed to be the first generation of homo-aquatus, the dawn of the oceanic master race. Then the anti-splice backlash kicked in and the UN shut the whole thing down. The kids grew up in care homes then got pushed out to fend for ourselves. We spent a few years in the fishing trade off the Gulf of Mexico but the locals started getting restless, we were too successful and they didn't like the competition. Luckily, the aquatic hab community saw the wisdom of taking us in."

Erik climbed down from the pilot's station, pausing on the ladder. "We're fifteen minutes from docking, Phae."

She nodded and turned to me. "We good? Should be in range of a smart node by now."

I checked my smart, finding a new ID had been uploaded: Hubert Plympton, Special Agent, UN Federal Security - Criminal Investigation Division. *Hubert? Fucking Mr Mac.* "Yeah, we're good."

Renewal's Medical Director was named Dr Julieta Perales, a handsome and elegant woman who probably spent just as much on rejuve as Theodore, the retired actor. She was also a lot less pleasant to deal with. "I really can't see how we can help you, Agent Plympton," she told me, apparently relaxed and unruffled behind her desk. "Naturally, when we heard the news and realised one of our former patients was responsible we conducted a thorough review of his time here. However, I can assure you there were absolutely no indications anything like this would occur. Our ethical code would have dictated that any warning signs be notified to the relevant authorities." She gave a tight, professional smile. "There really isn't much else to tell you, and I'm sure you're familiar with the statutes regarding disclosure of medical records, even after death."

"Exemptions apply in cases of Global Security," I told her. "Otherwise, I wouldn't be here."

She maintained her smile, giving a smooth and evidently rehearsed reply, "I'm aware of the exemptions and if you can show me a warrant from the Security Council..."

"Over half your patients are aquatic hab residents," Phaedra said. "Referred as per your contract with the community justice system. Right?"

Perales' smile flickered, just a little. "Quite right."

"The justice minister is very fond of me. Kind've a surrogate daughter thing. I'd hate to have to call him."

I saw the doctor's face darken as pragmatism warred with innate medical bureaucracy. I decided Phaedra had poked her a little too hard and said, "We don't need full access, in any case. I'm more interested in the treatment Schiffler received here, specifically the immersion element."

"I assure you our immersion therapy meets the highest industry standards and is subject to regular independent review."

I gave her a smile of my own. "Then let's just call this a surprise inspection, shall we?"

"There wasn't anything unusual in Mr Schiffler's treatment profile," Perales told us a short while later. We stood around an immersion couch in one of the clinic's treatment rooms as she called up various holo-stills from Schiffler's sessions. "Relaxation scenarios alternated with situations that forced him to confront the damage his behaviour inflicted on himself and those around him." She tapped a finger to the hypodermic armature fixed to the side of the couch. "The procedure is pharmalogically assisted to enhance the realism."

"So they're high as a kite when they're in there?" Phaedra asked.

"Mild hallucinogens only, no opioids or stimulants."

Phaedra squinted at a still of several naked female bodies in mid-cavort. "That looks pretty stimulating."

"We find a reward-based structure to be the most effective. A carrot-and-stick approach, if you will."

"Put him through something shitty and then ease the pain with porn." Phaedra shrugged. "I can see that."

I watched the stills roll: A young man behind a dumpster bleeding out from a stomach wound. A hot-tub blow-job from a model just dissimilar enough from a famous actress to avoid a lawsuit. A middle-aged woman screaming in maternal anguish as tears streaked down her face. A mountain-top looking out over a sunlit valley that resembled something from an old fantasy flick. I was about to let it slide by when I noticed a structure in the foreground; white marble pillars arranged in a circle.

"Stop it there," I said. "That doesn't seem to fit with everything else."

"Ah, yes," Perales said. "A recent addition, but an effective one. It's called the Temple of Serenity. The specifics of the design vary according to the subject, but it's intended to enable the patient to connect with their spiritual side, provided they have one, of course. In this case, Schiffler being vaguely paganistic in his beliefs, a Greco-Roman style was deemed the best choice."

"How exactly do you connect someone with their spirituality?"

"Well." Perales crossed her arms, getting defensive. "You don't. Not really. But there are particular centres of the brain that respond to certain stimuli and convey the… impression of what Bhuddists like to call 'enlightenment'."

"You mean, you dope them up and trick them into thinking they've seen the face of god in an immersion sim?"

"The path to recovery is never a straight one, Agent Plympton. And the subject invariably realises on waking that the experience was a simulated one. However, the sensation of a spiritual awakening persists in the memory. An awareness of the wider universe is important when combating addiction."

I studied the image a moment longer. It seemed a slender lead, but it was the only indication of a connection to cult-like behaviour. "Fire it up, Doctor," I told Perales, taking off my jacket and climbing onto the couch. "Just the serene temple thing, and hold the drugs."

I've never been a fan of Immersion. It was too expensive prewar and all that time spent with Consuela's increasingly embittered consciousness had soured me on the whole thing. But I'd never doubted the power of it, the insertion of a new reality into the brain with sufficient accuracy that you just don't question it. Compelling for some, addictive for others, and I'd recently come to terms with the fact that I had an addictive nature. So I did my best not to enjoy the feel of a sun-warmed breeze on my skin, or drink in the fresh mountain air as I marvelled at the impossibly beautiful valley below. *Don't forget, it's all a lie.*

I walked across a field of long, green grass towards the temple, marble pillars shining white in the late afternoon sun, the breeze blowing autumnal leaves from a nearby copse of maple across my path. The temple itself held no secrets that I could see, just a circle of paving stones surrounded by seven pillars. I dimly recalled seven pillars having some kind of religious significance but couldn't place it. Otherwise, I found nothing. No vaguely worded inscriptions inviting a close examination of the soul, no mysterious symbols in need of interpretation. Just the pillars and the view.

Maybe it's supposed to teach the virtues of patience, I wondered as the minutes ticked by and nothing happened. The sun's rays shimmered like multiple searchlights through the drifting clouds, painting the valley below an enchanting range of colours, and nothing happened. *You really need to be stoned to appreciate this.* I opened my mouth to speak the end-sim codeword Perales had given me, then hesitated as I noticed the clouds had stopped drifting. In fact, it had all stopped. The maple leaves were frozen in the air, the swaying grass now stiffened like spikes. But the air, the air was definitely getting colder.

Something flashed in the sky, bright enough to make me turn away, tears streaming from my eyes. When I looked again the clouds were gone and the sky had turned black but for a small pinprick of light. It started to pulse as I watched, flaring then diminishing in a regular rhythm that I realised matched the beat of my heart. It grew bigger with every pulse, the light varying in colour from white to red, to blue, then green. The effect was mesmerising, even without the drugs.

The pulsing abruptly stopped, the light now a single transcendent star commanding every facet of my attention. I heard the voice then, female, un-inflected but somehow utterly compelling. "From light..." The light began to swell, shimmering as it did so. "...we are born." The light burst apart, birthing a massive spider's web of glowing gas that surrounded me on all sides. "To light we return," the voice continued as the gaseous web began to coalesce. My physics was pretty limited but I'd seen enough pop-science docs to know this was a representation of the birth of the universe, a single massive release of energy coalescing into physical reality under the pressure of gravity. Stars began to ignite a second later, thousands, millions, every colour and shade. The effect was impressive, even emotional, and I could only imagine what it felt like for a long-term junkie stoned on hallucinogens.

"From light we are born to light we return," the voice repeated, once, then twice, then again and again, the words overlapping until it became a discordant babbling mantra, maddeningly inescapable.

Then silence.

After the babbling silence was a shock, leaving me stunned as I floated in my new born universe.

"Your light, Randall," the voice said, returned to its previous emotionless but compelling cadence. The stars began to shift around me, slowly at first, then clumping together with increasing rapidity, the sky becoming black as it formed a single shimmering image in the void. A woman's face. A woman in her fifties with a very sad smile: Lisabet Holstom. "Your light resides in her, Randall," the voice told me, its previously empty tone now stern and commanding, a high priest sending a supplicant on a holy mission. "Set it free. Set all of them free…"

Holstrom's face began to glow brighter as the voice spoke on, strident and booming now: "FROM LIGHT WE ARE BORN TO LIGHT WE RETURN!"

I tried to close my eyes against the now blinding glare of Holstrom's image but found I couldn't. The sim had evidently been coded to prevent Randall averting his gaze at this moment. Holstrom's face began to flicker, a thrumming migraine inducing pulse that seemed to pry its way into my brain as the voice boomed on and on.

"FROM LIGHT WE ARE BORN…."

"Bolero!" I shouted out the end-sim code word. "Bolero! Get me the fuck out of here!"

I surfaced with a hammering heart and what felt like a pick-axe buried in my skull. The tremble in my limbs was so severe it took a few seconds for me to drag myself into a sitting position.

"I didn't know!" Perales was backed up against the wall with Phaedra's gun pressed into her cheek, hands raised and all composure vanished. "I swear!"

"Your vitals went haywire," Phaedra told me, keeping her eyes locked on Perales. "Near fatal levels. Looked like this bitch was trying to kill you."

I looked down at my hands, making fists until the tremble faded enough that I felt capable of standing. "The temple," I said, advancing towards Perales. "Did you come up with it yourself?"

"No." She shook her head, as much as she could under the

pressure of Phaedra's weapon. "Most of our sims are third-party software."

"So where'd you get this one?"

"I need to check the records."

I nodded to Phaedra and she stepped back, allowing Perales to pull a smart from the pocket of her lab-coat. "We have a long-standing contract with Sensory Realities," she said, calling up the relevant company site. "They're mainly involved in the games sector but they also have a therapeutic arm."

I punched the details into my own smart. More grist for Janet's mill.

"That sim turned one of your patients into a mass murderer," I told Perales. "And you didn't notice."

"Our monitoring protocols are strict," she insisted. "But non-invasive. We only intervene when the patient's vitals start to spike. Which is extremely rare, and never happened in Schiffler's case."

"Must've been an incremental thing," I muttered, turning back to the couch. "Increased the conditioning with every session. What I saw was the final iteration, by the time he experienced it, Schiffler would've been so steeped in the creed of his fake enlightenment it was probably just another holy vision."

My eyes went to the couch's hypo-armature. "Are hallucinogens used in corrective immersion?" I asked Perales.

"Well, yes," she said. "Bringing about a personality change requires at least some form of pharmacology."

Corvin and Blair. Both recipients of extensive immersion. With Vargold's links to the justice system, how difficult could it have been to add a little something extra to the mix? Corvin gets spliced into a werewolf and Blair a human bomb. No such extremes had been needed for Schiffler, I suspected because Vargold's reach didn't extend to this clinic, just the software they used.

"Thank you for your time, Doctor," I said, pulling on my jacket. "We'll be going now. It's in your best interests to forget about our visit."

CHAPTER 20

"THE THERAPEUTIC ARM of Sensory Realities is run as a non-profit," Janet said, her holo-rendered face pale and indistinct in the bright St Barthélemy sun. We'd found a cafe near the beach to make the call, Phaedra sipping a mint-julep whilst I worked my way through a whole pitcher of iced-tea and tried to ignore the soul-sucking blue emptiness above. "Guess who their principal donor is?"

"Astravista?"

"Actually, the money comes from a charitable trust registered in New York which receives donations from several different sources. But dig down a few layers and you find Astravista as the main donor. The interesting thing is the principal trustee, Konstantin Wallace. He's ninety-six years old and has an academic career going back six decades, social sciences, anthropology and bio-chemistry. Clearly a bit of a polymath. Numerous published papers and a few books, burgeoning media career in his forties, turned up on some docs and talk shows, appointed to the UN Scientific Advisory Committee for a while, then fell off the radar shortly after the Rapture Wars. Ten years later he resurfaced in Korea."

"Haunai Genetics," I said.

"That's right. Kruger finally got us access to an unedited historical data-set. Wallace's listed as a non-executive director, but the financial records make it clear he was the principal investor. Since the company was wound up the senior officers seem to have had a remarkably unlucky time of it. Two died in a freak road accident and a third went missing on a hiking trip in Nepal. Wallace's the only Board Member still around."

"He still in Korea?"

Janet shook her head with a grin. "It looks like you get to return to your roots, Wallace is in Scotland. He bought himself a private island in the Hebrides a few years ago. I'm sending through some schematics. He hasn't skimped on security so I'm not sure how you'll get in there, assuming that's what you want to do."

"Vargold?" I asked.

"Still digging. He's been on the feeds again, though. The *Jason Alpha* is only a week away from its maiden voyage."

Jason Alpha, his grand design. It had to be linked to all this. Had Rybak and the others posed a threat to it somehow?

"Keep at it," I said and closed the call.

"Pretty lady," Phaedra observed, cheeks contracting as she sucked julep through a straw. "You're a lucky fella."

"I'm aware." I rubbed my temples and risked a glance at the sky, managing a good three seconds before my eyes shut tight as the dizziness swept through me. "Don't suppose Erik's sub is capable of a transatlantic crossing?"

The sub sat in the quietest corner of the docks that formed Salacia's base, resembling a giant torpedo with a bad skin condition. A hundred metre long round-nosed tube, its hull covered from end to end with small triangular crenellations of irregular size. "She used to be the *USS Olympia*," Erik said. "One of the last attack subs built for the US Navy. Fusion core reactor and hybrid hydro-jet screw drive. She was sitting in mothballs in the San Diego yards until Aquatic League Security let me buy her a few years ago, secret weapon kinda thing. Just in case. We named her the *Tethys*."

"What's that's stuff on her hull?" I asked.

"Sonic baffles. Like the inside of a recording studio, only bigger. Confuses sonar. They're retractable so overall speed isn't affected. Should get you to the Scottish coast in just under four days."

"Weapons?"

"Thirty Fire-lance torps. Faster and more sophisticated than anything else in the water these days. We make them ourselves so, y'know, military secret and all. I'll kill you if you tell anyone." He gave an apologetic shrug. "Sorry."

I watched Phaedra carrying her gear onto the sub. "Guess she had to pull a lot of strings to make this happen."

"Not really. Everyone's mighty pissed about what Schiffler did. More so now it turns out he wasn't some random nut. The rest of the world needs to know they can't fuck around on our turf. Most folks choose to live down here to get away from all that shit."

In addition to Phaedra and Erik, Aquatic League Security had seen fit to send along what I assumed to be their version of a special ops squad. There were six of them, all products of the defunct Aqua-Utopian Movement judging by their mods. They stowed their gear and started prepping the sub with happy efficiency, displaying the kind of keenness that came from long-term training and zero combat experience.

"They've been waiting for something like this their whole lives," Phaedra explained. "The Movement envisioned a war between land and sea once the inevitable apocalypse kicked in."

I spent much of the journey studying the schematics of Wallace's island hideaway and going over the background material Janet had uploaded to my smart. Much of it consisted of Wallace's scientific papers and copies of his books. The science stuff was mostly lost on me, but the books made for more interesting reading. The first, entitled, 'Towards Ascension', was an optimistic treatise on humanity's prospects in the post-fusion age. *For millennia we have struggled to free ourselves of the mud from which we grew,* Wallace wrote in the introduction. *Our struggle has been a painful one, our path ever obstructed by superstition, prejudice, dogma and the thousand other frailties to which our species is prone. But now, through the wondrous agency and insight gifted to us by the extraordinary accident of our evolution, an infinity of possibility awaits us, in the stars.*

"Poor bastard," I muttered, calling up the next book. "I guess you were in for a shock."

Predictably, Wallace's next book, 'Ascension Lost?' written not long after he resigned his position with the UN two decades later, had a decidedly bitter tone, though the underlying message remained the same: *The mud proved far more difficult to scrape off than I assumed. An inability to grasp the narrowness and greed inherent in our species has ever been the flaw of the scientific mind. It has become increasingly clear to me that, if we are to finally begin our journey to ascension then those capable of grasping its possibilities must forsake this planet. Our cradle has become our prison. We are like a mental patient who, having been given the key to our cell door, sits in the corner and weeps with indecision, so terrified are we of what awaits us outside.*

I skim-read most of the rest, finding much of it a somewhat grim history of the last sixty years, though Wallace did find perverse cause for optimism in the CAOS war: *Can it be, that in seeking to enslave our poor in an orbital gulag, we have inadvertently created a launch pad for ascension? Now, drifting above us, is an entire generation of humanity who have never been mired in the mud. A new culture has risen, a culture born in the fires of revolution, scoured clean of sentimental attachment to this speck of unremarkable rock orbiting an unremarkable star.*

But it was the final chapter that I found most interesting, particularly the conclusion: *I have never been one for superstition, nor do I wish to succour the cowardice of agnosticism. However, I can't resist the conclusion that there is wisdom and insight to be found in those myths produced by the pre-enlightenment mind. The Ragnarok of the Vikings and the Armageddon of Christian tradition reflect a fundamental understanding of our tenuous position on this planet. On an instinctive, perhaps primal level our forebears knew our time here was finite, a truth lost in an age where technological wonder has been matched by all-too-human horror. If we are ever to ascend, we must once again grasp this essential, inescapable truth - to prosper, we must leave this world behind.*

I found Erik and Phaedra on the bridge, pondering a map of Wallace's island on the tactical holo as they discussed assault scenarios. "We're only fifty klicks away," Erik said. "Euro-Fed drones regularly patrol the coastal approaches so we'll have to go stealthy to get close enough for a landing. It'll reduce our speed to five knots, but I can't see a way past it."

I took a close look at the holo. The island was called Gruinard, two klicks long by one klick wide, and heavily forested apart from the three acres where Wallace had constructed his mansion. Red dots around the coast and interior indicated the most likely nodes for his security net. "Anthrax Island," I murmured.

"What?" Phaedra asked.

"Gruinard was a test site for the British bio-weapons programme in the twentieth century," I said, repeating what I'd read in Janet's info package. "It was uninhabitable for decades. Even after decontamination it remained unsettled until Wallace bought it. The trees are all new, accelerated reforestation. Hugely expensive but I doubt he worries much about that kind've thing."

"Nice of him to provide so much cover, anyway," Erik said, tapping icons to highlight a spot on the island's northern shore. "Our insertion point. The beach on the south side is way too obvious. You'll need to get suited up, Inspector, assuming you want to come along. Don't worry about trying to keep up, the suit has a propulsion system. On landing, one team will strike out directly south, tripping the security net and hopefully drawing off most of the guards. They've got instructions to exfiltrate after a brief engagement. Should give us a reasonably uninterrupted approach to the mansion. We force entry, grab up Wallace, retreat to the insertion point for exfil. In and out in fifteen minutes."

"Very slick," I said, feeling a pang of guilt at bursting his bubble. He'd really been looking forward to playing commando. "But it won't be necessary. D'you have a boat I can borrow?"

The sky was getting dark by the time I rounded the headland and steered for Gruinard's gently sloping southern shore. Somehow the gloom made the roofless horror of it all more tolerable, an echo of the starlit void I'd looked out on for so many years. The boat was a small rigid-hulled inflatable with an electric outboard, rigged to run at near silence so the guards on the beach didn't notice my approach until I'd begun to ride the surf towards the narrow strip of pale sand. I waited until the hull scraped bottom then killed the outboard and hopped over the side, sloshing my way to shore with hands raised, my smart glowing blue as it displayed my ID. The real one this time.

"You are trespassing on private property," a guard informed me. He was dressed in standard combat gear, body-armour, enhanced optical rig and a state-of-the-art carbine raised so that its laser dot centred on my chest. The dot was quickly joined by two more as a pair of guards came to a halt a short distance away. "We have authority to use lethal force…"

"Yeah, yeah." I tossed the first guard my smart. "Tell Mr Wallace that Fenrir's here to talk about Ragnarok."

CHAPTER 21

WALLACE'S MANSION CONSISTED of a series of inter-linked one-storey units, the architecture all straight lines and right angles that somehow managed to work amongst the wooded backdrop. I counted a dozen guards in addition to the trio that escorted me to the front door, and assumed there were at least the same number in concealed locations. Wallace evidently took his security very seriously. We came to a halt at the door where the guard growled terse jargon into his mouth mike. After a short pause he nodded, handed me my smart and walked back to the trees with the rest of the escort. The door opened a few seconds later, revealing a tall dark skinned man who looked to be about sixty, meaning he hadn't bothered with rejuve for a while now.

"Inspector McLeod," he greeted me in a gravelly baritone, expression cautiously intrigued rather than concerned.

"Mr Wallace," I said. "Thank you for seeing me."

"I'm always happy to converse with interesting people. And who could me more interesting than a dead hero?" He stepped aside, beckoning. "Please come in."

The interior was surprisingly spartan, polished floorboards, nondescript furnishings and no objets d'art that I could see. However, Wallace clearly shared an interest with Holstrom. Five free-standing and very tall bookcases stood in the centre of the space, every shelf full. They were arranged around a desk like monoliths in some ancient stone circle. I couldn't see a data terminal anywhere but the desk held what I recognised as an antique typewriter.

"Paper and ink can't be hacked," Wallace explained, noting my interest.

"But people can," I said. "Quite successfully, as it turns out. And I've got twenty-five bodies to prove it." I held up my smart, displaying the images from the Rybak murder scene. "Wanna see?"

No denials, no outrage, just a grim smile before he turned and nodded to an alcove beyond the bookcases where a teapot and cups sat on a table between two armchairs. "My evening ritual. Will you join me?"

He poured tea as I took a chair, choosing the one facing the window. "Earl Grey," he said, setting the teapot aside. "I hope that's acceptable."

I eyed the steaming beverage he set before me with no intention of touching a drop. "Never had it."

"If I'd given the word," Wallace said, sinking into his own chair and crossing his legs, cup and saucer in hand. "My men would have killed you on the beach and your body would never have been found. Nor would any law enforcement agency have expressed an interest in your demise."

"Disadvantages of already being dead, I guess."

He bared his teeth in a brief smile before sipping some tea. "Well, quite. But, please, do try the tea."

I shrugged and leaned forward to take a sip, finding the taste slightly raspy but not unpleasant.

"Small pleasures, Inspector," Wallace said. "When you get to my age you begin to appreciate that it's in the details that life offers the greatest rewards."

I glanced around. "I suppose it helps if you have a fucking big house to enjoy them in."

Another smile, shorter than the first, then a raised eyebrow. "Fenrir?"

"Fed Sec's codename for me during the war."

"Ah. Surprisingly portentous, but not quite accurate. You see, Fenrir will be one of the agents of destruction at the dawn of Ragnarok, not a would-be saviour."

"A saviour from what?"

That seemed to give him pause, his brows creasing in mild surprise. "It appears you're not quite the great detective after all. You really don't know what he's planning?"

"You mean Vargold?"

"Of course."

"It's his ship, the great big doodad that's going to secure the future of humanity. At least partly inspired by you, I would guess. The key to ascension. Rybak and Holstrom knew something that threatened it, a design flaw maybe, something screwy with the funding. It's Vargold's obsession, all he cares about…"

"No." Wallace's tone held a surprising amount of anger, expression hardening as he set his tea cup and saucer down with a small rattle of china. "Can your vision really be so narrow? You are the product of a society, and a war, where insight, reflex and cunning were necessary for survival. Do not limit yourself so." He reclined once more, elbows resting on the armrests, fingers steepled as he spoke in a gentler tone, coaxing, encouraging; a teacher's voice. "You are right to focus on the Ad Astra project and the ship it produced. And you are correct in that Othin was influenced by my work, at first through my books and papers then directly when he unearthed the patents produced by Haunai Genetics and decided to seek me out."

"Rapid morphological change," I said. "Werewolves and human bombs."

"A perversion of truly great science. If you've read my work you will know I had become increasingly frustrated by our continual failure to pursue ascension. It struck me that our attachment to this planet stemmed in no small part from the fact that, in a very real sense, it is our mother. It shaped our evolution and eventually gave birth to us. To leave her behind, to escape the womb, we needed a rebirth, not technological in nature, but biological."

I recalled something Janet had said, back when we were chasing a monster through the Slab. "Post-human."

"Exactly. Imagine a new strain of humanity unfettered by environment. A being that could change its body instantly to adapt to any conditions. If that could be achieved then perhaps we wouldn't be so fearful of opening the door to our cell."

"But it never happened. You shut down Haunai Genetics. Why?"

He closed his eyes for a second, expression unchanged as he said. "Human trials produced... unexpected results."

He reopened his eyes and I stared into them, reading the strange mix of guilt and certainty. "You sick old fuck," I said.

A soft, humourless laugh escaped his lips as he said, "It was, in fact, the least of my crimes."

"Meaning?"

"You seem to have some acquaintance with history, Inspector. Have you ever heard the name Hernan Cortes?"

I shook my head. "He a mass murderer too?"

"Actually, yes. But he's better known as the most successful Conquistador of the sixteenth century, a man who brought down the Mayan empire with only five hundred soldiers and a few cannons, securing much of Mexico for the King of Spain. Perhaps his most famous exploit, however, came after he captured the port of Vera Cruz in 1519. When it became apparent that many of his men were leery of proceeding further into the Mayan heartland, Cortes burned his ships. It could easily be read as the act of a megalomaniac driven mad by lust for gold and glory. But I've always seen it as an extremely rational act, the perfect example of brutal pragmatism. For Cortes to succeed his men must be denied the opportunity of retreat. From that point on, achieving their goal was not a choice but a necessity." Wallace leaned forward, eyes intent on mine. "Do you begin to see now? Does understanding begin to dawn?"

I frowned at him, bafflement mingling with impatience. "I'm getting tired of this lesson, old man…" I trailed off as my smart started bleating; Janet with a priority message. "We're not done here," I told Wallace, getting up and wandering over to his monolithic bookcases before answering the call. "Yeah?"

"We finally got somewhere with Vargold," Janet told me. "Took a lot of research but it's solid."

"What's solid?"

"Turns out Vargold had a family after all. One of his early relationships bore fruit, as it were."

"He's got a kid?"

"Not anymore. He met the mother when she interned at Astravista during the start-up days. Her family were ultra-fundamentalist neo-Catholic types, no sex before marriage, yadda yadda, so they kept the relationship secret while it lasted, which doesn't appear to have been very long. He dumps her, she finds out she's pregnant, parents kick her out. Vargold doesn't want to reignite the romance, but he does agree to be the daddy. He buys her a Yin-side apartment, big annual settlement, pays for a private school when the kid's of age. A thousand points if you can guess the name of the school."

I remembered Vargold's words back at the bar: *The governance of the planet beneath us is in the hands of those who have never balked at murder. Nor have they always been so discriminating.* "January Gardens."

"Bingo. And the kid's name…"

"Jason," I said. "As in the Argonauts." I glanced back at Wallace, sitting silent and still in his chair. "It's almost time to call Sherry," I told Janet. "I should have the whole picture in a few minutes. Get everything tabulated and ready for transmit when I call back. Copy it to all the news feeds, widest possible distribution."

I closed the call and moved to stand opposite Wallace, feeling the absence of a weapon very acutely and hoping he could hear the intent in my voice. I was fully prepared to break some fingers if he didn't start being less opaque. "Why did Vargold name his ship after his dead son?"

"His ship," Wallace muttered with a slight shake of his head. "It's not a ship. It never was."

"Then what is it?"

Wallace's gaze snapped up and I saw that his previous calm was gone now, the placid mask vanished to reveal a scared old man with tears shining in red-tinged eyes. "Lisabet and Craig," he said, voice raw and tremulous. "They were his warning to me. I have children, grandchildren and great grandchildren, and all of them are currently residing off-planet and easily within Othin's reach." He flapped shaking hands at our surroundings. "This… You think it's my refuge? It's my prison. He gave me a choice, you see. Ascend with my children or stay and witness the cleansing fire."

"Fire?" I moved towards him, ready to drag him from the chair and wring it out of him, and I might have, if the window hadn't exploded.

Ingrained muscle memory saved me, sending me into a roll, eyes shut tight, mouth yawning wide and hands clamped over my ears to shield against the eardrum shattering boom of a grenade. Wallace wasn't so lucky, the blast tearing his chair apart and kicking him halfway across the room, clothes shredded by flying glass, his aged flesh leaking blood from a dozen places. He managed to cling on to consciousness, shuddering on the floor as he tried to heave himself upright, eyes swivelling towards me, locking onto my gaze. I think there may have been some apology there, some attempt to secure forgiveness, or at least understanding. Or maybe it was just the last glance of a terrified old man. Anyway, I had only a few seconds to ponder it before an operative in full combat gear stepped through the remains of the window and blew most of Wallace's upper torso to pieces with a burst of carbine fire.

More due to luck than judgement, I'd landed with the coffee table between me and the intruder. As the carbine's laser dot flicked towards me, I managed to hook my foot under the table and heave it at him. He quickly batted it aside, but the distraction gave me enough time to surge to my feet. Attacking a fully armed and armoured operative with my bare hands might sound like something I'd do, but I've never really been that dumb. I fled towards Wallace's free-standing library, diving between the bookcases. The carbine barked out another burst, powdered wood and shredded paper cascading around me as I rolled over Wallace's desk then lay flat. A two second delay then the high-pitched metallic cacophony of the antique typewriter being blasted to pieces. A jagged piece of metal landed close to my hand. One of the keys, a bakerlite 'x' attached to a long twisted shard of steel.

"Philistine," I muttered, fumbling for my smart and hitting a preselected icon.

A flat boom from the front of the house indicated the door had been blown in, confirmed almost instantly by the thud of combat boots as a secondary team made their way inside.

"Flank left," said the one who had shot Wallace. "Target is unarmed."

My gaze returned to the twisted piece of metal and I snatched it up, rising to a crouch. I waited until I saw the shadow of the operative's boots in the gap between the floor and the base of the desk, then launched myself up and over in a single movement. He reacted with annoyingly professional swiftness, stepping out of reach of my probably ineffectual weapon and centring the carbine's laser dot on my chest, finger tightening on the trigger.

A low buzzing sound, a rush of displaced air from the direction of the shattered window and the operative no longer had a head.

I sprang forward to claim the carbine as the corpse collapsed, whirling about and spraying rounds in a wide arc without bothering to aim, forcing the secondary team to take cover. The magazine fired empty and I dropped, snatching another from the headless operative's bandolier, slamming it into place then reaching for the stun-grenade on his belt.

"Taking this outside," I said into my smart. "Be ready."

I thumbed the grenade's activation switch, counted to three and tossed it over my shoulder. I waited for the bang then sprinted towards the window as carbine bullets cut the air in my wake. Outside, I hurdled one of Wallace's guards, lying on the patio with his throat cut, and ran for the trees. "Drop on my mark," Mr Mac's voice blared from the smart as I ran. It seemed a very long way to the trees and my back itched in expectation with every stride.

"Drop!"

I threw myself flat, scrabbling around until I could aim the carbine back at the house. One operative was already down, just as headless as the first. The remaining four attempted to respond with a standard manoeuvre, two spraying the treeline with covering fire whilst the others backed into the house. Four bullets cut the air over my head, fired at a rate of one per second after which four more corpses lay headless on Wallace's patio.

"Any more inside?"

I looked up to see Mr Mac emerging from the trees with carbine in hand. Beyond him, Simon rose from the undergrowth, the long barrel of his sniper rifle still trained on the house. "Not that I saw." I got up, looking around to count the bodies of Wallace's security team.

"They weren't my responsibility," Mr Mac said, in an off-hand tone which made me want to shoot him. "We should get going," he went on, apparently oblivious to my murderous impulse. "Unless there's something else you need here."

I glanced back at the house. There may have been something to learn in Wallace's part-shredded library but I knew there was no time to find it. Anyway, I had the answer I came for. *The cleansing fire.*

CHAPTER 22

SIMON AND MR Mac had used an amphibious microlight to get to Gruinard, all stealth materials and micro-jets. It sat bobbing on the swell just off the craggy northern flank of the island, requiring a short but bone-chilling swim. I was obliged to sit double with Mr Mac, wedged in behind him and shivering as Simon climbed into the pilot's seat. "Got a mini-drone overhead," Mr Mac said, holding up his smart. "Shows another squad sweeping the island from south to north."

"Vargold's being thorough," I chattered.

"Let's hope they didn't think to bring any anti-aircraft stuff." He raised his voice as Simon fired up the jets. "How'd he know where you were, anyway?"

"Wallace said he was a prisoner. Vargold probably gets an alert every time someone pays a visit."

"You cut it pretty fine this time, Alex. Thirty seconds sooner and we'd have been out of position."

"I had complete faith in your abilities."

Simon completed his preflight and glanced over his shoulder. "Destination?"

I showed him a set of coordinates on my smart screen. "That's out to sea," he said, frowning.

"I have friends waiting." I gave an annoyed grunt as Mr Mac shifted his weight. "Let's go."

We were in the air within the minute, skimming the surface at ten metres and throwing in the occasional jink to frustrate any optical tracking. The sky was fully dark by the time we reached the coordinates, Simon's thermal imager picking up the tiny blinking spec of *Tethys's* beacon. I placed a call to Phaedra. "Bring her up. We have a lot to talk about."

"The whole world?" Phaedra squinted at me across the tactical display. "Seriously?"

"No," I said. "Just this planet. The world's a lot bigger than that now. It's kind've the whole point."

"How?"

"His shiny new interstellar space ark. Not sure of the details yet."

"We need to call the UN. This just got way too big…"

"Uh, Phaedra, Erik," one of the crew broke in, looking up from the main comms terminal. "Dunno if it's relevant, but every news feed on the planet just went crazy. Something about an attempted assassination upside."

"Play it," I said, a hard knot of grim understanding forming in my gut. *We forced his hand.*

The tactical holo shimmered into the form of a CNN news anchor, face set in that earnest yet sombre mask they use when things really go to shit. "…reports from the Lorenzo City Primary Care facility confirm Mayor Arnaud is currently undergoing surgery. His condition is described as extremely serious and medics would not be drawn on his chances for survival. The Mayor's name may not be familiar to many viewers but he's a highly important figure in the orbiting community - a decorated war veteran, former police chief, and recently elected mayor of the most populace orbital habitat. More importantly, his attempted murder is being blamed on a Federal Security operative…"

A pause as the anchor put a finger to his ear-piece. "I'm

told we now have footage of the event in question. Viewers are advised the content is graphic."

The display shifted into a view of Arnaud at some ribbon cutting ceremony. One of the new Yang-side parks by the look of it. He was into the first few sentences of his speech when it happened, the view momentarily turned chaotic as whoever held the camera was jostled aside. Then screams and gunfire. The camera refocused, revealing Arnaud dangling as something large and hairy lifted him off the ground. Another of Vargold's morphs, presumably not long out of corrective immersion. The view got shaky again as the gunfire intensified. The thing holding Arnaud had been about to close its jaws on his throat but the barrage of fire from the phalanx of bodyguards proved sufficient to shatter its skull.

The image froze on Arnaud's prostrate form as the anchor's voice-over resumed. "The mayor's injuries are said to consist of compression trauma to the throat and multiple lacerations. Acting Lorenzo City Police Chief Sherrilynn Mordecai refused to comment on the assailant's identity or motive, stating merely that the investigation is progressing at a very rapid pace. However, a spokesperson for the CAOS Central Governance Defence Ministry was quick to point out parallels with the murder of Astravista co-founder Craig Rybak at the hands of a man widely suspected of acting as an agent for UN Federal Security. Many commentators have also linked the assassination to the recent tragic demise of Chief Inspector Alexei McLeod, the Lorenzo City Detective who identified Rybak's murderer. Inspector McLeod and several colleagues died in an as yet unexplained shuttle accident following the successful capture of notorious gangland figure…"

"Turn it off," I said, punching Sherry's personal ID into my smart.

"Hey," Mr Mac said as the holo blinked off. "I didn't get my mention. I'm notorious, apparently."

I ignored him, watching the 'message sent' icon blinking and praying she saw some significance in my caller ID: Newface1.

She picked up after two full minutes, voice cautious. "Who is this?"

"Sherry..." I began.

"You fucking dick!"

I held the smart away, wincing at the volume.

"I knew you couldn't be dead! I would've felt a whole lot better-"

"Listen! We don't have time..."

"Fuck you! Is Joe there? I wanna swear at him too."

I didn't say anything for a second, hearing her anger leech away in a long sigh of realisation. "Joe's gone," I said. "Janet, Timor and Leyla are on Cerberus Station."

"What the hell happened?"

"Vargold. It's all him. Rybak, Joe, Arnaud. All of it." I laid it out as quickly and clearly as I could, everything that happened from Rybak's murder to my meeting with Wallace. "You have to call CAOS Military," I said. "Get them to seize the *Jason Alpha*."

"Don't you get it, Alex? As far as anyone up here is concerned, Fed Sec just tried to assassinate the man most likely to win the next presidential election. Everything's in uproar or lock-down. Central Governance just went into emergency session and every hab's alert status has been set to red. It's likely they'll vote to suspend helium 3 shipments within twenty-four hours, and you can guess what the UN's reaction to that will be. CAOS Military won't shift a single missile turret away from Earth just now, that's even if I could get through to someone with high enough authority to give the order."

"You need to try. Yell as loud as you can, to anyone who'll listen. I'll be in touch when I know more."

I shut down the smart, reluctance battling necessity as I stared at the screen. "Don't suppose the Aquatic League has a space program?" I asked Erik.

He gave an apologetic shrug. "Sorry. Guess no one felt the need."

"Nearest launch-port is in London," Mr Mac said. "But we'd need to hijack a shuttle, and make it past the UN security patrols, all now on a war readiness footing."

I sighed and punched in another ID from memory. "Guess we'll have to think of something else." The call was answered within five seconds, no greeting, just expectant silence. "Captain Alexei McLeod," I said, knowing voice recognition would confirm my ID. "Grey Wolf."

The ship's approach became audible only when it got within fifty metres, and even then it was little more than a slight whine above the bluster of the sea. Its presence became more obvious when the engines raised spume from the waves as it slowed to a hover barely ten feet above the Tethys. I looked up to regard a swirling smear in the sky, formless and impossible to define. After a brief pause, the smear flickered and faded, revealing a matte black hull configured into a sleek and familiar shape. *The design specs I brought back from Ceres. Guess they couldn't resist it.*

A square of light appeared in the underside of the black shape before a rope ladder unfurled its way onto the upper hull of the *Tethys*. "You should head back to Salacia," I told Phaedra, reaching out to snare the ladder. "Get your authorities to make some calls…"

"Forget it," she said, hefting her gear. "You need soldiers. We're it. And this is our planet."

I glanced over to see Mr Mac giving Simon a questioning look. The mercenary replied with an expressionless nod. "Looks like he's got a sentimental bone or two, after all," Mr Mac said, turning back to me, face guarded. "Doesn't mean I do."

I took a firmer hold of the ladder and began to climb. "Well, that's a big surprise."

CHAPTER 23

THE PILOT WAS blank faced as she nodded her head at the comms terminal. We'd burned clear of Earth orbit a few minutes back, slipping through an electro-magnetic haze of military scanners without a blip. A pair of cold blue eyes stared up at me from the holo with the laser-like focus I remembered. "Actually, it's General these days," he said in response to my terse greeting. "Central Command was very impressed by our last op."

"Congratulations."

"I seem to recall you promising to kill me if you saw me again."

"Which I guess is why you sent the ship and didn't feel the need to come along."

"I have responsibilities, Captain. Covert Ops is now on stand-by to execute its war-plan. Something I'm keen to avoid, if possible."

I glanced around at the ship's interior, all curves and no hard edges or sharp angles. It made for an aesthetically pleasing but not necessarily comfortable environment. I wasn't relishing the three hour journey to Cerberus. "You got any more of these?"

"Sadly no. She's a prototype, still undergoing evaluation."

"She got a name?"

"Covert Insertion and Extraction Vehicle Mark One."

"Imaginative. I'm afraid she'll get a few dings in the paint-work before this is over."

"Understood. You have some form of plan, I assume?"

"Yeah. Stop Vargold's ship by all means necessary. Any intel that might help would be appreciated."

"We know Vargold left the Slab five hours before the assassination attempt on Arnaud, his shuttle's flight-plan indicates a routine visit to Hephaestus. I had an agent on station there but they went dark shortly after his arrival. The last package I received confirmed the *Jason Alpha* was being prepped for an early maiden voyage."

"So you've been watching him for a while now?"

"We watch everybody, you know that. Especially someone with his access and influence."

"And yet you managed to miss his fiendish planet-destroying master plan."

The General blinked and punched an icon on his own display. "All the intel we've gathered on the *Jason Alpha* and its capabilities," he said as a package uploaded to my terminal. "Includes hacks for the on-board security systems, atmospheric controls and the main engines. You'll need a hard-interface to upload it and Vargold's security software is dynamic and partially AI-driven, so expect it to adapt quickly."

"To come up with this contingency, you must've had your suspicions for a while."

"Basic military strategy, Captain. Always have a contingency. Besides, it may have become necessary for CAOS Defence to co-opt the *Jason Alpha* in the event of another Fed Sec attack." The display shifted to a tactical graphic showing the *Jason Alpha* on approach to Earth orbit. "I had our tactical people run some attack sims. It doesn't look good." He paused and when he spoke again I heard something I'd never expected to hear in his voice; uncertainty. "This is all I can do. CAOS Military will be unable to assist, they're expecting a UN armada to come streaking out of Earth's atmo any second. I've tried to persuade Central Command otherwise, but after Ceres they're not in a trusting mood."

"Then it's lucky I've got my own army," I said and killed the comms feed.

"*Scheisse,*" Kruger said, eyeing the tactical display with understandable trepidation. "More heavily defended than anything we faced in the war. Wouldn't you say, Herr Oberst?"

I'd convened a council of war aboard the *Aguila* shortly after docking with Cerberus. Kruger had been elected to speak on behalf of those veterans with an interest in lending a hand, most having volunteered in response to Riviera's request. He considered the display for a second, eyes tracking over the thick net of bots and the four Seraphim-class corvettes in close escort around the rectangular bulk of the *Jason Alpha*. "Vargold's people," Riviera said to me. "All mercenaries?"

"According to my intel," I said. "Though we can bet there's a few true believers amongst them. Lotta people with unresolved grudges out there."

"Armament on the *Jason Alpha* itself?"

"Minimal. Long range optical scans indicate some ad hoc additions to the outer hull, cannon turrets for the most part, some chaff dispensers too."

"Which raises the question," Janet put in, "How exactly does Vargold intend to wipe out a planet with a lightly armed ship?"

"Perhaps he intends to crash it," Kruger suggested. "A big beast like that would create an impressive crater and expel a large amount of matter into the atmosphere. Nuclear winter scenario."

"It doesn't have enough mass," Lucy said. "No, he's going to fry the place."

She squirmed a little as all eyes turned to her. "How?" I asked.

Lucy laughed, as if the answer were obvious, then stopped when she realised it wasn't, to us anyway. "The whole purpose of the Ad Astra project," she began, "was to produce a propulsion system capable of traversing an interstellar distance within a typical human lifespan. The ship is basically a contained singularity event; a shit-load of mass condensed into a super-dense form in order to produce a miniature astrophysical jet. It's the jet that provides the thrust. The great technological feat here is that Astravista found a way to contain and direct the jet. All down to magnetic fields apparently."

"Contain and direct," Riviera said. "Like a huge rocket nozzle."

"Or the ultimate flamethrower," I said. "Point the rear end at Earth and blast off. Destruction and ascension in one glorious moment."

"He'd need to be within lunar orbit to do it," Lucy said. "And have the ship pointed at Proxima, if he's really interested in getting there."

"Run the numbers. Find us a likely destination point based on its current velocity."

Her fingers danced over the icons for a few minutes before the result flashed up on the holo. The *Jason Alpha* hovered over northern Europe, the most densely populated sector of the globe. *Happy accident or by design?* I decided it didn't really matter.

"Just under eight hours from now," Kruger said. "Not much time to prep an assault."

"It'll have to do," I said. "Do you have any ordnance capable of stopping that thing?"

Mr Mac cut in before Kruger could reply, voice soft but intent, "Can we discuss the rather large invisible elephant standing in the corner?"

I met his gaze, for once finding no sign of humour. "Which is?"

He nodded at the planet on the holo. "Why exactly are *they* our responsibility?"

"If not ours, then whose?" Janet enquired, her dislike of Mr Mac now palpable in the narrow stare she fixed on him. "Or are you worried there's no profit in stopping it?"

"I'm worried we're all going to die trying to save a world that doesn't give two shits about us, and never has. And what exactly did happen at Ceres, Alex? I think we have a right to know."

"It's not relevant..."

"Fuck that!" I'd never seen him actually angry before, face red, eyes wild and lips trembling. A near psychopathic rage was usually a pre-requisite for people in his line of work, but somehow I'd always thought him above such things. *Just another scumbag gangster after all.*

"What were they building there?" he demanded, rage subsiding but not by much. "Tell us why we need to risk our lives for a planet that wants us all dead?"

"What is he talking about?" Riviera asked.

"The ship that brought us here," Mr Mac said. "It's not an original design, is it, Alex? Want to tell them where it came from? What it was built for?"

My gaze tracked across all of them as I fumbled for the right words, but it was Lucy who spoke. "A fleet," she said. "Fed Sec was building a fleet of stealth ships. They were gonna destroy CAOS and take back Earth-space. We stopped them."

"Thank you for your honesty, my dear," Mr Mac said. "Which brings me back to my original question."

"They were gonna kill a shit-load of people," Lucy said. "Not politicians or generals or rich bastards who own big corporations. Just people. That's why we stopped them. That's why I'm up for stopping Vargold."

The silence stretched as I scanned their faces, seeing more sombre contemplation than reluctance. "I'm not conscripting anyone," I said. "But I'm doing this. We didn't win a war to become what we fought against." I levelled my gaze at Mr Mac. "You want out, fine. Bribe yourself a place on a shuttle and go rebuild your empire. When this is done, I'll start chasing you again and we can do our pointless dance until we're both old or dead."

His anger disappeared as he looked again at the holo, grinned and shrugged. "I'll be expecting a full pardon when this is over."

"Not in a million years." I turned back to Kruger. "Ordnance?"

"We have a stockpile of fifty plasma shrikes," he said. "They're old and the targeting systems will need to be re-calibrated, but they're in full working order. If we score hits with the whole load..." He shrugged. "Maybe."

"Not enough," Lucy said, running some more numbers. "Best-case scenario, you render the *Jason Alpha* sixty percent inoperable, and that leaves the propulsion system undamaged. You'll need a nuke to stop her."

"We don't have a nuke," Kruger said. "Given enough time we could convert one of our old fission reactors..."

"There is a nuke," I said, meeting Lucy's gaze. "Her engine, right?"

"Sure. Fuck up the magnetic containment fields and she'll come apart like an egg the instant she powers up. The engine's in the heart of the ship, though, so it can't be done from outside."

I turned to Riviera. "Boarding party."

He shook his head. "The escort will take out any ship we have before it gets in range."

"Any ship but one."

"Even a stealth ship would be spotted, their defensive net is too tight. We would need to punch a hole." I watched him study the display in silence for a long time, gaze losing focus as he ran multiple attack scenarios through the tactical computer that formed his brain. We'd had our differences over the years but I'd never discounted his abilities. When it came to micro-grav combat tactics he had no equal. "Can it be done?" I asked after a full minute had ticked by.

"*Si*," he replied softly, fully focused gazed now fixed on the display. "But it will be messy."

"Was it ever anything else?"

CHAPTER 24

"COME ON, YOU lazy old cow!" Lucy aimed a kick at the nav-console, the trode-tiara on her head lighting up red to indicate pilot distress. She'd gone into a deep sulk upon being told she had to fly the *Aguila* rather than take charge of the Covert Ops stealth ship. "No way she's a better pilot than me," she had grumbled back in the Cerberus docking bay, jerking her head at the professionally taciturn woman checking over the stealth ship's landing gear.

"Yeah," I said. "That's why I need you with me. Think I'd trust anyone else to shoot this hoop? Forget it."

It had been enough to mollify her, but her frustration with the aged freighter's handling became more evident the closer we came to lunar orbit. Maintaining station among the ragtag fleet that had launched from Cerberus wasn't easy, given the souped-up engines and manoeuvring thrusters added by their mod-happy owners. There were thirty ships in total, all crewed by veterans willing to volunteer for Riviera's ad hoc fleet. There wasn't a matching type among them and every hull was decorated in the graffiti that seemed to be a Cerberus trademark. The number surprised me. I'd been expecting more than a few to share Mr Mac's reluctance; they all had the scars and prosthetics to testify to a genuine and justified grievance against the planet we were trying to save. But Riviera's word, taken with

Kruger's support, had been enough to secure us a decent sized attack-force.

The burn to lunar proximity took the better part of three hours where the fleet settled into a geosynchronous orbit over the southern pole. Riviera calculated that the bulk of the moon would shield us from both Earth-based and CAOS scans. The reaction of either side to the appearance of a fleet of armed vessels at this juncture was unpredictable and I didn't want to risk any unfortunate consequences. CAOS news feeds had been mostly shut down since Central Governance formally declared an existential threat, but the Downside stations were still blaring out a constant commentary on the unfolding crisis. All in all, it didn't paint a pretty picture.

"The UN Security Council has enacted the Global Defence Protocol, requiring all member states to place their military resources under UN Central Command... Offers from the Vatican to act as intermediary in negotiations with CAOS have so far gone unanswered... Reports indicate all off-planet Federal Security resources have been recalled to Earth orbit..."

"ETA thirty minutes until we show on the corvettes' long range scans," Riviera told me. "Better prep your people."

I nodded and made my way to the cargo bay where my assault force waited. Cerberus's military surplus included enough combat ready vac-suits for everyone but they were all wartime vintage, no shiny new Pendragons here. Luckily, Kruger's people hadn't skimped on maintenance, so they were fully operational, if lacking in firepower. To compensate, the force carried a mix of up-to-date assault rifles and grenade launchers, apart from Janet who maintained her strict anti-gun policy even now.

"It's all been checked," she told me as I ran a critical eye over her suit's seals and power couplings. "Timor was very thorough."

I moved back to meet her gaze and knew there was nothing I could say to make her sit this out. A shared hero-complex was probably one of the things that bound us together. "It won't just be bots this time," I told her. "Real people, and they need to die."

She gave a short nod and forced a smile. "I know."

"Are we there yet, Dad?" I turned to see Phaedra standing with Erik and the rest of her people, all suited-up and bristling with weapons. The novelty of taking their first off-planet trip seemed to have faded pretty quickly. The reality of restricted and decidedly non-aromatic surroundings had a tendency to bleed the wow-factor from spaceflight. I could also tell they were missing the ocean, this was the first time any of them had spent an appreciable time away from a large body of water.

"Half hour to go," I said, raising my voice to address them all. "We've been through it already but it pays to be clear. I lead Alpha team to the bridge." I nodded at Leyla, now sufficiently recovered for micro-grav combat, Janet and Timor. "Beta," I gestured at Mr Mac, Simon and Phaedra's people, "escorts Lucy to the engine room. We need maximum damage and maximum confusion. If we take the bridge or the engine room this thing is pretty much over." I paused, knowing the occasion called for some rousing words but finding myself at a loss. "You know the stakes," I muttered finally. "End of the world. All that shit."

Mr Mac gave a brief but loud snicker. "Wow, Shakespeare lives."

"Oh, fuck you."

"Alex," Lucy said via the voice-comm. "Looks like their outlying scout-drones picked us up sooner than expected. We're getting a transmission from the *Jason Alpha*. No encryption. They're asking for you."

Vargold wants a chat. What the hell? "Put it through."

A pause then his voice came through the cargo bay speakers, as unwavering and softly confident as before. "Inspector McLeod?"

"Mr Vargold."

"I see you've been very busy."

"You've been busier. I'm guessing there's no point in asking you to call the whole thing off?"

A faint sigh of amused dismissal. "That would make me a coward, like Craig or Lisabet."

"That why they had to go? Had a crisis of conscience and decided they weren't on your programme anymore?"

"Craig spent months trying to drown his weakness with drugs and sex. To no avail it seems. He covered his tracks pretty well, but not well enough and it became apparent he had requested a covert meeting with Fed Sec, at Lisabet's urging and, I suspect, with Wallace's connivance. I really shouldn't have allowed him that typewriter. Strange, the three people besides myself that did the most to make this happen, with scant need of encouragement I might add. And yet they all fall victim to cowardice at the final moment."

"I guess the prospect of orchestrating planetary genocide will do that."

"It was fairly inconvenient, forcing me to adopt an accelerated schedule. Still, Craig's demise did give me the opportunity to point an accusing finger at Fed Sec when the time came. For what it's worth I do regret the necessity of involving you, but a martyred hero garners more sympathy than a drug-addicted business tycoon dying in a brothel."

"All so you can play out your avenging angel fantasy. Your son's death was terrible, but fifty billion charred corpses won't bring him back."

"I'm aware of that. I'm also fully aware that I may very well die today, as are the people who have joined me in this endeavour. I greatly wish you would too, Inspector. After all, an objective observer might well conclude, given your history, that you're on the wrong side."

He paused and I said nothing, drawing a satisfied grunt from the speakers. "I see the thought had occurred to you, too. And why wouldn't it? They made you a slave for the crime of being born in orbit. They made you fight a war, torturing and killing for years. They maimed your wife and made you put her out of her misery. And let's not forget their little project at Ceres. And these are the people you want to save."

I glanced over at Phaedra, black and white eyes steady in her silver grey face, fully confident in me. "There are people and there are people," I told Vargold. "Spliced, modded, or pure as the genetic snow. But they're all just people. Good, bad, crazy or just trying to get through life. Then there are delusional pieces of shit like you. I'm going to kill you, Mr Vargold. Not just because you're a genocidal nutcase, but because you killed my friend, and he was better than you."

I told Lucy to kill the comms-feed and requested a sit-rep from Riviera. "It's already working," he reported. "Two corvettes and a swarm of bots already moving to intercept. Vargold may be a businessman, but he's no admiral. All helmets on. Prepare for deployment in under ten minutes."

We watched the first phase of the assault unfold on the cargo bay holo, the *Aguila's* optics relaying the flurry of explosions as the bulk of the Cerberus fleet engaged the bot-swarm surrounding the two corvettes. The Cerberus ships moved in small groups, attacking in relays according to a preset pattern, firing short but intense missile salvos and cannon bursts then immediately going evasive. Their escape manoeuvres seemed random at first glance but in fact followed similar vectors designed to drawn the corvettes further and further away from the *Jason Alpha*. Although Riviera's overall strategy seemed to be working, it soon became apparent that Vargold hadn't recruited complete idiots as a large portion of bots broke away from the main group and made straight for us.

"Flak boats, you're up," Riviera commanded. "Fast movers on the flanks. Lucy, time to do your thing."

The *Aguila* gave a shudder as Lucy cranked the main plasma-drive up to maximum, obliging us to take a firmer grip on our hand-holds as the g-forces kicked in. The holo showed a wall of explosions directly in our path as those Cerberus ships equipped with flak-guns blasted away at the approaching bot-swarm. Inevitably, a few made it through. I counted one ship destroyed and another two badly damaged before the faster ships swept in from both flanks to complete the destruction of the bot-swarm, leaving clear space between us and the two other corvettes. They were putting up a flak-screen of their own, a half-circular shield of blossoming orange flame growing larger by the second as Lucy set course for the *Jason Alpha*.

"Now's the time," I heard Riviera say, receiving an immediate and terse response: "Roger that. Three seconds. Stand-by."

It was only a small flicker on the holo, a burst of light as the pilot of the Covert Ops ship fired off four of Kruger's plasma shrikes at once. Two were caught by the flak screen, flaring so bright the holo whited out for a second, then faded to reveal the sight of the remaining pair impacting on one of the corvettes. A plasma shrike won't detonate on contact, instead the depleted uranium warhead will cut through successive layers of armour and deckplates until its on-board AI detects it's gone as deep as it can and decides to ignite the half-tonne of highly energised plasma in its reservoir. So there was a short delay before the rear of the Corvette's hull blew apart in two near simultaneous explosions. Its flak screen died instantly as it rolled on its x-axis, spewing debris and bodies, atmo burning away in a red flash.

"I'm hit," the Covert Ops pilot reported in a clipped wet sounding grunt. I noticed the ship's stealth mode was off and she was now a small black arrow streaking towards the second corvette. The arrow began to jink as the Corvette shifted its flak barrage, corkscrewing ever closer as explosions chased it across the void.

"Fire your ordnance and withdraw," Riviera ordered the Covert Ops pilot.

"Targeting's down," she replied, then gave out the kind of deep, grating cough that told of a bad chest wound. "And it wasn't just the ship that took a hit. McLeod, you there?"

"I'm here," I said.

"Tell the General I always thought he was a prick."

"Happy to."

She waited until the corvette was at point-blank range, less than a kilometre, before firing all her remaining plasma shrikes. At that distance, she had no chance of surviving the resultant explosion, but then, neither did the corvette.

"Fast movers take point," Riviera said as the shattered hulk of the corvette drifted out of view. "Clear the road."

The smaller ships formed a wedge formation half a klick ahead of the *Aguila*. They were mostly converted racing skiffs or joyriders; fast, one or two person craft, their unarmoured hulls augmented with unsightly weapons pods. They blew through the remnants of Vargold's bot-swarm in a few frenzied but costly seconds, half-a-dozen or more falling victim to interlocking cannon and missile fire, but they'd done enough to get us where we needed to be.

"One pass over the upper hull to clear the on-board defences," Riviera told the surviving fast-movers as the *Jason Alpha* loomed in the holo, a dark, oddly featureless monolith about a quarter the size of the Slab. "Turn for home," Riviera ordered as the fast-movers swept over the hull, leaving numerous fiery flowers in their wake. He overrode the resultant chorus of dissent with a harsh bark. "If this doesn't work we're dead anyway. Return to Cerberus. They'll need you when this is over."

The holo turned red as Lucy activated the targeting system and a circular reticle appeared dead centre of the *Jason Alpha*.

The *Aguila* auto-fired two plasma shrikes the instant the reticule stopped pulsing, both missiles spiralling through lines of tracer fired by the cannon the fast-movers had missed. One was blasted apart two hundred metres short, but the other made it through. Unlike the other shrikes, it had been modified to detonate a few micro-seconds after impact, doing minimal damage to the target's superstructure but leaving a nice big hole wide enough to accommodate the *Aguila*.

"Hold on to your lunch," Lucy grunted, the strain of concentration telling in her voice as she took us through the storm of cannon fire, throwing the bulky freighter around like a stuntship. A few hard, percussive thumps indicated we were taking hits, forcing Lucy to even more extreme feats of g-pulling dexterity. Janet and I were obliged to grab hold of Timor as he lost his grip and almost went tumbling through the cargo bay.

"Helluva party, boss," he gasped, grinning behind his visor.

The ship shuddered as something much bigger than a cannon shell impacted on the hull, a brief haze of grey smoke filling the bay before being whipped away as Lucy vented the atmo. "What was that?" I asked her.

There was a pause before she replied, voice dull, "A bot kamikazed into our starboard side. Damage is… manageable. You'd better get ready, sixty seconds to touchdown."

"Weapons hot!" I told the boarding party and disengaged the safety on my primary weapon, a Ruger 10mm recoilless assault rifle and grenade launcher combo. Big and heavy, it was a micro-grav only weapon and had no non-lethal mode which suited me just fine today. I turned to the holo as Lucy took us into the jagged rent torn in the *Jason Alpha's* upper hull, the forward lights illuminating a broad deck beyond. From the General's intel package I knew this to be the *Jason Alpha's* central rec area, a broad plaza of gymnasiums and eating tables where those chosen for the first journey to the stars would spend their off hours. Judging by the few dozen bodies floating about we'd caught some crew members in the middle of watching Vargold's great triumph on a huge holo display that now filled the darkened interior with aggravating strobe-light. Lucy hit the retros at exactly the right moment, the *Aguila* rearing back and settling onto the deck with a surprisingly gentle clunk of magnetic clamps.

"Exterior scans show no opposition," I said, skipping through the camera feeds. "That won't last." I hit the ramp release button and Phaedra's people were the first out, suit-thrusters blazing as they deployed in a loose perimeter.

"Colonel, Lucy," I said. "Time to go."

No response, just the sound of her breath, choked and close to a sob. I cursed and propelled towards the bridge, finding her still in the pilot's seat staring at Riviera's inert form. The starboard window had shattered under the impact of the bot along with a good sized portion of the hull. Riviera's upper half had taken most of the blast, his optic array floated in pieces from the remnants of his helmet visor amongst a haze of crimson droplets.

No time, I thought, fighting down the rage and clamping a hand onto the rear of Lucy's suit, hauling her from the seat. "We gotta go." She allowed herself to be dragged outside before struggling free, her breath harsh in my 'phones as she tried to control her grief. I took the carbine strapped to her thigh and pushed it into her arms, staring into her eyes until the sobs faded. "Use this only if you have to. Leave the fighty shooty stuff to the others. Your job is the engines. Upload the hack and get back here. Don't wait for us."

"Where's Riviera?" Janet asked.

"Dead." I ran through my suit's various scans and stopped at thermal as it picked out a cluster of glowing smears approaching from a port-side corridor. "Company's on its way," I said. "Best get to it."

"That's our cue, my dear," Mr Mac said, patting Lucy on

the shoulder before favouring me with a mock salute. "Onwards to glory, my captain."

"Don't fuck this up, and if she dies you better have beaten her to it."

I watched them form up with Phaedra's team and burn towards the stern then turned about, aiming for the corridor my heads-up display indicated as the most direct route to the bridge. "I'm primary infiltrator," I told Leyla and Timor. "You two are flank-guards. Janet, stick to me like glue."

As expected, all undamaged exits from the rec concourse had sealed against hard-vac the moment the fail-safes detected a hull-breach. "Running overrides," I told the others, as we halted before the sealed doors. I slotted a data stick into the door control and punched icons on my wrist console. "No way to know how long it'll be before Vargold's security AI changes the codes so move quickly."

I raised the Ruger as the doors irised open and fired a grenade into the corridor followed by a two second burst of 10mm. More than enough to shred the two suited-up Astravista Security mercs sent to greet us. "No prisoners," I added, somewhat redundantly.

We blasted through three corridors in quick succession, meeting piecemeal resistance for the most part. They came at us in pairs or alone, displaying either poor training or suicidal courage. Most wore tech-suits rather than combat models and some had weapons incapable of piercing our armour. Here and there, we came up against an experienced and well-armed veteran, but without back-up they didn't have much chance. It was clear to me they were struggling to form a cohesive response to the assault; Vargold's plan hadn't envisioned anyone being nuts enough to try a boarding operation.

"Oh give it up, you stupid FUCK!" Leyla yelled, the last word punctuated by the point-blank burst of carbine fire she put into the head of a particularly stubborn merc. He'd held us up for a full thirty seconds before one of Timor's grenades took his arm off. Still he'd tried to resist, fumbling for a frag with his remaining arm as we closed in.

"What are these people on?" Timor wondered, breath ragged over the comms.

"Fanaticism," Janet told him. "Always a potent drug."

A shudder ran through the ship and the surrounding walls began to shift, the detritus of combat swirling about then abruptly smearing onto every hard surface. My suit's boots thumped onto the deck and the Ruger, suddenly heavier than an anvil, tore itself from my grasp. "Vargold's initiated the spin," I said, grunting as I raised my now-leaden arms to tap a sequence into my console. Behind us a sealing bulkhead slammed closed and dust blew away from the vents in the walls as I replenished the atmo. "De-suit," I told the others, hitting the quick release on my breastplate.

We climbed out, Leyla concealing a wince as she put weight on her partially healed leg. I was tempted to leave her here to guard the suits, but knew we had no time for the inevitable argument. We pressed on towards the bridge, the sudden absence of armour instilling a sense of nakedness. I'd had the foresight to stow a carbine as a secondary weapon and I also had the Colt strapped under my arm, both coming in very handy when what can only be described as a howling mob came charging at us from a side corridor.

They came at us in a frenzy, many with untreated wounds or burns. They were either unarmed or wielding makeshift clubs, falling over each other in their desire to get at us. I saw a uniformly wild cast to their eyes, the same blind devotion I'd seen in Blair's gaze before he went into bomb-mode. Also, many were screaming, the words a chaotic babble at first, becoming clearer as they surged closer. "From light we are born…"

I put the carbine to my shoulder and fired off a long burst, drowning out the screams. About a dozen went down, followed by a dozen more as Leyla and Timor opened up. The bodies piled up quickly, but still they came on, clambering over the mound of corpses, screaming out their mantra even as the bullets tore them apart.

"Alex!"

I turned, finding Janet standing in the path of a second mob, claws fully extended as she awaited the onrush. I moved to her side and started firing, cutting down the first rank before the magazine emptied. I reached for my Colt, but they were on us before I could clear the holster, clubs and fists raining down. I backed up against the wall, kicking out and trying to free the Colt. A wet splash across my face and the press of bodies was gone. I collapsed to my knees, head reeling from multiple blows, dragging in air and shaking the confusion away. I staggered to my feet, Colt raised and saw Janet wreaking havoc.

She moved like a whirlwind of flesh and claws, scattering the mob before her, body after body slammed into the walls with spine-shattering force. She would pause now and again to finish one who managed to get close enough to land a blow, claws clamped onto head and chest to expose the neck before her fangs tore most of it away and she hurled the corpse at the remaining mob. I retrieved the carbine from beneath a decapitated corpse and reloaded, staggering to Janet's side and unloading an entire magazine into the seething mass of crew.

Silence descended as the carbine fired empty. The crew lay around us, bloody and twitching, the wounded still babbling their inane creed. "...to light we return..." I knelt beside a young woman little older than Lucy with a gaping hole where her throat had been. I pulled up her sleeve to reveal the forearm, picking out the tell-tale hypo-marks in the flesh.

"Fanaticism to order," I said. "Undergoing the same immersion treatment as Corvin and the others was probably a pre-requisite for recruitment to this merry band. We're lucky he didn't have time to splice them, too."

Janet made a small sound and I saw she was fighting down a sob. "Had to be done..." I began but she shook her head.

"I..." She paused to swallow, fully-fanged and blood-spattered features rendered even more nightmarish as she turned to me with a smile. "I think I'd like to announce my formal retirement from the Lorenzo City Police Force."

I reached for her hand, feeling the claws recede as I squeezed. "Just one more thing to do."

CHAPTER 25

"LOST SOME OF your mer-people getting here," Lucy told me via the comms array I'd salvaged from my abandoned suit. "Had to ditch our suits a few decks back. Looks like Vargold sent most of his trained people to guard the engines." Her cam-feed played over the cavernous expanse of the *Jason Alpha's* engine room, huge magnetic generators and power relays the size of trains. A number of bodies were scattered about, including two with silver-grey skin.

"Phaedra?" I asked.

"I'm here." She stepped into shot, her face showing the strain of recent combat. "Erik isn't."

I swallowed commiserating words. Sympathy wouldn't help just now. "Grieve later. We have a job to do. Lucy, how long to run the hack?"

Lucy's cam hesitated before swivelling towards another body, this one still alive and propped up against a power relay. "Through and through to the lower abdomen," Lucy said as Simon knelt to apply a field dressing to Mr Mac's wound. "I was too eager… Came through the door too quickly… He took my bullet, Alex."

I watched the image linger on Mr Mac's bleached features. "The hack," I said.

Her cam swung towards the main control terminal where

a data stick blinked in the input port. "It's already uploaded, but the AI's fighting back. Every time I initiate a shut down sequence, it finds a way to reverse it."

I pushed aside the readout visor and fixed my gaze on the door ahead. The last one before we made the bridge. "Should be able to help with that shortly. Stay on comms."

The door shuddered in response to my command, opening then closing like an industrial cutting machine as the ship's AI fought it out with the General's hack. Luckily, it hadn't fully adapted yet and the door finally stuck halfway open, allowing me to peer through to the bridge beyond. I could see only one occupant, a tall figure with long dark hair, standing before a large flickering holo display. He didn't bother to turn as I made my way inside, the others following close behind. A brief scan of the bridge confirmed it; Vargold was all alone now.

"So you sent everyone you had left to stop us," I said, striding forward.

He merely glanced over his shoulder before returning his gaze to the holo. It was a forward view largely obscured by the moon's bulk, a blue, thumb-sized half-circle slowly cresting the lower hemisphere as the *Jason Alpha* maintained its course. Vargold continued to regard the view as I came to his side, arms folded and face serenely contemplative. Deciding this wasn't the time for subtlety, I slammed the carbine stock into the small of his back, sending him to all fours with a shout of pained surprise.

"Were you under the impression," I said, filling my fist with his hair and dragging his head back as I pressed the carbine's muzzle into his temple, "that I was fucking about here?"

He replied with a teeth gritted smile, grunting the words out. "Did... you... think... I was?"

"Gonna need you to shut this ship down, Mr Vargold."

"Can't." His smile broadened. "Won't."

I moved back and tapped an icon on my comms controller. "Kruger, you reading this?"

"Alles ist klar, Herr Hauptmann."

"Any problems?"

"Casualties heavier than expected, but we have the ship."

"Set course, maximum thrust. Then get clear."

"Jawohl."

I accessed the bridge controls and switched the holo to the port-side optical array. I saw Vargold shudder as the image came into focus, one of the escort corvettes, badly damaged and trailing debris from the hole Kruger's assault team had blasted in its side. Fortunately its thrusters were still operational, bringing it about and commencing a full burn towards the *Jason Alpha*. "Five hundred twenty-seven seconds to impact," Kruger reported. "Punching out now. Best of luck, Herr Hauptmann."

"Not one boarding party, but two," I told Vargold. "Something you might have learned if you'd actually fought in the war; always have a contingency." I trained the carbine on his knee and put a bullet through it, leaving him convulsing on the deck, choking down screams. "Your great project is about to become a lunar debris field, and I think you should stay and watch the show. After all, you paid for it."

He clenched his teeth and blinked up at me, his expression markedly less pissed than I wanted it to be.

"Alex!" Lucy's voice, shrill and urgent in my ear.

"What?"

"The main drive just started powering up. We're less than seven minutes from going to relativistic speeds."

I glanced up at the holo, watching the blue half-circle continue to ascend above the grey arc of the moon.

"Won't be... everything I... wanted," Vargold rasped. "But enough..."

A ship this size slamming into the Earth at relativistic velocity... Nuclear winter kind've thing.

I dragged Vargold up, forcing his head forward to expose the small round bump in the flesh behind his ear. *Sub-dermal smart, he's got a direct neural link to the ship.* "Shut it down," I said, pressing the carbine's muzzle harder into his flesh. "Last chance."

A deep, guttural laugh, then he spoke, voice rich in amused satisfaction, "From light we are b-"

The carbine burst blew his head apart and I let the twitching corpse fall to the deck. "Lucy, you have to shut down the engines."

"I can't. The hack just isn't taking. It's slowing the fusion reactions, but not enough…"

Another voice broke into the comms, laboured and heavy with suppressed pain. "What if… we… remove the hack?" Mr Mac asked.

"It'll power up in seconds," Lucy said. "At the current trajectory…" She trailed off.

"Better… than the… alternative, wouldn't you… say?" Mr Mac enquired.

"Has to be done manually," she said in a small voice. "We don't have time to code up a remote link."

A very short pause. "Then… I suppose you'd better… be on your way, my dear." I watched him nod to Simon, the mercenary helping him up and half-carrying him to the terminal. "Escort her back… please," Mr Mac told him, nodding at Lucy. "You'll find triple… your usual fee in your account… as promised."

"Three hundred and fifteen seconds," Lucy told him, voice receding as Simon pulled her towards the exit. "Otherwise the trajectory will clear the surface…"

I watched Mr Mac slump against the terminal, hand reaching out to rest on the data-stick before Lucy rounded a corner and he was lost from view.

"Back to the suits," I said, running from the bridge with the others at my heels. We sprinted through successive corridors, leaping the mound of corpses and making for the junction where we'd left the suits. As we ran Mr Mac's voice provided an unwelcome commentary I couldn't bring myself to mute. "I... never told you... why I deserted, did I, Alex?"

"Doesn't matter now," I said.

"There's no mystery," he went on. "I was afraid... plain and simple. I knew... none of us were coming back. I asked Consuela to come with me... Did you know that?"

I climbed into my suit and hit the rapid-seal command, the constituent parts closing around me. "And I'll bet she told you to get lost."

"Actually, no. Believe it... or not she was just as scared as I was. But she had... something I didn't, she had you. So... she stayed."

I accessed the *Jason Alpha's* systems, finding the attitude controls still off-line which meant we were stuck in a gravity environment. I checked to ensure the others had successfully suited up, then blew every hatch between us and the recreation deck. "We'll have to bounce," I told them. "Jump then hit your thrusters."

It was a bruising and difficult journey, the suits taking considerable damage as we repeatedly collided with hard surfaces, ricocheting along the corridors until we scraped through the final set of doors to be greeted by the welcome sight of the *Aguila*.

"I kind've... loved her, Alex," Mr Mac said, voice fading now, words coming in wheezy grunts. "Been feeling... guilty about it... ever since. It's... the main reason I never... had you killed. In case... you were wondering."

"And I thought it was because we've always been such close friends." I jumped, the suit's power-assisted limbs taking me to a height of twenty feet before I hit the thrusters and covered the distance to the *Aguila* in a single bound, landing with the kind of force that made me wonder why my ankles hadn't shattered.

"No... words of admiration for me?" Mr Mac enquired with a small chuckle that quickly turned into a gasp. "Even now? I'm... heroically sacrificing myself, here."

"Then it'll balance your account." I groaned, rising from a crouch to see Lucy landing nearby, Simon and Phaedra's people close behind. "Lotta bodies left in your wake."

"All those bastards… deserved it. One way… or another… You'll talk to Oksana and Bao… Won't you? I'd like them to know."

Lucy was first on board, the rest of us following to collapse into a jumble of suits as the ramp sealed behind us. "Yeah," I muttered, struggling free of the crush. "I'll talk to them."

"Thank you." A pause as he checked the readout. "Sixty-three seconds. You… really need to… get a move on."

The *Aguila* lurched as Lucy disengaged the landing gear. Then came the stomach dragging acceleration as she brought the main plasma thrusters on line and gravity faded. "We're clear," Lucy reported. The cargo bay holo flickered into life, showing the receding shape of the *Jason Alpha*, soon rendered a dark speck against the vast backdrop of the moon. "Thought you'd want to see it," Lucy said.

"It's time," I told Mr Mac.

"Just one thing…"

"It's time!"

"You still… haven't told me… how you caught me." I could hear the smile in his voice, enjoying my anger even now.

"The Rodins," Janet told him.

"Ah." A soft sigh of resigned frustration. "Of course. But I just… couldn't resist them. Every Achilles… has his heel, eh, Doctor?"

I watched the *Jason Alpha* drift towards the edge of the moon's arc, ever closer to the blue half-circle.

"You were right," I said. "You would never have come back from Langley. The ex-filtration plan didn't include you. Given your erratic behaviour Covert Ops considered you an expendable asset. Needs of the mission, they said."

"Yes... I thought as much." Another pause. "It... wasn't just guilt that stopped me, Alex. You know that, right?"

"Yeah, I know."

Two seconds of silence, then a faint snick as he removed the data stick. As Lucy promised the main drive came online almost instantly, flaring bright like a second miniature sun before giving birth to its jet. The stream of super-energised matter extended to over a thousand klicks in the space of a few micro-seconds, sending the *Jason Alpha* into the moon's surface faster than any human eye could hope to capture. I saw the moon tip on its axis as the energy release shattered much of its southern polar region. Vast chunks of moon-rock spun away, a few zipping past the *Aguila* and compelling Lucy to put her through a series of evasive manoeuvres. The larger rocks rose from the surface and tumbled about before slowly subsiding back into the main body. By the time the debris field cleared, the moon had gained a titanic new geographic feature, possibly the largest crater in the Solar System.

"I estimate six percent loss of mass," Lucy said from the bridge. "Earth's tidal patterns are gonna be pretty weird from now on."

"We'll get used to it," Phaedra said.

I accessed the news feeds, hearing a chorus of confusion and panic. *Potential first strike by CAOS forces... UN Federal Security insists it has taken no off-planet action... CAOS Central Governance denying all responsibility...*

"Well, at least they haven't started shooting."

I cracked open my suit and floated free, Janet doing the same before pressing herself against me. She stank of blood, but I didn't mind. "You were saying, before," I said, pulling back slightly to run a hand through her gore-matted hair. "About retirement..."

THE END

ABOUT THE AUTHOR

Anthony Ryan was born in Scotland in 1970 but spent much of his adult life living and working in London. After a long career in the British Civil Service he took up writing full time after the success of his first novel Blood Song, Book One of the Raven's Shadow trilogy. He has a degree in history, and his interests include art, science and the unending quest for the perfect pint of real ale.

Discover other titles by Anthony Ryan:

The Raven's Shadow Series
Blood Song - Raven's Shadow Book I
Tower Lord - Raven's Shadow Book II
Queen of Fire - Raven's Shadow Book III
The Lord Collector - A Raven's Shadow Novella

For information on where to find these books, free audio downloads, news and general wittering about stuff he likes, check out his blog at: http://anthonystuff.wordpress.com

Follow Anthony on Twitter: @writer_anthony

Printed in Dunstable, United Kingdom